SHIELD
of the
MIGHTY

Books by Connilyn Cossette

OUT FROM EGYPT

Counted with the Stars
Shadow of the Storm
Wings of the Wind

CITIES OF REFUGE

A Light on the Hill
Shelter of the Most High
Until the Mountains Fall
Like Flames in the Night

THE COVENANT HOUSE

To Dwell among Cedars
Between the Wild Branches

THE KING'S MEN

Voice of the Ancient
Shield of the Mighty

THE KING'S MEN

2

SHIELD
of the
MIGHTY

CONNILYN
COSSETTE

BETHANYHOUSE
a division of Baker Publishing Group
Minneapolis, Minnesota

Published by Bethany House Publishers
Minneapolis, Minnesota
BethanyHouse.com

Bethany House Publishers is a division of
Baker Publishing Group, Grand Rapids, Michigan

Printed in the United States of America

Library of Congress Cataloging-in-Publication Data
Name: Cossette, Connilyn, author.
Title: Shield of the Mighty / Connilyn Cossette.
Description: Minneapolis, Minnesota: Bethany House, a division of Baker
    Publishing Group, 2024. | Series: The King's Men ; 2
Identifiers: LCCN 2023059771 | ISBN 9780764238925 (paper) | ISBN 9780764243141
    (casebound) | ISBN 9781493446544 (ebook)
Subjects: LCGFT: Bible fiction. | Novels.
Classification: LCC PS3603.O8655 S55 2024 | DDC 813/.6—dc23/eng/20240103
LC record available at https://lccn.loc.gov/2023059771

Cover design by Jennifer Parker
Cover photography by Todd Hafermann

Author is represented by The Steve Laube Agency.

Baker Publishing Group publications use paper produced from sustainable forestry practices and postconsumer waste whenever possible.

24 25 26 27 28 29 30   7 6 5 4 3 2 1

For the people of Israel.

May the Lion of Judah give you strength as you fight for your home and your children. May you find *shalom* that surpasses all understanding as you await freedom for the captives and grieve the fallen. And may your eyes be lifted to the One who alone can rescue his treasured people.

I stand with you. *Am Yisrael Chai.*

THE GREAT SEA
WEST MANASSEH
JORDAN RIVER
Bezek
PHILISTINES
EFRAIM
Beit El
Naioth
Ramah
Michmash
Gilgal
Geva
Jericho
Ashdod
Beit Shemesh
Kiryat-Yearim
Gibeah
BENJAMIN
Ashkelon
Azeka
ELAH VALLEY
JEBUSITES
Gaza
Lachish
Maresha
SALT SEA
YEHUDAH
Be'er Sheva
Arad
SIMEON

The LORD is my rock, my fortress, and my deliverer, my God, my mountain where I seek refuge, my shield and the horn of my salvation, my stronghold.

Psalm 18:2 HCSB

A psalm of Ronen ben Avidan

The anointed one shall abide by the counsel of the
   Most High,
The voice of the Ancient One to light his every step

A shield to both the humble and the valiant,
His mighty fortress offers refuge to all who call on the
   Name.

From ashes and dust shall his glory arise,
a diadem of splendor to grace the head of the lowly.

His scepter lifted high shines justice across the Land,
Heavenly righteousness, like a river of gladness, flows
   from his throne.

Selah.

PROLOGUE

Zevi

1043 BC
MITZPAH, ISRAEL

Long live King Saul!"
The shouts of the tribal leaders gathered in the valley echoed off the stony cliffs below our hiding place. A thrill buzzed in my chest as I met the wide-eyed gazes of my three cousins lying in the weeds beside me. Then, as if by silent accord, we too lifted our own voices to exalt the man who'd just been anointed the first king of Israel.

Finally there would be someone in command of the squabbling sons of Yaakov. Someone to inspire the tribes to fight under one banner. To mete out justice and make our enemies pay.

And as soon as I was old enough to join them, I would have my own vengeance as well.

For the space of five breaths, I was back in Zanoah, choking on ashes and shivering at the bottom of a half-full underground cistern as the feathered monsters of my nightmares stalked the streets.

"He's *huge*!" exclaimed Gavriel, yanking me out of the gut-churning memory. "Our enemies will lose their bowels when they see him coming! I can't wait to see them turn tail and run." His fists clenched, jaw twitching. My cousin was nearly as hungry for battle as I but would have to wait two years longer than me to join the army.

I nudged him with an elbow. "Soon enough we'll *both* march in the king's ranks. Carrying weapons you've made."

Gavi's eyes flared, then took on a far-off look. "Perhaps. If I had the right tools and an actual supply of iron ore instead of scraps from old tools and broken knives."

Avidan reached over Shalem, the youngest of us, to clap Gavi on the shoulder. "You do some pretty impressive things with those bits and pieces, cousin. Maybe one day the king himself will wield one of your swords in battle."

When Gavi suggested he, Avidan, and I sneak onto this rocky ridge above the meeting where a new king would be chosen, I'd initially hesitated. Our families had come to Naioth to celebrate the autumn festivals a week ago and would remain until the booths we'd built for Sukkot were disassembled before the arrival of a new moon. All our fathers would have our heads if they knew we'd snuck down into the valley before dawn to meet Gavi outside Ramah and then walked an hour to Mitzpah in order to spy on the gathering of elders and tribal leaders. But the temptation to see a king selected by lots was far too enticing. So I'd agreed, with the understanding that Shalem—our spoiled younger cousin—was not to be included in the scheme.

But of course Shay had followed us, like the little sneak he was. And like usual, I got talked into letting him stay because I'd always had a soft spot for the boy.

"I wish I could go fight too," Shay muttered.

The corners of Avi's mouth twitched down, his expression full of similar dismay. As Levites set apart for sacred service, neither of them would see battle. And truly, that was for the best. Though built like a warrior, Avi's true strengths lay with his silver tongue, not warfare. And Shalem, with his brilliant mind and tender heart, would more than likely be among the vaunted leadership of priests and prophets who lived and taught in Naioth, the community founded by Samuel the Seer just outside the city of Ramah.

I did not look forward to leaving behind the young men who'd embraced me as a cousin soon after I'd been adopted into their family, and as a friend even before that, but my path was clear. I'd spent nine years preparing for one thing: taking up a sword against the Philistines. The only thing that had changed was that instead of simply joining the tribal army of Yehudah in my twentieth year, I would now fight in the army of a united Israel under King Saul.

"I thought the king would come from Yehudah's lineage," said Shalem, his keen mind snagging on an ancient blessing bestowed on Yaakov's second-eldest son.

We'd been shocked when Samuel eliminated Yehudah from consideration. In fact, a large contingent of my fellow Yehudites had even stomped away in protest. But once the lot had fallen on the son of Kish, a Benjamite who towered above everyone around him by at least a handspan, doubts seemed to melt away.

We had a king, and an impressive one indeed. That was all that mattered.

"I don't care which line inhabits the throne," I said to Shalem, "as long as the Philistines are crushed once and for all."

It did not matter that the man I called father was a Philistine. Nor that his sister, my aunt Eliora, was the kindest of women. The rest of their kin deserved no mercy. Not after I'd been dragged off to be sold in Ashdod with the few who'd survived the slaughter in Zanoah. The screams of children being ripped from their mothers' arms still reverberated through my dreams.

"Let's get closer," said Gavriel, his body nearly vibrating with anticipation.

I shook my head. "We're already at risk of being seen."

Although my cousin's jaw ticked, he remained in place, just as I knew he would. The three of them had looked to me as their leader since we were boys. But there were times I wondered if their confidence in me was misplaced. They would never know the things I kept locked in the darkest places of my soul.

As the shouts acknowledging Saul's new headship died away, the tribal elders began to chatter amongst themselves while the priests conferred in a tight group, but the insistent bleat of a *shofar* soon brought them back to quick order.

Samuel, the prophet and judge revered as the very mouthpiece of Yahweh for most of his life, stood beside Saul and lifted high a hefty scroll. "These are the words of Adonai Elohim, as recorded by our forefather Mosheh in the wilderness. Hear now and obey."

With a practiced twist of his wrists, the seer unrolled the parchment and began to read the ancient statutes for Israel's king in a commanding voice that rang through the valley. Not only did they include a warning for a leader who would seek to enrich and lift himself above those he governed but an admonition to transcribe a personal copy of the Torah. It ended with a promise that as long as the king listened and obeyed those commandments all the days of his life, his descendants would sit on the throne of Israel forever.

Samuel gestured for the new king to kneel on the ground at his feet. "Do you hear these words, Saul ben Kish? And will you, chosen of the Most High, heed them until your final breath?"

"I will" came the answer, after the briefest of hesitations.

As the crowd looked on in hushed awe, Samuel gestured to one of the Levites and exchanged the scroll for a horn of oil, then anointed Saul as king of Israel while offering blessings to Adonai Most High. Golden oil trickled down Saul's face and dripped from his full beard into the dirt.

I'd attended many convocations in Kiryat-Yearim where my family lived, led by my grandfather, the head of the Levites assigned to protect the Ark of the Covenant. And I had participated in sacred gatherings that Samuel himself presided over in Naioth, where Avi and Shalem lived with their own families, but never had a moment seemed so holy, so significant as this one. Even if we were caught spying today, I would never regret being witness to this assembly.

However, once the gathering began to disperse, I breathed a bit easier, grateful the thick weeds had successfully shielded us from the view of anyone below the ridge. Even though the four of us had tangled ourselves in a fair amount of mischief, I'd only allowed myself to be reckless once, and the result was the scar that sliced through Shalem's black brow—a constant reminder of my failure to keep him safe that day.

With a jolt, I forced the memory aside. "Time to go."

"Something is happening. Men are crowding around Saul," said Gavi, sliding forward to peer over the lip of the ridge. "We need to get closer."

"They are probably just offering blessings," said Avi.

"No," Gavi pressed. "Those look like warriors. I want to hear what is going on."

"We don't have time," I said. "We'll barely get back before the evening meal as it is. We'll never hear the end of it if they figure out where we were."

"I don't care. I'm going down there," Gavi said, coming to his feet.

"You are going to get us caught," said Avi, making a grab for Gavi's arm.

Gavi sidestepped Avi with an arrogant smirk. "I want to see what sort of men he chooses for his guard."

I gritted my teeth. "Not ones who disobey orders."

Heedless of the tension between us, Shalem bounced up. "I want to see the warriors too."

"No," Avi and I snapped at the same time. Shay's golden eyes went wide.

"If he wants to be a fool, he can bear the consequences," I said, placing a hand on Shay's slender shoulder. "I doubt the king's men will forget the boy drooling over their weapons. But the three of *us* are leaving. Now."

Gavi sneered at me with the disdain he usually reserved for his stepfather. "You may be older than me, Zevi, but I haven't been a boy in a long time. I can take care of myself."

I glared at his retreating back, frustration pounding through my body. But what could I do? I may have been the unspoken leader of my cousins for almost a decade, but he was right that we were no longer children. Sooner or later, our paths would diverge. Avi and Shalem would remain in Naioth to learn their sacred duties while Gavi and I took up swords to fight for Israel and the king who'd been appointed here today.

But there was a scar at the base of my right thumb that would always remind me of the promise I'd made to my cousins, one I held just as sacred as the blood-soaked vow I'd made as I was led away in chains from Zanoah while it burned.

I would hold to both until there was no breath left in my body.

1

Zevi

1040 BC
Beit El, Israel

A spray of cold rain whipped across my face as I peered at the hills to the southwest. Just beyond them, an enemy camp lay spread over stolen terrain, mocking us with its proximity. And yet for reasons I could not comprehend, we'd done nothing. Nothing but camp here for months on end as snow and rain beat down on our tents while Saul's commanders remained silent.

My men were restless. *I* was restless. And no amount of hefting stones or hauling timber for the fortress we were building here assuaged the frustration of hundreds of soldiers who could barely recall the last time they'd raised swords against actual enemies.

I'd lost four from my squad over the coldest months, cowards who'd sneaked out of camp in the dark of night to run home, bored with the monotony and tired of waiting for the king to push back against the insidious creep of Philistines from the west.

I did not blame them for their impatience. I deeply respected my king, but I too was more than ready for Saul to rally us to battle. However, deserters deserved no mercy. There was no room for self-ishness in the ranks of Israel. We fought as one or we would fall, because the enemies that surrounded us were adept at slithering into the cracks between us.

The day my cousins and I had witnessed the anointing of King Saul, I'd naïvely assumed such divisions would have faded while fighting beneath one banner, but living in the army camp since then had disabused me of that notion. There was just as much distrust among the tribes as there ever had been. Unfortunately, the fractures that had formed between Avidan, Gavriel, and I when our young cousin Shalem disappeared had widened to chasms over the past couple of years as well.

I'd only seen Gavi a few times in those months, since he'd sworn his allegiance to Yonatan, the eldest son of Saul and high commander of the division stationed in Gibeah, while I remained in the larger division sent to Beit El in the hopes of deterring the Philistines from pushing any farther east. But the last time I'd crossed paths with my younger cousin, he barely acknowledged me, too busy charming the serving girl who diligently kept his cup full of drink while his companions shared bawdy jokes across the campfire.

As for Avi, he'd settled back in Naioth with his new wife to continue his Levitical studies, and I'd heard through my mother that they already had a child. I'd avoided Naioth since then, not because I did not miss my cousin, but because I could not shake the image of him standing before me, palm outstretched with a familiar white shell in its center. There'd been no accusation in Avi's green eyes as he'd offered up what he considered evidence of Shalem's survival from a wild animal attack, but I'd felt the indictment, nonetheless. I was the eldest. I should not have been swayed to let Shalem come in the first place. And I certainly should not have left the boy in a cave to be torn to pieces during the battle at Yavesh-Gilead. Yet another loved one whose death weighed heavily on my soul.

And I hated the hope Avi clung to even after his fruitless search across the river. Because from time to time, I felt it welling up in my heart too, and it took concerted effort to press it back down in the darkness where it belonged.

Shay was gone for good, and it was my fault.

"Captain." A young voice cut into my unwelcome thoughts. "He's ready for you now."

Turning to glance back at my commander's tent, I found his fourteen-year-old aide holding aside the door flap in silent invitation. I'd been waiting for nearly an hour since I'd received the summons but knew better than to let my annoyance show. It was Merotai's prerogative to keep me and any other man in his command waiting for however long he deemed necessary.

The youth kept his well-trained eyes on the ground as I stepped past him into the dimly lit interior. What I would not have done to assist a battalion commander in Israel's army at his age. The boy would go far once he was old enough to join and would likely step into my own hard-earned position when he did. However, I was grateful for all I'd learned over the past two years as I moved from a soldier to a leader of twenty to a captain of a hundred men. They were lessons that would serve me well as I moved up the ranks.

"Zevi!" Merotai greeted me from his seat at the low table near the far end of the tent. "Come have a seat. I apologize for the wait."

Silently, I took my place on the ground near the table. I'd have been more comfortable standing but knew better than to remain higher than the head of the battalion.

"Some wine, Tobi," said Merotai with a wave of his palm, and the boy jumped to fill two cups.

Once we'd both taken a drink, Merotai cleared his throat. "I'll cut to the heart of it, Zevi. We're going to war."

17

My muscles went tight, my stomach lurching as my pulse sped, but I kept my face perfectly blank. I swallowed hard, barely able to control the shocked exclamation that pushed into my throat. "When?"

"Within weeks," he said. "Yonatan retook Geva a few days ago."

An irrational flare of jealousy welled up. After all these years of waiting to meet my enemies on the battlefield, it was Gavriel who'd done so under Yonatan's command.

Merotai gestured to the east with his empty cup. "All reports say the Philistines are already on the move, preparing to retaliate."

The reclamation of the fortress at Geva was no small thing. The Philistines had been entrenched there for decades, within a stone's throw of Saul's home in Gibeah just to the south. But the weather had been brutal these past weeks, so I was surprised Saul had sent Yonatan to battle this early in the season. And yet it was not my place to question the decisions of my king.

"When do we march?"

"Not yet. We have some time. The rains will keep the Philistines from building up their forces. Those iron-wheeled chariots cannot slog easily through the mud. For now, I have a task for you."

"Anything." Not only was Merotai my direct commander, but he'd also been instrumental in my promotion to captain a few months ago. He'd taken me aside soon after Yavesh-Gilead and drawn a clear path for me to succeed him in leadership one day—a surprise, since his own son, Kyrum, was of a similar age. But the commander, a distant cousin of Saul himself, had been impressed with my performance in battle, untried as it had been, and said he saw great promise in me. Since then, Kyrum and I had become friends, and he served as one of my two squad lieutenants.

"It may take the Philistines a few weeks to stage their retaliation, but they will strike back. Hard. So, within the month, Saul expects us to not only be at double our numbers but also be ready to push the enemy back to their nests on the coastlands. Perhaps even into the sea itself."

Heady anticipation rushed in my blood, but I locked down the instinct to surge to my feet, allowing only one rebellious finger to tap against my leg under the table and release the tension in my muscles. Finally, *finally* I'd face my enemy. "My men are ready."

"I know. Which is why I have every confidence that you'll return with fully trained recruits."

"Return?"

"You and the other captains will sound the call to arms among your tribesmen. You are charged with bringing back at least one hundred men to add to your command—but not just any volunteers. Saul wants the best. You'll be seeking out those who require very little training to meet the Philistines on the battlefield, and those whose skills are already lauded among their own."

Not only had Merotai just given me a promotion to captain of two hundred in one stroke, doubling my command, but I would hand-select those I would lead into battle. Elation surged through my veins, but I kept my expression bland, even if one more finger joined the increasing tattoo against my thigh.

"You'll be given documentation for town elders to prove you come in Saul's name, along with necessary provisions. Chose five of your best to accompany you."

Names came to mind without much thought. Asher and Kyrum, who'd been the first to be added to my numbers, and whom I trusted implicitly. Lemek, who, like the rest of his Zebulonite brethren, was extraordinarily skilled with any type of weapon. In that, he reminded me much of Gavriel, but with less tendency toward recklessness. Mahir and Shimi, cousins who were built similar to my own father, once known as the bare-knuckle Champion of Ashdod.

My mind swirled with plans. Merotai may want me to recruit men already prepared for battle, but I'd developed a training

19

program for myself years ago, a relentless combination of exercises learned from my father that had honed my squad into a force to be reckoned with. With the help of my trusted men, we'd return with a hundred soldiers at the same level of preparation. A month was not very long, but it could be done, I was certain.

"However . . . this will not be your only mission," Merotai said, dragging my attention back to himself. "I have a special task for you. One that I am entrusting only to a few."

"I am honored, my lord."

"As you know, Saul is determined to not only drive our enemies from the Land but to raise Israel to a place of prominence." He swept a hand toward the south. "Our king is determined to build a powerful and influential nation, one visibly blessed by the hand of the Most High. For the past few months, Saul has been seeking skilled artisans to reside in and around the new fortress in Gibeah, men and women whose talents will aid in his efforts to transform Israel from a hodgepodge of shepherds and farmers to a kingdom that shines like a beacon to the world."

Realizing I was frowning, I pressed my mouth into a straight line as Merotai continued.

"Therefore, as you recruit soldiers, you'll also be on the lookout for metalworkers, weavers, perfumers, those who know horse breeding, who are talented with wood carving or making jewelry, and any other useful skill that might benefit Saul's efforts. Bring them to Gibeah when you return."

I blinked at the man I'd revered for the past two years, wondering if I'd misheard him. "You want me to talk craftsmen into leaving their homes and families?"

"They'll be well compensated. And given places of honor within Saul's court."

"I'm but a soldier, my lord . . ."

"And one of my best," he said. "Which is why it is so imperative you take this mission seriously. The reward for returning with not only well-trained soldiers but talented men and women—and tribute from the towns you visit—will be promotion to higher command."

Although I quickly wiped the disbelief from my face, Merotai must have seen my confusion.

"Our king is committed to building Israel into a nation to be respected among the nations," he said. "But to do so will require a great deal of resources."

I knew this firsthand. I'd been in the grand palace of a foreign king, and even as a boy in chains, I'd been impressed by the vastness of the Philistine fortress, the countless rooms and brightly painted murals on nearly every wall. I'd seen finely crafted clothing on well-fed royal bodies and the glitter of jewels around necks and fingers. It was true that in order to be counted among the wealthy nations around us, Saul would need a large amount of silver and gold. But did that mean I had to be a tax collector as well as a soldier?

"I see such potential in you, Zevi. Always have. It's why I have little doubt you'll one day take my position. And if you are successful in this mission, I guarantee that day will come sooner rather than later."

I was at a loss for words. Merotai was commander over the three thousand of us in the division encamped at Beit El and he held a position of great influence with his own superior, Eyal, and Abner, Saul's cousin and the High Commander of Israel's army.

I could not deny that such a future was enticing. But the idea of trying to convince others to understand the importance of such things was a daunting prospect, especially when words did not come easy to me. Thankfully, Asher was almost as skilled as my cousin Avidan in that respect. If I was to persuade town elders to not only send their young men to war but also to offer up both their artisans *and* their silver, I'd have need of his honey-coated tongue.

"What if they refuse?"

His brows arched high, as if the thought had never occurred to him. "The artisans? Or your tribesmen?"

"Either. Both."

"You'll convince them. I'm certain of it. After all, towns that refuse to support Saul will likely not be among the first to be defended by his army." There was an edge in his voice I'd never heard before. "Loyalty matters, as you know. I chose you for this position for a reason—even above my own son. Do whatever you must, because I expect Saul himself will be pleased that I chose so well when you return with plenty of recruits, artisans, and tribute."

It was both a promise and a warning. If this mission went well, then he and I both would reap the rewards. But if I failed, I would be letting down both my mentor *and* my king.

I lifted my chin and looked him in the eye. "You can count on me, my lord."

"Of that I have no doubt." He grinned, then slid a clay tablet across the table to me. "Here is proof that you come in the name of the king, with his royal seal, along with an explanation of Saul's requests. And these"—he handed over a scrap of papyrus—"are the towns you've been assigned."

My eyes swept over the first few names on the list. "These are Yehudite towns."

"Indeed," said Merotai. "You are a son of Yehudah, are you not?"

I nodded. Regardless of my adoption by Natan and Shoshana, and the ten years I'd spent in the Levitical community of Kiryat-Yearim, I was Yehudite by birth.

"And you hail from the *shephelah*?"

I swallowed hard as I nodded again. It was true I'd been born in the hilly region that bordered Philistine territory.

"Then you are the perfect man for this assignment."

22

Arguments sprang to my tongue. Not only had I been nowhere near that area since I was a boy, but many of the Yehudites were less than thrilled with a Benjamite on the throne—my task to convince them would be that much harder.

But I was a soldier. We obeyed orders without question. So instead of giving voice to such thoughts, I pressed them into a corner of my mind. "I understand, my lord."

"I knew you would," he said. "Send my son to me, will you? I haven't seen the boy for days."

Kyrum was no boy—he was almost two years older than I was, even if no one was aware of that fact since I'd entered the army under vaguely false pretenses. But I supposed all fathers had difficulty thinking of their children as grown. My own still ribbed me for foolish decisions I'd made as a youth—albeit with a twinkle in his eye that clearly expressed his affection for me. And although my father had made a firm vow not to shed blood except in direct defense of his family, the day I'd left to join Saul's army, he'd told me how proud he was of my firm convictions and my unwavering loyalty to Israel. As much as I wished I'd never endured the destruction of Zanoah, I could not regret crossing paths with the fearsome Philistine who would eventually adopt me as his own son.

"I'll send Kyrum directly," I said. "And of course, I mean to take him with me. He too has an eye for potential that will be advantageous in this mission."

Busy examining another tablet imprinted with Saul's insignia, Merotai hummed acknowledgment. "I'll see you back here in three weeks, Captain."

Dismissed, I stood and gave my commander a bow. When young Tobi pulled back the tent flap to allow my exit, I took a closer look at the scrap of papyrus in my hand. My attention snagged on the final name on the list as my stomach lurched and bile surged into my throat.

Maresha.

I was not only assigned the exact region where I'd spent my early years, but the town in which I'd been born. The town that banished me when I was nine years old, within days of my entire family dying around me.

2

Yochana

I won't marry him, Abba," I said, tucking a cloth-wrapped parcel into my herb satchel. "Tekoa is the very last man in the town I would choose. Even if I wanted another husband."

"Please at least consider him. He has a very prosperous trading business—"

"And that is his *only* redeeming quality." I directed a frown at my father. Usually I enjoyed our early mornings, when it was only the two of us stirring at dawn, praying together on the roof before the bustle of the day began. It had been a joy to continue our lifelong tradition after Ilan died and I returned to my father's home. I'd not expected an ambush today.

My father opened his mouth to protest, but I continued, determined to nip this idea before it grew deep roots in his mind. "Tekoa is awful. He either talks over me when I speak or explains things as if I am a child. His greatest talent is not his business acumen—it's bringing every single conversation back to his extensive wealth." Thinking of the pompous man, my nose twitched. "Besides, he

25

stinks. Last Shabbat, when he ate with us, I had to hold my breath the entire meal."

My mother bustled into the room. She must have overheard our conversation because she launched directly into admonition. "You cannot be so particular, Yochana. At least four others have come to your father this past year."

That they had. My husband had barely been in the ground when the first, Elishama the baker, had come sniffing around, looking for a mother for his unruly sons. Thankfully, my father and mother were kind enough to fend him off and had not told me until a few weeks later about his poorly timed pursuit. Back then, Ilan's death had been far too fresh and my heart far too crushed to even consider the next day—let alone the rest of my life.

But a few months later, my abba had come to me with yet another man's proposal of marriage. This time from the son of a council elder. The young man seemed honorable enough at first, but the more wine he drank, the more dismissive he'd become of my little shop and the perfumes, balms, and tinctures I made. Instead, he insinuated that my hours perfecting mixtures of flowers, herbs, oils, resins, and minerals would be put to much better use in the kitchen, concocting dishes to fill his well-cushioned belly.

The third suitor only took his eyes off my chest long enough to tell me how beautiful I was but otherwise only spoke to my father when he came to visit our home. At least my mother understood when I protested the man's fixation with my face and form, something my father did not.

The fourth one had been a traveling merchant who generously offered to take me off my father's hands. The man stated plainly that he needed no dowry, since he saw me as a means to more silver in his purse. At least *he* saw my work as an asset. I suspected Tekoa merely coveted my father's influence with the rest of Maresha's elder council.

"Then what will we tell Tekoa?" my mother said, her silvering brows furrowing deep as she leaned into my father.

I knew they both only desired my good. And since they had no sons, only three daughters, they worried for their future, even though my father was a well-respected elder of the town. But I'd fought hard to keep my shop after Ilan's death, and it would sustain us for as long as they lived, I was certain of it. Maresha was growing, little by little, and there was always a need for a medical tincture or a healing ointment.

Also, once Avigail, the wife of the head elder and my mother's closest friend, spread word about my perfumes among the other women in Maresha—making it clear she supported me unequivocally—I'd had steady business the past few months.

My shop was profitable and my family well-fed and safe. I needed nothing else to be content. Least of all, a husband. Once my sisters were of age to marry, I would remain with my parents, where I belonged, and care for them in their old age.

"Tell him I have no interest in marrying again right now," I replied as I slung my satchel over my head, settling it at my hip, and then freed my long braid from its strap. "I have no interest ever, really. I am more than happy as I am."

My father raised his palms in supplication. "But you are so young, daughter. You cannot *want* to be alone. You have many years ahead of you in this life."

That's what Ilan had thought as well. Nowhere among his many plans for us had been an enemy sword cutting those years tragically short. But one moment we were laughing together on the night of our wedding, and three months later, he was in the ground somewhere far away. So, for as many days as I had left on this beautiful earth, I would do what I loved in his honor.

"I am not alone. I have you both and Tifarah and Zerah. And I have my work, which keeps me far too busy to deal with a husband anyhow."

The concern in his eyes did not abate with my explanation. It only grew more prominent. "Ilan would not want you unhappy."

I flinched. Although my father's tone was gentle, his comment pressed into the grief just enough to cause a sharp pain. "Which is why I am grateful he left me a thriving business that has sustained me in widowhood and fills me with joy. I am content, and that is enough."

I pressed a kiss to both parents' cheeks before heading to the door. "I must go. I need to make a delivery before I open the shop. And don't you have a council meeting this morning, Abba?"

"I do." He frowned, looking oddly out of sorts as he straightened the mantle over his shoulders that denoted his authority. But I had no time to ask what weighty matter the council was discussing today. I had to get down to the caves.

"Then we both have work to do. I'll see you this afternoon." I headed out the door but had barely taken one step over the threshold when my mother made one last attempt.

"Are you *certain* you won't even meditate on Tekoa's offer? He can provide so well for you."

Without turning, I shook my head and waved a hand of farewell. Unless my parents could find the equal to Ilan, a man whose charisma and kindness matched his generosity, and who'd been my best friend from the time we were children, I had no interest at all.

I hurried through Maresha toward the gates. Most everyone was still abed, only a few women stirring while they fed animals, started cook fires, or carried empty jars on hips, eager to be the first to the well on this crisp, gray morning.

It had rained all day yesterday, leaving behind plenty of puddles for me to dodge. But at least the air was fresh and clean, and only the sweet tinge of smoke mixed with earthy forest green lingered on the gentle breeze today. I breathed deep of its perfume, loving the brisk tingle of cold against my cheeks and nose.

Once outside town, I headed down the sloping path until I was well out of sight and then darted onto a small footpath that wound around the eastern side of Maresha, where a series of ancient caves, carved by water and time, dappled the hillside. A few had been enlarged by human hands to use as burial sites on the other side of the hill. Others that reached deep underground, I'd been told, had served as a place of refuge when Philistines came to plunder Maresha in the past.

Just as the trail took an upward turn, a flash of movement off to my left caught my eye, and I came to an abrupt stop. Had I been followed? With my heart pounding a double beat, I slowly turned to peer over my shoulder.

Standing ten paces from me was a little brown-and-white dog, no higher than my knee, staring directly at me. I froze in place, not wanting to frighten her, and the two of us watched each other warily for a long time. The leanness of her face and ripple of ribs on her sides made it clear she was hungry, and the swollen teats on her belly told me she was nursing a litter. Some shepherds in the area kept dogs to watch over their flock, and it was likely the little brown dog was the offspring of one of them. She looked neither aggressive nor vicious, only dirty and starving, with an edge of desperation that nicked at my heart. I'd always had a soft spot for any sort of animal.

"I wish I had something to give you," I said, keeping my voice low.

She tensed, her too-slender body responding to my hushed words, then skittered backward, her eyes latched on me.

"I won't hurt you," I said, slowly lifting one palm with the foolish idea that perhaps she could see I meant her no harm. But with a puff of dust, she scrabbled away, darting under an overgrown oleander bush that clung to the side of the hill and disappearing from view.

Disappointed, I waited for a few long moments, hoping she

might reappear, but she'd likely slipped into one of the many caves to wherever she'd stashed her litter of puppies. I hated to think of them being vulnerable to wild animals out here.

Reluctantly, I moved up the trail. It was not as though I could do much anyhow. The dog would not let me near her and certainly not her vulnerable offspring.

It did not take me much longer to find the cave I'd been seeking. Ilan had taken me here a few times before, and the acacia tree that partially covered its narrow entrance was distinct. I paused for a moment, listening for signs of life inside, but only the sounds of the land awakening all around greeted me. Had I missed Noham and the others?

After a quick look around to make certain I'd not been followed, I entered the cave by turning my body sideways and pressing into the gap. Ilan had been tall but lanky enough he'd been able to slide through. I had the distinct memory of telling him that if he ate so much of my mother's lamb stew he'd not be able to fit inside his favorite cave anymore. I swallowed down the grief that always came with such reminders of my husband. Even if these bouts of sadness came less frequently than they had a year ago, they still pierced me through each time.

Once past the entrance, I pressed farther into the cave, but the cavern inside was dark, and the large hollow that I knew was three times my height was nothing but blackness. However, the tinge of smoke still lingered in the air. I'd missed them. Perhaps while I paused to watch the little dog.

A hand reached out of the emptiness, grabbed my wrist, and yanked me forward. I stumbled, barely keeping my footing on the slick limestone, letting out a cry. Another hand went over my mouth.

"Who are you?"

The voice was gruff, but I'd know it anywhere, even with my heart pounding loud enough to echo in this dark cave.

"It's me, Noham. Yochana."

My husband's friend released me immediately. "Yochana? What are you doing here?"

"Looking for you," I said.

"It's all right," Noham called out. "It's just Ilan's wife."

It had been a good long while since I'd been called such, and it made my gut ache. I was no one's wife anymore.

Three more forms moved toward us in the shadowy cave. "What's she doing here?" said one of them.

"Just light the fire again, will you, Mazer?" Noham said, then turned to me as his companions did his bidding. "We heard you outside and put out the light. How did you find us?"

"Ilan told me years ago this was the cave you two once used as a hideout. I figured you'd use the same one for this gathering."

Now that my eyes had adjusted, I could see him tip his head to the side. "And what do you think we are doing here?"

"It's no secret that you have been meeting together. And I overheard you and Mazer making plans in the market yesterday."

The two of them had never been quiet about their distrust of King Saul, nor for their hope that he would be replaced with a man of Yehudah. But I happened to pass by Noham's pottery stall when the two men were discussing meeting today at sunrise. I'd deduced that they were planning something to help speed Saul's deposition.

"I want to help," I said.

Noham scoffed. "And what can you do about those soldiers?"

"What do you mean?"

His brow furrowed. "There's a group of Saul's men in Maresha."

No wonder my father had been so agitated this morning. There was little that divided Maresha more than opinions over the king appointed to the throne of Israel, and if his men were sniffing around town, the council would have to deal with it. "For what reason?"

"Likely to recruit more fools to join his cause."

A memory sparked of Ilan striding off to battle with nothing more than a spear and a cloak to shield his body—the last moment I would ever see him. That precious body now lay in some foreign land in an unmarked grave. Because of Saul and his men.

"What will the council do?"

"Turn them away, I hope. The elders insisted they remain outside the walls for the required three days. I'd thought the soldiers would give up and move on, but they submitted to the demand."

The plague that swept through our village over a decade ago had devastated Maresha. I remembered little of the aftermath because I had been so young, but since that time, the council had been very wary of outsiders. Blaming a traveling group of entertainers for bringing the dangerous illness into town, the elders had decreed that outsiders would not step foot into Maresha without proving they were fever free for an entire week. It was a miracle Maresha had not withered into nothing during that five-year ban, but the fertility of our valley continued to draw trade, even if most of the buying and selling happened in the larger caves down below the city.

However, after a near-rebellion by the younger generation a few years ago, the council finally loosened the reins, and gradually the market in town began to thrive again. But still, no visitors were allowed inside the gates without proving themselves healthy for three days before entry. It had served us well, as no more devastating fevers had come through, and it also worked as a deterrent for those whose motives for coming to our town were less than upright.

"What do you plan to do?" I asked.

"Nothing for the moment," he said. "Zefanyah has no love for Saul. I'm certain he'll tell them to look elsewhere to bolster their numbers."

It was true the head elder on the council hated Saul even more than Noham did. His own son had died at the battle of Yavesh-Gilead two years ago, along with twelve others from Maresha. The victory over the Ammonites had come at great cost for our town and solidified the opinions of many that the man who wore the crown of Israel cared more for idol worshipers across the river than he did for anyone in Yehudite territory.

"They're likely here to collect silver as well as men. Saul is building a grand fortress in Gibeah that will serve as his palace. And of course he'll need to fund his growing army, won't he?"

"You're planning something, aren't you?" I said. "To replace him?"

"And if we are?"

I dug around in my satchel, drawing out the little packet of silver pieces I'd wrapped in linen. "It's not much. But Ilan would want you to have this."

Noham's brows flew high. "Are you certain?"

"I wish it were more." I was only a woman and could not join in whatever they were planning, but in this, at least, I could contribute.

However, if I was to continue to remain unmarried and living under my father's roof, I had to not only provide for myself but contribute to the family purse as well, so I had little extra to spare. Because though he'd been gently pressuring me to marry, as he did this morning, my father's lack of adamance was a direct result of my contributions. He had my mother and two younger sisters, and their future dowries, to consider, after all. Noham accepted the packet. "Thank you, Yochana. You do Ilan credit."

My throat ached. Coming into this cave had stirred up so many memories of my husband and all the hours we spent foraging for ingredients together. He'd loved trekking around the countryside, seeking out exotic plants and herbs for my concoctions, his curious mind always wondering about places far away from our isolated little town. When Saul's messengers came with a summons to war across the Jordan River, he'd been among the first to volunteer, hungry for adventure and trusting that he would return in victory. Instead, he'd not returned at all, slaughtered by Ammonites after being sent into battle on the front lines with a division of Yehudites, most of them untrained and barely armed.

So, even if I could only give a few pieces of silver to Noham's efforts, whatever they may be, I would do anything to see Saul removed from the throne of Israel. Because he may have won a victory that day that solidified his kingship in the eyes of many, but he'd sacrificed my husband for his glory. I would never forgive him or anyone else who groveled at his feet.

3

I leaned against the doorframe, crossing my arms against the chill as I cursed the gray sky. Only two customers had come into my shop so far this morning—a young mother looking for something to cure her infant's flaking scalp and a farmer's wife who used my beeswax and goat's milk balm to soothe her perpetually chapped hands. But the sky had been threatening to loose itself for hours now, and the market was virtually empty. Many of the merchants had already packed up their wares and headed for their homes. Perhaps I should do so as well.

If Ilan were still alive, I would simply climb the stairs behind the shop and take refuge in our cozy little room above. But I'd only spent one night there after news of his death had arrived. Then I'd begged my father to allow me to live with them again. I could not stand the sadness that lived inside what had been our happy home.

It was Ilan who'd taught me about plants and flowers in the first place. A legacy of knowledge he'd received from his grandparents, along with this shop. Now it was mine. The only thing I had of my very own. And I would not let it fail.

So, as the sky released its burden on Maresha, creating a rush of muddy rivulets in the street, I turned from the doorway. I had work to do.

After grinding down a variety of herbs and spices with a heavy pestle, I refilled my jars of ingredients and stacked them inside the large rosewood box under my workbench, which had been a wedding gift from my parents. Then I went to stir the mixture that had been simmering among the ashes within my wide-mouth oven, inhaling deep of the spicy-sweet elixir released by the heat. Blinking back the emotion that always welled when I worked with lupine, I left the perfume to infuse with the almond oil and went to fetch some tallow from the jar I'd purchased from the butcher yesterday.

I wondered if the kind old man would be willing to give me a few scraps for the little dog I'd seen this morning near the caves. I'd not been able to get the poor animal and her scrawny body out of my mind all day. Perhaps if this rain dried up, I'd take a quick detour on my way home this afternoon and see if I could get her to trust me. If anything, I could see that she had some food in her belly for the sake of her puppies.

Between the soft music of raindrops on the stony ground outside, the smoky warmth from the fire, and the sweet familiarity of measuring, mixing, and stirring different fragrant concoctions, I was so happily consumed in my craft that when I finally peered outside, I had no idea what time it was. The sky was still gray, rain showering down from time to time, but the open door lent just enough light that I only needed one oil lamp to work by. Perhaps I should have been disappointed that no one else came into the shop, but I reveled in the peace of a quiet afternoon spent creating. It was as close to Ilan as I would ever be again.

We'd passed countless hours as children collecting flowers and plants and then many more while we cultivated our friendship into something deeper over the years. Then, during the three short months of our marriage, we'd remained long into nights here in the shop, laughing, loving, and mixing new creations together. How could my abba think my heart could simply be mended by some other man, as if those precious days meant nothing?

Humming, I bent to riffle through the rosewood box under the workbench. There had been something missing from one of the medicinal balms I had been working on, and I was certain it was nutmeg. Searching blindly about with my fingers, I found the lumpy packet of nutmeg seeds buried beneath a thick sheaf of cassia bark and pulled it free.

"Shalom. Are you open for business?"

The deep voice startled a gasp from my lips. I jerked upright and spun, gripping the packet of nutmeg to my chest as my pulse pounded. A man filled the open doorway, his face obscured in shadow. I did not recognize the voice, but it held a hint of the soft Yehudite drawl this region was known for.

"Oh." I placed a hand over my thudding heart, willing it to slow. "Yes . . . I wasn't expecting any more customers with this rain. Is there something I can help you with?"

"Forgive me." The man took a step backward, looking almost off-kilter for some reason. "I'll come back another time."

I could not afford to turn anyone away. He may be the only customer I'd see for the rest of the day if this weather persisted, and it was rare that strangers entered my shop. It was almost always locals who had need of my skills.

"No, please," I said, placing the nutmeg on the workbench. "Come in. What are you searching for? A perfume? An ointment? A remedy of some sort?"

He looked hesitant, peering back over his shoulder into the rain.

Feeling a little desperate, I gestured toward my shelves and merchandise tables. "I have the best balms and perfumes in the region, and there are plenty to choose from. You are welcome to take a look."

Noticing that the sky had gotten darker while I'd been caught up in my work, I hurried over to the corner and used the wick of my one lamp to light another larger one, bringing a wash of light to the room.

37

A kick of nerves hit my stomach when I did. The man was a handspan shorter than Ilan had been, but he was built like a cedar tree. Even though he wore a hooded cloak wrapped around himself, his shoulders nearly grazed the doorway on each side as he passed over the threshold.

His arms were thickly muscled, bunching and flexing as he removed the hood of his sodden cloak to reveal thick, nearly black waves at his ears, a full beard, and brown eyes that somehow pierced right through me, even from across the room.

For a moment, I held my breath, my eyes going wide. Everything about this man screamed warrior. Could he be one of those soldiers from Gibeah?

"Peace be upon you," he said in a quiet tone as he stepped farther inside, "and may the blessings of Adonai fill this place."

All fear that this was one of Saul's thugs evaporated, and I let out my breath. No Benjamite soldier would know the greeting particular to the region around Maresha. Especially when the trace of accent I'd detected thickened as he spoke it.

"Peace be upon you as well," I replied, with a dip of my chin.

"It was the smell," he said, his gaze traveling to my worktable and then across the back of the room where a variety of herbs and flowers hung drying from the ceiling beams. "I was walking by your door, and there was something in the air . . ." His eyes moved to the cushion beside the oven where I usually sat, cross-legged, stirring whatever concoction I'd dreamed up and more often than not staring into the glowing embers, wishing there was still another cushion beside me. A number of ingredients lay haphazardly about on the floor, lidless jars and unwrapped parcels of dried herbs I'd been experimenting with this afternoon.

Warmth teased my cheeks. I usually kept my shop spotless when customers were about, but I'd been so engrossed that I'd left my mess all over. I restrained the urge to bustle over and tidy the area, but what was the use? The stranger had already seen my chaos.

And from the sound of it, he'd been lured inside by one of the fragrances I'd been mixing. The thought had a strangely warming effect in my stomach.

I cleared my throat. "So you are looking for a perfume of some sort?"

"I'm not certain," he said, his assessing gaze now taking in the shelves where ointments and balms waited inside ceramic pots made by Noham, a mutually beneficial arrangement Ilan had made with his friend years ago. Noham still supplied me with the small, lidded pots, painted with colorful swirling designs and marked by my own unique seal, which had been designed by Ilan himself as a betrothal gift to me.

However, one shelf at the very top of the wall held the most precious of my unguents. Not because of the ingredients inside or the mixtures of the different elements, but because they were housed in wooden jars carved by Ilan's precious hands and engraved with the contents and with the unique mark he'd made for me—a simple rendering of a blue lupine, my favorite flower, along with the three symbols that made up my name. These were items I would never sell for as long as I lived.

Ilan was always so adamant that my mark be used on the perfumes and not his own, saying that it may be he who owned the shop and who taught me to identify every plant and flower that went into my mixtures, but it was my sensitive nose and instinct for blending them that made the business thrive.

"How you are able to imagine which ingredients might complement each other or the perfect proportion of oils and fats to create potions that soak into the skin like water is beyond me," he'd always said.

For some reason, it was Ilan's wooden pots that the stranger seemed most drawn to, and he stepped forward as if to examine them more closely.

Needing a distraction, I grabbed for the closest pot and removed the stopper to allow the scent free. "This is one of my most popular healing balms."

He came closer, and as he did, I was able to see his face more clearly. I'd thought my Ilan was the most handsome man I'd ever seen, with his light brown hair and laughing gray eyes, but his face had had a sweet, boyish quality to it. This man's striking features were something altogether different.

The lines of his face were almost severe, and there was no levity in the mahogany eyes, as if something had drowned out the light. He bent toward me to smell the unguent, and I resisted the urge to take a step backward. There was no threat in his stance, and one scream from me would alert the merchants on either side of me, but there was something overwhelming about this man's presence that I could not explain.

"It's made with balsam, honey, rosemary, and just a touch of cedar oil. Pleasing, yes? Dry skin drinks it up like wine."

He hummed, noncommittal. "Yes, but that wasn't it."

"What do you mean?"

"There was something . . ." He shrugged those large shoulders, a pinch between his brows. "Spicy? Or perhaps like a forest? But also like flowers?"

That characterized quite a few of my scents, but if he had noticed that particular smell just before he'd come inside, chances were it was the mixture I'd been simmering over the fire for the past few hours. I hesitated for a moment, but out of curiosity, I collected the pot from where it still sat among the cooling ashes and took it to him, holding it up so he could breathe it in.

"This one?"

"That's it," he said, lifting his eyes to look straight into mine. They were rimmed with the darkest and longest eyelashes I'd ever seen on a man, as if they were outlined in kohl. "I've never smelled anything like it in all my life. . . ." He shook his head, as if unable to find words he needed.

40

My insides fluttered so hard that I could not breathe. This was *my* scent. One I did not sell to anyone. And this was the one that lured him into the shop? A pulse of inexplicable panic began to hum in my veins. "This one is . . . not quite ready," I hedged, setting the pot on the worktable behind me. "But I have many others I'd be glad to show you."

He furrowed his dark brows and pinned me with a far-too-assessing gaze, as if he could see the lie dripping from my mouth. "You have quite the talent."

A warm wave of something pleasant swallowed up my unease. Odd, that a compliment from a stranger should affect me in such a way.

"Thank you," I said, turning to scan a nearby shelf for something else to show him. "This one is neem oil with cypress leaves. A little unorthodox, perhaps, but I think it's lovely."

He accepted the pot of balm and turned his glittering eyes up to meet mine. "Is there . . ." He frowned, then took another long inhale. "Lavender in this?"

I sucked in a breath. I'd never known anyone to detect such a light scent before. I'd not used more than a few drops.

"Indeed there is," I said. "There was a bit of an off-putting smell because of the neem oil, and the addition of lavender made it much more pleasant. I've been told it's wonderful at keeping flies and gnats at bay, although I did not set out to make such a thing. The butcher had a sore on his hand from one of his knives and he used it to help with healing, but he also discovered that when he applied it liberally, the tiny creatures kept their distance. He was back a few days later for more. I'd added a few drops of juniper oil to the second batch, just for variety, and he said it worked even better. It was simply a fortunate accident."

Suddenly realizing I'd been rambling on at the stranger, I pressed my lips closed. My own family went glassy-eyed whenever I went into detail about some new blend I was experimenting with. He'd probably head for the door any moment, glad to be clear of my stream of useless knowledge.

However, instead of retreating, the man was watching me intently, the severe lines of his face having softened slightly. "You make all of these concoctions? Not your husband?"

I held back the flinch this question always inspired.

"I am widowed," I said, swallowing down the dregs of the ugly word. "This is my shop."

The man was silent, but there was a minute shift in his expression at my revelation. And still he watched me with such intensity that the back of my neck prickled.

"You are a stranger in Maresha," I said, fumbling for something to quell the odd sensation.

"I was born here."

My brows pitched high. "Indeed?"

He nodded, his tongue darting out to wet his lips as he looked away, his eyes taking in the boxes and pots of ingredients on my worktable, the herbs hanging from the beams on the ceiling. "I was sent away after the . . . plague."

"You were? You must have been only a boy."

"Nine."

I studied his face, searching for any hint of familiarity. I was barely six years of age that year, but I remembered little from that time, since my father had insisted we stay cloistered in our home for many months, terrified that our family would be swept away next. "Where did you go?"

"To live with relatives."

By the shuttered expression on his face, he had nothing further to say on the subject. I could respect that. There were plenty of things I had no desire to talk about with anyone.

"Have you come down to trade here, then?" The man was built like someone who spent many hours in the fields plowing and harvesting crops. Or perhaps he was a mason, used to carrying heavy rocks and cuts of wood.

"Just passing through." He reached to pick up another little jar from an assortment of medicinal ointments, removing the stopper to breathe it in.

"What's this one?"

I squelched a little smile. "It's a remedy."

He took another long inhale of the ointment. "It smells like . . . grass?"

I shook my head. "No. It's made from calendula and chamomile, along with some aloes."

The focus he kept on me as he waited for an explanation was already becoming familiar. I bit my lip to hide my amusement. "It's to soothe sores on one's . . ." I cleared my throat to keep from laughing. "Nether regions."

He jerked back, eyes wide as he set the jar back onto the shelf with a thunk, and I could not help but laugh at his horrified expression, along with the tint of color that brushed along his cheekbones above his black beard.

"Forgive me." I pressed my fingers to my mouth, trying to quell my laughter. "I could not resist."

Again, I expected him to spin around and head for the door, scandalized by my brazenness at speaking of such private things with a strange man. But I'd been making medicines for a long time now, and I'd lost any sense of embarrassment years ago. There was little I hadn't heard by now or ailments I had not been asked to prepare remedies for—even if sometimes those requests were delivered in whispered tones. My discretion was unwavering, and my customers knew it.

But instead of glowering at me as he had when he'd first come into the shop, the barest hint of a smile ticked at the corner of his mouth. And just that small shift changed his countenance from severe to . . . extraordinary. What would a full-on grin do for such a face? It would be difficult to look away, that I knew for certain.

"You must have a vast store of knowledge in order to create all of this."

He spoke as if my skills were something to be admired, as if after only this short meeting, he already held me in high esteem. Yes, there were many in Maresha who valued my work and frequented my shop, but there were just as many who avoided me in the marketplace, likely thinking I was far too bold to both remain in business alone and to refuse groom after groom.

"I've spent many years learning about the varieties of plants, trees, and minerals in this region. My husband taught me much of it, and he learned from his grandparents, who'd inherited the knowledge from their predecessors. I was told some of it came out from Egypt with distant ancestors who once served in the royal courts. Some of the more rare perfumes he taught me are supposed to be made with a breed of lotus that grows only in the Nile, so I've never had the opportunity to truly craft them."

My face flushed warm as he kept that steady gaze pinned on me. The intriguing amusement from before had drained away as I spoke, but his expression remained soft, almost tender in its curiosity.

It hadn't been since Ilan that I'd enjoyed the feeling of a man's attention. In fact, I actively avoided it, and here this stranger walked into my shop on a rainy day and I was overwhelmed by his presence and nearly desperate for just the promise of his laughter. What was this madness?

"What is your name?" His voice dipped so low it was almost a whisper.

"Yochana," I replied in a matching tone, my hands shaking.

A clap of thunder outside caused me to start, and I jerked back a step, knocking into my workbench with a jolt that made more than a few of my ingredient jars clatter together and set the pot of my personal perfume off-balance. It rolled from the bench and onto the floor with a crack, setting free the combined fragrances of sweet jasmine, cinnamon, honey, almond, and just a touch of cedar, along with a heavy dose of blue lupine.

With a gasp of dismay, I crouched to pick up the pot at the same time the stranger did, and we nearly crashed heads.

Even with my own perfume infusing the air, it could not overpower the alluring scent of the man only a handspan away. He must have bathed in a local stream this morning, as he smelled of fresh air and forest, with just the faintest trace of leather and green earth. I breathed in the heady scent, intoxicated by both it and his nearness.

"Don't let it go to waste," he said, scooping up the pot before I could and holding it at an angle so the rest of the liquid did not seep out of the fracture in its side. "It's too beautiful. Too perfect."

"It's not perfect," I said, "I'm sure it is missing something. . . ."

He gently placed the pot into my hands, the warmth of his skin brushing against my palms. "No. It is flawless. Beauty without parallel."

There was something odd in his tone, something that made me wonder if he was not speaking of the perfume. We stared at each other without speaking for the count of five breaths, but the moment I opened my mouth to ask his name, another man burst through the door. Both the stranger and I jolted to standing, as if we'd been caught stealing.

"Zevi!" said the intruder, who was tall enough he'd had to duck to enter the shop, just as Ilan used to do. "I've been looking everywhere. The council is finally reassembling. They've called us to speak."

"I'll be right there, Asher," said the stranger, whose name was apparently Zevi. Unlike the gentle tone he'd used with me, his words were commanding and his expression back to stone.

45

A tendril of unease trickled through my veins, and my shop seemed far smaller than it had a few moments ago.

"I barely convinced the council to let us speak today," said Asher, with a subtle glance toward me. "We can't tarry."

These men were meeting with the council? With my father? The trickle of unease now swelled into a river of apprehension. I'd been wrong. Zevi was not just some trader from up north, was he? I took a step backward, my gut roiling as I looked from one man to the other. The other man's accent was quite plainly from somewhere other than here.

"I said I am coming, Asher. Tell Kyrum and Lemek to meet us at the city gates."

"Already there," said Asher. "Awaiting your orders."

Realization solidified inside my skull. Zevi's authoritative tone and the way the man obviously deferred to him made the truth all too clear.

Not only were these two men soldiers who'd come to Maresha to take our young men off to be slaughtered under Saul, but it seemed the stranger I'd been so drawn to was the leader of the group.

I turned my back to them as they discussed some message Asher was to deliver to men named Mahir and Shimi, but I heard little of it, too busy setting my worktable to rights and chastising myself for entertaining any foolish notion of being drawn to a man like that. A soldier. My mind practically snarled the hated word over and over as I righted pots and pressed lids tight.

Zevi was one of the king's minions. Here to steal more of our young men to be sacrificed to his own glory. And I'd been lured in by his handsome face and some imagined spark of something between us. My stomach wrenched as I snapped closed the lid of the neatly divided wooden casket my sweet Ilan had fashioned to keep my ground herbs and spices fresh, glad that he was not here to witness my betrayal. If only I could undo the past half hour and tell the stranger that I was closed for business.

Fool.

From behind, Zevi's warm hand settled on my shoulder. "Yochana, may I—?"

I jerked away, spinning out of his grasp, and slammed a hip into my worktable. Pots and jars rattled like a warning.

"Don't touch me," My words came out in a half-growl.

He lifted both palms in a gesture of innocence. "I did not mean to startle you."

He looked so bewildered. Almost . . . hurt by my sharp demand. I briefly shut my eyes against the notion, slipped back behind the wall he'd breached with far too little effort, and shook my head.

"Just leave my shop. Now."

4

Zevi

W ho was that?" Asher asked, with an arch to his brow, his challenging glance reminding me of my younger brother, who shared his first name.

"Just a merchant," I said, annoyed with the gleam of amusement in his eyes and feeling oddly protective of the woman I'd just met, even if she'd unceremoniously booted me from her shop. "A perfumer."

"You talk her into coming with us?"

I flinched. Petitioning the perfumer to serve in Saul's court had been my first objective as soon as I'd smelled such overwhelming beauty outside her shop. I'd only recruited a few artisans along the way—a cobbler talented with boot-making, a man skilled at crafting leather and scale armor, and two metalsmiths. But given her skill with creating perfumes, medicines, and ointments, Yochana would surely earn a place of honor in Saul's court.

However, with the way she'd gone from smiling to scowling, I doubted very much she would consider joining our company, regardless of the rich rewards she'd be showered with by a king.

When I'd walked in earlier, drawn like a bee to a flower garden, I'd expected some wizened perfumer to greet me. A learned old woman, perhaps, who'd been mixing concoctions for decades. Or a grizzled merchant whose long trade in exotic spices was the basis for such intriguing fragrances.

Instead, I'd found a young woman crouching on the ground, searching under a worktable, humming to herself, and had been nearly struck mute at the sight of her.

I'd seen plenty of beautiful women in my lifetime. As a boy in Philistine chains, I'd seen women in the streets of Ashdod who looked like murals on a wall, their light-colored eyes perfectly lined with swirling kohl and their faces decorated with cosmetics that made their pale skin glimmer. And yet somehow this woman, this widow, tied my tongue in knots like no other.

The lamplight had kissed the alluring curves of her face, highlighting the smoothness of her olive skin, but it had not been just her beauty that had stolen what little words I had.

It was her voice.

The moment Yochana had spoken, her tone full of the gently drawling accent of Yehudah, I'd barely been able to breathe. It was almost as if my ima had spoken from beyond the grave in the particularly soothing way she'd done when I was a child. A river of calm had washed over me, until I forgot everything but the sound of Yochana's voice and the warmth of her sweet-smelling perfume shop.

Gone was my frustration with the stalling tactics of the elders—being made to wait outside the gates for three days, then to be inspected by a guard who looked in our mouths, peered into our eyes, and put his sweaty palm on our foreheads before letting us inside the town. Gone were the discomfiting memories of my childhood that had only grown louder and more shadowed as I'd wandered the narrow streets of my birthplace.

I'd almost retreated. Almost ran away like a coward, but the young woman had been persistent, inviting me farther into her shop with its bewitching fragrances and I was caught in some invisible snare.

Her knowledge of herbs and spices, flower and trees, was so thorough that I'd been in awe. If only my aunt Eliora could meet her. The two of them would no doubt talk for days about the varieties of plants in their gardens.

But the moment Asher had appeared in the shop, the woman who had been smiling and chattering only a few moments prior had gone silent, and the warm gray eyes that glittered with mirth as she'd teased me had gone flat. It was as if a cold wind had snuffed out every flicker of light in the room. But even if my instinct was to order Asher to wait for me outside while I pled for an explanation for the icy wall she'd erected, I had no time.

"How long do we have to come before the council?" I asked, pressing the enigma of Yochana's sudden change of attitude to the back of my mind.

"I was told they will tend to the needs of the townsfolk first and *then* we'll be allowed to speak."

We'd already waited three whole days as we ceded to their ridiculous demands. Everyone was itching to face the Philistines, so the agitation in camp was growing by the hour. Shimi especially had been threatening to plow through the gates, assert Saul's authority, and force the council to listen.

Tired of the stalling, I'd come close to giving the order to put Maresha behind us and head south to Lachish. We were frustratingly short of our recruitment goals, with less than ten days to return to Gibeah, and Lachish was the largest of the cities I'd been assigned. But something had kept me from giving the command to pack up our camp. Perhaps it had been the familiarity of the hill on which Maresha was built, or the sight of the limestone caves around its base where I remembered playing as a boy, or just a draw to the place where I'd spent the first nine years of my life—most of which had been happy—but the command to leave refused to pass my lips.

Instead, I'd told Shimi and Mahir to use the time to take the new recruits on longer runs through the hills, to stretch their endurance like never before. In between runs, Lemek worked with them on weapons training and was impressed by the talent we'd gathered along the way, sparse though it may be. We'd only managed to find sixty-eight soldiers willing to fight for Saul since we'd left Beit El, and five of those had left once they'd gotten a taste of my training regimen.

I'd known it might be a difficult task to inspire Yehudites who were still somewhat divided over Saul's kingship. But thousands of them had fought with us at Yavesh-Gilead, so it was maddening I was still so far from my goal. Hopefully all this hassle would yield a good number of recruits from Maresha, because my promotion to a higher rank was slipping away moment by moment.

"Where is Kyrum?" I asked.

"Found him at the inn, talking with some of the locals. He and Lemek will meet us at the gates."

After we'd finally been allowed inside Maresha, Asher had remained near the stone seats at the entrance to the town, awaiting word from the council. Kyrum said he and Lemek would try to get a head start on recruiting soldiers, so I'd parted ways with them at the metalsmith shop and set out to seek artisans in the marketplace. Instead, I'd been overcome with memories of my childhood as I wandered the town and then was lured into a perfume shop to meet the first woman who'd ever caused me to question the long-term plans I'd made for my life.

But I had a job to do. Orders to obey. So I tucked it all away and faced forward. Only forward.

Asher went quiet, sensing I was focused on the task ahead. He and I had met on the battlefield at Yavesh-Gilead, two strangers working together to bring down three angry Ammonites as if we'd trained together for years. He was the first to volunteer when I was given charge over a squad of twenty men, and he already knew

Kyrum well. The three of us had spent the last two years not only facing foes together but training men, marching endlessly, sharing meals around cook fires, sleeping under the stars, and guarding one another's backs. I trusted them both without reservation and knew they felt the same.

I wasn't certain why Merotai hadn't already moved Kyrum up the ranks, but I planned to petition for both him and Asher to be promoted to squad captains upon our return. They'd proven themselves plenty capable. If I failed this mission, I did not want either of them to be held back on my account.

Kyrum and Lemek met us not far from the city gates, their somber expressions doing little to bolster my hopes.

"Any prospects?" I asked.

"A few young men at the metalsmith shop said they would consider it," said Kyrum. "Two in particular look like they might be the type we are looking for."

Asher frowned. "That's all?"

"Talk at the inn was distinctly skeptical of the king," said Kyrum, with a sour look. "These Yehudites still think *they* belong on the throne."

A proud Benjamite and a distant cousin of Saul himself, Kyrum sometimes seemed to forget that Yehudite blood ran in my veins, but I could not fault his frustration with my brethren. We'd spent the last two weeks visiting six larger towns and a few villages in Yehudite territory yet we always seemed to leave with fewer men than originally showed up as recruits. I'd second-guessed my training tactics more than once along the way, wondering if word was somehow traveling ahead about my high expectations, but I refused to lower my standards. The men I led to battle must be prepared, especially against a well-trained, well-armed, well-fed force of relentless Philistine soldiers.

I sent Lemek back to camp with a message for Shimi and Mahir about the council meeting and continued on with Asher and Kyrum on either side of me, where they'd been for every other skirmish I'd faced in the past couple of years.

We approached the gates to join the gathering of townspeople standing witness to the elders as they mediated a dispute between two farmers. Apparently, one was accused of moving the boundary stones on the western edge of his land. The council came down on the side of the accuser and ordered restitution. Their fair treatment encouraged me, as did the next case brought before the council, in which great compassion was shown to a widow who'd been caught stealing a basket of bread to feed her two young children. But when Asher, Kyrum, and I finally stood before the seven men who made up the elder council of Maresha, their expressions were as hard as the stone seats they occupied.

As had been the pattern from the first town we visited two weeks prior, I stepped forward to address the council. Although I was still annoyed by their obvious stalling tactics meant to frustrate us enough to move on, I would show them the respect due their office.

I bowed low, hoping my deference would be appreciated. "Shalom, my lords. I am Zevi ben Natan. I have been sent here by King Saul of Gibeah with a plea for your assistance." Asher moved to hand the clay tablet with the royal insignia to the leader of the council on his seat of honor at the center of the group. I allowed him a few moments to read the message from King Saul before speaking again. "As you can see, Saul is looking for men who are both skilled and willing to join—"

"You are Yehudite?" The elder spoke over me.

I paused for three breaths, startled by his interruption. "I am."

He narrowed his eyes as he looked down at me. "From where?"

From the moment I'd seen Maresha on that scrap of papyrus from Merotai, I'd dreaded this very question. I'd foolishly hoped to leave unscathed, but apparently this was not meant to be.

I let out a slow breath, willing my voice to remain neutral. "I was born here, my lord. To Abiyel ben Gaddiel."

There was a muffled gasp from somewhere in the crowd behind me, and a couple of the council members looked visibly shaken. Although I did not turn my head, I could feel Asher and Kyrum's eyes on me as well. Although I'd never hidden my Yehudite heritage, I'd said nothing to the men I trusted most in my squad about being born here.

"You are *Abiyel's* son?" asked the head elder, a note of astonishment in his voice. "The one sent away after . . . after the plague?"

As the once-hazy memory of that day arose with surprising clarity, my throat went tight, and I swallowed hard against the burn. Although I did not recognize these men, it was more than likely that most of them were in the room when that decision was made.

"I am."

Whispers and murmurs grew louder at my back. Although Maresha had grown quite a bit, with higher walls and many new or rebuilt buildings along the narrow streets, it was certain that there were many who would remember my parents. And they would also undoubtedly remember that my three little sisters and my infant brother perished in the plague as well.

"Your father was a good man, an honorable son of Yehudah," said another of the council, one whose expression had softened considerably. "May he rest well in the arms of his fathers."

I gave him a nod to acknowledge the blessing but refused to let the chaos in my mind show on my face. I had a mission to fulfill here. I could not dwell on the past.

"As I said, we've been sent here to seek out those willing to fight against the Philistines. Time is short before we expect them to retaliate, so we are looking for skilled soldiers able take up arms immediately."

The leader spoke again. "And why should we send our young men to fight a battle in *Benjamite* territory?"

His disgust was evident in the way he leaned on the name of Saul's tribe, a prejudice I knew traveled back centuries to the rivalry between the sons of Leah and the sons of Rachel. I was just as proud of my Yehudite heritage as any other man in this region, but the time for strict tribalism had passed with the anointing of Saul. I tried to form an argument that might sway these men of stone, but my mind spun uselessly, my words mired in thick vexation. I could not collect the scattered thoughts in my head.

Thankfully, Asher knew me well and stepped into the gap.

"We are one nation, my lords," he began, his tone smooth and deferential in a way I would never accomplish with my blood pumping so hot. "Brothers bound by the blood of our fathers Avraham, Yitsak, and Yaakov and united by the covenant under Mosheh. As inheritors of the Land of Promise, we must stand beside one another in unity to fend off our enemies—or else risk annihilation."

As the son of a learned scribe, Asher had a way with words that was second only to my cousin Avidan. Surely this council would hear the truth in his persuasive argument.

Instead, the elder scoffed. "We've not had any trouble with the enemy to the west in some time. And have no desire to send any of our own to tangle with them. Look elsewhere for help."

"With much respect, my lord," Asher continued, undeterred by the man's adamance, "all Hebrew territory is in danger. We are surrounded on every side by those who either claim this land as their own or who desire to conquer it. Efraim and Dan are fully occupied, and their people subject to Philistine rule and enslavement. Saul has only begun to build his forces with the ultimate aim of freeing all of Israel from oppression. We've been successful against the Ammonites thus far, and even engaged a few Amalekites and Amorites since his crowning at Gilgal. We knew that the transition from divided tribal forces to a united one would not be easy, but Yahweh chose Saul ben Kish to bring us together against our enemies. Unless we *all* are willing to sacrifice for the sake of Israel—"

"We've sacrificed plenty for Israel, young man," snapped the elder. "We heeded Saul's call to fight for Yavesh-Gilead."

"Against our better judgment," interjected another council member to the right of the one who'd spoken highly of my father.

"Yes, especially with the threat he sent to dangle over our heads," said the leader.

There was no need to ask what he meant, as I well remembered the day Saul's messengers arrived in Ramah with the bloody foreleg of an ox and a call to rescue Yavesh-Gilead from the Ammonites, who'd threatened to take the right eye of each man, along with their city. It was true Saul had warned of stark consequences for those who refused to come to the defense of his distant kinsmen, but how else would he have spurred the ambivalent tribes to leave their harvest and go to the aid of the people of Yavesh-Gilead?

"We sent twenty-five young men to Bezek," continued the head elder. "Less than half returned. And did we receive any word of gratitude for such a sacrifice from Gibeah? Or any restitution for the widows and orphans made from the hastily planned attack? No. The only thanks we have received thus far is a demand for *more* blood." He lifted the tablet with Saul's message in the air. "And a shameless demand for silver to fund his throne."

"This is not a demand," I said, before Asher could respond. "It is a request to help build a respected kingdom and an army to be feared by our foes. Above all others, this town should understand the importance of preparing a strong defense against the Philistines."

"Which is why we have no men to spare," he said. "There is little threat at the moment, but we will not leave Maresha defenseless in order to protect Saul's new fortress. Let the men of Benjamin come to his aid."

"You must understand, young man," said the elder who'd spoken highly of my father, his tone far kinder than the others. "This town has lost too much. We are still rebuilding after the plague stole so many of our young people. Coupled with the losses after the battle in Yavesh-Gilead . . ." He shook his head. "We cannot spare any more. Not for a battle that does not touch us."

I clenched my fists, my teeth near to grinding. The shortsightedness of these people was astounding. Did they not see that Saul's ultimate goal was to protect *all* of the tribal borders from our enemies? I may not have lived in Maresha for many years, but I'd seen firsthand how ruthless the Philistines were in Zanoah, and the thought of such a thing happening here made me ill. The enemy was practically within spitting distance.

"We are not here to take all of your young men," I said, "only those who are especially skilled. If we do not stop the Philistines up north, they will only be emboldened. This city will be even more vulnerable than it is."

The head elder narrowed his eyes on me. "Do not lecture us, young man. You left Maresha when you were a boy. You may have grand ideas of defeating the Philistine army, but we have lived alongside them our whole lives, just like our fathers did and their fathers before them. We will offer up no more sons to your king."

"It is just one battle," I said. "They will return within a few weeks."

"Do not take me for a fool, Zevi ben Abiyel. Saul is building an army. And he wants our best to fight for him, defend his walls, and build his kingdom. Who will be left to guard us? Old men? Women? No. You'll have none of our young men. Nor our silver."

It was as if their ears were made of stone. I gestured toward the tablet the man still held in his hand. "The king has promised to come to the aid of any cities who support his cause."

"This is not a promise," said the elder, dropping Saul's message on the small table at his side with a clatter. "It is simply another threat."

A corner of the clay tablet crumbled at the rough treatment, and I feared it may have cracked.

"If you will only—" I began.

The elder lifted a flat palm, decisively cutting me off. "This council meeting is adjourned."

I inhaled deeply through my nose, counting my breaths as frustration boiled under my skin. Merotai had made it clear that I was to report directly back to him about any towns that refused support of Saul. Objectively, I understood the reasons why it was necessary for Saul to know such things, since unity was imperative if we were to have any chance against the Philistines, but my gut churned at the thought of going back with the name of Maresha on my lips. Something about it made me feel unclean, as if I were spying on my own people.

And yet, they'd never meant to listen to us at all. This had only been a show to prove to the people of Maresha that the council had no plan to bow their knee to a Benjamite king.

I'd known that some Yehudites were still antagonistic toward Saul, even after his decisive victory at Yavesh-Gilead, and we'd encountered a few towns over the past weeks that were reluctant to comply. But they'd all wisely submitted, putting forth a few recruits and offering assistance in the form of silver and supplies, knowing it would serve them well to publicly support the anointed king—and serve them poorly to refuse. The elders of Maresha were endangering their own people with their stubbornness.

In the few moments it took for me to build a secure wall around the impulse to lash out at the stiff-necked elders and shepherd my chaotic thoughts along a more orderly path, the elders had vacated their stone seats and most of the crowd had dispersed.

"Well," said Asher, turning to me. "That was a disaster."

I grunted in agreement, scrubbing a hand over my beard as I scowled at the retreating backs of the elders.

"When were you going to tell us you hailed from this town?" asked Kyrum.

"It wasn't important," I replied. "I haven't lived here since I was a child."

He frowned. "Does my father know?"

"He knows I am Yehudite."

Kyrum's brows arched high, but he said nothing more. Obviously, it didn't matter to the elders whether I was from this town or not. They'd wiped out any chance of adding to our numbers here. I would now have to persuade nearly forty men in Lachish to join us or go back without completing my mission. With such a disastrous failure, Merotai may relieve me of command altogether.

I shifted to gauge the position of the sun, which was already low on the western horizon. We could shake Maresha's dust from our sandals now and begin the short journey to Lachish, but Shimi and Mahir would likely have run the recruits into the ground today.

I turned back to tell the others we would break camp first thing in the morning, but as I did so, a figure near the edge of the crowd caught my eye. The woman from the perfume shop was standing near the city gates with a small basket in one hand, watching me, and from her place twenty paces away I felt her gaze on me like a brand.

Unlike when she had invited me into her shop and rambled freely about her perfumes and balms with such passion, Yochana's unwavering glare was just as cold-eyed as the men on the judgment seats. With an expression full of loathing, she gave one disgusted shake of her head, and then, with her spine as straight as a rod of iron, she turned to walk out of the gates of Maresha.

"Tell the men to rest up," I found myself saying, my eyes on the woman's retreating form. "I'll meet you back at camp later."

Without giving myself a moment to question my reasons for doing so, I followed her.

5

Yochana

My sandals scraped on the limestone as I bent to peer into the next cave, holding my breath as I listened for any sign of the little brown-and-white dog. The basket of scraps I'd begged from the butcher swung precariously from my arm as I crouched lower to search the shadows. There were countless caves in this area, so perhaps I was wasting my time trying to find her.

I waited for a few more moments, listening for the scrabble of claws against stone or perhaps the whimpers of puppies, but other than the echoing coos of a few doves who'd made their nests in the cave, all was silent.

The sun would be going down soon, and perhaps it was time to admit defeat and go home. I'd needed the time to cool my blood after witnessing the council meeting and Saul's brutes demanding both soldiers and silver to build his kingdom.

I could not believe I'd fallen for the seeming interest of that man—Zevi ben Abiyel or Natan or whoever he was. I did not remember him or his family, even if my father seemed to think

Zevi's father was someone worthy of honor. But it did not matter. He may have been born in Maresha, but he was Saul's man and that made him my enemy.

The true mystery was what he'd been doing in my shop in the first place. Why waste his time with a widow when his goal was to recruit soldiers?

"What are you doing in that cave?"

I gasped, nearly dropping my basket as I whirled around. As if my thoughts had conjured him out of air, suddenly Zevi was here, peering at me curiously while I collected myself. The surprising and stupid thrill that went through me when I realized he'd followed me was almost immediately swallowed up by alarm. I was alone in a secluded place near dusk with a stranger.

As if he sensed my fear, he backed up a couple of steps, hands splayed. "I am not here to harm you. I vow it. Only to talk."

Something about the way his voice deepened as he spoke the promise made me think he was sincere. But still I glanced to my right and left, bracing myself in case I needed to run. I had the advantage of knowing every cubit of this area and long enough legs to outrun him, I was certain.

"I have nothing to say to you," I replied. "Leave me alone."

"Have I caused some offense?"

I scoffed. "Your mission here offends me. So, do what the council told you: go recruit elsewhere. And stick your greedy hands in someone else's purse."

"I take it you are not among Saul's admirers?"

Thinking of the silver pieces I'd given Noham this morning, I folded my arms and simply smirked at him.

"What is it with this town?" he murmured.

"I think the council made their position quite clear. We've sacrificed far too much to participate in another of Saul's campaigns."

Zevi studied my face in silence, his scrutiny unnerving.

"And what did you sacrifice?" His gaze did not relent, even if his words were surprisingly gentle. My nerves buzzed with the odd idea that those deep brown eyes could see right to the center of my pain.

"I'm a widow. What do you think?"

"Your husband was at Yavesh-Gilead?" A flicker of compassion passed over his expression, but I refused to believe it. He'd deceived me before; I would not fall for his manipulations.

Looking away, I nodded as my throat burned. I hated the name of that city and had refused to speak it since word of Ilan's death had come to me. Saul may have won that battle, but I had lost everything.

"May he rest in peace in the arms of his fathers," said Zevi, sounding almost sincere.

I was saved from responding by a canine whimper off to my left. There, in the shadow of a wide oleander bush, was the dog I'd been searching for. Her big eyes were on the basket dangling from my arm. She must have smelled the scraps.

"There you are," I cooed, my voice low and soft. "I've been looking all over for you."

She watched me with suspicion, her body rigid with tension. I was certain if I made a move toward her, she would run. So instead, I slowly reached into my basket and retrieved a bloody piece of sheep fat and tossed it over the ten paces that lay between us, close to her front paws.

In a lightning-fast move, she snatched up the meat and licked her chops as she looked at me expectantly. I tossed her another small piece and sank down into a cross-legged position on the ground as she ate.

Refusing to check over my shoulder to see if Zevi had left already, I talked in a quiet voice to the dog, telling her how I'd been wondering where she was and asking where she'd hidden her puppies, as if she would supply me with the answer. I tossed another piece of butcher scrap, but this time, I shortened the distance of my throw. The dog glanced at me warily but then dashed forward to snatch up the food in her teeth.

Again and again, I tossed meat to the dog, each time a little closer, until finally she slid toward me on her belly and came within only two paces. She kept her golden eyes on me as she gnawed at the last lumps of fatty gristle I'd tossed into a bloody pile.

"What was his name?" came Zevi's voice, so low and quiet the afternoon breeze nearly snatched it away. So he'd not left after all. The small kindness of trying not to startle the dog made me answer.

"Ilan. Ilan ben Reuven."

Zevi sucked in a quick breath, and the dog twitched at the sound, pausing mid-chew to look at the man behind me for a moment before going back to her meal.

"I remember him."

Shocked, I turned to peer at him. "You do?"

"He lived with his grandparents, didn't he? Above your shop?"

I blinked at him in surprise. "He did."

"I knew your shop seemed familiar," he said. "He and I were friends, of a sort."

"What do you mean?"

"There was a group of us boys who ran around together in Maresha when we were small. I don't remember him well, just that he was a lot taller than me. And he was always looking for flowers to bring to his grandmother."

My heart ached at the reminder. Ilan had adored his grandmother. When she died two years before we were supposed to wed and his grandfather passed just a few months later, Ilan was devastated. Thankfully, my father had given his blessing for our marriage to be made complete a year sooner than planned so Ilan would not be alone.

"And I remember that his parents died, just before my family."

I caught my own breath at the depth of grief in those words, along with the realization that it must have been more than just his parents who'd died in the plague. I was tempted to ask about who else he'd lost when the dog made a noise, her eyes on the empty basket on the ground beside me.

"I'm sorry," I said, scooting it toward her. "I have no more. The butcher only gave me a few scraps." After a moment, she trotted forward to sniff at the woven basket, examining the outside first and then pushing her nose down to the bottom. I thrilled that she no longer seemed afraid of me. "Perhaps I can bring you something in the morning."

"If your husband fought at Yavesh-Gilead, he must have understood the threat we are facing."

"You haven't lived here for a decade. You know nothing about Maresha."

"I know better than most what the Philistines are capable of," said Zevi, a hint of something dark in his quiet voice. "If only your council could see what fools they are being."

"My father is one of those fools," I snapped, jolting to my feet in a rush that startled the dog. She darted off, slipping beneath the oleander bush. The overgrown plant looked to be covering yet another small cave, and I wondered if perhaps she had her puppies tucked away inside.

Zevi appeared shocked for only a moment before his expression went bland. "Then perhaps you can convince him to plead with the others to put their support behind Saul."

I scowled. "Why would I do that?"

"Maresha's proximity to Philistine territory already puts it at risk, Yochana. You know this. Saul is committed to shoring up the borders of Hebrew lands and retaking the territory that has been stolen, but he needs the support of all the tribes to do so. The council is putting Maresha in an extremely precarious position with their stubbornness."

His words were carefully chosen, but the undercurrent was more than clear.

"So you're saying that unless we give our money and our blood to Saul, we'll just be left to the Philistines if they attack?"

"I am saying our king values loyalty. We have to be united if we are to keep the enemy from making further inroads to our territories."

I could not argue that we were vulnerable here. Maresha was not a large city like Lachish, which boasted thick walls. We had little in the way of riches that might entice our enemies, but the Philistines had long coveted the fertile land that spread out around us.

Even if Maresha itself had been fairly safe for as long as I'd been alive, Yehudites had been fending off sporadic attacks by the Philistines for so many decades it was simply a fact of life in this region. Plow. Fight. Plant. Fight. Harvest. Fight. Over and over. It was as certain as the ever-spinning circles of time. And I, like many, feared the cycle would not end until the true Anointed One sat on the throne—the son of Yehudah prophesied by Mosheh who would execute justice, apply Torah perfectly, and usher in lasting peace. Until then, Israel would likely endure year after year of harassment, invasion, and uncertainty.

As it was, many people in the shephelah did not bother to build permanent homes. What was the point? The Philistines would come and burn them down anyway. The territory of Yehudah had exploded with population growth over the past few decades, either from natural reasons or from those fleeing occupied areas like Dan and Efraim, yet many still chose to remain in tents like our ancestors.

If the Philistines turned the full force of their armies on us, we would be like defenseless lambs against a horde of hungry wolves. It made me loath to admit it, but a well-trained Israelite army would be a great deterrent to the sharp-toothed beasts that crouched just beyond the western hills.

"Even if I wanted to speak to my father," I said, "I could not change his mind or that of the council."

His jaw twitched, his expression hardening. "Then this town will suffer."

I narrowed my eyes on him. "So you *are* threatening us, then."

"The Philistines are ruthless, Yochana. You cannot imagine how depraved . . ." He paused, shook his head once, and then cleared his throat. "You do not want to know what awful things they do to women . . . to children." His voice warbled on the last word, and something deep inside told me Zevi spoke from experience. Regardless of the mistrust I held for this man, I could not help the surge of compassion that welled up.

"I may have only sparse memories of this place," he continued, "but I don't want to see any of my brethren come to harm. Least of all Maresha."

I was surprised at the note of tenderness in his voice, as if he truly cared about the fate of his birthplace. And for as much as I hated Saul, there was much truth to Zevi's argument that we were susceptible to attack. "The elders will not change their minds. There's nothing to be done."

He went quiet for a moment, his eyes tracking to the place the little dog had disappeared beneath the oleander bush. He swung an intent gaze back on me. "There is. *You* can help protect Maresha."

I recoiled. "Me?"

"Your perfumes, Yochana. I may just be a soldier and know little about such things, but your talent is undeniable. You should not simply be making concoctions for farmers' wives and local townsfolk. Those remedies and balms are far too precious for that. They should be experienced by everyone—foreigners, royalty, the whole world."

A swirl of warmth moved through my stomach at his admiring words, but confusion swiftly cooled the sensation. "What do my perfumes have to do with the safety of Maresha?"

Zevi took a step closer, his expression intensifying. "I wasn't only sent to this region to recruit soldiers. I seek artisans with skills like yours."

I blinked at him.

"Saul is building an army, yes, but also a kingdom to rival other nations. Your perfumes should be worn by King Saul, by his wife, and those he appoints to high places. Their beauty would make Pharaoh himself seethe with jealousy. You should be famous, Yochana."

I'd had others say I should sell my perfumes outside Maresha, perhaps in the large market at Lachish, but I had no interest in doing so. I was content with my little shop and the locals who valued the fruits of my labor. I needed no accolades.

I scoffed. "You ascribe far too much to my simple concoctions."

"There is nothing simple about the things you create." He stepped closer until I could see the dark rim of ebony that surrounded the rich mahogany of his eyes. The lure of his potent gaze was undeniable, even if I barely knew anything of the man behind them. "I may have only been in your shop for a short time, but since I walked out the door, I could think of little else than the fragrance you wear now."

I held my breath, reluctantly intrigued by both his words and the man himself. Had my husband ever looked at me this way? As if nothing else in the world held the same fascination as my face? Although I'd known Ilan since I was three years old and his companionship had been the bedrock of most of the years that followed, I could not say that I'd ever felt such intensity between us. I had no words to describe the draw I felt toward this man—this stranger. My lips tingled, my pulse raced, my hands trembled, and it took me a few moments before I could remember the original path of this conversation. "And what does any of this have to do with Maresha?"

"The king will richly reward someone with a talent such as yours. And would assign much credit to the town you hail from."

I lifted a skeptical brow. "You think my *perfumes* will convince Saul to protect Maresha?"

"I think that if you come with us to Gibeah, the resistance of the elder council will be overlooked. Maresha and those who live within its borders would be firmly under Saul's protection."

The vivid image he drew snapped the strange tension between us in two, and I jolted backward a step. "Go *with* you?"

"You would have a place of honor in Saul's court, Yochana. There would be no lack of reward for you and your family, and no need to fear that they or Maresha would be left vulnerable. Loyalty is of utmost important to the king."

Stunned by his audacity, I stared at him with my jaw slack. He wanted me to leave my home and my family on only his word that the king would protect Maresha because of my perfumes. What had I been thinking?

I didn't want to be famous or have my perfume on the neck of the usurper who'd killed my husband. And neither did I believe that my fragrances—no matter how lovely—would convince the villain to care about Maresha in the first place.

Ilan had been convinced he was serving our town and our people by running off to war when Saul's messengers came with their bloody ox leg, and my gut revolted at just how close I'd come to being swayed by false promises as well.

Zevi had been sent here to convince us to hand over more young men like Ilan to be sacrificed to Saul's ambitions and our meager earnings to build his kingdom. And I'd nearly been taken in by his pretty words and empty flattery. It had taken me nearly two years to rebuild my life without my husband, and I had no intention of giving that up for anything. Least of all a man who bowed at Saul's feet.

I pointed to the poisonous plant sprawling over the entrance to the dog's cave. "I'd rather eat that oleander than ever step foot in that liar's palace."

Ignoring the shock on Zevi's face, I turned my back on him and walked away. Zevi may think my father and the elder council were fools for not heeding his warnings, but truly the only fool this day had been me.

6

Zevi

I stood watching the place where she disappeared for far too long, half wishing she'd come barreling back down the rocky path with a mouth full of curses for me and half glad she'd left before I lost my temper at her smart mouth and sharp tongue.

Infuriating woman. How could she be so cavalier about the safety of this town? Of her *own* family? She was just as hardheaded as her father and the rest of the council. She'd refused to listen, her gray eyes sparking black fire that made my blood sing with attraction as much as it burned with fury at her stubbornness. Could she not see that I was trying to save Maresha? Save *her*?

My attention slid to the tiny portion of the cave entrance I could see between the thick oleander branches, where the little dog had slipped into the darkness. She probably had a brood hidden away in there. Yochana's singular focus on the animal, even when I'd been so desperate to sway her, had been at first frustrating and then, after a few moments, utterly fascinating.

Most Hebrews either reviled dogs or feared them, but she

showed such tender compassion for the nursing mother. I'd not been able to take my eyes from the woman as she patiently spoke in the same sweet and low tone that had lured me in just as easily, nor could I keep my thoughts from Igo, the dog who'd been my companion since the day my father had rescued me from slavery.

In fact, as Yochana soothed the dog and fed her scraps from the basket she carried, a startling memory of that very day had washed over me. I'd been so confused when an enormous Philistine with ivory plugs in his earlobes, tattoos swirling over his muscular body, and a gigantic dog by his side purchased me from the king of Ashdod. But when he spoke to me in my own tongue and then left me for a few moments with only his frightening beast to guard me, I'd sat on the ground and let my head drop into my hands as my throat burned with tears I refused to let fall. To my shock, the dog had whined with an uncertain shake of his tail, then plopped down beside me, laid his big head on my lap, and licked my hand. Igo and I had been friends from that moment on. Without his comfort, my months in the land of the Philistines would have been far more difficult. And far more lonely.

I blinked away thoughts of the past and instead turned toward the Philistine threat in the west. These people had so little under-standing of their enemies. Maresha was not a strategic strong-hold, but Israel's foes did not care. They wanted this land and had no compunction about terrorizing whomever stood in their way. Zanoah had not been of any worth to them, after all, and I had witnessed the people in that town suffer unspeakable indignities.

Something had to be done. I had enough to carry without drag-ging around the weight of my hometown's safety on my shoulders as well. I'd not thought of this place in years, but now that I saw it, the ghostly voices of my parents and my siblings pled for my action from beyond their graves.

And yet what could I do? Neither the council nor Yochana would heed my warnings, and I had no power except over my own men. I had a job to do and orders to obey. I'd have to leave Maresha in the hands of Yahweh and the king he'd appointed to watch over her, no matter how much it set my teeth on edge to walk away from Yochana and whatever intoxicating spell the woman had cast on me.

The sun was nearly down, so I headed for the camp we'd made just to the west of Maresha, within a glade that lay in the skirts of one of the many forested hills that made up the shephelah region. The smell of roasting fowl met my nose long before I approached, and my stomach took the opportunity to remind me I'd not eaten anything since this morning.

As if he'd sensed my imminent arrival, Asher's head popped up the moment I stepped out of the trees, and he left behind the meal he'd been eating to come greet me. From the looks of the small bones my men were stripping clean with their teeth, they'd come across a large bevy of quail sometime today.

"Captain," Asher said, extending a cup to me. "We wondered what happened to you. I was about ready to send Mahir and Shimi over the hills to see if the Philistines had taken you captive."

The flash of memory that hit me in that moment was so overwhelming the breath was knocked from my lungs—the acrid heat of burning homes in my nostrils, the terrified wails, the feel of large hands dragging me from the cistern, even the trickle of hot urine down my leg as I saw what the soldiers did to the two girls I'd been hiding with before they cut their throats.

Frustrated that such images had somehow been unlocked from whatever box I'd kept them in over the past decade, I forced my hands to remain still as I accepted the drink from Asher. Then I slugged it back in one draft, focusing on the bittersweet burn in my throat and the wave of heat that expanded outward from my belly instead of the ugly past that insisted on being dredged up by my presence in this town.

"Just making plans for our journey to Lachish," I lied.

Kyrum joined us, still gnawing on a leg bone. "Are we heading out now?"

We'd marched through the night a couple of times since we'd left Gibeah, mostly to beat storms that threatened to blow across our path in the daytime, so it was not inconceivable that the men would expect it now. I was certainly tempted to put this place at my back, but somehow I could not form the words that would command them to break camp and go.

I would certainly never admit to the men in my command that at the heart of my hesitation was a woman who'd rebuffed me twice in one day. Instead, I caught Lemek's eye across the fire and waved him over.

"How are the new men doing?" I asked him.

"Fairly well," said Lemek, scratching at the jagged scar that traveled from the corner of his left temple to his jaw. A distinct mark that made him look nearly as fierce as my own father. "Most are green, of course, but a few have shown some real talent. Three in particular are skilled in both left-handed and right-handed fighting. They'll be excellent with slings."

"How's their endurance?"

"Not bad," he said. "A few lost their stomachs this afternoon after their second run in the hills. But none gave up."

I nodded my head, considering. "Excellent. Let's give them one more night of rest. We'll leave for Lachish tomorrow."

"Haven't we been here long enough?" asked Kyrum. "We only have a week to get back to Gibeah."

His question tapped at a nerve. I fixed him with a stern look. "Lachish is only a short distance from here."

"No disrespect meant," he said, palms raised in surrender. "Just wondering how we'll make up for being so short of our goal."

"I am fully aware of the issue. We'll make up the difference in Lachish. It's a far larger city and not nearly as insular as Maresha."

I had no basis for this assertion, since the only people I'd ever met from the city of Lachish had been a few Yehudites at Bezek just before the conflict in Yavesh-Gilead, and at least one in particular had been vehement in his hatred of Saul. But I would not let on that I had trepidations as well. I must appear confident at all times for the men who looked to me for leadership.

"Did you convince that perfumer to come with us after all?" Asher asked.

Annoyed that he'd noticed who I'd followed after the council meeting, I took a moment to collect my thoughts.

Kyrum frowned in confusion. "What perfumer?"

"A woman." Asher's voice was full of teasing insinuation. "A beautiful one."

I'd never in my life been so tempted to slap a palm across another man's mouth except, perhaps, for my cousin Avi after he rambled on with some long story. But I held back the instinct to knock the teeth from my friend's jaw and kept my expression bland.

Kyrum's brows lifted. "Is she talented enough for Saul's court?"

Reluctantly, I nodded. "She'd put the best in Pharaoh's palace to shame."

"That good, is she?"

"She's worth ten of any other artisan I could bring," I admitted, knowing it was the truth. "The fragrances she makes are like nothing you've ever smelled in your life."

Asher grinned. "And you know how Saul loves to please his wife."

That I did. Everyone knew how much Saul valued his wife, Ahinoam. We'd been told to give her equal deference to the king himself whenever she was in residence at Gibeah. Perfume that rivaled that of the queens among the other nations would be highly sought after to be certain. Not only would Yochana have the choicest of materials to create new fragrances at Saul's expense, once word traveled of her expertise, young men and women would flock to Gibeah to soak up her knowledge. Frustration began to roil in my chest again. Why could she not see how this position would benefit her and her family?

"She is not interested in coming," I bit out.

"Didn't you tell her she would be rewarded?" Asher asked.

"Of course. Nothing I said convinced her."

"Perhaps, in this matter, actions are better than words. . . ." said Kyrum.

I flattened my lips, arms crossed over my chest. "Meaning?"

He lifted his palms. "You are the one who said creative tactics might be necessary."

When I'd considered having to lean on artisans to get them to comply, I'd never once considered that one of them would be someone like Yochana. Nor that my return to Maresha would stir up so many memories.

Just before I'd walked into Yochana's shop, I'd been overtaken by such a vivid memory of my parents I'd barely been able to breathe. And suddenly I was five years old again.

Walking to the market between my ima and abba, each holding one of my hands, I could barely contain my excitement. Abba had promised I could select a special treat from the baker's stall, and I'd been dreaming of a cake filled with honey-sweetened cream. I'd been telling my ima about how I planned to share my treat with my friends when she came to an abrupt halt right there in the street. She bent over, holding her swollen belly, and let out a groan that made my insides hurt.

"Ima? What's wrong?" I asked, as my father dropped my hand to come to my mother's aid.

"Lavona?" There was panic in my father's voice that I'd never heard before as he looped his arms about her. Tears sprang to my eyes. What was wrong with my ima?

Eyes closed, she moaned again, leaning into my father's embrace, but then she took a long, deep breath and opened her eyes. "It's time, Abiyel. Take me to the midwife."

"Oh! It's time!" *My father smiled, and though tears continued to pour down my cheeks, the sight of it made my stomach stop pinching so tight.*

My mother turned to me, startled to see that I was crying. "Oh, my sweet boy. Fear not. I am well. You will just have a baby brother or sister very soon."

"I will?" I wiped my tears with the back of my hand.

She nodded, leaning to press a kiss to my forehead. "And you will be the very best older brother. You will always protect your siblings, won't you?"

I nodded my head vehemently. I didn't know much about babies, but I would do anything for my ima.

Before I could say anything more, she flinched and groaned again, clutching at her belly. My father swooped her up in his arms, and I followed as he strode through the marketplace, where people called out blessings for the coming child.

I remembered little of the next few hours, just that when I woke the next morning, I had a sister. And for the next few days, an army of women fed us and insisted my ima remained abed until she regained her strength.

She was always so strong through each of her children's births, and even up until the day she worked herself into the grave caring for us. And though I couldn't quite remember the shape of her face, I knew that this town meant everything to her, and I still would do anything for my ima. I may have failed to protect them all in life, but I refused to see the place that held the bones of my parents and my siblings desecrated by the Philistines because of a few stiff-necked elders.

Without Saul's protection, the town my father and mother loved so much would be among the first to fall, so I had to give Maresha a chance. Even if it meant employing some of those creative tactics Kyrum spoke of.

I knew I could make Yochana understand how truly precarious

Maresha's position was here, but I had no time to convince her. She was as stubborn as Avi had been when I told him to return to Naioth when Shalem followed us to the army encampment at Bezek. If only I would have listened to my gut then, ignored his argument, and forced them both to go home, Shalem would not be gone now.

If I'd learned anything from our young cousin's disappearance, it was that sometimes decisions had to be made for the good of others and explanations made later—or not at all. In this instance, it was not only Yochana's well-being I had to consider but that of the entire town of Maresha.

The answer to my problem was simple, but it was not one she would like. In fact, she may very well hate me. But I saw no other way forward without leaving the town exposed, allowing my mission to be compromised, and having everything I'd worked for go up in flames.

"Do whatever you must." Merotai's words had not been a mere suggestion but a command. And just as I expected unquestioning obedience from my own men, I could not ignore a direct order from my commander. As soon as the plan solidified in my mind, and before I could question my own decision or consider what Yochana might have to say about it, I explained my idea to Asher, Kyrum, and Lemek.

I had failed Shalem with my inaction, allowing myself to be swayed by his emotional plea, but I would not make the same mistake again. Yochana was coming with us to Gibeah, whether she wanted to or not.

7

Yochana

I'd had enough of rain, so I was glad the sky was somewhat clear as I passed through the gates just after daybreak. The two guards stationed at the entrance barely glanced in my direction as I walked by. They were used to me venturing out of town this early to seek wild herbs and flowers in the fields and forest glades.

Taking the path that led around to the southern slope of the hill our town was built upon, I found my way back to the cave where I'd seen the little dog last night, glad that even though I'd been furious at Zevi for trying to manipulate me and at myself for nearly being swayed by his flattery, I remembered exactly which oleander bush the dog had slipped under when she fled.

I'd not been able to keep her off my mind all night, and I was certain she had a litter hidden in the cave. If I'd not been so distracted by Zevi and his ridiculous demands that I leave my home and family to come with him to Gibeah, I could have checked for myself.

My younger sisters would be devastated to discover I'd left

them behind this morning, since they'd begged to come see the puppies for themselves, but I feared their innocent exuberance might frighten the mother into moving her brood. They'd fussed and cajoled until bedtime, but I'd been firm, telling them that once the dog came to trust that I meant her and her offspring no harm, I'd bring them along.

Once the girls finally took to their bed and my mother drifted off to deliver food to our elderly neighbors, I told my father that I'd witnessed the council meeting and asked what had happened to Zevi's family.

He'd let out a deep sigh, staring into his empty wine cup. "His father, Abiyel, was a most righteous man and his mother a gentle woman whose children adored her. Abiyel was one of the first to perish when the plague hit, and since there was so much fear about what was happening and how it was spreading so quickly, no one came to Lavona's aide." He shook his head, his tone full of regret. "It shames me now to think of how consumed with fear we were in those days, how untrusting of Yahweh to walk us through the valley shadowed by death. Yet through sheer strength of will, Lavona nursed her children, alone. One by one, they died within a week before she too was swept away. In fact, we thought all in the house had succumbed until Zevi emerged a few days later—pale and emaciated—but alive."

The knowledge that Zevi lost more than just his parents in the plague had caused a spike of pain in the center of my chest, one that was surprisingly sharp when the man was little more than a stranger to me. "Why was he sent away?"

"With so many sick and dying, there was no choice but to send him north, to his mother's relatives. I sent him with Tuval, back when he was only my apprentice, up to Zanoah. I never heard what happened to him, other than the report from Tuval who said Lavona's family grudgingly gave him shelter after he guilted them for nearly turning away a child of their own blood. They must have adopted him as one of their own since he called himself by a different name before admitting his true identity."

My father had gone quiet for a long while, his gaze on the wall across the room as I imagined a younger Zevi and what it must have been like for him to not only endure the deaths of his entire family but then to be sent to a town far away, to people he'd likely never met and who resented his presence.

Suddenly, my father spoke again, his voice a low rasp. "There was a moment I considered bringing him into our own home. But I could not, not with your mother pregnant with Zerah and you so young and vulnerable. He was a danger."

I blinked at my father in disbelief. He'd considered an orphaned *child* a danger? I'd always thought my abba a compassionate man and fair in his council rulings and could not comprehend such a decision.

Later, as I lay on my bed with the girls breathing evenly beside me, I wondered what life would have been like with Zevi in our household. Would he be the same stone-faced man I'd met in my shop? Or would he, given the same love and care my sisters and I enjoyed, be in possession of a lighter heart, of a full and quick smile? The fact that I spent far too much time wondering what that smile might look like unsettled me. Would Ilan be horrified to know that after such a short time, a stranger's face had filled my dreams last night?

Annoyed with myself, I shook off thoughts of Zevi. He was gone. Thankfully, the council had sent him and his cohorts away empty-handed. Just before I left home this morning, my father had told me the town guards reported the soldiers' camp had broken before dawn and headed southeast. Hopefully the unease that had plagued me over the past couple of days would finally dissipate and I could return to the contentment I'd found since I'd emerged from the darkness of my grief.

I came upon the oleander covering the dog's cave and slowly

pressed the splayed limbs aside to seek out the entrance. The opening was smaller than I'd guessed, just large enough to crouch and squeeze my full body through the gap. Once I'd crawled fully inside, before my eyes fully adjusted to the dim, a low growl came from a few paces away. I held my breath and peered in the shadows at the back of the shallow cave where I could barely see the outline of a small animal. I shifted my body, allowing more light to infiltrate the cave. There was the little dog, her eyes gleaming yellow in the meager sunlight, her teeth bared as she let out another growl of warning.

At that moment, I realized two things. First, just behind her was a nest of tiny, squirming puppies looking as though they'd only been born a few days before, and second, the mother dog was not only protecting her brood but three quail carcasses, one of which she had gripped in her paws. A hunk of flesh she'd torn from the bird was clenched between her teeth, dripping with saliva. She growled again, the warning deeper this time, and quite menacing for an animal that barely came to my knee.

I slid backward so she would know I did not mean to steal her treasure, but gone was the sliver of trust I'd earned yesterday. The most surprising thing was not that she'd found food before I arrived with my basket of table scraps but that it was clear she'd not hunted the quail on her own.

There was no trace of feathers in the cave. The birds had been carefully plucked. And the meat was not raw and bloody but fully roasted. The enticing smell of it filled the cave.

Yet the only people who knew about the dog's hiding spot behind the oleander were myself, my sisters who I'd left sleeping in the bed we shared, and Zevi.

Surely not.

There was no reason for the man I met yesterday to feed the dog. He'd not even acknowledged the animal in his determination to talk me into going to Gibeah. But how else would these quail be here in this cave, if not for Zevi taking the time to bring them to her before he and his men left Maresha this morning?

The dog's growls grew more fervent. So after dumping the scraps I'd brought into a pile for her to consume later, I backed out of the cave and into the soft morning light trickling through the low bank of clouds overhead. I fought the wild tangle of oleander limbs and stood to brush the dust off my skirt.

If Zevi had indeed brought the quail for the dog, there must be *something* good in him. Most Hebrews viewed dogs either as herding animals or as wild and dangerous. Whereas I had a weakness for any sort of living creature and had applied more than a few healing ointments on sheep, goats, and, yes, even a few herd dogs over the past couple of years.

Perhaps beneath his gruff countenance and thick armor there beat a heart that held the same tenderness as mine for animals. Maybe I should not have judged—

A hand went over my mouth, another slithered around my shoulders, and my body was swiftly yanked against a larger one. Before I could think to scream, someone spoke directly into my ear. "I won't hurt you."

Even in my confusion, I had expected the accent to be Philistine, perhaps some wandering villain who had slipped over the hills to snatch unsuspecting women. Instead, the familiar Yehudite drawl incinerated the small vine of tenderness that had just begun to snake its way through the stupid cracks in my heart.

I struggled hard against Zevi's hold, cursing myself for being fooled again. . . . I'd been right to begin with. He was nothing but a liar. A deceiver. A man with no honor. Fear and betrayal mixed into an explosive fury that roiled and bubbled up my throat. I bucked hard again, stomping on my captor's foot and flailing my limbs with all my strength, but he was immovable.

Asher, the man who'd come to fetch Zevi at my shop, came

out of the brush, chuckling. "She's a wild one, Zev. Are you sure this is worth it?"

Behind him was the other soldier I'd seen them with at the council meeting. I was outnumbered and at their mercy.

Instead of responding to Asher, Zevi spoke to me. "Yochana. Stop. You'll injure yourself."

I was nearly as furious with myself as I was with Saul's lackeys. I'd made it all too easy to be snatched. Zevi must have overheard me tell the dog I'd come this morning. But it didn't matter how I'd gotten myself into this mess. I had to get out of it. Or die trying.

I threw back my elbow at the same time I sank my teeth into the fleshy part of Zevi's hand. He grunted but kept his palm pressed to my mouth, ignoring the pain I was inflicting.

He spoke directly into my ear, his breath warm on my skin. "I know you are angry, but you gave me no choice. I have to obey my orders. So you can either come with us quietly or we can gag you. What will it be?"

I bit down harder. He would get no cooperation from me.

He huffed a loud sigh. "Asher. Headscarf."

With a faintly apologetic expression, Asher obeyed, snatching the headscarf off my hair. Then, in some incomprehensibly coordinated move between them, Zevi released my mouth just as Asher slipped the fabric between my teeth, wrapped its length around my head, and tied a secure knot at my nape. I glared at Asher with all the fury boiling in my veins, snarled muffled curses against my captors, and made another attempt to slip out of Zevi's hold.

Soon my hands too were tied with a short length of rope. Then, so swiftly I could not take a breath to protest, the world tipped over as I was slung over Zevi's thick-muscled shoulder and we were on the move. I bucked my body and slammed my bound wrists against his wide back, but one strong arm was locked around my hips and the other was like a vise on my legs, preventing me from kicking him in the face. Not that I didn't try my best to do so.

As we entered the trees, I caught one final glimpse of Maresha before it slipped out of sight, and suddenly the anger that had consumed me from the moment I'd heard Zevi's voice in my ear iced over and cold dread took its place.

The Philistine soldiers and others in the enemy tribes that surrounded us were notorious for violating captives. Even if the Torah forbade such things, many Hebrews disregarded Mosheh's laws. And after what just happened, it was clear these men had no integrity. I may not be a waif of a woman, but I *was* a woman. One of these large and capable men could overpower me, let alone three of them together.

My eyes and nose burned as I realized the truth of my position. I was a widow. I came and went of my own accord and sometimes wandered for hours looking for wildflowers and herbs. A few merchants may notice I'd not opened my shop today but would probably assume I was ill or so lost in my work I hadn't bothered to open the door, since I'd been known to do that before.

It would likely be hours before anyone would notice I was missing, and within that time, these men could take me anywhere, do anything, and I was completely helpless.

In fact, it may not be until nightfall that my family would question whether I was missing. But then again, I'd slept at the shop before when I'd lost track of time in my creations. For the first time since Ilan died, I cursed the freedom caused by my widowhood.

My world flipped again as I was tossed into the bed of a wagon atop a few sacks of grain. These men must have coerced a good amount of tribute for the king from the towns they'd visited before mine. Thankfully, my town had stood firm against Zevi's manipulation, and the only thing in this wagon meant for King Saul from Maresha was me. Pride for my father and the other council members filled my chest. They'd refused to bow down to Saul and his ruffians. And I would do the same. Zevi could drag me all the way to Gibeah by my hair but I would never bend a knee to the man who'd killed Ilan.

When Zevi pulled himself into the wagon beside me, I attempted to flip over, but my head thwacked against something wooden. I let out a startled yelp against my gag.

"Stop fighting, Yochana," he said, maneuvering me with a firm but gentle hold until I was cradled by sacks of grain. Then he smoothed his hand over my temple, as if he actually cared about the tender spot already forming there. "I have no desire for you to be hurt."

I scoffed and turned my face away. As I did, I saw what my head had knocked against—the rosewood box filled with dried herbs and flowers, spices, and resins that I kept under my worktable. Beside it were two large baskets stuffed full of my oil jars and fragrances and balms. There were even jars of my best perfumes from the small cellar under the floor. It looked as though someone had simply grabbed whatever they could carry and haphazardly stuffed them into the baskets. A couple of the stoppers had broken free in the act, and the smell of myrrh and juniper met my sensitive nose.

No wonder Zevi had been hanging around the market that day. He must have planned this treachery from the very beginning. While I'd been wrapped up in fantastical notions that he was truly listening to me and valued my creations for their own sake, he'd instead been cataloging which of them he would steal and take to his king.

"I would not have done this if it wasn't necessary," he said in a voice meant only for my ears. "I know you don't believe me, but I'm doing this for your good. And for Maresha's."

I may have been taken in before by Zevi's tricks, but I would not let it happen again. I swallowed hard against the burn of tears that welled in my throat, refusing to let them fall in front of him or even turn my head in his direction.

After a few moments, he let out a sigh. "All right, then."

The wagon trembled as he jumped out of the bed and onto the ground. A black wool blanket was thrown over me, blocking out the light before the wagon jerked, setting into motion as it took me away from my home.

Alone and in darkness, I let the tears come.

8

By the time the wagon shuddered to a stop, trails of salty tears had long dried to my skin. Sore from bumping along atop lumpy bags of grain and numb from futile hopes of rescue being dashed by hour after hour of travel, I barely reacted when the blanket was lifted and the sharp spill of sunlight seared my closed eyelids.

"Are you well?"

I opened my eyes to find Asher peering at me over the rim of the wagon bed instead of his captain, whom I'd pointedly ignored each of the numerous times he'd checked on me during the long trip.

Seeing my confusion, Asher answered my unspoken question. "Zevi had to deal with a situation in camp. An altercation between a couple of recruits. But I promised I would take care of you."

I narrowed my eyes but otherwise remained still.

"We won't hurt you. I swear by all that is holy we mean you no harm."

I knew nothing of Asher, other than he was a soldier, but something about his tone told me he truly meant what he said.

"Now, Kyrum and I can get up there and pull you out of the wagon, which will not be pleasant for any of us, or you can do it yourself. What will it be?"

At least he was giving me a choice, which was more than I could say for his captain. So I awkwardly maneuvered myself upright and looked around. I could not see the rest of Zevi's company through the thick trees all around, but rhythmic shouting in the distance sounded like some sort of training exercise with a large group, and a fearsome one at that.

I scooted to the tail end of the wagon, where Asher and Kyrum lifted me out of the bed and set me on the ground. At some point during the journey, Zevi had taken the gag out of my mouth, leaving it hanging about my neck, but my wrists remained tied.

"Let's give her a chance to tend to her needs," said Asher over my head.

"How? She'll run off if we untie her," said Kyrum.

Asher grinned. "Have you ever known a man who could outrun me?"

Kyrum chuckled. "Not a one."

"Well then," Asher said, with a wink toward me. "I think Yochana understands the situation just fine."

They led me to a thick stand of bushes not too far away and, blessedly, did untie my wrists. Stationed a few paces from me on either side, they turned their backs and gave me a few brief moments of awkward privacy.

But my freedom was short-lived, since the moment I was finished, Kyrum retied my wrists together with the rope, much tighter than Asher had done, looping it around in a complicated twist and then knotting it securely. But I would not give him the satisfaction of complaining at the painful constriction and said nothing as the two of them took me back to where the wagon stood and made me sit at the base of a large sycamore. Exhausted, I leaned back against the trunk and let my eyes close.

"What is going on in camp?" I heard Kyrum ask Asher.

"Not certain. Mahir said there was a clash between some of the men. Zevi might need to send a couple of them away."

"Oh? I'll bet he was none too pleased."

"No, he was not. We need every man we can get."

"Certainly doesn't look as though we'll return with the entire one hundred. We'd need close to forty, if not more now."

"Have some faith, Kyrum. Have you ever known Zevi to fail at any mission your father has given him?"

There was a long pause. "There's a first time for everything."

"You worry too much, my friend," said Asher. "The three of us have been in plenty of precarious situations before. It'll sort itself out one way or the other."

Kyrum only grunted in response.

It thrilled me that Maresha had thwarted Zevi's ability to complete his mission. But I was surprised Zevi's commander was Kyrum's father. That must be an odd dynamic when the two of them seemed such good friends—or so I assumed from the few interactions I'd witnessed between them.

Asher began to whistle a low tune, and after a while I peeked at the man, who sat with his back against the wheel of the wagon a few paces away from me. Long limbs crossed at the ankles, he looked the epitome of relaxation, but his eyes roved the area with a careful vigilance that reminded me of his captain.

Kyrum seemed to have disappeared from the small clearing.

"Do you have siblings?" Asher asked when he caught me watching him, as if he'd pulled a subject of conversation from the blue sky overhead. I pressed my lips into a firm line. I was in no mood for a friendly chat with one of my kidnappers.

Asher lifted a hand, spreading his fingers wide. "I have five sisters. And *I* am the youngest. They gave me no lack of grief as a boy, of course. Tying me up. Slathering cosmetics on my face. Once they told me my eldest sister had been eaten by a lion in the woods. Made me sob my little heart out for hours, even after she 'miraculously' came back to life." He shook his head, chuckling to himself. "And though they are grown and married, they still tease me relentlessly, always pestering about when I'm going to take a break from being a soldier to marry and dragging their maiden friends in front of me at every opportunity." He rolled his eyes but then scrubbed his fingers through his beard. "But I would cut out my own liver before I would ever see harm come to them. You understand?"

I furrowed my brow in confusion.

"And Zevi? He knows this very well. He told me to treat you like one of my own sisters."

He had? What an odd request for a man who'd stolen me from my home.

He peered at me. "Did you know him? Back when you were children?"

I shook my head.

"So he walked into your shop yesterday and saw you for the first time? Interesting." He hummed to himself and then went quiet for so long a rush of frustration caused me to blurt out.

"*What?* What is so interesting about that?"

"Only that he was insistent no one but he lay a hand on you. And he must have checked on you under that blanket at least a dozen times in the few hours we traveled here."

I scoffed. "And what does that matter? I am nothing more than the prize he's bringing back to his king."

"I know it may not seem so right now, but he is a good man," said Asher. "The best one I know, really."

I rolled my eyes.

"It's true, even though I've only known him for a couple of years. We met at Yavesh-Gilead, just after the battle."

My gut hollowed at the name of that horrid place where Ilan had been sent like a lamb to slaughter.

"I saw him, though, during the initial assault on the Ammonite camp. He was in one of the companies who went in first, right before dawn. I'll never forget the sight of Zevi blazing through the enemy camp, cutting down every foe as if they were made of nothing more than straw." He shook his head, staring off into the distance as if reliving that moment. "I was the first to volunteer for his initial squad of twenty when Merotai gave him leadership soon after the battle. Kyrum and I had known each other before, so it was a natural fit. But it was not until after the battle as we pursued the remaining Ammonites that I saw exactly who Zevi was.

"Our squad came upon a band of Ammonites that had overtaken a Hebrew farm near the King's Highway. He feared that if we made a frontal attack, the fiends would kill the family members held captive inside, since we'd seen at least a couple of children and a woman from a distance. Zevi devised a plan to have one of us go in looking as if he'd been waylaid by bandits, to ask for help while the rest of us snuck around the back. But Zevi would let none of us put ourselves in such a precarious position. He took off his armor. Left his sword with me and concealed a dagger under his tunic. Then he insisted that Kyrum and I rough him up enough that he appeared to have been battered by thieves. I'd never had anyone—let alone my squad leader—ask me to not hold back a punch that would bloody his face. I'll spare you the details, but his plan was perfect. The Ammonites fell for the ruse, and before they had any time to suspect something was amiss, he'd killed one and placed himself between the family and the other Ammonites. The rest of the squad eliminated the lookouts before going in to secure the home, so somehow Zevi fought off four Ammonites by himself and kept the family safe until we blew through the door."

I was reluctantly spellbound by his story, fighting off the instinct to ask for more details. And I had to admit that hearing Zevi put himself in front of women and children with little regard for his own life shifted my opinion of him ever so slightly.

"So you see, there is a reason we are so loyal to our captain. He's proved himself on and off the battlefield to be a trustworthy leader and a man of great honor. In fact, if I had a brother, I'd want him to be just like Zevi."

"Well, your *brother* kidnapped a woman. Why would a man of honor do such a thing?"

He let out a long sigh. "He may be my friend, but he is still my superior and not obligated to explain his reasons for his orders. But I trust his judgment. Even in this."

Movement by the wagon caught my eye, and something in my chest fluttered at the thought that Zevi had returned. But it was only Kyrum riffling under the blanket in the bed of the wagon for something. What was wrong with me? Anticipation should not be coursing through me at the thought of a man who'd taken me from my home. Apparently I was still the same fool who'd fallen for his ruse back in my shop.

Kyrum looked up and noticed me watching. He dropped the blanket back over the goods and narrowed his eyes.

"You're back," said Asher, pulling my attention to Zevi, who'd returned to the clearing, his face a storm cloud as he met my gaze.

"Did you send them away?" Kyrum asked, coming around to lean against the wagon.

"No," said Zevi. "It was a dispute that had more to do with bad blood between clans than anything. They both know they are on their last chance with me and vowed to fight the enemy, not each other. I have a feeling that once they go to war together, they'll forget their prejudices."

Asher nodded, then gave me a knowing look. "Battles make brothers of strangers. The three of us are proof enough of that."

It also makes widows, I thought, but held my tongue as Zevi came near, blocking out the sun as he towered over me. I refused to look up.

"Are you well, Yochana?" he asked, his voice low and soothing. As if he cared. As if my name itself was something to be handled with gentleness.

I shook off the shiver that went through me at the odd thought and pursed my lips. I may have spoken with Asher out of curiosity, but I was not going to give Zevi the satisfaction of having broken my resolve.

Removing a satchel from his shoulder, he crouched down in front of me, his back to Asher and Kyrum. He removed a loaf of bread from the bag, along with a couple of figs, a chunk of what smelled like roasted venison, and a small wineskin, laying them atop the empty satchel. "You need to eat."

I turned my face away, even as my stomach snarled. I wasn't certain how long it had taken us to travel to wherever we were, but I'd not eaten anything since just after dawn when I set out to feed the little dog—a moment that seemed like days ago now. That I'd ever considered Zevi to be compassionate because he'd gotten there first with a few quail was almost laughable. Now he was trying to do the same with me, lull me to complacency with the illusion of concern. But I was no animal. I would not be swayed so easily.

Zevi's hands were suddenly on the rope Kyrum had tied around my wrists, his fingers working at the complicated knot. "Why is she bound so tightly? Which of you did this?"

"Just doing as you asked. Thought you wanted her not to get away," Kyrum replied.

Zevi turned to peer at Kyrum over his shoulder. "I told you I did not want her harmed in any way. Her skin is *raw*."

Kyrum's jaw twitched. "Apologies, Captain."

Zevi ignored the admission and unbound my hands. My skin prickled as soon as the constriction on my wrists was released, but I refrained from sighing in relief. Zevi's fingers brushed over the stinging skin, bringing a surprising rush of gooseflesh to my arms that I hoped he did not notice.

"Now eat," he murmured. "It's been too long."

But I only pressed my lips together and gazed off to the side.

"I know you hate me." His voice was so deep and low that the words were meant only for me. "But I have a good reason for this.

Maresha's safety—and therefore your *own* family—is at stake here. I must convince Saul that the town deserves protection."

I scoffed silently but did not look his way.

"I know you do not trust the king. It's clear to me, now more than ever, that many of our brethren feel the same. Saul *is* a fair man, Yochana. One who takes his mandate to fight for Israel seriously. But he is not a fool. He must have the full support of *every* Israelite in this war, or the enemies around us will continue to gnaw at our territory, taking pieces of the Land bite by bite, and soon there will be nothing left. We must be united, or we will cease to exist altogether."

His passionate argument left my mind spinning. What he said did make a good bit of sense, but the idea that I could do anything to counteract the elders' spurning of the king's edicts was ridiculous.

"I cannot stomach the thought of Maresha being destroyed, Yochana. If only you knew what I have seen . . ." His voice trailed away. He dropped his head with a deep sigh, and I chanced the barest of glances at him. His broad shoulders were hunched, his nearly black curls askew, as if he'd been running his fingers through his hair in frustration. He looked tortured. Haunted.

Against my wishes, two things bubbled up inside me: curiosity about exactly what it was he'd experienced that made him willing to kidnap me, and the preposterous urge to stroke my hand over those unruly curls in a soothing gesture.

The impulse was so shocking that I sucked in a sharp breath through my nose and snapped my chin to the side, glaring at the sunset-pink clouds over the trees to the west. I had no idea where I was, but surely, if I got away, I could find my way to a trade road somehow. I needed to go home. My parents and sisters would be beside themselves with worry once they realized I was gone. I could not allow my natural inclination toward compassion to nip away at my resolve in any way.

"Please eat," Zevi rasped, holding the loaf of bread in front of me. "Much longer and you'll faint from hunger and thirst."

He was right, of course. My insides clawed at me as the scent of the bread hit my nose. I could either continue to refuse sustenance and be weak or take the offer and have plenty of strength to escape.

I had to get away, and there was no possible way to do so if I was physically compromised. I would never overpower these soldiers, and even if I was long-legged, they'd made it clear I could not outrun Asher. I would have to outsmart them instead. And I had to be clear-minded and sharp if I wanted to do so.

So, as much as it galled me to let him think he'd worn me down, I turned my hand up and accepted the bread.

"Thank you," Zevi said, his voice full of relief. "There's watered-down wine to fortify you as well."

As I took a bite of the soft bread and my entire body celebrated the taste in my mouth, I felt his intent gaze on the side of my face. But I still refused to turn my head.

After a few long moments of silence, he let out an amused sigh and then stood to his feet, ordering Kyrum to come back to camp with him to discuss their foray into Lachish tomorrow and Asher to keep his eyes on me while I ate unfettered, then ensure I was carefully bound with something much softer than rope.

Keeping my eyes on the horizon and pretending not to listen, I reached for the wineskin and untied the spout to take a long, refreshing drink. I'd let Saul's man think he'd won this battle for now, but *I* would win the war.

9

Zevi

LACHISH, ISRAEL

Tossing aside extraneous thoughts not inherent to the mission in front of me was usually easy enough, taking little more than a stern focus and a firm knowledge of my duties. But nearly every step I'd made away from camp had been dogged by thoughts of Yochana. Even now, as we passed by the large assortment of tents pitched outside Lachish and then through its impressive and ancient gates, I could not get her out of my mind.

The woman was stubborn. That much was certain. Her refusal to eat or drink anything on the journey to the camp in the valley of Eshkol had been nothing short of impressive. And she'd barely given me a glance since she'd fought me like a wildcat when I'd captured her outside Maresha. She would likely put half the men of Israel to shame in battle. The place she'd bitten my hand was still tender.

I understood her anger, even if I could see no other way to ensure Maresha's protection. And though it irked me that she refused to look at or speak to me, I had to admire her tenacity. It paired perfectly with her talent and beauty to make her more captivating, almost frustratingly so. If only I could make her understand my reasoning. Make her see that she could, in fact, sway the king to see her town as an asset and not a holdout in his push for unity among the tribes.

At least she'd eaten something. I hated thinking of her going hungry or being hurt in any way. If I'd not known that Kyrum meant no harm in tying her up in a way that had chafed her soft skin, and the thick knot was only a product of his rough nature as a soldier, I would have ordered the man to report to me for punishment later. It was why I'd captured her myself near the dog's cave instead of Asher or Kyrum. They would not have intended to hurt her, as neither man was reckless, but the thought of anyone else touching her made me feel like hitting something. Or someone.

Having her out of my sight to go talk to Mahir and Shimi about the fight between recruits had been bad enough, but leaving her behind at the camp with Asher, whom I trusted just as much as Avidan or Gavriel, still made me deeply uneasy. Hence the distraction that continued even while I stood before the council of Lachish, with Kyrum on one side and Lemek on the other, making the very same appeal I had to the elders of Maresha.

Thankfully, these men were far wiser and had agreed to listen to the request from Saul without delay. And although a few of the ten elders seemed to waver back and forth during our conversation, ultimately they gave their blessing for us to set up recruitment just outside the gates. Within only a short period, a group of men ready to serve were lining up to speak to Lemek, who would test their skills, and tribute from the city was being loaded into the wagon, their offerings recorded and watched over by Kyrum. If only Maresha had done so, I wouldn't have had to take Yochana in the first place.

And yet as I walked through the market of Lachish, hoping to find a few more craftsmen—preferably ones I didn't have to kidnap—I reminded myself that what I'd done was necessary. Her skill, along with the perfumes and balms that Asher and I had taken from her shop in the dead of the night, would ensure Saul would forgive Maresha's refusal to support his throne in any way. I had no choice.

Besides, it had been far too easy to break into her shop. If the two of us could slip inside the town's walls and easily dodge three careless guards patrolling the streets, then so could our enemies.

Maresha's council had grown far too complacent over the past couple years of relative quiet in the region. And far too comfortable in thinking that Lachish and the Yehudite militia would come to their aid in the case of a Philistine raid. They were playing with fire. And Yochana's perfumes would be the way to ensure Maresha did not end in conflagration, like Zanoah had.

We'd been careful to watch for anyone following us to the valley of Eshkol to the east of Lachish, but no one had pursued us. I'd worked hard to make it look as though Yochana herself had cleared out her belongings from the shop, hoping it would make her family think she'd run off for some unknown reason. I'd even taken the time to latch the door securely. If anything, I hoped the ruse would keep anyone from guessing the group of soldiers they'd booted from their town made off with a widowed perfumer, no matter how beautiful she was.

But just the same, I'd instructed Asher to hide her if anyone came looking while I was gone. We'd be gone by tonight anyhow. My plan was to round up as many recruits as we could here in Lachish and then march through the night to get as close to Gibeah as possible, while doing our best to seek out a few more recruits along the way. I was running out of time, and we were still short of the goal Merotai had given me.

The city of Lachish boasted a bustling marketplace spread

throughout its center and along some of the streets, but I was so distracted that I passed by the vast majority of stalls and shops until I arrived at a metalsmith forge at the far end of the market, impressed by the well-made farm implements hanging from the hooks. Forcing aside thoughts of Yochana, I hailed the smith and entered his shop, hoping he'd be more receptive to my proposal than she had been.

However, I soon discovered it was not the master who was interested in joining us but his son. The young man had been looking for an opportunity to use the skills he'd learned from his father on weapons instead of farming tools. He spent a good while talking to me about the lack of iron ore in the region and lamented how some Hebrews went to Philistine territory to have their iron repairs made. The young man vowed to go home, pack, and meet us at the wagon within the hour. He may not be the master metalsmith his father was, but he was willing and enthusiastic. I did not doubt he'd be of use to Saul.

In truth, he reminded me so much of Gavi and his obsession with weapons that it caused a flare of melancholy for the presence of my cousin. He would more than likely tease me for my choice to take Yochana but would understand my reasons. He was just as committed to Saul's goals as I was.

If only Yochana would see the necessity of offering her talents to the king like the two of us had done.

Again, my rebellious thoughts had returned to the woman I'd left at camp. I'd made certain Asher kept her hidden. The recruits may be skilled and ready to fight, but that did not make them safe company. A lone woman in an army camp might make any unprincipled among the group get the wrong idea about why she was there.

Just after I parted with the young metalsmith, I happened across a weaver's stall. The fabrics were different than anything else I'd seen in the market, the colors vibrant and the patterns far more complicated, looking almost foreign in their design. I knew little about cloth, but surely textiles like these might be interesting to Saul and his court.

Two women were in the stall, both turned away from me. The weaver herself sat at her loom, and nearby another woman was cross-legged, trying to untangle a messy spool of saffron-colored yarn. They were far too engrossed in their conversation to notice me hovering nearby.

"Did those traders really have purple yesterday?" the woman with the yarn asked, grimacing as she tugged at the yellow thread.

"Yes," the weaver replied, with a thick accent I could not place, but it was most definitely not Hebrew. "From Tyre, they say. Such deep colors. Very fine. Would look pretty in my fabric."

"You purchased some?"

The weaver laughed. "No. No. No. I would need sell all my cloths to have only little jar." She made an expansive gesture, as if frustrated at her inability to explain herself in a language not her own. "Those traders need go to rich city if ask such a price."

Phoenician purple, extracted from some sea snail up north, was difficult to procure and, as the weaver said, very costly. Only the rich and royal could afford to wear such rare colors. Perhaps I should ask the woman how to find these traders and send them toward Gibeah. But the two women still did not notice me as they continued chatting.

"Such a strange boy they had with them," said the first woman. "Did I hear you talking in your own language with him?"

"Yes!" said the weaver, her hands finally going slack on the threads in order to look at her friend. "*No one* speak the language of my island. His talk not perfect, but he say a man in Tyre speaks my words. He learn quick the words for greetings and things. But it seem like he *always* know my words! Like I was back on my island, if only a little time."

There was sadness in her voice, and I wondered how a woman

from some far-flung isle would be here weaving cloth in Lachish. But more, I wondered about the boy she'd spoken of. I'd once known someone who was able to learn foreign words with barely any effort and could mimic any accent or sound with astounding proficiency.

But it couldn't be the same boy, the one whose blood I'd seen in the dirt among a swarm of hyena prints . . . could it? If Avi were here, I knew what he would say: that somehow Yahweh had led me to these women and that I should never have given up hope. But I'd had my hopes dashed so often in my lifetime that the idea Shay might have survived had seemed no more tangible than a breath of mist. And yet I could not convince my feet to turn and walk away. If there was even a slight chance, I owed it to Shalem to make an attempt.

A strange feeling of being outside my own body followed as I found myself moving closer and my mouth opening to ask, "This boy you speak of, did he have a silver streak"—my hand floated up to touch my dusty hair, just above my right eyebrow—"right here?"

The woman with the yarn frowned at me, startled by the interruption. "Why? Do you know him?"

My pulse thrummed, sudden desperation crawling up my throat. "Please, just tell me. Was there a streak of silver in his hair?"

The weaver spoke up. "Yes! I never see a young one with such a mark. And too, he had a . . . how do you say?" She made a slicing motion through her right eyebrow.

"A scar," the other woman cut in. "Yes. There was a scar on his brow. I remember wondering if he'd been in some sort of fight."

Not a fight. Just a run-in with a tree branch on a day I'd neglected to make certain he was safe.

The revelation that Shay may truly be alive had the same effect on me now as when I'd been struck in the head during the assault on Yavesh-Gilead with the pommel of an Ammonite sword. The ring of it had vibrated for what seemed like an hour in my skull.

My vision went hazy, and my legs turned to water. I had to grip the weaver's table to keep from sinking to my knees.

I'd not believed Avidan when he'd said Shay still lived—had practically mocked him for insisting that the boy had survived. Still, he'd refused to give up the search for weeks, until circumstances forced him to. And when he'd returned home with Shalem's small knife in hand, I'd only taken it with me as a reminder of my young cousin, a reminder of how I'd failed him—not because I had any hope. In fact, I'd not even accepted the other evidence he'd offered me, a white shell I'd given Shay many years before, because it had hurt to even look at it.

Had I actually left my fifteen-year-old cousin alone to fend for himself, confused, wounded, and terrified in a foreign place like Avi had insisted? If what these women said was true—and I doubted the odds of anyone else having such a unique blend of distinctive features—then yes, I had.

Because of my single-minded focus on vengeance, I'd ignored Avi's pleas for help and then left *him* to wander alone, looking for Shay.

I'd failed him, Avi, the people of Zanoah, and so many others.

And yet, perhaps all was not lost. If Shalem was alive and with these traders the weavers spoke of, he had to be close by. If I'd not remained in Maresha for Yochana, I might have come across him here in the market. But there was no use cursing the decision I'd made yesterday. If I could bring him home, perhaps sharp-toothed guilt would stop gnawing at me every time I saw Shay's little knife in my pack among my belongings.

I *had* to find him.

Suddenly, the sharp focus that had eluded me all day was back.

"Where is he?" I asked the weaver. "The boy?"

The woman shrank back at my demanding tone, her eyes wide. With the way my blood was rushing and my mind spinning, I must look a fearsome sight.

I forced myself to take a long, deep breath and tried again with a gentler tone. "Please. I suspect the boy you met was my cousin Shalem. He had a silver streak in his hair, like you saw. A scar in his brow. And had an inordinate talent for learning new words and mimicking accents. He's been lost for two years . . . taken away by traders. I *need* to find him."

The two women shared a long look and what seemed to be a silent conversation about whether they should tell me. To my relief, the foreign weaver gave me a sad little smile.

"I . . . I don't know for sure," she said. "The Phoenecians come only for a day, I think. They go north? I hear one man say they go to meet ships in Ashdod."

My teeth gritted so hard pain shot through my jaw. Of all the destinations in this part of the world, Shalem and these traders were headed to the place I hated the most, the city I'd been taken to by my captors after the fall of Zanoah.

The last place on this earth I could go was the port city on the Great Sea. It was an enemy stronghold where my men and I would instantly be recognized as Hebrews by our speech and dress. But if Shay was on the trade road, perhaps I could catch up before he passed over into enemy territory. Once he was on the other side of the shephelah, he would be completely out of reach. But whatever I had to do was worth the cost if I could restore Shay to the family that still grieved him so deeply. To make right what I'd gotten so very wrong two years ago by ignoring the narrow threads of hope Avidan had brought me in the form of a white shell and a small flint knife.

Without another word, I left the women standing slack-jawed and headed for the gates of the city. I'd have to devise some explanation for my sudden change of plans and why I was delaying our return to Gibeah without making my men think I'd lost my mind.

Looking out over the small sea of faces, most of them unknown, I prepared myself to speak to those who'd joined us. We'd only added fifteen to our number in Lachish, bringing us to a total of seventy-eight, which made little sense in a city that size. Kyrum and Lemek said that although initially quite a good number lined up to volunteer, quite a few changed their minds when they were subjected to the test we'd used to determine their endurance and agility, or when they realized they would be expected to leave their families and farms immediately.

But there was little time to stew over whether my standards had been too high or why there were so few men willing to defend their fellow Hebrews. Shay could be halfway to Ashdod by now. I had to get us north as quickly as possible without raising suspicions.

I'd never defied orders before, and it set my teeth on edge to push the edge of those boundaries, but I planned to continue recruiting along our new route, so I was technically still on mission. Besides, we had an entire week before we were expected back. The moment I found Shalem, we would turn northeast, march double time, and report to Gibeah. Merotai would never know the difference.

For now, though, I needed to push aside the inevitable roiling in my stomach that always happened when I spoke to a crowd of more than five people. Since I hadn't yet explained myself to Asher, I did not have the luxury of having him speak for me, so I pressed my rebellious emotions into a box, cleared my throat, and waited for all eyes to be on me before speaking.

"I am honored you have joined our company," I said, ignoring the buzz of nerves in my throat. "You represent the best of Yehudah, men of honor and skill willing to sacrifice for our people. For *your* families." I paused to let my gaze drift from face to face, hoping my sincerity would sink deep.

My attention snagged on a familiar face. I'd been so spun up over Shalem when we left Lachish that I'd not taken a second look at the recruits we'd added to our numbers, so I was shocked now to see one I recognized. He was a bit older than most of the others, a touch of silver at his temples and with the bearing of a grizzled warrior.

His name was Rezev. Two years ago, just before I'd led my cousins across the Jordan River near Bezek, we'd come across his group. He had hated Saul with such passion that I could not fathom now why he would volunteer to join my company. Thrown off by his presence, it took me a few moments to gather my wits enough to continue.

"You know what is at stake here," I said. "The Philistine army is mighty, well-trained, and heavily armed. We need more men with skills and determination like yours to drive them from the Land given to our forefathers. Therefore, I've made the decision to go north and continue our recruitment efforts. Prepare to depart within the hour."

A ripple of confusion moved over the crowd as I let out a long breath of relief that the speech was over, whispers and nudges betraying the recruits' shock at the contradiction in orders I'd had Mahir and Shimi give them earlier today.

My own men were likely just as taken aback but were far too disciplined to act surprised. I'd banked on that training. I was their captain and under no obligation to explain myself—even to Kyrum or Asher.

One of the recruits lifted a hand. "Captain, what's with the woman tied up over there behind those trees?"

My ears rang for a moment. I'd not been prepared for questions about Yochana. I'd purposefully kept myself from even looking in that direction since we'd returned from Lachish. I'd had too many other things on my mind and refused to let myself be distracted again. I thought she had been well-hidden in the thick woods. But someone must have wandered outside camp and come across her and Asher.

I forcefully snapped myself out of my momentary haze. "She's my concern, not yours."

Another soldier spoke out. "Does that mean we get to choose women of our own along the way too?"

Scattered laughter bubbled up, but I refused to let my expression change, though my blood was boiling. With the same fury I channeled into my sword when I faced an enemy, I stared at the two fools. "She is here on direct orders from the king. And you will not so much as *look* at her." I narrowed my eyes. "Do I make myself clear?"

I waited, my body tense as a newly strung bow, until they both dropped their eyes and sheepishly nodded. I doubted I would face any more direct challenges to my authority, even if whispers continued behind my back. But regardless of my distractions over the past couple of days, I'd been preparing myself for this battle against the Philistines for the past ten years and felt compelled to ensure they understood the gravity of what we were facing.

"And don't think for a moment that this slight delay means we will go easy on you, because the Philistines will not. They steal, burn, rape, and destroy anything and everyone in their way. They want our land. They want our homes. They want our women and children as slaves. We *must* stand in the gap for Israel or there will be nothing left of her."

There was no more confusion on the faces of the men before me now, only thoughtful and respectful attention.

"We have a grueling march ahead of us," I said with a note of dismissal. "I hope you can keep up."

Immediately, the crowd scattered to break camp, and within moments, all who remained was Kyrum beside me. He must have a thousand questions swirling in his head about my change of plans, but thankfully he trusted my judgment enough to hold them back.

When I'd first met Kyrum, I'd expected he might be resentful of my position, especially when it was his father who'd placed me over him.

Until the day he'd saved my life.

We'd been sent to deal with a group of bandits that had been attacking travelers on the road between Anathoth and Jericho. Since Kyrum was from Anathoth, he knew the area better than anyone, and it took little time for him to scout out the area. Deciding it would be best for us to split up to scout which cave they were hiding in, Kyrum and I went one direction and Lemek and Asher the other. Unfortunately, the bandits must have seen us coming, because I was attacked from behind near the entrance to a large cave and knocked unconscious with a rock. When I came to, Kyrum was standing over me, knife in hand, and Asher and Lemek had arrived to join the fight. We'd left behind five dead bandits and all my doubts about his loyalty in that cave.

He was a brilliant soldier, solid and fearless, and though I hated to lose him, I was certain his father would promote him to lead his own company soon. I would make certain of it once we returned to Gibeah. He'd earned it after two years submitting without complaint to the command of a younger man. I was grateful to have reliable men like Kyrum and Asher by my side. But I was not ready to explain my reasons for going north to men who looked to me for leadership.

So instead of satiating the curiosity I could practically feel vibrating off him, I did not even turn my head as I spoke. "Find those two fools and send them home."

"With pleasure," he replied, already moving to obey my orders without question. I would take no chances with Yochana's safety by retaining dishonorable men, regardless of how short I was of my recruitment goal.

"Forgive me, Captain, but may I speak with you?" said a gravelly voice off to my left. I turned to find Rezev, looking far humbler than he had two years ago at Bezek, when he'd spat out insults about Saul and mocked Gavi's Benjamite heritage. At least he'd saved me the trouble of seeking him out.

"Do you remember me?" he asked.

"I do. And I remember that you were not among the king's admirers. Why are you here?"

He dropped his chin, nodding. "It's true. Like a good number of my tribal brothers, I saw Saul as a wrongly appointed king, occupying a throne that should be inhabited by a man of Yehudah. But I was wrong."

I was stunned. The man I'd met at Bezek had been so hostile and suspicious of me and my cousins that I'd changed my plans to go to war with my fellow Yehudites and instead fought among a company of Benjamites at Yavesh-Gilead.

"What changed your mind?"

His gaze met mine with piercing intensity. "You were there at Gilgal, weren't you? When Samuel brought down the storm on us?"

I nodded. I had indeed been among the throng gathered at the sacred place a few weeks after Saul's decisive victory over the Ammonites.

"You know I was not in support of Saul then," said Rezev. "I was there for the spoils alone, and honestly hoping that the Benjamite would fail miserably. But who could refute Samuel's true status as a prophet of Adonai after that tempest?" His eyes tracked off to the distance, both of us remembering the violent storm that had arisen shortly after Saul's crowning. The prophet had spoken harsh words about Israel's demand for a human king and then called down the sky on us as both a warning and chastisement. None who were there would ever forget the terror of that day.

"One thing I know for certain now is that Samuel is the mouthpiece of Yahweh. And although I don't understand why he chose a man of Benjamin to inhabit the throne when Yehudah was given the royal blessing, I have learned not to question Adonai's will. Only to obey."

I stared at Rezev in slack-jawed shock. "You truly want to fight in this company? In Saul's army?"

"If you'll have me, I would be honored," he said. "I know you have little reason to trust me. But I vow that I am not the same man I was before."

I took a few silent moments to contemplate my decision. I had nothing to prove Rezev was truly loyal to Saul, but we needed every willing man to fight the Philistines, and I hated to send another away, especially after losing the two Kyrum was dispatching now.

"You *will* respect my authority," I said. "Regardless of your age and experience."

He gave a firm nod. "I am here to fight for my people and to expel the enemy from the Land, not advance in the ranks. I'll leave that to those with enough talent and ambition to do so."

I stared at him, narrowing my eyes for a good long while as I waited to see if he would squirm. But he endured my pointed scrutiny without flinching. Finally, I let out a sigh. "Don't make me regret it, Rezev."

He grinned, revealing a large gap where a canine tooth was now missing, a possible victim of the war at Yavesh-Gilead. "I won't, Captain."

"All right, go on with the others and prepare to move north."

With a respectful bow, he turned to go, leaving me baffled and very much wishing my cousins were here. I could almost hear Avi going on about the miracle of the man we'd met at Bezek transforming so drastically and Gavi telling me I was a deluded fool for believing him. And perhaps I was. But right now, I had to focus on the youngest of us.

Shalem needed me. And I would not let him down this time.

10

Yochana

At least they left off the blanket this time, if not the bindings.

Flat on my back in the wagon bed, I'd watched the sky go from gray to flaming red to purple and now to black. After an entire day of boredom, while Asher chattered at me with almost-bothersome cheerfulness about his home in a small Benjamite village, Kyrum had come back to the clearing to announce that Zevi had ordered the group to march through the night. Once again, I'd been packed up like one of the many sacks of barley beneath me and put into the wagon. Asher and Kyrum were careful not to divulge our destination around me, and Zevi himself had not returned.

Perhaps he'd forgotten about me. Found some other unsuspecting woman to chase after in Lachish. It annoyed me that the thought inspired a twinge of sickness, so I kept my gaze on the stars, plotting the ways I might escape my captors, until my eyes were too heavy to keep open.

When I awoke to the soft slant of sunrise against my face, the wagon was at a standstill.

I twisted my body until I was sitting up and sucked in a sharp breath when I recognized the landscape around me. This was the valley of Elah. I'd been here before with Ilan, just after we married, to harvest resin, which was especially effective in healing balms and to soothe itchy rashes and burns. The groves of terebinth trees the shallow valley was known for were heavy with red fruit, and their sharp resinous smell permeated the air around me. Excitement surged through my limbs. I didn't know why Zevi would lead his men in nearly the opposite direction, since he'd been so driven to return to Gibeah, which lay to the northeast, but I didn't care. I knew where I was and how to get back home.

Now all I had to do was get free.

Kyrum and Asher once again removed me from the back of the wagon and gave me just enough space to tend my needs near the wide stream that ran along the bottom of the valley, where I could at least wash my face and hands.

The fertile area was thick with high grasses and blooming with colorful flowers. My feet itched to explore the sloping hills and seek out new varieties of flora that I'd not seen before around Maresha. As we walked the short distance back to the wagon, I noticed a cluster of deep purple iris, and a plan began to formulate.

"Would you mind if I picked a few?" I asked, gesturing with my bound hands toward the regal stalks. "They are so rare around Maresha, and I don't have any in my case."

Asher and Kyrum glanced at each other, some silent conversation going on between them.

"Your captain wants me to make perfumes for his king, correct? The oils from iris make some of the best fragrances and last longer on the skin."

Of course the best perfume was made from the bulbs, left to sit dormant for a few years in the cool cellar Ilan's grandfather

111

had dug into the limestone beneath the shop, but I needed only the papery blossoms.

"I don't see what it could hurt," said Asher as he withdrew a knife from his belt. "How many do you want?"

"As many as you'll let me carry," I said, although I needed only one. "Since I cannot boil them down while you are dragging me all over the countryside, I'll have to let them dry, but they'll still retain scent."

In truth, dried flowers would be practically worthless to make the sort of perfume that would please a king. It was fresh blooms, plucked at the height of their scent early in the morning, that yielded the best smell, but thankfully these soldiers were ignorant to such nuances in my craft.

Asher did as I asked and cut at least twenty irises near the ground, following my instruction to take care with the petals, and then laid the fragrant bouquet in my outstretched arms.

Once we returned to the wagon, which had been guarded in our absence by another of Zevi's men, one who barely glanced at me before disappearing into the brush, I asked Asher to spread the irises in the sun to begin drying, but I'd already crumpled one of the blossoms in my palm.

As before, Kyrum left the clearing, returning with two bowls of stew leftover from yesterday before once again leaving me alone in Asher's care. I wasn't certain who was cooking for this group of soldiers, but I'd not been surprised that it contained fresh venison, along with some wild roots and a few unevenly chopped herbs. It was as if I'd conjured the perfect dish to be set before me.

Could this really be so simple?

I held the bowl to my lips, taking a sip of the broth. Then I twisted my expression into displeasure. "Ugh."

"What is wrong?"

"So bland," I said.

Asher sniffed at his own bowl. "Seems fine to me."

I shook my head. "It's desperately in need of rosemary, pepper, and—" I paused, pretending to think—"perhaps some coriander."

Asher's eyes went wide. "You are a cook as well?"

"What do you think? I deal with herbs all day. My husband's grandmother, who taught me her trade, said I have the best sense of smell she'd ever seen." That, at least, was the truth. Whenever Ilan and I played together in her shop, his grandmother had taught me to distinguish between subtle scents.

I took another sip and put my bowl down, shaking my head. "I'll just go without."

Asher frowned. "Zevi wants you to eat."

I shrugged. "I'm not that hungry."

He set down his bowl, leaning forward with a look of desperation. "You don't understand, Yochana. He may be my friend, but the man practically threatened to relieve me of my own stomach if I didn't ensure you were fed."

I stifled my amusement at Asher's panic. "I have three of those spices in my box. If you'll fetch them for me, I'll fix the stew to my liking."

"Are they marked?" he asked, already standing to fulfill my request.

"They are," I said. "As long as your captain did not destroy my box when he stole it."

"He told us to treat your belongings with the utmost care," he said as he reached for my rosewood box in the wagon bed. "Which was quite the feat while we were climbing over the walls of Maresha in the middle of the night."

"A couple of stoppers came out of their jars," I said, letting my bitterness flow freely. "I smelled them immediately when your *friend* threw me in the wagon."

He stopped riffling through my jars and linen-wrapped packets for a moment to look me in the eye. "That was my fault. The basket tipped as I lowered it down over the wall with a rope. Zevi just about knocked my head from my shoulders. I thought I was able to replace the stoppers in time, but they did spill a little of their contents. I'm sorry."

He sounded genuinely apologetic for the loss.

"And yet no apologies for taking my things in the first place. Or, worse, taking me from my home?"

He shrugged. "I'm a soldier. We follow orders."

"Even if they're wrong?"

He returned to searching for the herbs I'd requested. "That's not up for me to decide."

I shook my head, incredulous. "What if your captain ordered you to do something truly horrible?"

He held up a packet of rosemary in victory, and I nodded.

"Zevi may not be perfect, but he is trustworthy," he said. "He always has good reason for whatever he commands us to do. And he, in turn, trusts his commander, who answers to Saul's high commander, who answers to Saul himself."

"And you trust King Saul?" I scoffed, doing nothing to hide my bitterness.

"I trust the God who placed him on the throne. So unless I am ordered to do something that violates the law of Mosheh, I will obey."

His answer shocked me. I would never have guessed that he would be so devoted to Yahweh.

"And you don't think kidnapping a woman is wrong?"

He tilted his chin, considering. "You are being taken to the king, to serve in his court. You will be thoroughly rewarded. Not taken into slavery or being violated. If I thought you were in true danger, it would be a very different story, regardless of my loyalties." After what he'd said about his sisters, and the way he'd spoken of Zevi's sacrifice for the woman and her children across the river, I believed him.

If only *I* could believe the same of his beloved captain.

"The pepper should be near the bottom," I said, as he continued looking through my box of dried herbs and spices. "In a linen packet." I knew very well it was in a stoppered jar, since black pepper was far too potent and would allow the smell to permeate waxed fabric, but I needed the time.

I let him wrestle with the contents as I completed my own mission, then sat back with my bound hands in my lap. Hoping to appear relaxed, I plucked at a thread of conversation from yesterday. "You said your sisters hassle you about marrying. Why are you so reluctant to do so?"

"Because I am a soldier," he said, pausing to look at me and holding up the packet of coriander seeds.

I nodded in confirmation. "And you fear leaving your wife alone if you are killed in battle?"

He frowned, digging again for the pepper. "No. I trust Yahweh to care for those I love. But we are at war, and I cannot step away from my duties for a year right now."

The reminder sent new pain into my heart. Mosheh had said a man was to be excused for a year to enjoy his new wife. And yet Ilan had chosen to ignore that directive. If he had obeyed, he would still be here, and I'd not be in this mess.

"Perhaps once we push the Philistines out of Benjamin and Efraim I'll give in to my sisters and take a wife. But as it is, the women in the Land are far too vulnerable. So, for now, I will obey the orders of my captain and my king and fight until the women and children of Israel are safe from the invaders."

A niggle of guilt prodded at me. Asher really was a good man.

"I'm wrong about the pepper," I said, done with my ruse. "I think it's in a jar as well, with black spots around the rim."

Zevi too had insisted he was following orders, but bringing me to Gibeah did nothing to further the cause of our people's freedom from Philistine threats and oppression.

I had no time to contemplate such things as Asher had returned with the three spices. I accepted the offering as best I could with my wrists still bound, then added a few pinches of the rosemary and crushed coriander to his bowl and mine.

I took a sip of the stew. "Much better. It would be best to steep the flavors for a while over the fire, but that will have to do."

Asher grinned at me. "As long as I don't have to explain to Zevi why you did not eat, then I am satisfied."

Pretending to enjoy my meal, I watched over the rim of my bowl as Asher devoured his own and reminded myself that I had to get free, by any means necessary. I could not miss the chance to run when I knew exactly where I was—and before Zevi returned. Because even if he'd been scarce since yesterday, I doubted he would go much longer before checking on the prize he'd been taking to his king.

It took only a quarter of an hour before Asher went pale. He wiped at both corners of his mouth, where bubbles of saliva had formed, and then a hand went to his middle.

"Something's not right . . ." He turned aside to violently heave the contents on the ground.

I wasted no time in jolting to my feet as he continued vomiting, and then, trying my best not to worry about the man I'd just poisoned, I ran.

"Yochana! Stop!" he called out before loudly retching again. He staggered to his feet.

Another wave of guilt swept over me, but I refused to halt my flight. This was my only chance. I dodged terebinth trees, pulse outpacing my feet. I longed to have my hands free so I could run faster. But I had to get as far away as possible before trying to free myself from my bonds.

Between the blood rushing in my ears and the rush of wind that suddenly whipped through the trees, Asher's words were lost, but so were the footfalls of my pursuer.

Suddenly, arms wrapped around my waist, jerking me to a halt.

"Where do you think you are going?" Zevi said.

I struggled against his hold. "Away from you!"

He pulled me tighter against his body. "Yochana. Stop fighting me."

"I won't."

"Please." The plea was little more than a rasp as he pressed his face into my hair. "Please. I cannot . . ."

I would not apologize for trying to flee, but the raw ache in Zevi's voice startled me to stillness. I counted five breaths, waiting for him to finish, but he remained silent. Frustrated, I spun in his hold, too late realizing that it would put us nearly nose to nose, but I forced my words to come out evenly. "What? What can you not do?"

Still gripping me tight, he met my eyes, and I was struck with the impression that this was not the same man who'd gone off to Lachish yesterday with bold confidence but instead the quiet and intense one who'd walked into my shop. It was as if he'd pulled back the curtain from a window into his soul, and all I could see behind it was a deep and pulsing sadness that I was intimately familiar with. Zevi was a man practically overflowing with grief and regret.

I could not take my eyes off him as I whispered, "What happened to you?"

He stared at me, raw misery on his face, as we breathed in tandem. Then he blinked, twice, and suddenly he was once again the brash commander of his unit, posture stiff, eyes blank, and his jaw again set like granite. He dropped his hands from my waist but did not retreat. "You poisoned Asher."

My stomach curdled. "It's only a little nausea. He'll be fine in a couple of hours."

"What did you give him?"

"Iris petals."

He shook his head, his eyes dropping closed briefly. "Of course you did."

"I was told Asher was fast. I had to do something to slow him down."

He huffed. "None faster. But, unfortunately for you, I am a close second."

"Just let me go."

"I can't do that."

"No. You *won't* do that."

He gave a slight shrug. "I told you I have orders—"

"Yes. Of course. Orders from your king to kidnap women."

He let out a sigh. "I don't have time for this right now. You poisoned Asher. I need to make certain he is all right."

"I told you, he'll be fine. I know flowers and *all* their uses." I gave him a smug smile.

"Noted." He tugged my arm and began to walk back the way I'd fled. "Let's make sure you haven't killed my second-in-command before we split off from the company."

"Split off?" I asked, tripping along behind. "You . . . you are taking me with you?"

"It's clear I can't take my eyes off you," he said, "and I have a mission to complete."

"I thought you were in such a hurry to get back to Gibeah and drag me before Saul. What changed?"

Without faltering a step, Zevi continued on, pulling me behind him, but I thought I heard him murmur, "Everything. Everything has changed."

11

Zevi

I didn't like the looks of the sky. It had been gray before we left the rest of the camp near the town of Sokho in the valley of Elah, but now the clouds were dark as iron and threatening to unburden themselves on our heads. We'd need to find shelter soon.

I remembered this village perched high on the hillside among the trees from when I was a boy. My father had had a distant cousin who lived nearby, and we'd come to help with his harvest from time to time, but I did not remember the man's name. I'd hoped to at least recruit a couple of men here to keep up the appearance I was working solely for Saul's benefit, but while Kyrum and Lemek spoke with other villagers, I'd quietly inquired of the head elder whether any traders had come through, hoping Shalem's captors had stopped here as well.

I had no luck on either account.

I feigned confidence as we went back down the hill, having learned that particular skill long before I'd faced an enemy on a battlefield. I would not show weakness before my men. I'd not told anyone, even Asher and Kyrum, the true purpose of our detour, but there was a moment, after I'd caught Yochana running, that I almost told her. Almost revealed the desperate drive to go after Shalem at the expense of the mission.

Having recovered from his bout of vomiting before the group left, Asher insisted on coming, even if there was still a tinge of green to his pallor. He did not fault Yochana for her attempt at escape and actually lauded her sharp-witted scheme with the iris. *"She'd make a fine spy,"* he said with a wry grin. *"Our enemies would never know what hit them if we sent her into Philistia armed with that dangerous box of hers."*

He and the others who'd volunteered to come along had remained in a small clearing partway up the trail with Yochana while we ventured the rest of the way. It was probably not the wisest decision to have her come with us in the first place, but after what she had done to Asher, I knew she would not give up. All of us would be much more diligent from now on—especially me.

The pleasantly acrid smell of smoke greeted us on our return to the clearing. Someone had made a fire, and a hasty spit held the remains of a large bird. It seemed they'd done some quick hunting while we were gone. Yochana sat near the fire, her eyes on the flames, while Rezev entertained the rest with an account of a skirmish with Philistines a few years back.

Thunder rumbled in the distance as those around the fire noticed our return. Yochana glanced up for only a moment, giving me a scowl before dropping her eyes back to the flames. But that was far better than when she'd been ignoring me. There was a strange sense of relief at finding her here, as though I was a ship returning to port after a long voyage.

I shook off the strange idea. She was intriguing, yes, and admirably strong-willed, but she was a means to an end. One that was becoming more and more necessary with each failure at recruiting more soldiers for Saul.

"Any luck?" asked Asher, coming toward me with a skin of beer in hand.

I accepted it and tipped it to my lips for a long draft, then wiped my mouth with the back of my hand. "None interested in leaving their families so close to Philistine territory."

In truth, I was more frustrated they'd not seen a boy with a silver streak in his black hair. "Everything all right here?"

Asher made a small gesture over his shoulder toward Yochana. "She didn't try and run off, if that's what you are asking."

Kyrum joined us, a frown pinched between his brows. "Remind me again why we brought her with us."

"I told you—" I began, but a scream from behind us had me spinning around, heart pounding and eyes searching for whatever was threatening Yochana.

Instead, they landed on a young man named Eliyah from Lachish, who had somehow pitched hands-first into the fire. With a shout, Rezev leapt up to pull the soldier from the fire while Yochana stood by with her bound hands awkwardly outstretched in horror.

Rezev lowered Eliyah to the ground, muttering assurances that all would be well as the young man shook violently. Asher asked for Yochana's headscarf, which she gave willingly, then soaked it in some water and carefully wrapped Eliyah's right hand in the wet fabric while the soldier trembled and cried out in anguish at even the slightest pressure on his flaming red skin. Thankfully, he'd twisted his body as he fell, sparing his left hand the worst of the burn he'd sustained to his right.

"We need honey," Yochana said, as if it were she and not me in command of my men. "Someone is bound to have some up in the village. If we had time, we could tap a terebinth for sap, but he needs relief now. I saw some calendula on the way up here." She turned pleading gray eyes on me. "You have to untie me. Please. I can help him."

The soldier cried out again, the sound of flaming agony taking me back to a time I had no interest in revisiting. I could not let him suffer, even if it meant letting Yochana go. I took my knife to her bonds, and she gave me a look of such gratitude that it filled my chest with relief.

"Lemek and Kyrum, go back to the village and get honey. I'll take Yochana to find the plant she needs." I gestured for her to lead the way, but within only a few steps of leaving the clearing, the sky opened and a deluge poured down on us.

Undeterred, Yochana pressed on down the hill at a trot, her head moving back and forth as she searched for the flowers she'd seen. I had no idea what to look for, so I kept my eyes on her, where they seemed to naturally land anyhow.

Water sluiced from the sky like a flood and rivulets streamed past us on the rocky trail, turning the ground to mud. Yochana slipped, her sandal sliding out from beneath her, and I grabbed her arm before she could go down.

"Let's go back," I said, "wait for the storm to pass over. It's moving quickly."

She shook her head, heedless of the water sliding down her cheeks and trickling off her jaw. Her brow furrowed, eyes full of concern. "I can't let him suffer. I'll find it."

She was knowledgeable about healing balms and herbs, but as she'd shown me with the little dog, she was also deeply compassionate. I could not deny her the chance to help alleviate Eliyah's pain, so I released her and we kept going.

After another few minutes of skidding down the muddy path with one hand over her eyes to keep her vision clear, she gestured to something off the trail. "There! See those little flowers! I knew I saw calendula."

"I'll go," I said, squinting at where she pointed. I could barely see a thatch of small yellow flowers on a narrow ridge about fifteen paces from where we stood, bobbing their heads in the constant patter of rain.

"No. You'll smash the petals with your big hands." She ignored my protest and darted off the trail into the tall grasses, slipping again and again as she pressed forward toward the flowers.

"Be careful!" I called out, but my voice was swallowed up by another loud rumble of thunder, so loud that it echoed in my chest, and the rain seemed to come down harder, funneling into muddy streams down the hillside. A flash of lightning in the distance between clouds made my skin prickle.

"Got them!" Yochana cried, lifting the plant she'd yanked from the ground, its spindly roots dangling in the air, and giving me such a breathtaking smile that my heart tumbled out of my chest and directly into her capable hands. It didn't matter that her cheek was streaked with mud and her tangled hair was a sopping, matted mess. I'd never seen anything more beautiful in my life.

And then, to my horror, her eyes went wide as a river of muddy water poured over the ridge and swept her feet out from beneath her. She went sliding down the slick hill so quickly it was as if I blinked and she was gone.

Her scream was snatched by the wind as I bellowed her name and tried to follow after her, but the ground was too soft and my own feet began sliding. I spun around and went back to the trail where, although muddy, the packed earth and rock remained fairly solid. I ran down the hill as fast as I could, my pulse clamoring in my ears.

"Zevi!" she called out, and I felt her fear at the center of my bones. She'd grabbed onto the branches of a large bush as she slid by and was now hanging on with white knuckles, water and mud flowing down around her.

Leaving the trail, I scrambled toward her, terrified she would go sliding toward the deep gully below. "Yochana! Grab my hand!"

Her eyes were so wide I could see the whites around her gray irises. But she reached for me, and once I had her hand in my grip, I gave her only a moment to get her feet beneath her before I hauled her toward me.

"You all right?" I asked, entangling my fingers with hers to keep her securely at my side. If another rush of water came at us, I refused to let her be swept away from me.

She lifted her other hand, the plant she'd risked herself for battered but secure in her fist. "I still have it."

I huffed a rueful breath. "Of course you do. Let's go."

Veins pumping with a potent mix of victory and fear, I headed for the trail. Each time we skidded through the mud, I drew her closer, until we were pressed together, side by side as we climbed. Once the ground was finally stable again, we paused for a breath, staring at each other with our fingers still entwined. All I wanted to do was pull her closer, wrap her in my arms where I knew she would be safe, and never let her go.

She blinked, breaking whatever spell had us in its thrall, and flinched away from me. Reluctantly, I let her go. "Are you hurt?"

"A little bruised and maybe a few scrapes but nothing broken. Well, except for the flower stems, but I kept the petals safe."

I tipped back my head, letting the rain fall on my face as I let out a long, slow breath. "I thought you were . . ." I let the words trickle away. How would I even describe my terror as she slid down that hill without revealing the depth of my fascination with her? All I knew was that I needed for her to be safe.

And that meant I should probably let her go.

It would be so easy to do so. She wasn't that far from Maresha, a five-hour walk, perhaps, and I'd already untied her. She'd risked her life for one of my soldiers, a stranger, and she deserved better than to be dragged before Saul against her will. I dropped my gaze to hers and let the moment stretch long, the words that would release her hovering on my lips.

"Zevi!" Asher came flying down the trail with Rezev close behind. "What's going on? We heard shouting. Why are you two covered in mud?"

My throat was too thick to speak.

"We're fine," said Yochana, lifting her crushed plant. "A little mishap, but I have the calendula. Let's get back to Eliyah."

Asher glanced over at me, a pinch of confusion on his brow, but he turned and led the way up the hill. Rezev walked close behind Yochana, his posture protective as I followed a few paces behind, battling with myself over whether I regretted not letting her go.

12

Yochana

I was covered in mud. My dress was soaked through with filth and my hair matted. As I applied the salve I'd concocted from the honey Kyrum had fetched from the village and what remained of the calendula petals, I could feel my skin going tight as it dried. But none of that mattered when Eliyah's right hand was still flaming red. My discomfort was nothing to what he was going through.

He was a brave one, though. Silent as I tended him—or perhaps just unwilling to let the others know how much pain he was enduring. But I could tell that just the slightest brush of my finger against the inflamed and blistering skin was agony. He shifted and winced and held his breath.

"Perhaps when I have my box of herbs again, I can add something for the pain. But I hope this gives you a bit of relief."

"Thank you," said Eliyah. "What was that you put in the honey?"

"A few calendula flowers."

"And you had to chew them first?" He gave me a wan look, probably unsettled by the idea of my saliva coating his injury.

"Normally I would boil them, then collect the essence for the salve, but that takes time. I had to make do."

"I guess animals lick their wounds, don't they?" he said with a little chuckle.

"That they do. In fact, the old woman who taught me my craft insisted saliva helped cut pain, so I probably did you a favor." I winked, and the young man laughed. It was good to see him doing so instead of blinking back tears and shuddering in his determination not to reveal weakness to the men around him.

"It shouldn't take too long to heal," I said. "As long as you keep applying honey and don't use that hand."

"I'll be careful," he said. "I'm more accurate with a sling in my left anyhow."

I lifted my brows, stunned. "Surely you don't want to still fight?"

Eliyah stiffened. "I can fight just as well with my left hand as with my right. I've made a commitment to serve my people, and I will not renege. We've lived in fear long enough."

The thought of this sweet young man going to battle turned my stomach, but I sensed there was nothing I could say that would sway him from continuing on. I could only pray his path would not end the way Ilan's had.

"Well, if you want to have the use of both hands in the future, you'll keep using the salve."

"I'll do my best."

I patted his shoulder. "You are very brave, Eliyah. You will make a fine soldier."

"I'm excited to finally serve my people. Especially under Captain Zevi ben Natan."

"Oh?"

He leaned in. "I talked with some others, and they say he's a legend in the making. The man has no fear on the battlefield. And he's the youngest among those who were promoted to captain after Yavesh-Gilead."

"Was he indeed?" I leaned in a little as well, eager to hear more about Zevi.

A nod. "He was commended right there on the battlefield by none other than Saul's son Yonatan for his courage and skill. Learning from him will be an honor. I only pray he will not send me home like the others."

I furrowed my brow. "Which others?"

"He sent home two men after they made comments about—"

"Time to go!" snapped Zevi loudly from only a pace or two behind me. I flinched at the abrupt order and spun away from Eliyah to glare up at the man he so admired.

Zevi returned my look with a blank one of his own. "We've wasted too much time here. We have two more villages to visit by dark." Then he turned to Eliyah. "You ready, soldier?"

The young man stood, his burnt hand tucked behind his back. "Yes, sir. I am."

"Good. Don't make me regret keeping you in this company."

Eliyah shook his head. "I won't. I vow it." He lifted his bandaged palm and then, with a slight blush on his cheeks, lifted the other instead.

I had a thousand questions but was given barely time to take a breath before we were once again heading back down the mountain. The rain had washed out a few places on the path, but Asher and Rezev were kind enough to help me navigate since Zevi marched at the head of the group, his pace astonishing for a descent down a muddy pathway.

When we came to the spot where only an hour before I'd slid down the hill on a river of mud and debris, the memory of the moments after Zevi had rescued me rose up. Perhaps I'd only imagined it, but I'd had the oddest sense that, had I run, he would have let me go.

What had not been my imagination, however, was the way he'd hurtled down that hill to save me and how he'd clutched me to him once he did, as if I was something precious, and then kept me close to his side until we were on firm ground again.

I didn't know what it meant, or why he'd left me unbound after the mudslide. Perhaps it was simply that he trusted his men would not let me get away or because I'd risked myself to help Eliyah, but something had shifted that I could not explain.

All I could do now was keep up with Zevi's ridiculous pace and tell myself that no matter what had happened up on that muddy hillside, the next time I was presented with an opportunity to run, I needed to take it.

After a couple of hours, a caravan of three wagons appeared in the distance, stopped at the side of the road, probably bogged down by the mud.

Zevi suddenly ordered a halt, and Asher and Kyrum passed a confused look between them. This was the second time Zevi had stopped to speak with someone since we'd parted ways with the rest of his company. Not long before we'd climbed up to the mountain village, he'd jogged off alone to talk to a few field laborers and then ran to catch up with us before wordlessly continuing on.

"Take a break," Zevi said. "I'll go see if these people need help."

"I'll go with you," said Asher.

"No." Zevi's reply was so short that Asher flinched.

As if he immediately regretted the rebuff, Zevi softened his tone. "I don't want them to think they are being overtaken. Traders like these are always on the lookout for bandits. Rest the men beneath those trees." He gestured to a shady spot a few paces from the road. "I'll be back shortly."

There was nothing for Asher to do but obey, so he gave Zevi a curt nod and ordered us to take a break in the shade. Asher stood a couple paces away, guarding me as always, but as Zevi closed the distance between himself and the traders, his eyes were on his captain.

Kyrum joined him, also watching Zevi approach the caravan with a palm raised in greeting.

"What's he up to?" murmured Kyrum in a low voice.

I feigned disinterest by scrubbing at the dried mud on my legs in a futile attempt to slough the itchy debris from my skin.

"Not sure," replied Asher.

"He never stops like this. He usually marches like Pharaoh's chariots are on our tail."

"I know." Asher sounded annoyed, whether with Zevi's odd behavior or Kyrum's question, I had no idea.

From the corner of my eye, I could see Zevi speaking with one of the traders. There was a fair amount of gesturing toward the north from Zevi and then some head shaking from the man.

"If we stop to talk to every merchant and farmer we pass," said Kyrum, "the battle will be over before we get back."

Asher did not respond. And in the distance, we watched Zevi turn and begin to make his way back to our group. But instead of his normal confident stride, his eyes were on the ground, his broad shoulders slumped, and his pace anything but swift.

"They need help?" asked Asher when Zevi was within ten paces.

Looking strangely defeated, Zevi shook his head. "Just waiting out the rain so their wheels don't get stuck. Let's go."

Asher frowned but did not argue, and neither did the other men. But there was a distinct air of unease as we overtook the caravan, and the curious traders watched us pass by. Zevi remained silent, his handsome features drawn. But I held my tongue and kept walking, reminding myself that whatever was bothering him was none of my concern.

We visited two more villages, and two men in each volunteered to join the fight against the Philistines, but somehow Zevi's dark mood deepened, along with the tension among the group. Eventually, no one spoke at all, until Zevi ordered a hasty camp pitched not too far from the trade road and Asher, Kyrum, and a few others slipped off to hunt. Rezev built a fire while I tended to Eliyah's hand, which already looked less angry, and the young man joked about keeping his clumsy feet far away from the flames this time. I laughed at his self-deprecation, glad he was no longer in such agony.

"I must thank you for what you did for my son, Yochana," said Rezev. "The captain told me how you risked yourself to retrieve those flowers."

"Your son?" I blinked at him in surprise, looking back and forth between the two. I'd certainly not noticed any resemblance between them before, but now that I was paying closer attention, there was a similarity in the shape of the eyes and the line of their jaws, although Eliyah must favor his mother, with his more refined features and lighter coloring that contrasted his father's craggy and timeworn appearance.

"My youngest," said Rezev, turning an arched brow on Eliyah. "And the most stubborn of the lot."

Eliyah grinned, although there was an edge to it. "Just like my abba, who insisted upon coming along."

"Of course I came. You have little concept of what you are facing, son."

All of the humor fled from Eliyah's young face, and the resemblance to his father was suddenly much more clear. "I may have never fought in a battle, but I remember the day they came to our town, Abba. So I know *why* I am fighting and for whom, and that is what matters most."

"The Philistines attacked Lachish?" I asked.

Rezev shook his head. "We came to Lachish after our town was destroyed ten years ago. We are from the south, almost to the borders of Simeon's territory. The Philistines came out of nowhere one day in the middle of the dry season. Set fire to our crops. Slaughtered anyone they encountered in the most heinous ways you can possibly imagine." He paused, swallowed hard before continuing. "They took a number of women and children with them into Gaza, including two of my daughters. My wife . . ." He stopped, his voice trailing away as he seemed to choke on the words.

"My ima died protecting me," Eliyah continued for him. "She hid me in a cellar underground and fought them off like a lioness until her final breaths."

Rezev cleared his throat. "An apt description of my Dinah. She was a lioness in every way. If only I'd not been delivering grain to Lachish that day . . ."

"You could not have known what was to happen, Abba."

"That does not assuage my guilt," he replied, his tone mournful. "Nor does it change the way I reacted to her death and the loss of my two girls."

Although I hated to prod at what was obviously a tender place for both these men, I found myself asking, "How *did* you react?"

Rezev winced. "Not with any wisdom, I'll tell you that. We'd lost everything. Eliyah barely escaped as the flames consumed the house. So he and I went with the few families who escaped the destruction and pitched our tents outside Lachish. I went to work in someone else's fields during the day and spent the evenings lost in drink. If it weren't for a kind neighbor watching over Eliyah . . ." He frowned, dropping his head in shame.

"You were grieving, Abba. I knew that," Eliyah said.

"My grief did not give me leave to become the hardened fool I was, drinking my life away, ignoring my son. . . . I was alone on an island I built for myself and blaming Yahweh for how he'd failed me. For taking my sweet girls and my love."

I flinched, his words cutting close to the bone. "You blamed Yahweh?"

"Along with everyone else," he said. "I blamed the men of our town for not being more vigilant. I blamed the elders of Yehudah. I blamed Samuel."

"The prophet?"

He nodded. "It was his sons judging at Be'er Sheva. If they'd been anything like their father, the Philistines would not have dared encroach on our lands."

It was true that Samuel had led our people to victory over the Philistines a number of times over the past few decades. And with each successful battle, he'd become more and more respected by the tribes—although there were many Yehudites who still doubted his motives.

But my father had told me that Samuel's sons were terribly wicked. They took bribes. Used local women for their pleasure. And ignored the needs of the people, including their safety. No wonder the Philistines had capitalized on the weakness. When the outcry became too great to ignore, Samuel had removed his dissolute sons from power, but the damage had been done, and Israel began to fervently demand a king.

But instead of placing a man of Yehudah on the throne as everyone expected from the prophecies of old, Samuel had anointed a Benjamite. One whose urgent call to battle had killed my husband before we'd been married a full season.

Perhaps I'd not been lost in drink in the worst of my grief, but I had lost myself in my work and even shut out my family in many ways, which is probably why my mother and father were so driven to find me another husband. And why I'd been so adamantly against even the thought of someone new. Of course I blamed Saul for my husband's death, but did I blame Yahweh as well?

I had to admit that the answer was yes.

I'd always delighted in the festivals given to us by Adonai, adored hearing stories of our ancestors and the way Yahweh had raised up Mosheh to deliver his beloved people from Egypt. I had spent nearly a decade learning about the myriad plants, flowers, and trees the Creator had spoken into existence and been awed at the ways they lent themselves to healing, to sustenance, and to pleasing the senses.

But since Ilan had died, the colors in my world had been dull. I'd absorbed myself in my craft but without the carefree delight I'd gloried in before. If it hadn't been for Zevi dragging me away, I would likely not have given a thought to traveling beyond the borders of Maresha and would have been content to remain buried in my work and isolated in my shop forever. I'd built my own island, just like Rezev had.

"What changed?" My question was little more than a whisper, but I was almost desperate for the answer. "How did you find your way back?"

"I let go," he said. "I realized that my understanding of Yahweh was far too small and that I had no right to demand he bend to my will."

"What do you mean?"

Rezev then told me about what happened at Gilgal, a few weeks after the battle at Yavesh-Gilead. Noham and the men of Maresha had returned before Saul had been anointed before the people there, so I'd not heard how Samuel rebuked the people gathered to witness the crowning, nor how he called down a terrifying storm on their heads. But it had impacted Rezev deeply. He'd realized that Samuel was indeed a prophet of the Most High and that although Yahweh was angry with Israel for rejecting Him as their king, he *had* chosen Saul to sit on the throne. He'd shown mercy instead of destroying us when he had every right to do so for our unbelief and rebellion.

"I will never forget my wife," said Rezev. "Every day I wonder what would have happened if I'd just not gone that morning to market. And I still grieve my girls every day, wondering where they are and if they are suffering. But I trust that Yahweh knows."

My heart pinched tightly at the devastation in his voice, but I understood it well.

"I am a different man than I was two years ago," he said. "As the captain will certainly attest."

"You knew Zevi before?"

"We had a brief encounter just before the battle at Yavesh-Gilead," he said, looking chagrined. "And not a pleasant one. I'm grateful he's been good enough to let me serve under his command."

"Did you fight in the same unit?"

"I don't think so," he said. "From what I understand, he went into Yavesh-Gilead from the north with the Benjamites under Yonatan. The men of Yehudah volunteered to go in first with Saul. We struck from the south."

My mind snagged on his surprising statement. "Volunteered? Saul didn't command you to do so?"

"No. The king gave a rousing speech before we crossed the Jordan River, saying that he himself would be first on the battlefield to free our brothers from the Ammonites. Even back then, when I hated the man, I was impressed by both his courage and his clarity of purpose—as were the Yehudite commanders. They practically clamored to fight under his banner."

When he returned to Maresha with news of Ilan's death, Noham had been insistent that Saul forced the Yehudites to go first into the enemy camp. He'd made it sound like my husband was an innocent lamb thrown to the wolves by a ruthless king. I'd never known that Saul's feet had gone before Ilan's onto that battlefield. All this time I'd blamed Saul for his death, but truly, it was Ilan who'd chosen to go in the first place. He'd been so passionate about protecting our people and fighting for our right to live in peace in the Land given to us by Yahweh that he'd eschewed the law that told him to remain with his bride for a year. No one had forced him to do so.

As I wrestled with the dizzy array of revelations, Eliyah spoke up. "So you now see why I am so determined to fight the Philistines.

I couldn't do so when I was a boy, but I am of age now. And I'll fight them one-handed if I have to."

Rezev reached over to clasp his son's shoulder. "And I will be right next to you, so that no more women or children have to suffer the horrors the Philistines brought down on our innocent village."

I could not speak for the emotion that rose in my throat as I watched the sweet interaction between father and son. I lifted my eyes to see that the hunters had returned, but Zevi was not among them. In fact, I'd not seen him since we'd first set up camp.

From a short distance away from where he stood watch over me, Asher caught my eye, and he gave me a little shrug as if to say he didn't know where his captain had gone either. I gave him an apologetic smile in return, hoping he knew that I'd meant him no real harm with the iris. And he gave me a wink that told me I was forgiven. His lightheartedness was such a contrast to Zevi's stormy moods that I almost wished I was drawn to him instead of his captain.

I partook of the antelope Zevi's men roasted over the fire at the center of camp, then settled on the ground, surrounded by a number of men who were already snoring after such an arduous march. I scowled up at the stars, uncomfortable in my mud-encrusted skin, trying not to care that Zevi was off by himself in the darkness, that he seemed almost tortured after crossing paths with the traders, or how much it bothered me that he'd not spoken a word to me since he'd rescued me from the mudslide.

I awoke to a hand shaking me gently by the shoulder, my name whispered not far from my ear. Disoriented, I blinked up at the black sky, the stars a bright canopy above me, and when then the hand shook me again, I gasped.

The hand moved to cover my mouth. "Hush. Yochana. It's Zevi."

I flinched away from the touch but did not make noise as I looked up at the shadowy figure hovering over me.

"I need you to come with me. Quietly," he whispered.

"Where?" I whispered back.

He shook his head, indicating he would not say. The audacity of this man. After all he'd done, I should simply trust and wander off into the night with him?

But then I remembered his concern about Eliyah's burnt hand. And that he'd had every opportunity to hurt me since he'd taken me—before that, in fact, when he'd found me alone near the dog's cave. I'd been nothing but vulnerable, and he'd barely laid a hand on me, other than to rescue me from the mudslide and tie my wrists together. And even then, he'd been careful not to wound me and livid when Kyrum had done so.

Besides, my curiosity about where he'd been for so long was almost overwhelming. And so, with a silent prayer that I was not being an utter fool, I stood and followed him out of the firelight, where it seemed only Kyrum was awake, taking his turn at watch.

Once we were far enough away that no one would hear, I spoke up. "Where are we going?"

He must have heard the trepidation in my voice because he paused and turned to face me, starlight illuminating the face that should not be so fascinating to me.

"I know you have no cause to believe me, but I will not hurt you. Please. Give me your trust for just a few minutes. I vow not to abuse it."

"You kidnapped me, Zevi."

He winced. "I know."

I waited for an apology. For an indication that he was contrite and ready to take me back to Maresha, but instead he kept walking. Stunned at his stubbornness but not willing to be left alone in the dark forest, I skittered to keep up.

The sound of rushing water met my ears before I saw it

glimmering in the moonlight through the trees. By the time I caught up to Zevi, he was already standing on the bank of a wide stream, moonlight sparkling on the surface as it hurried along. "What are we doing here?"

"You looked uncomfortable," he said. "Your dress . . . it's stiff with mud. I thought you could use a chance to bathe."

My eyes went wide. He'd seemed so preoccupied with the march and his men and whatever it was he was searching for that I'd assumed he'd barely given me, or my comfort, a second thought. "You want me to bathe with you standing here?"

He lifted both palms. "I will turn my back, I promise."

I huffed. "And I should believe the promises of a man who stole me from my home?"

He dropped his chin. "I know you have little cause to trust me. But there are reasons you don't understand about why I did what I did."

"Then explain it to me!" My voice echoed across the water, startling something out of the brush.

Zevi's sword was out in a flash, and my heart slammed into my throat as two sets of eyes reflected the moonlight. Gooseflesh crawled up and down my arms until the yellow eyes blinked away and whatever had been watching us ran off into the night.

Zevi sighed, lowering his weapon. "That probably was only a couple of foxes, but there are far more dangerous things out here. This may be your only opportunity to immerse yourself without an audience before we make it to Gibeah. So go wash. Kyrum's watch is over soon, and I want to get you back before anyone notices."

"Why?" I asked.

His jaw twitched. "You have so many questions, don't you?"

"Perhaps if you gave me answers I would not have so many questions."

He groaned, running a hand through his thick hair. "Fine. I'll tell you my reasons. But first, get in the water. You stink."

13

Zevi

Her jaw dropped at my rude remark, but the stubborn woman had to be miserable in that mud-encrusted dress, and the last thing I needed right now was for her to dig her heels in for another argument. Thankfully, my audacity paid off. Even though she glared at me, she stepped forward into the stream.

She hissed at the shocking chill of the water, and a shiver jolted her body. I wished there was somewhere warm for her to bathe instead of this swift stream as the breeze swept through the narrow valley with an icy bite. We were used to endlessly marching through sleet, snow, blazing heat, and pelting rain while carrying weapons and heavy armor, but she was not a soldier.

Besides, we were running out of time. The last thing I needed was anyone else questioning why I'd taken off with her in the middle of the night. I'd already fended off questions from Kyrum when I appeared at the campsite to whisk her away. Obviously, he was confused and frustrated with my decisions since Lachish, just as Asher was. And perhaps they were right to be upset. So far there'd been no evidence of the Phoenician traders the weaver had spoken of, and therefore no clear trail to Shalem. It was more than likely I'd led my squad and the new recruits astray for nothing.

Although I'd spent the last few hours tromping through the woods alone, struggling with my tumultuous thoughts, I'd come to the conclusion that I had no choice but to continue this course. In fact, as much as the weight of regret had grown since I'd taken Yochana captive at the caves, it was even more imperative I take her to Saul or return having completely failed in the mission I'd been charged with.

After giving herself a few moments to adjust to the cold water, Yochana walked farther into the stream until it passed her knees, and then, after another short pause while she shivered head to toe, she plunged into the flow, submerging herself to the neck without a word of complaint.

The woman was a wonder. It was difficult to squelch my fascination with her and turn away.

I doubted she would run in the middle of the night, especially in this wild country, but there was no way to know for certain, so keeping my eyes pinned to the trees instead of peering over my shoulder was an exercise in restraint. But above all, I wanted her to feel safe with me. To trust that I would not violate her or her privacy. So I remained at attention, scanning the darkness for any hint of danger while staying attuned to her movements.

"All right, I'm in the stream like you wanted. Now explain yourself," she said, a tremble in her voice as she shivered in the water. "Tell me how you can kidnap a woman with no remorse."

If only she knew how deep the roots of my many regrets traveled. I took a slow breath and lifted my eyes to the brilliant sky. After so many days of storms, broken only by bouts of endless drizzle, to see the stars clearly above us was a relief.

I had no reason to tell her about my past. No imperative to reveal myself to a woman I'd known only for a few days and who'd

immediately hated me for serving in Saul's army, the very thing
I'd worked half my life to achieve.

I loved my family. Adored the parents who'd adopted me into
their home and offered me kindness I never expected. Their children called me brother and looked up to me as their elder sibling.
But this compulsion to just be near Yochana, to be *known* by
her, was like nothing I'd ever experienced. The peace I felt in her
presence was almost as intoxicating as the delicious fragrance
that lingered around her, even when she was covered in mud. And
I simply could not contain my need to help her understand who
I was. And why.

"My father is a Philistine," I said, wishing I could see her face
and know how the revelation landed.

"But . . . I thought you were born in Maresha. My father said
he knew your parents."

"I was. But, as you know, when the plague took them, I was
sent away."

"To Zanoah."

I twitched, again tempted to turn around and look her in the
eye. How had she known?

"My father is on the council," she explained. "He was part of
the decision to send you to your mother's relatives."

I found it interesting that she'd discussed me with her father,
but I wasn't at all surprised he had been involved in the decision
that had altered the course of my life so drastically.

I ran a hand over my face, sifting through memories of that
time to select ones I could bear to speak of. "'Relatives' was a very
loose term for who they were. They were distant cousins, with no
recollection of my mother and no true concern for her orphaned
son." I couldn't keep the bitter note from my voice as I recalled
how they had balked at taking me into their home and how the
man sent to deliver me coerced them into opening their door. He'd
tried to hide that he'd had to promise a few pieces of silver for my

keep, but I'd heard every word of the sharp exchange and would never forget the apology on his face as he turned and walked away.

"They hurt you?"

My chest squeezed painfully, not because of any particular memory but because there was such naked empathy in her voice, as if it hurt *her* to think of a child being treated like a burden.

"Not physically, no," I said, with a shrug. "They just . . . didn't care. I was an extra mouth to feed and a pair of hands to labor in the fields. Their daughters, however, Tera and Chelah, were merciless."

Speaking their names aloud was difficult. The girls had been fourteen and fifteen, both expected to marry that year, and they had tormented me day and night. They mocked my dead family. Told me Yahweh should have killed me too for how worthless I was.

But I refused to dwell on what they had said. Looking back now, they were not much more than children themselves, and their parents ignored them nearly as thoroughly as they had me. Made no secret that they were eager to be rid of them when their bridegrooms finally took them off their greedy hands.

I cleared my throat, steeling myself to continue. "None of it lasted long, anyhow. The Philistines attacked Zanoah three months later and killed all of them."

Yochana's swift intake of breath was loud in the still night, over the rush of the stream, but I pushed on. I'd wanted her to know me, after all. "I was taken to Ashdod, destined for slavery, most likely in one of their profane temples."

I blinked away one of the more potent memories from my weeks in that repugnant city: the hollow-eyed women and children I glimpsed in the courtyard of Dagon's sanctuary during one of my rare outings with Lukio. As a boy, I'd not truly understood the reason for such bleak expressions, especially for people dressed in finery as they greeted worshipers carrying votive offerings. But gradually I'd come to understand exactly what indignities I had been saved from.

"When I was taken to the palace courtyard, taken before the king of Ashdod himself, someone came to my rescue."

Strangely enough, I'd seen Igo, Lukio's enormous gray dog, before I'd seen the man beside him. My young mind conjured the idea that I'd been brought there for the purpose of being ripped apart by the beast. But when my eyes next landed on his master, the Philistine I would come to understand was the feared Champion of Ashdod, I'd been both scared out of my mind and utterly fascinated.

He had looked twelve cubits tall to me. Covered in scrolling tattoos that traveled the length of his thick-muscled arms and across his expansive bare chest. Large ivory plugs filled his earlobes, and his oiled braids came nearly to his waist. The men who'd sacked Zanoah dressed in battle garb and feathered headdresses hadn't looked nearly as frightening. And then there were his eyes. One green and one brown. So startling in their inconsistency that I'd had a hard time keeping my focus from moving from one to the other for a long while.

And yet it was the man the entire city called Demon Eyes who had rescued me.

"Lukio purchased me from the king. I struggled hard as he dragged me from the courtyard, terrified he was going to feed me to his giant dog." I could not help the huff of quiet amusement at the memory. Igo had been the gentlest of creatures and a fiercely loyal companion. He'd been terrified of his own swishing tail at times. A spike of latent grief pierced me. He'd been gone for years now, and I missed his reassuring presence every single day.

I swallowed the lump in my throat. "It turned out Lukio had spent his youth in Hebrew territory, having been taken into a Levite family when he was a boy."

"Truly?" Her disbelief was palpable even without seeing her incredulous expression.

"He kept me safe in his villa for a couple of months until he found a way to send me to the very same family."

"He sent you back to Hebrew territory alone?"

I shook my head, still able to feel the rumbling of the wagon beneath me as I lay beside Igo's warm body under a covering of palm fronds while we snuck out of Ashdod.

"He sent me with Shoshana, a Hebrew woman he'd known as a boy, who'd also been enslaved by the Philistines." I would never have guessed I would someday call Lukio's beloved Shoshana my ima as we'd fled, especially since I'd been certain Lukio was dead that day. But I should have known the Champion of Ashdod would not be permanently separated from the woman he'd loved most of his life.

"Within a week, he had escaped Philistia and followed us to Kiryat-Yearim, where they married. They took me into their home and claimed me as their son. The entire clan claimed me, really." Including Avi, Gavi, and Shay, who were as good as brothers to me. Brothers I'd wronged in so many ways.

"Kiryat-Yearim. Isn't that where the Ark of the Covenant is?" she asked.

"It is. My father's family is charged with its safekeeping."

"Have you seen it?"

"No. It's hidden somewhere. But I've seen the effects of its presence."

"What sort of effects?"

There were plenty of things I could say to her: the extraordinary health of those who lived there; the way Elazar's family flourished and prospered; how women well past childbearing years were blessed with children. But I smiled to myself, knowing what she would be most captivated by—Eliora's garden.

"My father's sister began tending a garden in Kiryat-Yearim not far from the family compound soon after the two of them fled from Ashdod as children. It is like no other garden you have ever seen. There are so many varieties of plants growing there—herbs, vegetables, fruit, berries, and flowers—that I don't have names for half of them. It is as if *anything* planted in that soil flourishes. Twice the size as anywhere else, maybe more. The flavors are sweeter, deeper, lusher. The potency of the spices and herbs stronger. Eliora's garden is so famous that travelers from all over bring seeds, cuttings, and roots for transplanting there. Although my aunt now lives near Ramah with my uncle Ronen and their children, our family continues to tend and expand upon what she began. I doubt there is any sort of plant in the world that does not thrive in that place. It's like the Garden of Eden, truly."

I could almost feel Yochana's fervent gaze fixed on my back. Again, I wished that I could introduce her to Eliora. They would no doubt be fascinated by each other's knowledge.

Another icy breeze curled around my bare legs, reminding me that Yochana would feel it more acutely in her wet clothes and Kyrum's watch would soon be over. "We need to return to camp. Are you ready?"

She ignored my prompting. "I still don't understand. How does your adoption by a Philistine and life in Kiryat-Yearim lead you to kidnapping me?"

I almost laughed. Somehow in unspooling my history, I'd actually forgotten why I'd begun to tell her about my past. I owed her an explanation, even if it was a vague one.

"Because although I was rescued, most of the people the Philistines take captive are not." I tried to force away thoughts of the two girls I'd tried to save that day in the king's courtyard, and the women who'd been dragged away while their daughters screamed for them—not to mention Tera and Chelah's anguished cries—but the memories had been stirred up.

"The Philistines are not bound by the battlefield laws Yahweh gave us through Mosheh. So they have no restraint in how they wage war. Women and children are not exempt from their unspeakable atrocities. They plunder and pillage and rape and burn simply because we are Hebrew and they covet the Land given to us by the Creator. And they do it in the name of their foul gods, who delight in spilled blood and the destruction of innocents. If Lukio had not come to my rescue, I'm sure I would either have been dead within days or wished I was."

I chanced turning my face slightly in her direction because I wanted her to get a glimpse of the determination in my expression. "And I have been waiting—no, *aching*—for the day I could finally repay them for all they took from me and from our people. I have spent nearly every moment of these last twelve years honing myself into the soldier I am, vowing I would meet them on the battlefield not only as a warrior but in command of a company of warriors."

Not as I once had been—a weak and terrified child unable to do anything more than wet myself as the two girls I hated were brutally raped in front of me. My belly burned as the intrusive thought slipped through a crack in the wall I'd built around them so long ago. Every bone in my body went cold, but instead of leaning into the horror, I grabbed ahold of the vow I'd made to myself that day. "I will *not* give up my chance to face them."

"So why take me? I can't fight the Philistines. I am just a woman." Her teeth chattered as she spoke with exasperation. She needed to get out of the stream before she froze to death.

I shook my head. "No. You are not just a woman. You are the most talented perfumer in Yehudah. Perhaps all of Israel. And as I told you, those talents can ensure that Maresha is protected by Saul."

"So that gives you the right to take me by force?"

"You refused to listen to reason—"

She spoke over me. "No, you did not give me a choice. You came into my shop to manipulate me. Lured me in with your pretense of interest. Then you followed me to the cave with inflated ideas of riches and fame and far-fetched notions that my perfumes will save my home."

"They are *not* far-fetched. Don't you understand how much your skills will be valued by the king and his court? You will be in a position to ask whatever you desire and he will lay it at your feet. Anything! There would be no need to worry that he would punish Maresha for the elders' stiff necks and closed purses. Can you really say you would not do *anything* to keep the town—your family—from suffering the way Zanoah did?"

She was silent for a few long moments. "And what makes you so certain that he would listen to me?"

I'd seen how particular Saul was about who and what he surrounded himself with. From the mighty men who made up his personal guard to the materials that went into the building of his fortress, only the best would do. There was no doubt in my mind that Saul would do anything to obtain the unparalleled beauty crafted by Yochana's hands.

"Because you can take a pile of leaves and squashed flowers and turn them into a masterpiece."

"So why not just take the perfumes as tribute?"

"It's not enough."

"But you said my perfumes will convince the king to protect Maresha. Why drag me along?"

The tether on my restraint snapped, and I whirled around to fully face her. "Because I failed!"

She'd left the stream and now stood a few paces away, soaked through, shivering like a leaf in a whirlwind, her eyes huge in the moonlight. I'd shocked us both with my honesty, but I had to make her understand why I'd made such a desperate decision. Why, without her, the vow I'd made as a child might turn to ash.

"If I bring you with me, he will forget that I have failed my mission in persuading my own countrymen to fight for him. I cannot jeopardize my command, especially when everything I've worked for is so close within my reach."

"So I am a sacrifice, then? For your ambitions?"

"No, that's not at all—"

She pulled her arms tighter across her body. "Tell me, Captain, how is what you did any different than what the Philistines did to you?"

I recoiled, hard. I'd been wounded in battle, had plenty of scars to prove it, but no dagger had ever cut so deep as her accusation, nor the truth she'd just hurled at me.

An icy breeze slithered through the trees, and her entire body jolted with another racking shiver. What a fool I was to keep her out here so long while spewing my guts at her feet. I'd meant to give her the chance to be clean, not die of exposure.

With experience born of over a decade of shutting off turbulent emotions, I shoved the pain and guilt away and straightened my shoulders. "You need to warm up. Let's get you to the fire."

A strange look wafted over her features, her brows furrowing as if she'd actually heard the door slam closed on any further explanation of my actions. For a hopeful moment, I thought she would relent before I lost my patience and wrapped her up in my arms just to stop her shivering.

Instead, she gritted her teeth against their incessant chattering and pinned me with a defiant look. "Fine. I'll go as soon as you tell me who you are looking for."

"You know my mission. I need more soldiers. Now, let's go . . ."

She shook her head. "You are not looking for recruits among the traders. Something changed in Lachish. I want to know what—or who—we are chasing north."

Running my fingers through my wild hair, I groaned. How did she see through me so clearly? Asher and Kyrum, who knew me almost as well as Avidan and Gavriel, had not seemed to guess my true reasons for veering away from our original plans.

It was plain she would not give in, and I was almost desperate to get her back to the fire. I threw up my hands and gave her the truth. "My cousin. All right?"

Her long eyelashes fluttered with confusion. "Your cousin?"

"Yes. The boy has been lost for two years, because of me. I happened across information in Lachish that he is with traders traveling north toward Ashdod. But he's gone. I missed him. Or perhaps it was just a false trail in the first place. Either way, I've lost him. Again." I swallowed hard against the glut of sorrow in my throat.

"Oh, Zevi . . ." The whisper of my name on her lips was like a flame in some deep part of me. It took every drop of restraint in my well-trained body not to pull her into my arms and bury my face in her hair like I'd wanted to from almost the first time she smiled at me in her shop.

"Please, Yochana," I rasped. "Let me take you back to the fire. I will tell you about Shalem on the way. I cannot bear to see you shivering like that."

Her eyes flared with surprise as she stared back at me, and I did not care if she saw my desire for her written on my face. It was no use trying to hide it. I'd already given her most of my secrets tonight. What was one more?

The little nod she gave me sent relief sluicing through my body. "All right. Start from the beginning."

14

Yochana

Although my head told me I should not care, my rebellious heart ached for Zevi as he told me the story of four boys who should not be on a battlefield, running off to fight for King Saul. And when he spoke of his overwhelming regret for not sending young Shalem back and for letting himself be swayed into leaving the boy alone to be attacked by wild animals, I was glad for the darkness that surrounded us on the trail back to camp because I could not help the tears that sprang to my eyes.

I'd not expected him to be so honest with me about anything, let alone the horrific things he'd endured as a child. He'd spoken of the destruction of the town he'd been sent to live in, and the people who'd been so awful to an innocent child, in such a detached way. As if it had happened to someone else. And yet I sensed he'd been aching to tell someone these things, if only to purge himself of the horrors he'd experienced.

Why he'd been so open with *me* of all people was a mystery that kept me awake for a long time after he left me by the fire, before

turning back the way we'd come. He'd most likely returned to the
stream where I'd washed, since he was nearly as filthy as I'd been
after rescuing me from the mudslide.

Having taken over the watch for Kyrum, Asher had watched
his captain walk away with a pinch of bewilderment between his
brows. Even his trusted men seemed just as mystified as anyone
else with his behavior.

I did not want to be intrigued by the enigma of Zevi. Or heart-
sick at the idea of his young cousin wandering by himself in the
wilderness across the river, hurt and frightened after an encounter
with hyenas. Or angry on Zevi's behalf at his mother's relatives
who'd treated him so harshly. And I certainly did not want to
imagine the suffering he'd endured at the hands of the Philistines—
especially when I suspected the reality of what he'd experienced
was far worse than he let on. And I certainly did not want to feel
like throwing my arms around him and soothing his pain.

I *wanted* to escape. Wanted to go home to my family and my
shop where everything was safe and familiar.

I still knew more or less where I was. Knew that the trade road
we'd been traveling would take me right back to Maresha. But
since the mudslide, I'd been unbound and had not thought more
than fleetingly about ways to get away from Zevi and his men.

Instead, I'd been captivated by the country we'd been walking
through, by hills and valleys I'd never seen before. The colorful
varieties of wildflowers and blossoming trees painting the land-
scapes around us were endlessly fascinating as well. My fingers
itched to explore them, and my nose twitched with compulsion to
divine their fragrances. I also had to admit that I was not frightened by these men anymore. They'd had plenty of opportunity
to mistreat me since they snatched me from the cave, but instead
they'd defended me, watched over me, and trusted my expertise
when Eliyah had been burned. And then, of course, there were
the things Rezev had said about Saul, and about his grief-induced

anger, that refused to stop echoing in my mind, convicting me of ugly things I'd hidden deep inside my heart.

With my body and mind exhausted, I finally fell asleep, but Zevi had still not returned. When I awoke to the sound of his voice ordering his men to get moving just after dawn, barely giving any of us time to eat our paltry rations of stale bread left over from Lachish, I tried not to let my gaze linger on the shadows beneath his brown eyes that told me he'd gotten less sleep than I had. But it made little difference. He may be the captain of this group of soldiers, a man of war who'd taken me against my will, but he was also a boy who'd been wronged by the people who should have cared for him and who'd been traumatized by terror no child should ever endure.

If anything, I finally understood why he seemed so burdened all the time. He may have broad shoulders, but the man hefted around an unbearable load of responsibility for those around him. For his cousins. His men. The town that had sent him away as a boy. He was like no other man I'd ever met. And although I still had not fully forgiven him for taking me against my will, I had to grudgingly admit that his justifications for doing so were beginning to make sense.

The elders of Maresha were notoriously stubborn. Even my father regularly complained about Zephanyah, the head of the council, and about a few others who he sometimes joked were made of the same granite as their judgment seats. Perhaps the relative peace in the region during the latter years of Samuel's leadership had lulled us into a false sense of security. The battle of Yavesh-Gilead had been far away, and the conflict with the Philistines now was off in Benjamite territory, but what if Saul's army did not succeed in keeping them up north? What if, like Zevi warned, they got bold and swarmed us en masse from the south *and* the west? Yehudah's volunteer militias were scattered and largely untrained.

If my talent for perfumery could actually make a difference in whether the king viewed Maresha as an asset to his kingdom instead of a rebellious outlier, why *wouldn't* I do my best to help? As much as it galled me to give in after Zevi had given me no choice but to come along, the more I considered the stakes, the more I could feel my once-stony resolve melting like wax. I could not bear to think of my own family, my precious little sisters, being subjected to the horrors Zevi had described.

I'd been lost in my own mind as I walked between Asher and Kyrum, but a murmured comment from one of the recruits behind me caught my attention.

"I thought we were going to Gibeah," the man said.

"Me too," said another, his voice pitched low. "If we don't go east soon, we'll miss the entire battle."

Thankfully, a sharp glance backward from Asher abruptly silenced the gossip as we continued pressing forward at a swift but not unbearable clip. I suspected Zevi's altered pace was for my benefit, since I remembered how Kyrum had mentioned he usually led them at practically a gallop.

Ahead of us, Eliyah marched along quietly beside his father. When I'd checked his palm this morning shortly before Zevi had given the sharp command to march, it looked much improved. Perhaps he'd be able to use it in the fight against the Philistines after all.

About three hours after we'd left the campsite near the stream behind, Zevi came to an abrupt standstill, then with only a swift gesture for the startled company to halt in their tracks, he bolted into a run while everyone stood watching in confusion.

It did not take long for me to decipher why he'd acted so strangely. Off in the distance was a lone figure trudging along the trade road, head down. There was no question in my mind who Zevi guessed it could be. Unbidden, my heart kicked up its own pace as he neared the figure, who appeared to be a dark-haired, slender youth, and I found myself praying that his cousin had been found. That just a little bit of the burden he carried might be assuaged.

Everyone stood in hushed confusion as their captain spoke to the young man, but there was plenty of tension buzzing in the air.

In the distance, Zevi reached into his pack and then handed something to the youth—some food, perhaps? But instead of bringing the young man along with him, Zevi turned back toward us, his shoulders slumped.

My stomach twisted. He'd told me if the traders who had Shalem passed into Philistine territory there would be no hope and that we would be near that boundary by midmorning. Which meant the boy's wispy trail was most likely lost for good now.

I was shocked by the strong urge I had to run to Zevi, to wrap my arms around his waist and absorb some of the devastation he had to be feeling after his hopes were crushed. I told myself it was simple compassion and not because last night near the stream he'd given me a look that sent a wave of staggering heat all the way to my toes.

"This is ridiculous," said one of the men behind me. "Are we going to stop for every beggar we see?"

"I agree with Sakar," said another. "This is not what I signed up for. I thought we were going to fight Philistines."

Rezev turned around with a frown on his craggy face. "You'll do as your captain says and keep your mouth shut."

"What are you doing here?" Sakar shot back. "I thought you hated the usurper."

"Mind your choice of words," said Rezev, his tone going deeper with a hint of threat. "And I'll mind my own decisions."

I'd assumed that because these men had signed up to join Zevi's company that they too were loyal to Saul. But apparently there were more shades of loyalty among this crowd than I guessed.

"You have no authority over me, old man," said Sakar.

154

"If you don't want to be here," Kyrum interjected, his tone void of any emotion, "then why don't you turn around and go back to Lachish? No one is forcing you to remain."

I nearly scoffed aloud. I'd certainly not been given the same choice.

"This is nothing but a waste of time," said Sakar.

His friend smirked. "Especially when the so-called leader of this company is too busy panting over this woman he dragged along to focus on the mission."

"You have no idea what you are talking about, soldier," snapped Asher, seeming annoyed for the first time since I'd seen him in my shop. "Like Rezev said, keep your mouth shut and be ready to march when the captain returns."

"Or what, *Benjamite*?" The sneering response was an invitation if ever I'd heard one.

To my surprise, Eliyah interjected. "You have no right to talk to our superiors that way."

"We're just saying what you are all thinking." Sakar wiped his mouth with the back of his hand. "But then again, maybe you hope to have a turn with her when he's finished."

Nausea flamed in my throat at the insinuation, but there was little time to react because Eliyah suddenly barreled past Kyrum and threw a punch with his left hand that landed directly in the center of Sakar's smirk.

Chaos exploded around me.

Asher pushed me behind himself as Sakar's friends retaliated against Eliyah and a couple other soldiers who'd sprung to his defense. Kyrum plunged into the fray, grabbing young men by their tunics and yelling for everyone to stop. But the tension brewing over the past couple of days had already boiled over and all semblance of civility was lost. Curses flew as fast as fists while those who wisely abstained from entering the fight called for the rest to settle down.

And then, suddenly, Zevi was at the center of the roiling stew of masculine rage. He grabbed for Eliyah in an attempt to pull him off Sakar, but the young man did not register his captain's presence. He pulled back his arm to throw another punch, and his elbow connected with Zevi's mouth.

Zevi didn't seem to notice or care that he'd been struck. He slipped his arm around Eliyah's neck and jerked him backward, bellowing for him to stop at once. At the command, the young man twisted around in Zevi's hold and went pale.

Everyone went quiet, wide eyes on their captain as he stood bleeding from the corner of his mouth, chest heaving after what was likely a mad dash toward the mayhem.

"Asher?" Zevi said, strangely composed. "What is going on here?"

"Fools shooting off their mouths," Asher replied.

Zevi's brows arched as he slowly cast his gaze over the faces of the men: some full of shame, some annoyed, and some completely unrepentant. I expected a lecture or a tongue-lashing, but Zevi said nothing as he released Eliyah and then wiped the trickle of blood from his chin with his thumb.

"We're are heading back to camp now instead of continuing north." His tone was strikingly calm after what had just happened. "You can either go forward with us or you can go back. There is no room for in-between." The warning was as clear as his firm resolve.

He gestured west. "There is a spring just past that stand of trees. You have a quarter of an hour to refresh yourself. But remember this . . ." He paused, seeming to meet each man's eye before he spoke again. "You are here to obey orders, not question them. If you can't handle that, then go."

For the span of seven heartbeats, everyone stared at Zevi. He'd not raised his voice as he laid out his expectations, even if he'd drawn a stark line in the dirt. In that moment, I understood exactly why he'd been given command of this unit and how uniquely gifted he was as a leader. No wonder his men followed without question. If he was as iron-willed on the battlefield as he was with his men, the Philistines would have reason to fear the helpless boy they'd once dragged off to slavery.

"Now!" he barked, and immediately everyone scattered.

Rezev and Eliyah, however, remained in place. The boy stood beside his father with his head down, looking so painfully ashamed it made my stomach hurt.

"Captain," said Rezev, "I must apologize—"

"No, Father," said Eliyah, stepping forward and looking Zevi directly in the eye. "I am to blame. I threw the first punch."

Zevi flinched in surprise. "You did?"

I opened my mouth to speak up for him, but Asher beat me to it. "Only to defend Yochana's honor."

Zevi's dark eyes flicked to me, almost as if he'd forgotten I was there, and then back to Eliyah. "Is that true?"

The young man shrugged. "It is. But only because Sakar has little control over his mouth."

"You know him, then."

Rezev spoke up. "The fool lives in a tent not far from ours. He's notorious for his disrespectful ways with women."

Zevi's eyes slipped to me for another breathless moment, then he turned to Kyrum and with two fingers gestured in the direction Sakar and his friend had gone. On whatever silent command his captain had given, Kyrum followed. Somehow, I suspected it would be the last I saw of the two.

"How's your hand?" Zevi asked.

Seemingly thrown by his captain's concern, the young man looked down at his palm as if he'd forgotten it was attached to his own arm. My wrapping was more than half undone and the red skin exposed. "It . . . it hurts, Captain."

"Have Yochana rewrap it before we leave." Zevi dug into the pack still slung over his shoulder and retrieved the little pot of ointment I'd made with the honey and calendula, handing it to me with little more than a fleeting glance. "Rezev and Asher, come with me."

Rezev gave a nod, then patted his son's shoulder reassuringly before following Zevi in the opposite direction of the stream.

Eliyah and I stood silent as the three of them began an intense conversation beneath the shade of a wild olive tree on the far side of the trade road.

"He didn't send me away," the young man muttered. "Why didn't he tell me to go?"

I had no answer for him, other than ones that were not mine to share. So I ignored the question and turned a smile at him. "Thank you for standing up for me."

"I don't know why the captain has you with us. But it's not for . . . *that.*" His cheeks went a little pink. "Sakar has a filthy mind. Always has."

I bit back a smile. There was something so innocent about Eliyah. I hated that he was on his way to war. No wonder his father insisted on remaining at his side.

"How's the pain?" I asked as I reached for his hand and began unwrapping the strip of headscarf.

He shrugged. "Tolerable."

And yet he hissed when I reapplied the balm. I rewrapped the makeshift bandage and tied it tighter this time. "Let me see your other hand."

He lifted it, sheepish as I examined his abraded and bruised knuckles. I clucked my tongue and applied a little of the balm to those injuries as well, hoping it might help speed his relief.

"I appreciate you coming to my defense, but no more brawling or you'll undo my healing."

"Yes, my lady."

I lifted a brow. "None of that. I'm just Yochana."

He gave me an endearing smile that nearly had *me* ordering

the young man to go home. He was entirely too sweet-natured to be a soldier. But like Zevi, he'd endured the unthinkable at the hands of the Philistines and was just as determined to go to battle.

Noting that Asher and Rezev had left Zevi, who was now sitting beneath the olive tree with his eyes pinned on the western horizon, I told Eliyah to go find his father at the spring and crossed the road to the man who'd somehow taken over the majority of my thoughts.

Once in front of him, I waited until he slowly lifted his eyes to meet mine before speaking. "Your mouth is still bleeding."

One shoulder shrugged. "I'll survive."

I held up the pot of balm. "This should help."

The opposite corner of his injured mouth twitched. "Am I to believe that whatever you put on me won't make my lip turn black and fall off?"

Confused, I blinked at him for a few moments, until I realized he was teasing me for what I'd done to Asher. "I guess you'll just have to trust me, won't you?"

I crouched down in front of him, swiped a small glob of sticky balm from the pot, then lifted a glistening finger to his face. I hovered there for a couple of breaths, suddenly realizing what I was about to do.

My gaze darted up to meet his, and his words from before floated through my mind as I stared into his dark brown eyes. *You can either go forward . . . or you can go back. There is no room for in-between.*

It was the defeated curve of his shoulders after he'd realized that the boy on the road was not his cousin that made the decision for me. Zevi may have taken me from Maresha, but such shameful behavior seemed an aberration. Everything I'd heard and witnessed over the past few days pointed to a man whose honor ran bone deep. He'd wronged me, but he didn't deserve to be in pain any more than Eliyah did.

So, I took another deep breath and set my finger on the corner of his mouth.

I expected him to flinch at the contact, but he sat very still, almost as if he was afraid to breathe. I smoothed the balm over the split in his lip and then pressed gently, hoping the bleeding might stop with pressure. However, as I did so, my own blood rushed in a great torrent, and my hand trembled.

Unnerved by my own brazenness, I kept my eyes on his mouth, trying not to think about how close I was to him or how good it had felt to be tucked close to him on that muddy hillside.

Zevi inhaled slowly, his chest stretching as it filled with air, and my eyes darted up to meet his. They were a fathomless deep brown that simmered with both shadows and heat. An answering warmth spread from where my finger remained pressed to his mouth, down my arm, and into my chest.

Everything about him intrigued me: his face, the scars that marred his olive skin along his thick arms, the gaps between the few secrets he'd shared with me at the stream. I'd grown to love Ilan over time, and our childhood friendship easily transitioned into married companionship, but Zevi drew me to himself in a way my husband had never done.

Startled by my disloyal thoughts, I dropped my hand and sat back on my haunches, desperate for a little distance. "The bleeding has stopped."

"Asher told me what Sakar said." His gaze hardened. "That will *never* happen again. I assure you."

I shrugged one shoulder. "Eliyah hit him plenty hard enough."

Zevi's mouth quirked. "I know, I saw the aftermath. However, Sakar and his friend have already been dismissed." But then his fists clenched on his knees, his expression turning apologetic. "I should have considered the implications of bringing you north with me. The rumors it would cause about you."

I waved a hand through the air, dismissing his concern. "I've learned that I cannot control what others think of me, only my own actions. Otherwise I would have given up my shop when some of the townspeople said a woman should not own a business without oversight."

Zevi frowned. "How did you manage to keep it?"

"I went before the council. Made my case for continuing my trade as a widow."

His dark brow quirked. "The notoriously *stubborn* council of Maresha?"

I grinned, thrilled by the glint of amusement in his expression. "The very same. And they granted my request. Although I must admit that it might have had more to do with Avigail, the head elder's wife, who told me that whenever she wore my perfume she couldn't keep the old goat away from her."

To my delight, he laughed, and his smile was just as devastatingly beautiful as I'd hoped it would be and smashed through what little remained of the wall I'd constructed to keep him out of my heart. He may not have given me a choice to come with him in the first place, but I had no more desire to run away.

I hated to bring up Shalem, since he'd been so obviously disappointed after speaking to the boy on the road, but my curiosity would not hold.

"So the boy we saw . . . it wasn't . . . ?"

His expression fell. "No. Just a youth looking for work up in Beit Shemesh to help his family. If he'd been anywhere near military age, I might have taken him with us, but all I could do was give him some food and send him on his way."

"I'm sorry."

He shook his head, gaze drifting off toward the northern horizon. "Shalem is gone. Probably far into Philistine territory by now. I failed him again." He scoffed. "And now I've failed my men too. No wonder they are fighting. They have no confidence in me."

I'd been right that he'd been carrying the weight of the world on those broad shoulders, and looking at him now, I did not see the man who'd kidnapped me. I saw the one who'd told me that my creations should be worn by royalty. The one who'd saved me from tumbling to my death. He'd given me a gift last night revealing his painful past and so I would give him the grace he'd not even asked for.

"That's not what I see," I said. "I don't know much about what happened across the river. But I see men who look to you with great respect."

He scoffed again, his eyes practically rolling back in his head.

"There were two sides to that fight, Zevi. Yes, there were a few grumblers questioning your decisions, but there were more who stood up for you, who look at you with open admiration. You may not notice it, but I've been watching carefully. Most of them are champing at the bit to go to battle under your command, either because they've seen you are honorable or have been told of your worthiness as a leader. They don't question your orders because they trust you implicitly."

He stared at me with open-mouthed surprise.

"As for your cousin," I continued, "unless you go plowing into Philistine territory alone, where you'd certainly be slaughtered, I guess you'll have to leave the rest in Yahweh's hands."

"You sound just like Avi. He said Yahweh knows where our cousin is and will reveal it in his own time."

"I thought Avi ran off to look for Shalem when you and Gavriel remained with the army."

"He did. He disappeared for months across the Jordan. But instead of bringing back our missing cousin, he brought home a woman."

I raised a challenging brow. "I'll bet *he* didn't have to kidnap her."

"No. He didn't." His lips quirked with amusement again, then pressed into a thoughtful line. "Although the way my cousin looks at his wife, I would not put it past him to do so if it meant having her near him always. To ensure that she was his, and his alone."

My throat went dry as his gaze dropped to my mouth, and I sensed that Zevi was not talking about his cousin anymore. My pulse kicked up as he lifted his eyes to mine, full of longing. "It may be your perfume that drew me into your shop that day, Yochana. But it was you who captured me first."

Shocked at his confession, I inhaled a sharp breath, but before I could reply, Asher called his name in the distance, announcing that the men were assembled up ahead and ready to depart for Beit Shemesh.

We stared at each other, awareness humming in the space between us for a few more moments before he stood and silently walked away, leaving me unguarded, unbound, and not far from the road that would eventually take me back home, should I head south.

And yet it took me only the span of ten short breaths to follow Zevi instead.

15

Zevi

I was a fool. A wretch of a man who could not see past his own nose.

Everything Yochana had said of me was true—including her accusation last night that I was no better than the Philistines. Self-recriminations dogged my every step toward the camp in the Elah Valley. If I'd not been leading a small company of men, I would have spilled my guts on the ground.

How had I lost my way so completely that I would take an innocent woman from her home to further my own ambitions? I was still convinced that she could benefit Maresha with her skills, but what right *did* I have to take her choices away? I'd spent my entire life cursing the elders for sending me away from my home, cursing my mother's relatives for treating me like a dog, and cursing the Philistines for taking me into slavery, and then I'd stripped her of dignity all the same—tying her up and throwing her into the back of a wagon like a sack of barley. The fact that she'd seemed to have suddenly softened toward me made it worse. I did not deserve her kindness. Did not deserve gentle words and tender ministrations from a woman like Yochana.

For some inconceivable reason, she was still with us. Striding along confidently between Eliyah and Rezev as if it had been her own decision to be dragged to Gibeah like a prisoner of war. Why hadn't she walked away when she'd had the opportunity? I could have sent Asher to escort her to Maresha, since he was the only one of us who could run like a panther and would likely have been back before the moon rose high. And yet, I was not just a fool but a selfish one. I wanted her close to me, even if I had absolutely no right to keep her.

By the time we neared the camp where we'd left the rest of the company, I was thoroughly disgusted with myself. The sun was already drifting toward the western end of the sky, but the men were still going through the arduous exercise regimen I'd devised for myself from things my father had taught me.

Even if he refused to lift a sword in war against an enemy, he had understood my ambition from the beginning and had showed me the techniques he'd used to build himself into the Champion of Ashdod. It was one of those same exercises the recruits were executing now as we approached, running with heavy stones over their heads up and down the steep incline above camp, their rhythmic chants echoing off the hills around. The sight should have invoked a swell of pride in me, yet all I could see was my failure.

I would not be returning in triumph with one hundred well-trained men. I'd barely be limping back with eighty, because the four I'd recruited yesterday had left after the fight this morning.

I charged Eliyah and Rezev with Yochana's safety since they'd already proven themselves to be loyal and protective of her and then Asher, Kyrum, and I went to find the men I'd left in charge of the camp. We found Lemek, Shimi, and Mahir at the foot of the hill, watching the recruits' progress.

"Well," I said, "how are they shaping up?"

"It may not be the numbers we hoped for," Mahir replied. "But they'll get the job done and that's what's important."

I doubted Merotai would see it that way.

"We've had a few more show up to join from surrounding towns," said Shimi. "We should be heading back with around eighty-five."

That was a surprise. But still, eighty-five was not a hundred. Anything less than the full number would be counted as failure. One more to add to my lengthy account.

Suddenly overcome by shame, I told Asher to explain the plans for our return to Gibeah and ignored the odd looks from the rest of my men as I walked away.

I needed to clear my head.

Heading west, I followed the wide stream that flowed along the valley floor, its stony banks reminding me of another brook I'd sat beside nearly two years ago, hours after the battle of Yavesh-Gilead.

I'd been in shock as I'd sat there on a fallen log, staring into the water, trying to drown out the screams of the numerous Ammonites I'd killed, while Avi and Gavi went to fetch Shalem from the cave where he'd been hidden.

All I'd ever wanted was to become a soldier, and I'd excelled at it that day, but I had not been prepared for what looking into the eyes of an enemy as he took his last breath would do to my soul. When finally I'd managed to lift my head and blink away the haze, I'd spotted an abandoned waterskin across the narrow stream. We'd left just such a vessel with Shay.

Hair prickling on the back of my neck, I crossed over to discover the leather bag shredded, flecked with blood, and surrounded by numerous claw-toed paw prints that looked to be made by a pack of hyenas. All I could see for a moment was Tera and Chelah lying in their own blood and the footprints of the animals who'd destroyed them around their bodies. I'd not even considered for a moment that Shay was still alive after seeing what I felt was clear evidence he'd been torn to pieces.

Now I'd lost him again because I'd insisted on staying in Maresha one more night to snatch Yochana like the vile predators who'd snatched me.

The woman I called ima would be ashamed of me. Shoshana too had endured the unimaginable at the hands of the Philistines before being taken captive in Ashdod. How would I ever face *her* after what I'd done?

Turning away from the stream and the memories it invoked, I followed a narrow path up the hillside that meandered through a grove of wild terebinths, their profuse red blooms blazing in the golden afternoon light. I vaguely wondered what miraculous remedy or ethereal fragrance Yochana could concoct from them.

Everywhere I looked there were reminders of the woman who filled my mind day and night. She would undoubtedly know the names and characteristics of each flower, tree, and weed on this hillside. The blazing gleam of sunlight off the brook below me was like the flashes of her fiery intelligence whenever she challenged me. And somehow, up on this hill where I could see nearly the entirety of the Elah Valley, from Azeka to Adullam, I could still smell her fragrance on the breeze. It curled around me, causing a peculiar ache to expand in my chest and growing ever more potent with each step.

I'd never considered a wife. My mind had been so consumed with my mission to rain vengeance on the Philistines that I'd rebuffed numerous discussions with my father about marriage and attempts by my mother to introduce me to one lovely young woman or another in Kiryat-Yearim.

However, a few months after Avi had returned to Naioth with Keziah, his young bride, I'd had the chance to meet her during an ingathering celebration, and I'd been struck at the strength of connection between them.

Just as I'd told Yochana, my cousin adored his wife. They already had one child and another on the way, and although I'd known Avi since he was a boy, I'd never seen him so joyful. So at rest.

I'd been surprised to realize I was a little jealous of his new-found peace. Of the easy laughter, the secretive smiles, and the gentle affection he and Keziah shared.

Yet as was my habit, I'd immediately pressed such longings into whatever small compartment they belonged in my mind and forced myself to focus instead on my purpose.

Until Yochana.

Until I'd walked into her shop and an earthquake had rattled my bones—at least that was how it had felt when everything I'd diligently tucked into its proper place had been shaken free all at once.

I came up over a small rise and out of the trees to find myself in a hidden glen. My breath caught in my chest as I took in the sight in front of me. The sun sat perched atop one of the low hills of the shephelah, painting the sky in vibrant purple and orange. I remained there, captivated by the masterpiece of color and light until it slid down over the territory of my greatest enemies and the first stars blinked in the heavens.

It was clear as the brilliant canopy above that Yochana held claim to my heart, whether she desired it or not. Not only had I wronged her by stealing her away in the first place, but I was also putting her at risk by keeping her with us. The fight that had broken out with the recruits this morning had been sobering. Aside from the awful things that had been said of her, she could have been injured in the chaos.

Also, we were not all that far from the serpent's nest the Philistines called Gath, a place where descendants of the giant Rephaim still resided—we could have been ambushed on the road at any point during our fruitless detour and were heading directly back into a war zone

True, Maresha might be at risk in the future if we somehow lost this fight, but for now the best and safest place for her was far from me. I'd find some other way to convince Saul to protect the town she loved. Regardless of the way everything inside me had shifted so profoundly and irrevocably from nearly the first moment I saw Yochana, I had to send her home.

For the second time in the last three days, I woke Yochana before dawn. I'd not been able to help but just watch her sleep for a few moments, giving myself permission to memorize her face in the flicker of torchlight, wishing I could inscribe it in my mind for always. Kneeling beside where she slept beneath the wagon, I allowed my eyes to trace over her brow—smooth in rest—her high cheekbones, the slope of her nose, and finally the enticing curve of her lips. What I would not do to slide my fingers into the thick chestnut hair that lay in waves around her head, caress the silken smoothness of her light olive skin, or have those lively gray eyes smile at me instead of pierce me through. . . .

But I had been selfish enough. I would not touch her. I had to simply drink my fill before she awoke and let that be enough. I whispered her name, bracing for her displeasure. But when her eyes fluttered open, she just looked up at me with hazy confusion.

"Zevi?"

My name in that sleepy rasp caused a buzz of desire in my veins, so I pulled back and lifted the torch a little higher. "My men are getting the recruits ready to depart. But I need to show you something first."

She lifted one brow. "Last time you woke me, I nearly froze to death."

There was a touch of tease in her words, and I thrilled with hope that perhaps she didn't despise me after all, even if I deserved it. "Please, come with me."

She peered up at me for a few moments before nodding. The tidal wave of relief that tiny gesture inspired was on the edge of absurd. But it meant that though I'd wronged her, she held a small measure of trust in me. And I did not take that lightly.

Someone had given her a blanket last night, and once she slid out from beneath the wagon and stood, she pulled it tightly around herself to ward off the chill of the morning. Thankfully, it hadn't rained again, but the air was still full of moisture. I led the way through what remained of the camp, ignoring the curious looks of my soldiers and the questioning murmurs between them, and took Yochana along the path I'd found yesterday while the sky shifted from deep blue to gray.

She kept quiet as we followed the stream, but when I turned away from it to climb the hill, she paused. "I thought you were in a hurry to get your men moving this morning."

"I'm the captain," I said. "They'll wait for my command."

She lifted her brows but kept her thoughts to herself as we continued to climb. With my eye on the eastern sky, I'd timed our walk well, because as we came up over the last rise and through the trees, golden sunlight spilled over the horizon and illuminated the vast sea of blue that filled the glen I'd stumbled onto yesterday as I wrestled with myself.

Yochana gasped, hands flying to her mouth as she gazed upon the one and only gift I could ever give her.

"Lupines," she whispered. "Blue lupines. How did you . . . ?"

"The scent of them is embedded in my mind. Has been since the first day I came into your shop. As I walked up here last night to clear my head, the breeze carried this fragrance—your fragrance—to me and I followed it here."

She took a few steps to wade into the thick blooms, stirring their sweet essence, and then turned to face me. "These are my favorite flowers. The base of my own perfume."

"I know," I said, moving forward into the meadow myself,

drawn to her by instinct. "The fragrance follows you everywhere. Even covered in mud. I cannot get enough of it."

She blinked a few times, then frowned in bewilderment. "Zevi . . ."

Again I felt the impact of my name on her lips, but I put up my hands, cutting off the rejection that was sure to be next. "From the moment this fragrance lured me into your shop and I heard your voice, I have wanted to be near you. I cannot explain why. Only that there is something about you that calms me."

The chaos inside my mind had been there for as long as I could remember, at least since my family began dying off one by one, leaving me the sole survivor in a house of death. And although Natan and Shoshana were the best of parents, and I had no doubt they loved me, it took concerted effort to block out the noise.

I'd disciplined myself, learned to control the turmoil in my head in order to be a soldier—even taught myself to use those extreme emotions for my advantage in battle. But in Yochana's presence, it was effortless. How could I explain any of that without making myself sound like a madman?

"Being near you makes the storm in here"—I placed my hand on my chest—"go still. And even when you are scowling at me and putting me into my place—and rightly so after what I've done—I cannot help but be drawn to you the way the bees are bewitched by these blossoms." I gestured to the lupines all around us.

"Zevi, I—"

I interrupted again. "I'm not asking anything of you. Only forgiveness."

Her gaze scrutinized my face. "You want me to forgive you?"

"You were right. I am little better than the fiends who took me from Zanoah."

"That's not true, Zevi. I was too harsh."

"No, you weren't. I may not have violated you like they did me, but I harmed you just the same." My gut burned and my heart

171

pounded thickly as I spoke the entire truth out loud for the first time. I dropped my gaze to the blue flowers, unable to look her in the eye after such a horrifying revelation. "Just as I was taken to Ashdod to be sold for someone else's pleasure, I treated you as little more than a bag of silver to purchase Saul's goodwill for the town and to keep my command secure by distracting my own commander from my failures. But you are not a commodity to be bargained with. You are a woman of inestimable worth that I in no way deserve."

She stood perfectly still and silent, most likely disgusted and appalled, while the sunrise gently caressed her skin the way I never would.

"Asher will be here soon to take you back to Maresha."

She let out a little gasp. "You are sending me home?"

"I should never have taken you away. I will figure out another way to ensure Saul sees Maresha as an asset to his kingdom. I *won't* let anything happen to your family." I wasn't certain how I would avoid telling Merotai about the unwillingness of the elders to support Saul, but I would think of something.

"What about your mission? You are still short of your goal, are you not?" The concern in her voice was baffling to me.

"I'll find a way, but it will not be at your expense."

Her expression was full of confusion. "But you said I could help. That Saul will listen to me if I offer my talents."

Was she arguing to *stay*? "That doesn't matter now."

"Why not?"

"Because nothing matters more than your safety, Yochana. I've already put you in far more danger than I should have. Just like I did with Shalem."

"I do not feel endangered. I trust that you and your men will protect me."

I shook my head. "No. You must go back. This is my responsibility, not yours."

"If I can help my people, then I should go. Maresha is my home, Zevi."

"And it is *my* birthplace." I paused to take a deep breath, dropping my gaze to my feet. My attention snagged on one of the lupines I'd carelessly trampled. "You must understand that after I was sent away, I forced myself to forget. Dammed up every good thought of Maresha behind a thick wall. But as I walked through her streets, it came flooding out. My parents. My siblings. Everything. And I would dishonor their memory if I did not do everything in my power to ensure the survival of the place they loved."

"Let me help you, Zevi. We can *both* honor them, together."

Startled by how close she was now, I looked up and found the blue sea around us reflected in her gray eyes. I clenched my fists, restraining the instinct to reach for her. "You can help me by returning to Maresha where I can know that you are safe for now. If anything happened to you . . ."

I shook my head, angry with myself for putting her in this position. "You should be happily working in your shop right now creating treasures, not marching with a bunch of foul-mouthed soldiers who can't keep their eyes to themselves."

Her lips twitched. "Foul-mouthed, I'll agree with. But aside from what happened on the road yesterday, I've not felt disrespected by your men."

I resisted the urge to snarl. "That's because I sent home any who dared to do so in my presence."

She blinked at me in open astonishment. "Why would you do that when you are short of men already?"

"I told you, you matter more than the mission." I was shocked to realize that it was true. After having only one goal for so long, I'd discovered something—or rather someone—that meant more. I would take a demotion if it was necessary, but I would not risk her. Even if it meant disobeying direct orders from my superiors.

A mischievous breeze tugged a long piece of her dark hair across her face, and without thinking, I reached up to smooth it away from her mouth. She flinched ever so slightly at the touch but did not pull away. Instead, she let me skim the back of my hand down her cheek and across her jaw.

"If only . . ." I whispered. "If only I'd not been sent away. If I'd been allowed to remain in Maresha. So much could have been different. I know you loved your husband . . ."

She nodded, her eyes glistening.

"I don't begrudge the time he had with you. From what I know of him, he was a good man. But I cannot help but wonder, even if it is selfish of me . . . what would life be like if I'd known you all along? Found you first? I would have done anything to make you mine. At the least, I would never have endured the attack at Zanoah. I would not be so . . . ruined."

Her chin wobbled, and a tear trickled down her cheek. "You aren't ruined, Zevi."

My eyes followed the track of that one precious, undeserved tear until it dropped from her jaw to the dirt.

"I am. We both know it." I gave her a rueful smile. "I accept full responsibility for the choices I've made. So I need you to go back with Asher. I need you to be safe. Far from anyone who might harm you, including me."

Her brows pinched as she stepped in closer. "You won't harm me. You may have made a few bad decisions, but you are a *good* man. A *good* leader."

I frowned, still astounded that she'd not already walked away from me, as she should have. "I don't know about that. There are likely far better men than me to lead this company into battle."

"I couldn't agree more." The words had come from just beyond the tree line, but I did not need to turn my head to recognize the speaker. I knew that voice as well as my own.

I spun to find the man who'd fought at my side for almost two years, whose battle wounds I'd tended, and who I trusted almost as much as my own cousins, stepping into the blue-clad meadow, his sword in hand.

"But then, I already have someone in mind," said Kyrum, with a mocking little bow. "Me."

16

Yochana

As Kyrum came forward into the field of lupines with a sword pointed at his captain—his *friend*—Zevi shifted himself in front of me, his own weapon already in hand. "What are you doing?"

Kyrum sneered. "I've always known you were weak, even if you hid it well. I was just biding my time until you showed your underbelly. I appreciate you making it so very easy by bringing your little plaything along on this mission."

The suggestive arc of his brows and the lurid way he spoke of me made my skin crawl. I'd noticed Kyrum watching me a couple of times when Zevi wasn't around, but I'd never guessed he thought of me in such a way.

"I don't understand," Zevi said, undisguised pain in his voice. "You have been at my right hand for nearly two years. Since Yavesh-Gilead. I've thought of you as a friend—no . . . a brother."

Kyrum frowned, his disgust evident. "The worst two years of my life. Playing along as if I was another of your sycophants, like Asher. Calling you *captain* when it should have been *me*." He slapped a palm to his chest.

Zevi's breath came out in a huff, as if he'd been punched in the gut. "I had no idea. . . ."

"No. You didn't because you were too wrapped up in your own ambition to notice mine. But I have to thank you." He smiled, pointing the tip of his sword at Zevi. "Not only have you been so busy drooling after this woman that you didn't notice the alliances I've been making and game pieces I shifted in my favor, but you've been wandering off talking to beggars and farmers instead of doing the job you were sent to do. It was all too easy to finally claim what always should have been mine."

"What do you mean, shifting game pieces?"

Kyrum laughed. "Why do you think you could barely get eighty-five men to follow you to war? Especially when the men of Yehudah are clamoring to fight the Philistines?"

"You were undermining my efforts," Zevi stated, his tone bleak.

Kyrum shrugged. "Why do you think Lemek and I always volunteered to be the ones to recruit for you? Especially in Lachish, all it took was a well-placed rumor about your cowardice in battle and many of those who initially thought to join chose instead to go to Hebron, where captains with much better reputations are recruiting men to their companies. Of course, we were careful to enlist just enough fools to keep you in the dark."

Zevi flinched as evidence of yet another betrayal among his men came to light. "It was your own father who put me in command of this company."

"Oh, don't I know it," snapped Kyrum. "He did it to punish me. To teach me some ridiculous lesson about long-suffering or some such thing. But he'll have no choice but to elevate me now."

"After a mutiny?"

Kyrum laughed. "Of course not! I'll be promoted after I return the bags of silver you stole from the wagon when you ran off with your lover, too ashamed of your failure to face Saul."

Lemek joined him on the edge of the meadow, false apology

on his scarred face. "Sorry, Captain. He's giving me a share—and crediting me with uncovering your theft to his father. I have ambitions too, you understand."

If the burst of hot anger I felt on his behalf for this brutal betrayal meant anything, it seemed I had indeed forgiven Zevi for what he'd done. And I needed him to know. To show him that he wasn't alone.

I moved forward until I could feel the warmth of him in front of me and placed my hand on his back. He stiffened for just a moment, surprised by the contact, but then his shoulders relaxed slightly, and he leaned into my touch. He'd understood my silent message, I was certain of it.

"You two may fool some of the new recruits," Zevi said, "but you'll never convince Asher or Mahir and Shimi."

"Not to worry. We have plenty of witnesses to your treachery," said Kyrum.

A few more men stepped forward at his beckoning gesture, including Sakar and his friend. Apparently, Kyrum had not actually sent them home after Zevi ordered them dispatched.

"Besides," Kyrum said, "Asher won't be able to refute me, given you killed him."

I gasped at the same time Zevi groaned out a tortured, "*No. You didn't . . .*"

"I did everything I could to save him." Kyrum frowned deeply, sounding truly sorrowful. "But you stabbed him in the neck from behind. He never saw it coming."

Zevi shuddered in horror, just once, before going still as a wall of granite in front of me. I guessed that if he was not so committed to protecting me, then Kyrum, and possibly Lemek, might already be dead. But Zevi remained steadfast, not making the slightest movement toward his betrayers. For my sake.

Any unforgiveness I'd been harboring dissolved into nothing, replaced by acceptance that the feelings Zevi had admitted were echoed in my own soul. Until this moment, I'd not allowed the unbidden desires to take root, but it seemed they'd implanted themselves anyhow.

"Just let her go," said Zevi, his voice admirably calm. "You can do with me what you want."

"And why would I do that? She was valuable enough for you to snatch from Maresha. You made it clear how much the king will covet her skill. I'll bring her to Saul myself."

"I won't go with you," I said. "And I'll tell the king what you've done."

"No, you won't. Because, first of all, if you make a peep once we are back at camp, I'll let them have you." He gestured over his shoulder at the lecherous men from Lachish. "And if you say anything to Saul or anyone else, I'll make certain Maresha's treachery is uncovered and therefore left to burn the next time Philistines invade."

I blinked at him, confused.

"Oh yes. I know about the group planning to depose Saul and replace him with a Yehudite—and how most of the men on the council are funding their efforts. It didn't take long for a few of your fellow townspeople to spill their guts, especially when we paid for their drinks at the tavern." He tutted, shaking his head. "Saul will not look kindly on a town that is actively working against him. And I'll make certain your father is the first to be named as a leader of the coup."

All the blood seemed to drain from my head to my feet. My father was not an avid supporter of Saul but neither had he ever been involved in Noham's machinations. He was a kind and righteous man. It was *my* silver that had gone toward the plot.

Nausea flamed in my throat as conviction arose in my heart. I'd certainly had no right to judge Zevi for his sins when I'd been involved in a plot to kill the king. And after hearing Rezev's account from Gilgal, I was beginning to believe Yahweh himself had truly anointed Saul to rule Israel.

Shame settled over me like a shroud. *Adonai, forgive me.*

"Now, I really need to get my men on the road, so this little chat is over." Kyrum turned to Lemek. "Let's get on with it."

"When I say go, you run in a back-and-forth pattern as fast as you can," murmured Zevi, without turning around. "Don't stop."

"But—"

"Yochana. I'll give you as much time as I can, but you *will* run."

Dread clawed into my gut as Lemek stepped forward, along with another man from Lachish.

"Zevi," I whimpered, gripping his tunic with shaking hands. "I'm not leaving you to face them alone."

"It's all I have to give you," he said. "Just say you forgive me."

"I do. I do. Please don't—"

Suddenly, the two men lifted bows with arrows nocked, pointed at the two of us.

"Go!" Zevi said and sped forward, sword raised and a battle cry on his lips.

In a terrified daze, my body turned to obey, but I glanced over my shoulder before my feet could move. To my horror, Zevi's form jerked once, then twice before he'd taken more than a few steps. Pain shot through me just as surely as the arrows had done to him, and everything went hazy. I could still hear the echo of his insistent command to run away, but my legs refused to listen.

I spun around, a shout of disbelief bursting from my mouth as Zevi fell into the sea of blue lupines he'd brought me to, and without a second thought, I ran to him, throwing my own body over his pierced one.

As I shielded him, pleading for his life, Kyrum and his fiends sauntered forward.

"Take her," Kyrum said. "Tie her well and get her in the wagon. Don't forget to gag her. Can't have her flapping her mouth."

Two of them grabbed me and yanked me away from Zevi with

rough hands. I screamed for them to let me go. Screamed that he was dying.

"What do we do with him?" asked Lemek. "Cut his throat?"

My whole body went ice cold as Kyrum considered, looking around at the secluded meadow far from the camp.

"No. He can suffer for a while before he dies, just like I had to suffer under his command for almost two years." He crouched beside Zevi and snatched the iron sword from his grip. Then shook his head, scoffing. "If only my father could see his precious protégé now. Sorry, *Captain*, it's just your bad fortune he chose you over me."

I fought and kicked and screamed for Zevi, but the only glimpse I had of him before Kyrum's ruffians dragged me away was the man who'd stolen me, and my reluctant heart, spilling his precious lifeblood into a sea of blue lupines.

17

Not only was I too shattered to care that I was bound again, but there was little point in struggling against the ties at my wrists, nor attempting to push the gag from my mouth. Because unlike the first time I'd been taken captive, the men who held me now were anything but gentle. Lemek had trussed me with careful precision, checking and double-checking that his painfully tight knots were secure before forcing me back down the hill beside him, to the place where Asher's body lay in the weeds near the trail, still and pale.

He had been so kind and protective of me, even after I'd poisoned him. It broke my heart to see his lifeless body carried between the traitors who'd cowardly ambushed him. It made me ill to think that Kyrum would inform Asher's family by telling lies about Zevi murdering his closest friend. How his sisters would grieve such an injustice without knowing the true perpetrator. And how Zevi's family would never know the truth of his innocence.

I was fairly certain Lemek and Kyrum meant to throw me into the wagon without drawing attention, but when we arrived back at camp, there was a group of men standing in our way, including Shimi and Mahir. The two took in the sight of me, bound and covered in Zevi's blood, and jogged forward.

"What's going on? Where's the captain?" Shimi demanded, his

eyes searching behind us. When they landed on Asher's body, a horrified sound came from his mouth. "What *happened*?"

"A tragedy is what happened," Kyrum said. "One I would not have believed had I not seen it with my own eyes."

The snake sounded truly mournful, as if he'd not perpetrated the tragedy. I was desperate to free myself from the gag to scream the truth, but I was tied both with rope and with the threats Kyrum had made against me, my father, and Maresha. After the cruel betrayal I'd witnessed, I had no doubt he would go through with them.

"Were they ambushed?"

"No." He shook his head mournfully. "Far worse. Zevi betrayed us."

I groaned my frustration in the back of my throat, and Lemek squeezed my arm in an iron grip, warning me silently.

"No, that can't be," said Mahir, who I'd never actually heard speak before. "The captain would never—"

"I would have told you the same thing yesterday. But it's true. He and that *woman*"—Kyrum directed a sneer at me—"planned to run off with some of the silver we'd collected in tribute for the king. Asher must have discovered their treachery before they could get away because Zevi killed him." His voice warbled, and he paused as if overcome by grief. No wonder he'd been able to fool his friends for so long. He was a highly skilled deceiver.

"Zevi *killed* Asher?" Shimi's disbelieving expression gave me a shred of hope that he would reject such vile lies.

"If I hadn't seen it play out, I would not have believed it. Unfortunately, Lemek and I were too far away to do anything. And of course Zevi knew the exact place to cut his throat before he fled with his whore."

My skin burned with rage as Shimi and Mahir turned their gazes on me, and my head shook of its own volition. If only they could see the truth in my eyes.

"Now we know why he's been so secretive lately," said Kyrum, pulling their attention away from me. "Why he's been disappearing off and on since we left Gibeah. Talking to farmers and traders in the area to plan his escape route. And why he brought a woman along on a recruiting mission. It seems the two of them planned this from the beginning and the kidnapping itself was completely for show. Zevi did hail from her town, you know. They've likely been entangled for years." He'd certainly considered every aspect of his lies to make them sound entirely plausible. There was no way for me to prove otherwise. Besides, the word of a woman meant less than nothing before a court.

"That could be," Lemek said. "Especially when they were sneaking off together in the middle of the night."

As the entire group turned to gawk at me, my face went hot with embarrassment alongside the anger. I noticed Sakar and his friends laughing and whispering amongst themselves and had the horrible realization that with Zevi gone, I was truly at risk. It had been his commands and protection that had kept me from harm. Kyrum would indeed give me over to those lechers if I tried to fight back, I had no doubt.

As Kyrum had spewed his lies, more and more men had joined the crowd until most of Zevi's company now stood witness to my humiliation. And as explanations were relayed to those who hadn't heard the horrible accusations against their leader, more than a few curses were uttered against both of us.

"Where is the traitor now?" asked one of the men from the crowd.

Kyrum frowned, as if it grieved him deeply to relay the news. "He is dead. As is fitting for a killer like him. Asher—my friend—did not deserve . . ." He let his words trail off, covering his eyes with a feigned shudder.

A wave of disbelieving murmurs went through the group.

"What about *her*?" someone else asked with pointed disgust.

"She'll be taken to Saul. Justice must be done."

A lewd suggestion for carrying out punishment was tossed up from the back of the crowd, the words so vile I could not believe they came from the mouth of a fellow Hebrew. My body began to tremble as I took in the faces of the men who stood in judgment of me. A few appeared openly hostile, and others just looked confused. Some, like Rezev and Eliyah, regarded me with troubled expressions that made me think not everyone had swallowed Kyrum's lies. But even if it were so, there was nothing to be done. Kyrum was now in charge of this company, and I'd been branded a traitor.

My attention snagged on a small group of men who stood off to the side near the very back of the assembly. I blinked a couple of times in disbelief as my heart took up a hopeful rhythm.

Noham and another man I recognized from Maresha had joined this group. They must have arrived when we were pursuing Shalem north. I held my breath as I quickly dropped my eyes so Kyrum and the others would not see who I'd been staring at. But my pulse refused to calm. Somehow, my husband's friends had discovered where I was and had come to rescue me. After enduring the bruising grief of watching Zevi be shot and then being forced to abandon him in the meadow, the surge of hope in my chest was almost too painful to bear.

Wrapped in a makeshift shroud, Asher's body lay beside me in the wagon as we bumped along at the end of the company, a terrible reminder of Zevi's own body in that meadow, alone and abandoned to the elements. The idea of leaving him there without a proper burial, and knowing his family would never know the truth of how he'd died, made my heart weep.

There would never be a chance for me to tell him all the things I

wanted to say or to discover whether there could have been something for us beyond those moments in the meadow when he bared
his heart to me and I'd been in too much shock to respond with
the full truth hidden inside my own.

After what must have been a couple of hours jolting across the
rough terrain with my insides a mess of grief and fear, I startled
when the wagon came to an abrupt halt. I could hear the two
men who'd been walking alongside the wagon, driving the mules,
speculating over the reason for the standstill and concluding that
the storm brewing overhead must be at fault. A rumble of thunder
in the far distance seemed to back up their conjectures.

However, when urgent shouts echoed in the distance, I wondered if perhaps a storm of another sort was brewing. My heart
pounded as I lay helpless, breathing in the dusty wool of the blanket over my face and silently cursing the impressive knots that left
me vulnerable to whatever was going on outside the dark tent I
was imprisoned beneath.

When the patter of sandals approached the wagon, one of the
guards called out in a panicked tone, "What's going on up there?"

"Amorites," someone replied. "They've set up an ambush.
We've been sent to take your places because the new captain has
need of you. We'll make certain the contents of the wagon are
secure."

"You certain?" The guard's voice was colored with equal parts
fear and suspicion.

"Go! There's no time to waste!"

Suddenly, my heart was pounding—not from fear but from
relief. I recognized that voice. The black wool covering the wagon
bed was torn away, and while I blinked against the raindrops and
the light, Noham's face appeared above me.

The warm relief that had been pumping through my body instantly cooled. His was not the expression of a rescuer but that of
a man who loathed me. Confused, I tried to speak against the gag,

but instead of removing it, he reached over the side of the wagon and pressed a knife to my throat. I gasped and tried to move away, but I was solidly pressed between Asher's body and the edge of the wagon. I could do nothing but stare at Ilan's friend in terror.

"You make me sick," he spat out. "But at least Ilan died thinking you were a good and faithful wife instead of seeing you run off with your lover."

I shook my head with vehemence, hot tears pricking. How could he so easily believe the lies Kyrum had spewed about me? If only I could refute the slander.

"And not only whoring about with one of Saul's lackeys but spying on us as well." He sneered. "You should be stoned."

"Noham, we don't have time for this," said his companion. "There's Amorites coming. We need to get back to the group before anyone sees us."

"You're fortunate I don't have time or I'd be glad to tear you limb from limb," said Noham through his teeth, bubbles of saliva blooming in the corners of his mouth as the tip of his knife pressed harder. "But I have plans in Gibeah that don't include being discovered. So even if it's not the full justice you deserve, I can't have you telling anyone who we really are."

"*No!*" I tried to call out through the gag, but it was nothing more than a muffled moan as tears streaked down my face to join the stream of raindrops that were now coming down in earnest.

"I'll let them think these Amorites ended you." His grin was edged with malice as he leaned closer, his tone raspy. "But Saul . . . everyone will know that *I* ended that usurper's worthless life. Even if I have to lose mine to ensure a man of Yehudah inhabits the throne instead."

Helpless frustration burned through me. There had to be a way to stop Noham from going through with his plans to kill Saul. And perhaps Yahweh himself would intervene, but the murderous blackness in Noham's eyes made it clear that Zevi would not be the only one perishing today. The man with his knife to my throat was not the same carefree youth who had marched off to war with Ilan, both of them full of ideas of glory.

I let my teary eyes fall closed. Conjured up the blue meadow and the face of the stoic man who'd given it to me as a way to express the depth of his feelings. If only—

"Someone's out there!" Noham's companion hissed just before the distinctive thunk of a rock hitting the side of the wagon near my head jarred my eyes open.

Noham cursed, spinning away from me at the sound of a large body dropping to the ground.

"Drop the knife," said a voice that I instantly recognized as Rezev's. "Or I'll deal with you like I did your friend."

"I'm just making sure the wagon is safe from the Amorites."

"Are you now?" Rezev called, from some distance. "Because it seems like you are going after an innocent woman."

"Innocent?" Noham let out a bark of caustic laughter. "The whore deserves to die."

Something whistled through the air, and Noham slammed hard into the side of the wagon. He moaned, another low curse coming from his mouth.

Footsteps pounded toward the wagon from two directions, followed by a short scuffle, more foul words, and the sounds of men grappling and landing blows before all went silent.

The only sound I could hear was heavy breathing and the rain pattering down around me.

Had Rezev saved me? Or had Noham killed him too?

"You all right, old man?"

I thrilled at the sound of Eliyah's voice.

"Who are you calling old?" said his father. "I just knocked that young buck into tomorrow."

Eliyah snorted. "After *I* sent him reeling with a stone to the temple. With my *left* hand, I might add."

188

Rezev's response was as dry as the desert. "Just untie Yochana. We need to get moving."

As if he did not still have a singed hand, Eliyah bounded up onto the wagon, making quick work of my bonds with a knife before yanking the gag from my mouth.

I sucked in a grateful breath of rain-laden air. "Why are you two here? What's happening?"

"No time to explain," he said. "Dealing with your friend there set us back. We have to get out of here before anyone realizes you are gone."

"But the Amorites—"

He shook his head, cutting off my questions. "Later."

Sensing the urgency, I gave him a nod and followed him out of the wagon, my hands and feet still tingling with relief at being set free from the constrictive bindings.

I wobbled as my sandals touched the ground, and Rezev reached to steady me. "Can you run?"

"I can."

"Good. Don't stop until I say. Understand?"

The warning in his gravelly voice was very clear. I nodded my agreement, and then we were on the move, leaving Noham and his friend unconscious on the ground near the wagon and dashing into the thick trees nearby. With speed that belied his superior age and large frame, Rezev zipped through the trees, with me trailing behind and Eliyah close on my heels. I wondered what we would do if we crossed paths with the Amorites but knew better than to lift my voice to ask.

Rezev took us on a meandering trail, first heading northeast, then straight north, then veering back south. I did my best to keep up, but after we'd been running full tilt for at least half of an hour, maybe more, my legs began to tremble and my chest burned. I wasn't certain how long it had been since I'd eaten, but my reserves, fueled mostly by fear, were nearing their end. Still,

I would not be the reason why the three of us were attacked by enemies.

"Abba," called Eliyah, "Yochana is going to keel over."

Rezev came to a swift halt. "Take a break, then. I think we are far enough away now."

Glad for the cool air and the drizzle on my face, I bent at the waist, hands on my thighs as I drew in a shaky breath. "Just give me a moment. I can keep going." I sucked in another lungful of air. "They could be close."

"Those men? They'll be out cold for a while. I doubt they saw which way we came."

"No, the Amorites."

He laughed, and I startled at the jovial sound bouncing off the trees. "There are no Amorites."

Bewildered, I blinked at him. "What?"

"Mahir and Shimi made a show of spotting scouts in the trees," he said. "Kyrum and his stolen company are busy chasing after shadows."

"But . . . but why?"

Rezev reached to put one of his large paws on my shoulder. "There's no possible way Zevi betrayed us. I may have only known the boy for a few days, if you don't count the rough introduction we had before the battle at Yavesh-Gilead, but his loyalty was apparent to anyone with eyes."

My vision swam for a moment. "Then you don't think I . . ."

"Ran off with Zevi and silver?" Eliyah finished for me. "Of course not. And neither do Mahir or Shimi, obviously."

"So there really are no Amorites?"

Eliyah shook his head. "Just a ruse to distract from our rescue. We didn't expect for someone else to be there, though. Who was that?"

"My husband's friend from Maresha. He believed the lie that Zevi and I were acquainted before my husband's death and decided to mete out his own form of justice." I looked back in the direction we'd come. "But he also needed me silenced."

"For what reason?" asked Rezev.

"I'm the only one that knows he and his friend did not join the company to fight for Saul but to assassinate him."

Rezev's eyes went wide. "And how do you know that?"

I sighed, my face going hot with shame. "Because I gave them some of my own silver to do so. But after what you told me, Rezev . . . I was wrong. I'd been blaming the king for my husband's death and was caught up in things I did not understand."

With his arms folded and his expression drawn, Rezev looked down at me for a few excruciating moments that reminded me of times I'd displeased my own abba.

"Well, there's nothing to be done now. We need to get you back to Maresha. And then Eliyah and I will do what we can to prevent any attempt on the king's life. But, for now, we will trust Yahweh to watch over the man he's placed on the throne."

The image of my father's and mother's overjoyed faces at my return flashed through my mind. I could almost hear my sisters calling out my name and feel their arms wrapping around my waist as they clamored for my attention. But just as swiftly, the anticipation of a sweet reunion was replaced by the awful picture of Zevi lying in that beautiful meadow under the sky and what would happen to his body. And suddenly that was all that mattered.

"We have to go back," I blurted out.

"Go back where?" Eliyah asked.

"To where Zevi fell," I said, my throat burning at the reminder of the awful moment those two arrows pierced him. "I cannot bear to think of him not being buried. Leaving him to the wild animals . . ."

I let my words trail off, unable to speak of such horrible things. I'd not been able to bury Ilan when he'd died across the river, his resting place likely among countless other soldiers in some mass grave outside Yavesh-Gilead. He had deserved better. And so did Zevi. At least that beautiful meadow would be a peaceful resting place for a man with so much turmoil in his spirit.

"What really happened?" Eliyah's voice was so full of kindness that it brought another batch of tears to my eyes.

"He sacrificed his life. For me."

And at the very least, I would make certain his family knew the truth.

18

Zevi was gone.

The only evidence that he'd once lain in this field of blue flowers was two blood-soaked patches of earth. Eliyah and Rezev searched the rest of the area, while I spun in a slow circle, trying to make sense of the disappearance of his remains.

"There's no trace of him anywhere," said Rezev, when the two returned with bewildered expressions. "But there are no paw prints, so I don't think wild animals stole the body."

I pressed a hand to my chest, warding off the pain of the renewed thought of his body being desecrated in such a way. "I don't understand. Where is he?"

Eliyah shook his head, looking just as confused. "Could someone have found the body? Taken it somewhere?"

I spread my arms wide. "In this secluded place? Who would have come up here?"

Rezev ran a large palm down his beard, his gaze tracking over the meadow. "I'm sorry, Yochana. There's not much we can do."

My throat burned, and although I'd vowed months after Ilan's death to never again let myself wallow in despair, I wanted nothing more than to run home and cry into my mother's lap. Zevi had given his life to protect me, and now I was failing to protect him in death.

"What do we do now?" Eliyah asked his father.

"There's nothing to do but take Yochana back home."

Panic seized me. "No, we can't go. We have to keep looking. I have to make certain he is buried."

"He wasn't . . ." Eliyah began but then shook his head. "No. Never mind."

"What?" I pressed.

He grimaced, looking chagrined at whatever was going through his mind. "Are you certain he was dead?"

My breath caught at the question. Until now, I'd not given myself permission to listen to the quiet whisper in my heart. *Is the reason we've not been able to find his body because he'd actually* survived?

"I don't . . ." I bit my lip, torn between accepting the image of Zevi sprawled out, pierced through with arrows and perfectly still, and nurturing what could very well be a false hope. "I don't know. Maybe he could have lived? He's anything but weak. And it happened so fast."

"I really doubt it, Yochana," said Rezev, his tone apologetic. "I've seen plenty of arrow wounds in battle. From what you told me of the injuries, he could not have survived long. An arrow to the abdomen and the shoulder . . . And I've seen Lemek with a bow. The man is deadly."

Pain coursed through me as the tiny whisper went silent. "But then where is he?"

Rezev sighed, hands on hips and chin down. "I don't know."

"He cannot simply have vanished. We have to find him." I would not be able to rest until we did. And I was not too proud to beg. "Please, Rezev, we have to keep looking. At least for a while. There has to be some clue, somewhere."

"I agree, Abba," said Eliyah. "The captain deserves to be buried with dignity."

Faced with both of our arguments, Rezev pressed his lips together, contemplating. "All right. Let's keep looking."

Relieved by his acquiescence, I took a moment to drink in the glory of the blue lupines. "Where are you, Zevi?" I whispered, then sent a plea to the only one who knew exactly where his body lay.

Adonai, guide us to him, please.

We spent the next hour searching the hillside but found not even a broken blade of grass to give us any direction. Any footprints along the muddy trail would have been destroyed by our own on our way up to the hidden meadow. So, we descended back into the valley. A wide brook flowed westward, high from the recent storm. It slipped under a rough-hewn bridge made from a few weathered logs before curving north around the city of Azeka. We paused for a drink at a shallow ford, and I stepped into the water, groaning aloud at the cool relief. The sandals I'd been wearing when I left Maresha had not been made for the sort of walking I'd been doing over the past few days, and especially not a hasty run through the countryside. Stickers and brambles had made a hash of my skin, and blisters throbbed on my soles.

"Where next?" asked Eliyah.

Rezev shook his head, looking over the wide valley. "There are a thousand directions we could go, all of which may yield no answers."

"There is one that does," I said, frustrated by the resignation in his voice. "There has to be."

"I know what it's like to not know what happened to someone you love, Yochana." Rezev's voice was firm but kind. "Your parents are beside themselves with worry."

Without a doubt they were. They would be thrilled when I returned. And yet, however much I missed my family and my shop, being plucked from what had been safe and comfortable had opened my eyes to things I'd never imagined for myself.

Zevi had forced me to see how I'd undervalued the gifts Yahweh had given me. How I'd settled for a small existence and refused to consider that perhaps I'd been made for more.

What if I stopped holding on to what I thought my life should be and let Adonai determine my path? What would happen if I stopped gripping so tightly to what I held dear and opened up my hands instead?

I may not want to create perfumes for King Saul, but perhaps I could venture to Lachish once in a while to trade with people outside Maresha, maybe traders who traveled far afield. Who knew, maybe someday a perfume with my mark would grace the neck of some wealthy Egyptian woman, or Phoenician ones who resided in far northern Tyre or Sidon.

Something had changed deep inside me over the past few days. Because of Zevi.

If only he were here now, I would not be so fearful to accept his challenge to share my perfumes and balms with those outside Maresha, even if it meant leaving my home and going to Gibeah or Egypt or even Babylon at his invitation. As long as I was with him.

His beautiful words from the blue-clad meadow seemed to murmur along with the water that swirled around my feet. *"I cannot help but wonder, even if it is selfish of me . . . what would life be like if I'd known you all along? . . . I would have done anything to make you mine."*

Somehow, I knew that if it were Zevi standing here in this brook and I was the one missing, he would not give up.

So I would not either. Not until I knew for certain that he was truly lost to me and the man who'd been so tortured in life was at peace in death.

"No," I said.

Rezev frowned at me. "No, what?"

"I'm not going back. Not yet, at least. You don't have to stay here. You can go back to Lachish or on to Gibeah to fight with Saul if that's what you choose. I'm not leaving until I know what happened to him."

Rezev and Eliyah exchanged a look. And then Rezev gave the young soldier a nod.

"We're not leaving you alone," said Eliyah. "Especially after what you did for me."

"I would have done that for anyone."

Rezev gave a shrug. "Perhaps. But either way, I would never leave a young woman to fend for herself—" His words broke off, his eyes tracking over my shoulder.

I began to turn to see what had caught his attention, but his voice dropped low. "Don't look. There's someone watching from behind a tree just across the stream."

My pulse ticked up. Surely Kyrum hadn't followed us back to the valley of Elah, had he?

"Seems to be alone," Rezev said under his breath. "Eliyah, you stay with Yochana."

The young man huffed. "But, Abba—"

"You have one hand right now." Rezev glowered at his son. "Just pretend you're deep in conversation."

After a brief hesitation, Eliyah obeyed, letting out a laugh and patting my shoulder with an awkward grin that had to be transparently false even from fifty paces. I waved a hand through the air as if responding to him. The two of us were hopeless at pretense.

Then Rezev suddenly bolted with extraordinary speed for a man twice my age, plowing over the ford and onto the stream bank. I spun around to watch, holding my breath as he crashed through the brush. A sharp yell echoed across the water.

A few tense moments later, Rezev came out of the trees, pushing a young man along in front of him. The youth's black curls shone in the patch of sunlight that had broken through the clouds. By his height, I guessed him to be about fifteen or sixteen years of age, but without a shadow of a beard on his cheeks, I could not be sure. He certainly did not look dangerous in any way. Instead, he looked terrified.

Eliyah and I sloshed across the stream.

"All right, boy," said Rezev, poking the young man in the shoulder blade. "Tell us why you are spying."

The young man flinched away from the craggy-faced soldier, his voice trembling. "I'm not! I vow it. I just came back for a knife."

"What do you mean you came back?" asked Eliyah.

"I was down here earlier this morning"—the boy gestured at the stream behind us—"and dropped my father's knife. You haven't seen it, have you? He's going to kill me if I've lost his favorite one for good." All three of us relaxed at his pleading tone. He seemed far more frightened of his father than Rezev.

"No, I'm sorry. We've not seen it," said Eliyah, with a touch of amusement.

The boy's shoulders slumped, and he wiped a hand down his face with a groan. "I'm already in trouble for sneaking off yesterday."

"Why would you do that?" I asked.

"My ima is sick. And my abba's pottery wheel cracked the other day. It's unusable." He frowned, black brows pinching with frustration. "I was only trying to help, hoping I could find someone in need of an extra set of hands since I'd not been able to locate work in Azeka. But then, in Beit Shemesh, someone told me I should go home to my parents, so I turned back. I don't know what to do now, but I was told Adonai would provide."

At the name of Beit Shemesh, I realized I'd seen this talkative young man before. "You spoke with a man on the road yesterday, didn't you? One who gave you some food?" This *had* to be the boy Zevi mistook for his cousin.

He blinked at me in confusion. "I did. How did you know?"

"He was my . . ." I paused and gestured to Rezev and Eliyah. "Our friend. The captain of the company we were with."

His jaw dropped. "You know him? The man who was so kind to me?"

"We did. But I'm sorry to say that he is gone," said Eliyah in a gentle tone. "He was . . . attacked."

Oddly, the boy's lips curved into a smile, and he shook his head, setting those unruly black curls to bouncing. "No. He's not gone. Although I wasn't so certain when I found him."

Shock vibrated through my bones. "You *found* Zevi?"

He pointed over the stream about thirty paces away from where we were standing. "I did. Halfway on the bank and halfway in the water. Saw arrows poking out of his body and thought he was dead for sure. But when I got closer, he moaned, and then I recognized him from the road. He was barely conscious and not making much sense, but I was able to get him within sight of Azeka's gates before he lost use of his limbs and went down. One of the city guards helped me take him to my home."

My own limbs nearly gave out as relief coursed through every one of them. "He's alive?"

"For now. But he hasn't woken up. And truly, he doesn't look too good. My ima called the healer, who took out the arrows and applied a poultice, but he said there is not much more he can do."

Desperate prayers filled my mind. If Adonai had led this boy to Zevi, and then the boy to us, surely he would not take him now. Would he?

"Please." I pressed both hands to the heart that was beating at twice its normal speed, willing the sob building in my throat to dissolve. "Please take us to him."

"Of course," said the boy before his expression turned sheepish. "But first, would you mind helping me find my father's knife? He was happy to help your friend but furious that I was so careless."

"With pleasure," said Eliyah, his own relief palpable. "I wouldn't wish an angry abba on anyone." He gestured toward Rezev with a little grin. "Mine turns into a snarling bear at the slightest provocation."

Rezev scowled at his son with a hint of exasperation. "Just find the boy's knife, will you? This poor woman needs to see the captain."

199

19

Zevi

I smelled lupines again. I tried to draw in their fragrance, hold on to that elusive scent. But it hurt too much to breathe.

A cool hand smoothed over my forehead.

So hot.

Getting worse.

The words were disembodied, swallowed quickly by the black that held me down. But the hand felt good. Right.

Please. Wake up. The voice, low and raspy, came closer. *You promised not to let go.*

The sound was like a balm, sweet and soothing. I tried to plead for more, but my mouth would not obey.

The hand smoothed over my cheek, the feel of it like a freshwater spring in a desert. *Zevi? Are you trying to speak?*

I wanted to answer, wanted to open my eyes, but everything was so heavy. So painful.

Everything was gone, anyhow.

My cousins.

My men.

My vow.

Even her . . . Yochana. Her name cut through the terrible blackness like a burst of light.

I'd hurt her.

Loved her.

Lost her.

Again, that soothing touch caressed my skin.

I'm here, said the voice of lupine and honey. *I'm at your side.*

The words were a promise. Even inside this dark prison, I knew they had significance.

But my tenuous hold on consciousness was slipping away. I fought against the pull, tried to hold on to the fragrance, the voice that calmed my storm.

What can be done? said a deep voice, farther away.

The infection is deep, came the response, the sweetness edged with frustration. *I wish I had my box. I need herbs. Exotic ones. Things I've only heard about that can treat something like this—Oh . . . !*

A soft huff of breath brushed against my ear.

You gave me the answer already, didn't you?

I did not know the answer, but I knew I didn't want to disappoint that beautiful voice. I tried to pull myself out of the fiery blackness again, but I was bound by a thousand cords that held me captive.

Shhh. Rest now, it said, the silken coolness brushing over my face, my hair, before I felt a press of lips on my forehead. *I'll take you home.*

And I believed the voice. So, I stopped fighting against the darkness and let it wrap me in its soothing embrace.

20

Yochana

Zevi looked far too pale and small on the litter carried by Rezev and Eliyah. A man so full of vitality and strength should not be so helpless. He should be marching like the wind and barking commands, not vacillating between delusional mutterings, moaning, and horrible stillness.

Instead, I was the one repeatedly sniping at Rezev and Eliyah to be careful with their precious burden every time they jostled him or he groaned. But they were kind enough to say nothing, knowing it was only my worry that made me short-tempered and impatient.

It had been two of the longest days of my life.

I'd gladly take bumping along in the back of that horrible wagon, bound hand and foot, if it meant Zevi wasn't hovering on the edge of death.

If not for Osi, the boy who'd found him, and the kindness of his family, Zevi would never have survived.

I wasn't sure how he had gotten himself down from the meadow to the stream, maybe simply by the sheer force of his iron will. Or, more likely, Yahweh had given him some sort of divine strength to carry his wounded body down the hill and to where Osi had found him lying half-submerged in the freezing cold water.

All I knew was that I would be eternally grateful Adonai had preserved his life.

The arrow in his shoulder had gone straight through, making it fairly simple for the healer in Azeka to pull it out cleanly. It wasn't nearly as enflamed as the other wound and would probably heal well. If, that was, Zevi survived the other injury.

If it had not been for the thick leather armor Zevi wore, slowing down the arrow's impact, the one in his abdomen would likely have gone much deeper. As it was, the healer had been forced to dig out the serrated, bronze-tipped arrowhead. The wound was infected, swollen, and weeping pus, which meant fever had gripped Zevi in its blazing hold. He was delirious, sweating profusely, and like an oven to the touch. When he was not mumbling about his cousin Shalem, calling for me, for someone named Igo, and a few other names I did not recognize, he was terrifyingly silent.

It hadn't been until I remembered what he'd said about his aunt Eliora's garden being full of every kind of plant imaginable, and how the herbs within its soil grew with extraordinary potency, that I had some hope.

Perhaps I could have gone to Kiryat-Yearim myself and tried to return with what I needed, but we'd agreed that he was too near death to wait. We'd had to take him with us and pray that Yahweh would again preserve the thread of life Zevi was somehow clinging to.

Osi's family had been extraordinarily generous. Not only had they saved his life, they'd insisted on sharing what little food they had. Osi himself had given up his small cot for Zevi. The soldier's long legs hung off the end and his broad shoulders almost spilled over the sides.

To repay their kindness and use their pent-up energy to good use, Rezev and Eliyah hunted. They returned with a deer, which they butchered and prepared for drying on the family's roof. Osi's father had not only lost his pottery wheel, a heavy machine that had been passed down for three generations, to an irreparable split in the center post, but his severely deformed left foot prevented him from doing much else to feed his family. And although it did not stop her from offering every hospitality she could manage, Osi's mother was plagued with a cough that rattled her fragile frame day and night.

That, at least, I'd been able to help with. I'd asked Rezev and Eliyah to seek out a specific type of mallow plant, mullein leaf, and a few other herbs, which I then taught her to boil into a strong tea. Not only did the drink soothe the cough, but the spiced steam I taught her to inhale slowly as the pot boiled helped calm her lung spasms.

I wished that we could have done more for the family, but we'd had to set off at dawn for Kiryat-Yearim, knowing it would take us most of the day to get there, especially with Rezev and Eliyah each carrying an end of a litter they'd hastily constructed last night.

The only time I'd been glad that Zevi had been more or less unconscious was when we encountered what had once been the town of Zanoah. Although the Philistines had razed it a dozen years ago, only the crumbled remains of a few homes remained. Nothing had been rebuilt in all this time, as if some sort of curse still lay over its ashes.

As we passed by, I could not help but think of the things Zevi had told me about the horrors he'd witnessed there. Seeing Zanoah's fate with my own eyes changed that fleeting account of his tumultuous childhood into an undeniable reality. He'd experienced horrors no one, and especially no child, should ever face. No wonder he'd been so driven to rescue Maresha from a similar end. Even if he was wrong to force me into going to Gibeah, I was beginning to understand the deep pain that drove him to do so.

And I was glad he did not have to relive any of that anguish by seeing the ruins he'd been kidnapped from as a boy.

However, when he was out of danger from this horrible infection—as I prayed fervently he would be soon—I would tell him about the large group of tents pitched not too far from Zanoah, up on the hillside, where evidence of growing families abounded, of the group of children shrieking with laughter, and of the green wheat fields spreading across the valley. All signs that even after such devastation, life was still rooted here, pressing up through the ashes to seek out the sun.

A few hours past Zanoah, we came across some shepherds near Kesalon, who directed us to the foot of one of the many mountains in this hilly country. I hated to think of Rezev and Eliyah having to carry Zevi up the steep slope to wherever his family lived, especially after how long we'd traveled today, but father and son both insisted they were fine.

Just before we entered the little town, consisting of a surprising number of homes pressed into a clearing with enormous trees, two young women emerged from the woods, carrying baskets in their arms that overflowed with produce. They halted, staring at us with wide eyes.

"Shalom," I said, trying to keep the overwhelming fear for Zevi out of my greeting. "Could you perhaps direct us toward the house of . . ." I paused, trying to pluck a name out of my mind I'd only heard a few times. "Oh! Yes, Natan. That's it. He is a Philistine." I winced, hating the need to define Zevi's father that way, but there was no other designation I knew to give him.

One of the women, the older of the two, peered at me, looking wary. "Uncle Natan? What do you want with him?"

As I thanked Yahweh that I'd run into Zevi's family members without trying, the other one craned her neck, trying to catch a glimpse of the litter behind me. "Who is that you have? Is he sick?"

"Zevi," I said. "He's wounded."

The girls abandoned their suspicion at the name of their cousin, along with the produce baskets they dropped on the ground in their haste to run to his side.

"What happened?" cried the eldest.

"Oh no. He looks so awful," said the other, with teary eyes.

"He was attacked," I said. "Shot with arrows. I need plants from Eliora's garden. Or else I fear infection will overtake him."

Understanding filled their eyes.

"We just came from there." The eldest gestured to the spilled baskets. "We were bringing some of the harvest down for the townspeople, like we do every day."

"I'll go fetch Uncle Natan, Ami," said the younger woman, already moving toward the head of the trail the two had emerged from. "You take them up the mountain."

Ami gestured for us to follow. "It's quite a hike, but the trail up to Grandfather's compound is well-traveled, so it's not too difficult."

"You sure you'll be all right to climb that far?" I asked Rezev and Eliyah, wishing I had the strength of soldiers like them so I could help.

"Yochana," Rezev said, with a hint of exasperation. "The captain is dying. Stop asking us and *go*."

I did as he said, my stomach knotted at the reminder that Zevi had little time. Did I have the skills necessary to help him? Even if I'd learned much about herbs and ointments, I was not a true healer. And what if Eliora's garden did not have the plants I needed? Or the infection was already too pervasive?

Eliyah, always so perceptive, gave me an affirming nod. "We're right behind you."

Something about his statement bolstered my confidence. He believed in me, as did Rezev, or they would not have made this arduous trek carrying a heavily muscled soldier. And I had to believe that Yahweh had smoothed the way before us, not only by bringing Osi to Zevi, and these girls to lead us, but by bringing Eliora's garden to my mind in the first place.

So, the four of us began to climb the trail, which meandered back and forth up the steep slope directly through some of the thickest and most beautiful forest I'd ever seen in my life.

About halfway up the side of the mountain, Eliyah called my name. I dashed back to the head of the litter, heart pounding with terror. Had I been too late?

But Zevi's eyes were not closed, and neither were they blank. Instead, they were staring up at the leafy canopy overhead in bewilderment. "Trees?" he croaked out, through what had to be a parched throat since we'd not gotten him to drink much liquid in his delusional agitation.

My relief was as wide as the sky above, and I had to laugh at his bewildered question as I leaned over him. "Yes. Trees. Because we brought you to Kiryat-Yearim."

He blinked up at me. "You did?"

"For medicine from Eliora's garden."

He frowned, his fever-addled mind likely whirling in confusion. "Water," he rasped.

I yanked the water skin Osi's mother had given us from my shoulder and poured some into my cupped palm. I supported his head as he sipped from my hand for the first time on his own since we'd found him in Osi's home.

He coughed, then he turned his bleary eyes back up to me. "You aren't a dream? You're really here?"

I stroked his bearded jaw, just once. "I'm here."

"Zevi!" The shout from ahead of us on the trail barely preceded the sight of the most terrifying man I'd ever seen barreling toward us. Zevi may be a cedar tree, but this man was a mighty oak.

It was only because I saw Ami trailing ten paces behind him that I realized this enormous man, with black tattoos winding around his arms and holes in his lobes where plugs must have been, was the Philistine Zevi called Father. He came to a skidding halt on the other side of the litter, all attention on Zevi, and it was then I saw that he had two different colored eyes, one brown and one green, both of them full of devastation.

"Son." The heartrending word fell from his lips as he stroked the sweat-soaked curls from Zevi's burning forehead. "Oh, what did they do?"

The love this man had for Zevi, who was not of his blood—nor his heritage—was unmistakable. Tears filled those mismatched eyes, and my own stung in response.

"Abba?" Zevi croaked out, but then his eyes fluttered and he groaned.

I cleared the glut of emotion from my throat to focus on my mission. "He was shot with two arrows, and one wound is infected. I need herbs from your sister's garden right away."

As if he'd just realized I was there, Natan snapped his attention to me. "And who are you?"

"Yochana," I said, trying not to be intimidated by his intense gaze. "His—" I paused, uncertain of what to say. My cheeks warmed. What was I to Zevi? *His friend? His captive? Something else?*

There was no time for an explanation, so I merely said, "I know how to help him."

Natan peered at me for a couple of moments with those strange eyes before their corners turned up ever so slightly. "Ah. I understand. Well then, let's go."

Natan insisted on carrying one end of the litter as Rezev and Eliyah carried the other together, the three making quick work of climbing the rest of the way up the trail.

I did not know what to expect but was surprised to find that instead of only a few scattered homes, there was a well-organized compound not too far from the summit. Most homes were two stories and built around a central courtyard. And there were people everywhere. Men, women, and children swarmed us the moment we stepped out of the trees, expressions of curiosity and concern on every face.

I'd never imagined Zevi's family was so large, nor that he was so loved by the people who had adopted him. What he'd gone through as a child was horrific, and I was certain I only knew a portion of his story, but I thanked Yahweh that in his kindness he'd taken Zevi from the ashes of Zanoah to this peaceful place among cedar trees, oaks, and sprawling sycamores.

No wonder he was so burdened for others who had no refuge like this one. He may see his goal as vengeance on the Philistines for what they had done, but I wondered if the origins of his ambition to seek justice was because he had lived both lives—one of suffering and one of peace—and desired no one else to be trapped in the former.

A woman who barely came to Natan's shoulder pressed into his side. Zevi's mother, I guessed, since tears streamed down her face as she grasped her son's hand.

"It's all right, *Tesi*," said her husband, his tone soothing as he pulled her close and kissed her forehead. "Yahweh brought him home."

How strange to hear such deep faith and bedrock certainty in the God of Avraham from the mouth of a Philistine. When Zevi was better, and I was increasingly hopeful he would be, I would force the man of few words to tell me everything about how his father went from an enemy to a covenant keeper.

I felt the brush of a gentle hand on my arm and turned to find another woman with a concerned frown between her dark brows. "I am Galit," she said. "I've been told you need something from Eliora's garden?"

"I do. At least I hope you have the plants I need."

She smiled softly. "Let's go find out together, shall we? I am not Eliora, who knows everything about every plant in the garden, but she taught me well and left me in charge when she and her husband moved to Naioth years ago."

"Thank you," I said, but for some reason my legs would not move. I glanced down at Zevi, who'd once again fallen into fevered sleep, not realizing that an enormous crowd of people who obviously loved him were gathered around.

"I'll be with him," said his mother, her large hazel eyes red-rimmed. "Go, find what you need. If he wakes, I'll let him know you aren't far."

Somehow, without knowing anything about me, Zevi's mother understood that half my heart was lying on that litter. So, I trusted the woman who'd loved him for a dozen years longer than I had and followed Galit to the garden in search of a miracle.

21

Zevi

Before I'd even opened my eyes, I could sense a presence at my side: someone familiar, comforting, and overflowing with concern. A reassuring hand rested on my forehead for a moment, accompanied by the gentle murmur of my name, followed by a supplication to the Great Healer for my restoration and a plea for peace.

I waited until the prayer had come to an end before allowing my eyelids to peel open and seek out the speaker. One brown eye and one green eye met my slightly blurred gaze.

Abba?

When I blinked my eyes and turned my head, I recognized the room, the shelves on the wall, the lamp that flickered on the bench across from the bed. I was home. *Kiryat-Yearim.*

Confusion muddled my thoughts, swirling what lingered of my fevered dreams together with droplets of reality that I could not quite grasp. The blue paradise of the lupine meadow and Yochana's gray eyes full of wonder took focus before the black smudge of Kyrum's betrayal and Asher's murder cut through the scene, followed by the white-hot searing pain of Lemek's arrows.

"Yochana!" I struggled against the haze and whatever bound my feet. "They took her!"

My father pressed his large palm to my chest, restraining my movement. "Yochana is fine, son. She is with your mother and sisters."

The words made no sense. Kyrum and Lemek had taken her. I'd seen them drag her away while my body rebelled against any attempt to move.

"How?" I licked my dry lips and tried to swallow against the parched scratchiness in my throat.

"She brought you home to use plants from your aunt Eliora's garden to heal you. And she did, son. That woman of yours is a marvel. I've never heard of anyone understanding plants like my sister does, but she knew just the ones to bring down your fever and help the infection in your wounds."

At the mention of the places I'd been shot, my shoulder and gut throbbed. I'd known Lemek would not miss; he was far too proficient with the bow. So instead of running away, I'd run at him, desperate to draw his aim and knowing it meant my life was forfeit for Yochana.

I'd been shot with an arrow before, during a skirmish with some Amorites near Hebron last year, but it had barely grazed my thigh. This pain was much deeper.

"You are lucky to be alive. The leather armor you wore saved you."

"Gavi made it." My cousin would probably take full credit for keeping me alive and would never let me forget it. "But how did I get here?"

"Apparently, some boy in Azeka found you lying in the brook along the floor of Elah Valley." There was a foggy memory of a young boy with dark curls and deep-set eyes, but my fevered mind had told me it was Shalem. The boy must have been mixed into the muddle of my dreams. "Yochana will have to tell you the rest, but your friends carried you all the way here."

"Friends?" Of the two men I had considered friends outside my cousins, one was dead and one was a betrayer.

"Rezev and Eliyah. Good men. You'd not have survived without them. But as I said, Yochana will tell you more. She's barely left your side. I promised to stay with you because she'd not eaten yet today, and you know how your mother feels about that. She needed rest, as well. She has been so diligent with changing your bandages and applying the miraculous salve she concocted for your wounds. Your mother, Aaliyah, and Davina bustled her away a little over an hour ago to make certain her needs were tended."

That Yochana's talents had saved me was not a surprise. Only that she had somehow escaped Kyrum and Lemek.

"How long have I been here?"

"Three very long days," he said, the heavy smudges beneath his eyes proving just how worried he'd been in that time. He would have suffered greatly had I died.

And truly, I had resigned myself to doing so in that meadow. I'd lost Yochana. I'd lost Shalem, again. I'd lost my friends. My men. My command. There had been nothing left to live for.

"It's gone," I said. "I lost it all."

"What's gone?"

"Everything I've worked for these last twelve years."

"And what was that, son?"

"You know I'd been making myself into a soldier, Abba. You yourself taught me to discipline my body and mind to prepare for battle. But I've failed in everything. I failed my mission for the king. Lost the confidence of my men. And now I will never bring justice to the Philistines like I vowed to do."

I winced a little at the last proclamation. Regardless of Natan's heritage, I'd always been able to separate him from the rest of his blood. He wasn't an enemy. He hadn't been since the first day I'd known him. And now he was the man I'd called *Abba* for over a decade. I believed with all my soul that he and Shoshana saw me as no different from the rest of their brood. Besides, the three eldest of the lot—Aaliyah, Asher, and Davina—were not his by birth either. In fact, Davina was the result of Shoshana's own encounter with Philistine raiders. And yet I knew to my bones that Natan would die for any one of us without a second thought. But that did not change the way I felt about those who shared his heritage.

"Tell me about this vow," he said, without a hint of censure in his deep voice.

"I've always planned to fight them. To bring justice on those who destroyed Zanoah."

"I know you felt compelled to protect our people, your family. But you actually made a vow to avenge Zanoah?"

I nodded, knowing he would understand the gravity of such a thing. "On the day it fell."

Understanding moved over his features. "Oh, Zevi . . ."

"They deserve justice, Abba. After what they endured—"

"Tell me," he interjected. "You've never told me the entire story of the attack. I asked when you were younger, but you avoided the subject or said it was too much to speak of. I hoped you would tell me when you were ready, but you never said anything more."

I'd kept these horrors to myself on purpose, not wanting to taint the good life I had in Kiryat-Yearim with the ugly truth. But now that I'd told Yochana, I realized it was not so difficult to repeat. The sting of it had been softened by her calm and kind reception of even the worst things about that day.

Besides, I'd watched Natan love his family without condition or fail, and there was no reason to think, as I had when I was a boy, that he would love me any less for what had happened to me all those years ago.

And so, I told my father every dark, ugly detail of that horrible day. Of my terror as I cowered with Tera and Chelah in that plaster-coated cistern, listening to the townspeople scream, smelling burning homes and flesh, and enduring the torture when the monsters in feathered headdresses dragged us from our hiding place.

And then I told him the one thing I hadn't revealed to Yochana: That it was my fault.

He'd been silent, his face admirably blank as I spilled the blackness that had festered so long inside me, but now he scowled. "How could any of that possibly be your fault? You were an innocent."

I swallowed the hot spike of guilt in my throat, determined to finish what I'd started.

"Tera and Chelah had been particularly awful to me that day. They told me their father was going to feed me to the pigs he raised to sell to the local Canaanites."

I'd been terrified of those pigs after an elderly farmer had fainted in the mud and the despicable things finished him off. I'd loathed being forced to feed them each day and was certain their father made me do it on purpose, knowing my fear.

"I had run off, wishing I was anywhere but Zanoah, when the Philistines came through the same wadi I was hiding in. At first, I was fascinated by them. Their shining armor. The feathered headdresses. Their bright colored kilts and iron swords. They were like nothing I'd ever seen. So instead of running to warn the town, I sat there in the bushes, completely in awe."

"You were a boy, Zevi, captivated by soldiers—"

I put up a hand, shaking my head. "At first. But then I realized they were headed for Zanoah. And still I remained in place. Not because I was frightened, although I was. But because I wanted Tera and Chelah, and their parents, to be punished."

I could not look him in the eye anymore. I turned my head to stare at the flickering lamp across the room.

"By the time I was stricken with guilt for such a ruthless decision, I'd waited too long. I managed to find the girls and tell them to hide, but their parents were at the market, where the slaughter had already begun. And my warning did not save Tera and Chelah anyhow."

My father was silent, and for a few awful moments, I wondered if I should not have told him. But when he spoke again, his voice trembled with sorrow.

"Oh, Zevi. My son. Look at me." He placed his hands on my cheeks to turn my eyes back to his. "You were in no way at fault for what happened. Those soldiers were coming for that town no matter if you'd warned them. King Nicaro was ruthless and more than half-mad. You remember this. You met him. And he expected his soldiers and mercenaries to be just as cruel. And of course you wanted those who'd mistreated you to be punished. Any child would have felt the same—any adult, for that matter. You could not have known what would happen or have the ability to fully comprehend the consequences."

He paused. "Think about Arisa," he said, speaking of my eight-year-old little sister. "Would you expect her to carry such a burden?"

I considered how innocent the girl was, always collecting pine cones and snail shells in the forest. And how she'd climbed into my lap and looped her arms around my neck last time I was home to tell me about a squirrel that made off with one of *Doda* Miri's sweet cakes, her hazel eyes glittering with delight as she giggled over the funny creature.

I had been only a little over a year older than she was now when the Philistines came.

"You have always carried far more than your fair share, Zevi. You've been a champion for Asher, Aaliyah, and Davina since the moment we brought you into our home. You have guarded your siblings—and your cousins, for that matter—like a lion."

The reminder hit me like another arrow, and I huffed at the impact. "And yet I lost Shay too, again. I'm fairly certain Avidan was right and he is alive after all. I found his trail from Lachish but lost it within a day. Not to mention it's my fault he was lost in the first place."

My father frowned. "I am sorry to hear that, and I will admit you bear some culpability for taking him with you across the river. But you are not the King of the Universe, Zevi. I learned that lesson the hardest way possible, running away from Kiryat-Yearim when I was fifteen and thinking I could make my own way. Find riches and fame outside of this place and be the king of my own life. All it did was break my sister's heart, my parents' hearts, and keep me away from everyone who loved me. I may have been the Champion of Ashdod back then, wealthy and with every indulgence my selfish mind could imagine, but I was miserable. Lonely. And lying to myself about the dark pit I'd dug for myself."

He'd told me these things when I was younger, but I'd not truly understood the feeling of bleakness he'd spoken of until now. "But when everything went wrong, it was El Shaddai, the Mighty One, who broke me out of my chains before your uncles smashed through a wall to rescue me."

I knew the story of his return to Kiryat-Yearim well and would never forget when the man I'd then called Lukio appeared on the trail, battered and bruised. That was the moment I'd felt the first pulse of true joy in my chest since my family had fallen ill.

"Pursuing my own ways led to sadness, pain, and near death," he continued. "But I don't regret that pain because without my foolish ways, I would not have Shoshana, or any of my children, and I certainly would not have found you. Yahweh took my mistakes, my bad decisions, and my outright rebellion and turned it into something beautiful. Something worth far more than my mansion in Ashdod, my iron-wheeled chariots, or the gold and silver that once filled my coffers. And I'd give it up a thousand times for any one of you."

What would my own end have been, had he remained in Kiryat-Yearim instead of running away? I shuddered to even consider it. It felt odd to be grateful for his rebellion, but I was, just the same.

My father's voice grew stronger. "Somehow, while I was chasing after the world, Yahweh was still my shield. He shielded you and Shoshana on your flight from Ashdod. He shielded us during the battle at Mitzpah. And he has shielded us ever since we have come to live on this mountain. And though it pains me to think of my precious son on the battlefield, I have trusted him to be your shield since the day you declared you would be a soldier. And here you are, wounded but alive."

"But I lost it all. And I haven't told you how foolish I was with Yochana. . . ."

"Oh, I know exactly how you took Yochana." He frowned, and I felt the blood drain from my face.

"Does Ima know?"

"She does."

My stomach clenched. If I thought Lemek's arrows were painful, Shoshana's disappointment and, at times, the sharp edge of her tongue cut far deeper.

"We'll discuss that stupidity later. For now you need to heal and recover."

"But what do I do next? I've done nothing but prepare to be a soldier. I will admit Zanoah was not my fault, but that does not change the vow I made to avenge their deaths."

"And once you've had your vengeance—what then, son? There is no satisfaction in revenge. I watched my own enemy die before me and it did nothing to right the wrongs he had done—it was, at best, a hollow victory. You alone cannot bring justice to the Philistines. Only Yahweh can stand as a righteous judge. Leave vengeance in his capable hands."

"But they want the Land, Abba. Zanoah will be nothing compared to the whole of Israel if we do not stand against them. Should I just throw up my hands? Never fight again, like you?"

"I don't know your path, son. It may be far different than mine. But Yahweh does. He knows from the beginning to the end. So perhaps you should ask him instead. Let him be your shield, Zev. Let him be the shield to those around you. Maybe he will use you to protect them, and maybe he will rescue them all by himself. Either way, he is in control. Get out of his way and let him do what he does best."

I'd watched my father struggle to untangle from the life he'd built for himself in Ashdod, and I'd been there when he'd publicly submitted himself to the Covenant of Yahweh. I'd taken his physical training of my body to heart, but it seemed I had ignored his quiet shepherding of my soul. I would not make that mistake again. "How will I know which way to go, Abba? What choice to make?"

He was quiet for a moment, contemplating. "There is nothing wrong with fighting for our people, Zevi. It is a noble thing to sacrifice your life for another. But just as a soldier trusts his commander and a commander trusts his king, you must trust the King above all Kings to direct you. And as I've learned over these past years, the orders are more often whispered than shouted."

My father glanced up at the doorway, his sincere expression melting into an adoring one that told me without having to turn my head that my mother had entered the room. "Ah. Here they are."

Shoshana came into view, a sheen of tears in her eyes. "We heard you talking. I wasn't sure I should hope."

"Come kiss your son's face, Tesi," said my father, standing. "Then let him speak to Yochana. The poor girl has nearly killed herself caring for him."

My mother rushed to my side, happy to obey. It had taken me many years to accept her open affection, but now I welcomed it. I'd thought I'd never see my ima again as I lay dying in that meadow.

"You foolish boy," she chided. "I told you that if you were hurt, I would take my sandal to your backside."

I could not help laughing at the thought of my tiny mother trying to chase me down and bend me over her knee, especially when she'd never so much as raised a hand to me—though she'd raised her voice a time or two when I'd tested the bounds of her patience.

"And then to find out you *kidnapped* this lovely girl?" Now her tone grew more serious. "What were you thinking?"

My father quickly came to my rescue, slipping his arm around his wife. "Now, Tesi, I told him we'll discuss that later. Let's go for a walk now, shall we?" My mother frowned, not happy to let the matter go, but he tugged her along.

"We'll keep your younger siblings out of here for now, Zevi," he said, "but they will come flying in here as soon as they find out you are awake." On his way out, he murmured something to Yochana that I could not hear, and then all was quiet. But I could feel her presence lingering at the doorway, silent and still.

I waited, my heart beating an uneven cadence. From what my father said, I owed her my very life. She'd put aside what I had done, and in her compassion, had tended me for days, even though she could have left me to the fate I deserved for how I'd wronged her.

So although I would not keep her from returning to her home, I could not let her go without one more whiff of that lupine and honey-spice fragrance, the scent I hoped would stay with me before she was lost to me forever. I gathered every bit of the courage I normally used on the battlefield and called her name.

22

Yochana

I hadn't let myself believe that Zevi would actually survive. Too fearful that hope would raise its head and be trampled into the ground, again.

And so I'd spent every moment of these last three days in a state of willful numbness, mostly tending to Zevi's bandages, praying that the changes I saw in the infected area were not a product of my imagination, or staring at his chest rising and falling as I lay on the pallet Shoshana had made me on the floor near his sickbed. It had taken Shoshana and Galit threatening to bar me from Eliora's garden for me to take a break this morning and let Natan watch over his son.

But hearing Zevi's voice now, so much stronger than it had been in his semi-conscious ramblings, nearly broke my composure. As did the three words Natan had muttered when he and Shoshana passed me on their way out of the room.

"He's all yours."

He probably meant in the sense that they were leaving the two of us to speak privately, but I could not help but wonder if he'd purposefully left the meaning unclear. I'd learned a lot about Zevi's father in the past three days while living beneath the roof he'd built with his own hands.

He was unequivocally adoring of his wife, whom he sweetly called "Tesi," which I'd learned meant *little one*. He was unapologetically affectionate with her and his children—whether they resembled him or not—and he loved Zevi with every bone in his huge body.

So the allusion that he approved of whatever was between Zevi and me was weighty indeed. And it caused my mind to swirl with a thousand questions about what the future might look like now that Zevi had survived Kyrum and Lemek's cowardly attempt on his life.

But those were thoughts for another day. He may be awake, the swelling down, and the infection nearly gone due to the poultices, but he was still weak. Right now, I needed to focus on his continued healing, not the thrill that buzzed in my veins when he called my name.

I swallowed down whatever hot glut of emotion was clogging my throat, blinked away the wetness in my eyes, and strode into the room. "I hope you haven't pulled at my bandages. Or I'll be the one tying *your* hands together this time."

With only the briefest glance at his sickbed but not meeting his eyes, I headed for the washbasin to scrub any lingering soil from my hands.

"I've not moved," Zevi said, with a hint of amusement in his voice. "But do what you must."

I collected a stack of fresh linen bandages and the small jar of poultice I'd created from the wonders of Eliora's garden and approached Zevi's bed, which was pressed against the north wall of the chamber. Thankfully, there was plenty of light spilling in through the open door, overpowering the feeble flicker of the oil lamp opposite the bed, so when I tugged back the wool blanket that covered him, I could clearly see that even since this morning, the wound on Zevi's shoulder looked better than it had when Natan forced me to leave, insisting I do something other than worry over his son for a few hours.

I was amazed at the potency of the herbs that grew in the sprawling garden spread over several layers of terraces on the slope of Kiryat-Yearim. I'd not quite believed Zevi when he spoke of there being some sort of divine blessing on the soil of this mountain, due to the Ark's presence, but I could not deny that something otherworldly had to be at work for such profuse abundance. And the way my poultice worked on Zevi's wounds was nothing short of miraculous.

As I'd been doing for the past three days, I deftly ignored the fact that my patient was naked from the waist up, pulled back the long bandage that was wrapped around his middle, and leaned closer to inspect the wound beneath. No longer angry and oozing pus, the swelling had gone down significantly, and healthy pink was showing through what remained of the poultice on his skin. Relief welled up to dislodge a little more of the paralyzing fear I'd endured since I'd seen him shivering with blazing fever and with a wound that most men would already have succumbed to. I reapplied the ointment before covering the wound with a clean square of folded linen and readjusted the bandage to keep the treatment in place.

All this I did while not looking any higher than the man's chest, trying to pretend that the muscular body belonged to someone else, someone who had not told me a few days ago that he would have done anything to make me his. But every moment I tended him, I felt his eyes on me. When finally he breathed out my name again, I froze in place.

"Are you ever going to look at me?"

I swallowed hard against the unwelcome burn in my throat. I'd successfully held on to my restraint for three days and could not let his question undo me. I'd *been* the woman who cried for weeks straight over the loss of a man. Who could not walk into our empty home without crumbling to pieces. Once I'd crawled out of that pit, I'd vowed never to be that weak again.

But then Zevi's hand reached for mine, his fingers wrapping around my own, and tugged ever so gently. "Please, Yochana. Look at me."

So I did. And that was all it took. With one glimpse of his beautiful brown eyes gazing up at me with equal measures concern and longing, the spine I'd tried to fortify with iron turned to wax. My knees trembled and then gave out as I crumpled onto the floor at his bedside, laid my head on that strong chest, and wept.

He's alive. He's alive. He's alive.

The words repeated over and over in my head and my heart as I sobbed, barely able to catch a breath, and Zevi's other hand came up to slide into my hair, holding me close. Unable to stop the tears and the jerking of my shoulders as the dam broke, I let days of fear and uncertainty pour out of me.

I had no idea when this man had gone from captor to beloved. Perhaps it had been when he held me close after the mudslide, or when he revealed the pain of his past at the stream, or maybe it was before any of this began and he'd taken the time to feed a little dog. All of it was so confusing and complicated, but I did not want to fight the pull Zevi had on me anymore. I simply wanted to listen to his heartbeat thump against my cheek, strong and precious. This told me, even more than the visible healing of his wound, that Zevi was not lost to me.

When my tears were finally spent, I lay there, reveling in the steady beat inside his chest and the feeling of his fingers sliding through my hair, stroking with a gentleness that seemed at odds with his rugged and stoic nature.

Reluctantly, I lifted my head to meet the eyes of the man I'd thought for sure was dead four days ago. "I'm probably hurting you."

"I've never been more comfortable in my life." He grazed his calloused palm over my wet cheek. "But I wish you would not cry."

"I can't help it." I sniffed. "I thought you were gone, Zevi. I watched Lemek shoot you. I saw you fall like a stone, never imagining you could survive." I would never forget the image of him sprawled out in the lupines, having sacrificed his life—or so I'd thought—in an attempt to save me. "How? How did you get down to the brook with two arrows in your body?"

"I don't know. I remember the meadow and the arrows and then you being dragged away. Remember knowing I'd failed you as I stared at the clouds overhead. And then everything is hazy."

He went quiet, his gaze drifting over to the oil lamp as if his lost memories could be found within its orange flame. "I think . . ." He paused, blinking. "I think someone helped me walk."

"Who? Where did they come from?"

He shook his head. "It's very blurry and jumbled. All I remember is a man telling me to lean on him and a strong arm holding me up. Then he told me to drink from the stream, and after that, everything is mostly dark until a boy came. I thought it was Shalem."

"It's no wonder," I said. "Osi was the same young man you mistook for your cousin on the road to Beit Shemesh."

Zevi looked astounded. "The one searching for work?"

I told him of Osi's family and why the boy had been on the road that day and then, anticipating his next question, I explained how we'd come across him. Then I told him of Mahir and Shimi's loyalty and how they'd tricked the rest of the company into chasing imaginary enemies so Rezev and Eliyah could get me away.

Zevi ran a hand over his mouth and beard. "They really believed I did not betray them?"

"Of course they did, Zevi. They know how honorable you are.

They know you are not motivated by greed or easily lured into treachery by the wiles of a woman." I smirked at him.

His cheek twitched. "I'm sure it took little to convince anyone that you had me in your thrall from the moment I walked into your shop. Because I was."

My face went hot at the admission.

"I don't know how I will ever repay them for what they have done. My father said Rezev and Eliyah carried me here."

"They did. They refused to take more than a few moments' rest all the way to Kiryat-Yearim. And it's a good thing, because without the plants from your aunt's garden, you would not have survived. But oh, Zevi . . ." I squeezed the one hand that still held mine. "That garden. It's everything you said and more. You cannot imagine how many varieties of herbs are growing there. Plants Ilan's grandmother told me about that she'd only heard of growing in Egypt and Midian. I could spend ten years in those rows and still find new things. Galit knew exactly which plants I needed to help you and a few that I didn't know about from the coastlands— one in particular that I believe cut the swelling down as if Yahweh himself had touched you. There are trees from beyond Babylon that produce these lovely little pears . . ."

I let my words fall off, realizing that I was rambling again, and found Zevi grinning at me.

"Forgive me, I got carried away."

"No." He squeezed my hand this time. "I am glad. I knew you would love it there. When you meet Eliora, you'll have a thousand things to discuss—" His grin faded as he went quiet. Then he released my hand, and it felt cold without his touch. "Why are you still here, Yochana? Rezev and Eliyah could have taken you back at any time."

Had I misunderstood his overture in the meadow? My chest hurt at the implications. I'd spent the last three days trying not to allow my hopes to overtake my good sense, but I thought, at the least, he'd be glad I had remained.

226

"I don't need to stay," I said. "Your family is here—" I pulled back, embarrassed that I'd cried all over him.

"No." He reached for me before I could stand, his fingers weaving into mine, and then pulled me back to himself. "You misunderstand me. I want you here in Kiryat-Yearim. I never thought it would actually happen but imagined it plenty of times. And of course it seems you already have my entire family in your thrall as well. My mother has *never* threatened me with her sandal like that before."

I laughed. Shoshana was nearly a head shorter than me but full of fire. Heaven help Kyrum if he ever crossed her path. A sandal would be the least of that traitor's worries.

"But why, when you could have returned to your family after you escaped, did you choose to come find me?"

I'd asked myself the same question that day and again last night as I lay on my pallet watching Zevi struggle for life. But the answer remained the same. "Even when I thought it would only be to bury you, I was convinced I could not leave you behind. I belong at your side, Zevi. Always."

The admission was terrifying, but I needed him to understand. "Ilan and I had been friends since childhood, so when he approached my father to marry me, I never thought twice about it. I assumed he and I would live a long life together. But it wasn't meant to be. And I never thought I could ever feel this way about anyone after he was gone." I shook my head, uncertain how I would express it coherently.

There was a light in Zevi's eyes that I'd never seen before as he tugged me closer. "You mean that?"

"I don't know what it means," I said, "or where we go from here. All I know is that I had to find you . . . even if it was to say good-bye." And thanks be to Yahweh that I'd not had to grieve another man I cared for.

"So you truly forgive me for taking you?" His expression was so sincere and hopeful, but he at least deserved to be teased a little after what he'd done.

"Perhaps," I said, then leaned closer, lowering my voice as I let my eyes drop to his lips for just a moment. "But only because you sent me to the most astounding garden I've ever seen."

I'd once wondered what Zevi's authentic and unfettered smile might look like, and now I knew—it was full of sweet mischief and altogether dazzling. "I'd give you a thousand gardens if it made you happy."

I lifted a brow. "As long as you never tie me up and throw me in the back of a wagon again."

"And what will happen if I do?" The tilt of his lopsided grin grew dangerous. If I thought stoic Zevi was enticing, playful Zevi was devastating.

"You are aware that I know exactly which plants will incapacitate a man."

He slid his hand back into my hair as his voice went deep. "Your fragrance alone is more than enough to hold me hostage."

Whispers from outside the doorway cut through what narrow space remained between us, and I jolted back from Zevi, cheeks flaming and heart thundering. A small face peered around the doorpost.

Arisa. Zevi's youngest sister met my eyes, and her little mouth popped open at the realization that she'd been caught spying. The girl was adorable, big hazel eyes and freckles sprinkled over her face. She was the very image of her mother and the apple of her father's mismatched eyes.

"It seems your siblings have reached the limits of their patience," I said, coming to my feet as Jaru and Teitu appeared in the doorway on either side of Arisa, looking appropriately chagrined. Jaru was thirteen and with his golden-brown hair and height favored his father. A year younger than his brother, Teitu was a near-perfect mix of Shoshana and Natan and absolutely worshiped Zevi. I'd stumbled across him sitting outside the door a few times already in the past three days, head bowed and tears trickling down his cheeks.

I would not begrudge the poor children a minute more without seeing their brother. I waved them inside. "He's not ready to be on his feet yet, but he's going to be all right."

Needing no further invitation, the three flew into the room, but before I could move aside to let them welcome their brother back from the edge of the grave, Zevi grabbed my hand one last time. "This conversation is not over. Not by any measure."

I held to that sweet promise as I slipped back outside to allow his siblings time with the brother they adored but did not fool myself that Zevi would set aside the vow he'd made, or his duty to the king, to stay with me. So, with a prayer for strength on my lips, I headed back to the place where I'd found a great deal of comfort over the past few days while Zevi fought for his life.

Eliora's garden.

Zevi

I'd walked through these woods thousands of times since I came here when I was a boy. If I listened carefully, I could almost hear the shouts of four boys playing war among the trees and catch a glimpse of their shadows darting to and fro with a giant dog bounding along in their wake, a band of cousins made brothers by the slash of a knife to small palms and a vow—one that I'd broken.

I missed them.

I'd not let myself do so for a long time, because opening the door to what had happened between us two years ago allowed the guilt and shame of my failure to overwhelm me. But here, with only the cedars, the oaks, and the sycamores to witness my sadness, I threw that door wide open.

From the first day I'd come to this mountain with Shoshana, my cousins Avidan, Gavriel, and Shalem had invited me into their midst. There were no questions about who I was or where I'd come from, and certainly none about what had happened to me. They simply opened their little circle and made room for me. Of course it had taken some time to feel like I was part of them, and even when my role shifted into one of leadership, I still was never fully at ease. How could I be when I was so jealous? They'd never watched their families die or been sent away from their homes, rejected by others and then tortured and enslaved.

I liked playing at war and wrestling with my cousins. I liked that they didn't know anything about my past, and I liked being a part of their adventures. But I craved their innocence.

So when we lost Shalem because of my weakness for the sweet boy and his ability to cajole me into letting him tag along, I'd felt not only devastated at his loss but adrift without my cousins—my brothers. And nothing had been the same since.

Avidan lived in Naioth, studying Torah at the feet of Samuel and the other priests and learning his duties from the Levites who taught at the school of prophecy. My mother said there was talk from Avi about returning to his wife Keziah's hometown across the river so Avi could teach the people there about the ancient history of Israel. Which meant it might be years before I saw him again.

And Gavriel was a soldier, like me. Although barely twenty now, he'd found his place among the company of Yonatan, Saul's eldest son. His weapon-making skills were already highly prized, and I had no doubt he would be promoted among the ranks. But he was also adrift.

The last time we'd crossed paths in one of the army camps outside Gibeah, I saw how he'd embraced the life of an unmarried soldier, his cup full of drink and his arm slung around the waist of one of the serving girls. He'd dodged my questions about his family, although I knew he adored his mother and sisters, but he said he'd visited home only once since he'd joined the army. According to my ima, his mother was devastated and worried that she might never see her son again if he perished while fighting.

And truly, she had cause to worry, because I'd fought with Gavi at Yavesh-Gilead, and while he excelled as a soldier, he was extraordinarily reckless. The few times we'd crossed paths since parting ways to fight in separate companies, neither of us broached the subject of our lost cousin, but I suspected he carried a similar burden of shame for leaving Avi to search for Shalem alone.

And then, of course, there was Shalem himself. Younger than the three of us and coddled by his parents, he'd been equal parts frustrating and dear to me. With a brilliance that outshone the three of us, his quick mind always snatching up foreign words and what some might deem useless knowledge, he'd been destined for great things.

Instead, he'd ended up lost and alone and most likely enslaved to Phoenician traders. I'd considered going after him. What else did I have to do, after all? I'd been stripped of my men and my honor. On my own, I might be able to sneak back into Ashdod and seek word among the merchants about a boy with a silver patch of hair. Even if it had been many years since I stepped foot in that nest of vipers, I was certain I could find my way.

But I'd been stuck in my bed for nearly a week since I'd awakened, unable to do much more than lie there and stare at the ceiling. I spent a good couple of days stewing in my failures and thinking about how I could get back what I'd lost.

However, on the third day, I remembered what my father had said. *"Just as a soldier trusts his commander and a commander trusts his king, you must trust the King above all Kings to direct you. And as I've learned over these past years, the orders are more often whispered than shouted."*

And so I went quiet to await his command.

And when it came, accompanied by what only could be described as a weighty presence in my room, in my spirit, and all around me, I was as astounded by its clarity as I was relieved that I had direction. And when I discussed the surprising answer with my father, he admitted that he was equal parts proud of my willingness to submit to Yahweh's direction as he was terrified for me. But he reiterated that El Shaddai, the Mighty One, would be my shield and I could absolutely trust in his strength and righteousness.

However, the unfinished conversation with Yochana now lay before me, and I was not certain how she would receive it. Although she'd continued to tend to my wounds as they healed, we'd had little time alone, and once I was finally back on my feet, she'd been occupied either in the garden or off with my mother and sisters. And perhaps because she knew as well as I did that nothing about our situation was simple, I had the distinct impression that she'd been purposely avoiding being alone with me.

That ended today.

Taking one of the paths through the woods that I could probably follow with my eyes closed, I found the terraced gardens that perched on the side of the mountain, where my mother had said Yochana had gone to help Galit early this morning. I searched the leafy rows for the form that had become so familiar to me and was unsurprised to find her kneeling with her hands in the soil.

Galit's twelve-year-old daughter, Nadina, was seated beside Yochana, obviously enthralled by whatever Yochana was explaining to her, but I was far enough away that I could not hear their voices. Nadina gestured to one of the prolific reddish-pink blooms on a nearby flowering bush, and Yochana picked one to tuck behind the girl's ear. The smile on Nadina's face was as bright as the sun overhead. I knew how she felt. Yochana's intelligence and beauty were matched by her kind heart, and I was captivated.

I watched her pluck some petals from the same flower and rub them between her palms before inhaling their fragrance, her eyes closing as she considered its smell, probably imagining some new fragrance or balm she could create with its essence. I could watch her work for hours, fascinated as I was by her abilities.

True to their promise, my parents had voiced their shock and displeasure with my idiocy in taking Yochana from her home but also acknowledged that Yahweh used my foolish decision to save my life. They heartily approved of her, saying any woman who would forgive such an egregious sin was a woman of great worth. And she was indeed. There could be no better match for me than Yochana.

However, I had to obey my king. And I was not speaking of the man who currently inhabited the throne of Israel but the one enthroned in the heavens.

So, I took a deep breath, lifted a plea to El Shaddai that he would give me the strength necessary for what I needed to do, and entered Eliora's garden.

Nadina saw me first and ran to throw her arms around my middle. "Cousin Zevi!"

She'd been born only a few months after Shoshana, Galit, and I had escaped Ashdod, and from my understanding, her birth father had given his life for Galit and their unborn child. Nadina knew only my uncle Yonah as her father since, after years of patient effort on his part, he'd married Galit. But she was also well aware of the sacrifice made on her behalf.

"Where is Jaru?" she asked. The two of them were the closest of friends, born only a few months apart, but she never let her cousin forget that she'd been in the world just a bit longer than him.

"He and Teitu had chores to do at the house," I said, "but he'd be done faster if he had a little help." I gave her a wink, and after a quick good-bye to Yochana, she scampered off to find my brother.

And finally Yochana and I were alone, and thanks to the prolific bushes with their vibrant blossoms and thick foliage, completely secluded from the world.

"You're looking well today," she said, one hand shading her eyes.

"I'm feeling much more like myself."

Thanks to Yochana's care, poultices, and the tinctures she insisted I swallow, my healing had been extraordinary. And my mother's hearty vegetable stews, made from produce from this very garden, built my strength day by day. Other than persistent aches in my gut and shoulder, which I guessed might be with me for a while as my body healed inside, I was more than capable of doing what needed to be done.

"Where's Galit?" I asked, surveying the garden for signs of others.

"Daphna had her baby last night," she said. "Galit went to help with the rest of her brood, leaving Nadina with me."

Yet another of my aunts, although she was only about five years older than me, Daphna already had four children and now a fifth. I had so many cousins that I could not keep track of them anymore. Even my sister Aaliyah had been married now for a year to a local farmer and would make me an uncle again within a few weeks.

And yet I'd never seriously considered the idea of my own children. At least until Yochana. Until the idea of her body carrying a little one created from a union between us had taken root as I saw her kneeling before Arisa, listening to my sister chatter like a little sparrow about a wooden doll our abba had carved for her. But now the images of what could be flourished in my mind, nearly thwarting my objective in coming here in the first place.

I had to find the will to keep myself focused on the order I'd clearly been given by the Voice while on my sickbed. So, instead of dropping to my knees to plead with Yochana to be my wife, I took a deep breath and called on the skills I'd honed for setting aside distractions.

"I'll be leaving for Gibeah within the week," I said.

She came to her feet, brows furrowed as she blinked at me. "You . . . why?"

"I have to clear my name, Yochana. Not only have I been falsely accused of treachery but also of Asher's murder. If I do not refute Kyrum's lies, then my entire family will be dishonored. And worse, Asher's family could send a blood avenger."

Her eyes went wide. "They would do that?"

"As close as I was to Asher, I never met his family. They would have no cause to disbelieve Kyrum's claims. So, yes, if they discover I am alive, they could send someone to take vengeance on me. And I will not remain here to put my family in danger."

I paused before continuing. "When I go back, I am hoping that Mahir and Shimi will testify to my innocence before the king."

"But they weren't there when Kyrum made his betrayal known."

"No, but from what you said, they did not believe him. They know me, and I am certain they will stand on my behalf."

"You cannot know that, Zevi. What if Kyrum has turned them against you?"

I could not refute that, as it was entirely possible. Kyrum was silver-tongued; if he'd convinced Lemek to turn on me so easily, he might be able to confuse the others. Or convince them that testifying on my behalf would destroy their standing with Saul's army. Merotai was his father, after all, and might punish anyone standing against his son.

But I knew what I'd been told to do, and I had to obey a much higher authority than Merotai.

"I will trust El Shaddai to be my shield against Kyrum's lies. If I slink off like a coward and hide, and if I do not refute these accusations with the truth, my family will always be stained by dishonor. Even if none of it is true. I won't do that to them."

"But you could be put to *death* if Saul does not believe you."

I wished I could alleviate her fears, but she was right. I was a soldier and therefore must follow the chain of command, all the way to the very top—the lawgiver himself. And as had been so distinctly impressed upon me while I lay on my bed, struggling with Yahweh's strong command in my heart and mind, Kyrum had shed innocent blood and must be held accountable.

"Yes, I could. But I will do so knowing I have placed myself in the hands of the Righteous King."

She turned away, eyes back on the profuse green foliage that shielded us from the outside world.

"What about Rezev and Eliyah?" she asked, still not looking at me.

"What about them?"

"Will you take them? Have them speak on your behalf?"

"If they return before I depart and are willing."

The two of them had gone down to Azeka with my father three days ago to deliver goods to Osi's family. They'd taken a donkey laden with produce from this garden, along with other gifts of appreciation from my family, and one very strong cut of oak that my father would use to repair their pottery wheel. If I'd not still been gaining my strength back when they left, I'd have gone along to express my gratitude as well, but I trusted my father to pass along my thanks.

I'd also asked that a messenger be sent to Maresha with a note to Yochana's family that she was safe and would be returning soon. I'd planned to take her myself but would have to entrust her to my father now as well, since my new orders were taking me back east instead of south. At least she would be safe and back with her family, even if I felt in my bones that she belonged with me.

"And what about me?"

"You'll be returned to Maresha. I don't think I'll be able to retrieve your box of herbs, but I will try. I'm certain Galit will send you back with whatever you desire from this garden so you can rebuild your stock. I wish I'd not taken so many of your jars, but perhaps you'll come up with a few new fragrances using these flowers, and of course the remedies you created for me will be in high demand—"

"Not my shop, Zevi. I mean *me*."

"My father will make sure you get back safely."

An ugly growl came from her beautiful mouth, and she turned flashing gray eyes on me. "There you go again, making my choices for me. First you kidnap me. Then you make me love you. And now you leave me to grieve a second fool running off to his death?"

I tried not to smile, but in this instance, my famous restraint was useless against such an admission. "You love me?"

She pinched her fingers against the bridge of her nose, eyes pressed closed. She'd spoken of not being able to think of anyone taking Ilan's place until me, but I'd only dared to hope that she felt as strongly as I did, praying that the sweet intensity that had vibrated in the air before my younger siblings interrupted had not been my imagination.

I stepped closer to repeat, "You love me."

She opened her eyes and huffed. "Zevi, you just told me you are planning to go throw yourself on the mercy of the king."

I shook my head as I moved farther into her space. "I'm throwing myself on the mercy of the King I should have been trusting all along. The one who led the Champion of Ashdod to rescue me from slavery, the one who kept him alive to become my father, and the one who brought me into the shop of the most talented perfumer in the Land—whose brilliance saved my life—though I do not deserve her."

She pressed a flat palm against my chest as a shadow came into her gorgeous gray eyes. "There is something I haven't told you."

A flash of cold went through me at her ominous tone, one I recognized as the same fear I used to feel when I was young, that Natan and Shoshana would finally be done with my surly behavior and send me away.

But her warm hand was not pushing me from her—just the opposite. It felt more like trust and affection, even if something was weighing on her.

Oblivious to my silent battle, she continued, "You know that I was angry with Saul about Ilan's death. Furious. I blamed him for demanding that the tribes run to the defense of strangers across the river and sending my husband to his death."

"I won't force you—"

She shook her head. "This is not about that. This is about a plot to depose Saul. By any means necessary."

I blinked at her in profound confusion. "How do you know about such a plot?"

Her cheeks reddened. "I was involved. Well . . . not in any meaningful way. I did give some of my profit to the cause, but what's more important is that two of the men who've been leading the small group of dissidents in Maresha are now with your company. Or . . . well, they are with Kyrum on their way to Gibeah."

"I don't understand. No one from Maresha volunteered to go."

"They joined the group while we were traveling north. I recognized them in the crowd."

While I was chasing after Shalem. Not only had I not seen Kyrum's betrayal coming, but I'd been so distracted from my mission that I'd not realized traitors to the king had crept in. All the more reason to follow the direction I'd been given. It had been almost two weeks since I'd been injured, which meant these men were *already* in Gibeah.

"Did they see you?"

"They did. I thought perhaps they were there to rescue me, but they made it clear I was nothing but a liability." She then told me of how this man called Noham had come after her in the wagon. Apparently, I was more in Rezev and Eliyah's debt than I'd realized.

My stomach burned knowing Yochana had been in danger that day. "Why didn't you tell me any of this before now?"

"Because you were injured, Zevi. Near to death. What could you have done? Run off to save the king while your fever raged?"

"You should have told me."

She shook her head. "I may not have known you for very long, but I understand you well enough to know that you would have insisted on going the moment you heard. And I was right, since you already planned to go before you knew about Noham. And I don't know what I will do if—" Her words cut off abruptly, and her eyes glimmered with tears. I did not deserve her concern, but I was immensely grateful for it.

"I don't want to lose you again," she whispered. "It was as if those arrows pierced me too in that meadow."

I took a chance and placed my hand on her waist, drawing her close. I thrilled at the way she immediately melted into me. Nothing had ever felt more right than this woman in my arms.

"I cannot divine the future, Yochana, and all of this may go badly. But I do know that I want a life with you. What that looks like I cannot tell you. I swore allegiance to Saul and must fulfill my commitment to him and to our people. I cannot dishonor myself or my family with cowardice. And I cannot let Kyrum's lies testify against me any more than I can stand by while the king chosen by Yahweh is under threat of assassination. I have to go. You know I do."

She nodded, pressing her lips together. Encouraged that she'd not yet pushed me away, I lifted my other hand to cup her cheek. "However, just as you never thought to marry again, I never considered anything would mean more to me than being a soldier until I met you."

She leaned into my touch, so I let my thumb trace her lower lip. How would I ever deserve a woman of such grace and mercy? "We both know I cannot promise you anything until I know what my fate is with Saul. But if Yahweh sees fit to deliver me, I will come for you." I gave her a rueful smile. "That is, if you want me to."

"You had *better* come back to me," she said, sliding her arms up my chest and around my neck to pull me close. "Or I will hunt you down myself."

"Will you now?" I inhaled a deep lungful of the intoxicating scent I hoped would remain with me through whatever was ahead.

In answer, she closed the short distance between her lips and mine, setting my heart into a wild gallop and my head to swirling with the soft warmth of her nearness. Suffused with heat and a desire that only Yochana had ever inspired in me, I reveled in the sweetness of her mouth, the perfection of her wrapped in my embrace, and the thought that this strong and stunning woman had forgiven my transgressions against her and chosen me regardless of the ugliness in my past.

Knowing we needed to dampen the flame that had taken hold lest it burn us, but not quite ready to snuff it out, I took my lips on a journey across her jaw and pressed another kiss to the sweetly fragrant spot just below her earlobe.

"I will take that as confirmation of your intentions to chase me down if need be," I whispered against her warm skin.

She took a shuddering breath. "You'd do well to remember it, soldier."

I laughed. She was just as affected as I was but would never let me lead her around by the nose, I was certain. If Yochana were a man, I'd be honored to have her serve at my side in war, as her fortitude, quick thinking, and intuition were traits I sought out in the men I added to my company. And for the battle that lay ahead of us now, and more than likely in the future, I would need a helpmeet of such strength and faithfulness by my side.

"Who knew the hint of perfume in the air would alter my life so profoundly?" I said, keeping her wrapped in one arm while I stroked her back up and down with the other.

"Who knew the man who kidnapped me would steal my heart?" Her grin was full of mischief, bringing my greedy eyes back to her soft lips.

With a groan, I leaned my forehead against hers. "You'll never let me forget what a fool I was, will you?"

"Probably not. But I will also never forget that you fed the dog that morning." She brushed her nose against mine. "Why did you do that, Zevi?"

Thrown by the question, I pulled back to gaze into the gray eyes that, against all odds, now looked on me with such sweet affection.

"Igo," I said, with a shrug. "Remember how I told you that back in Ashdod my father had an enormous dog that I thought would eat me? That was Igo."

"He wasn't vicious after all?"

I chuckled. "Far from it. Not only was he the gentlest of creatures—although fiercely defensive of me—but he was my closest companion for many years, even above my cousins. I may have been enthralled by you in your shop, but it was your kindness to such a helpless animal and her pups that captured *me*. Perhaps it was ridiculous, but I hoped knowing I'd brought her food would help you see I meant you no harm. I would never have let anyone hurt you, and I am furious that I almost did. I still cannot believe I did not see Kyrum's treachery sooner."

She stroked my beard in a soothing manner. "I know. I wish I'd shared my suspicions of him."

I pressed my hand over hers. "What do you mean?"

She huffed a breath. "Sometimes he watched me when you weren't looking. And nothing about it was . . . innocent."

Heat shot up my spine. "He panted after you?"

Her eyes darted away. "I don't know that it was about me, really. More likely that he knew where your interests lay."

Although I disagreed with her first conjecture, because any man would be a fool to not want her, her second was probably just as true. In his final words to me, he made it clear that he coveted my command, and with it the approval of his father. Lusting after and then stealing Yochana was just another way to punish me for Merotai's regard.

"Kyrum will never be within a hundred paces of you again, Yochana. I vow it."

She slid her fingers into the unruly curls at the back of my neck, causing my skin to prickle with a much more pleasurable warmth. "I didn't tell you to stir up more reasons to be angry with him, Zevi. Only to say that he was a talented pretender. I half-doubted myself when he was with you and Asher. There was no hint of his designs for me or plans to betray you. Do not thrash yourself for being taken in. You are hard enough on yourself as it is." She pressed her lips to mine again, far too briefly. "You asked for my forgiveness, but I have a feeling you've not truly received it. And neither do I think you have released yourself from the self-incrimination and shame you've carried for so long."

"I am trying," I said. "Be patient with me. I want to be unfettered by it, but I've grown accustomed to the weight of the chains."

"Just come back to me and we'll find our way together, all right?"

"I want to be whole, for you." I kissed one cheekbone, lingering there for a moment to breathe deeply and thanking Yahweh for guiding me to her shop by that alluring scent, before moving to press my lips to the other. "And I want a lifetime of you at my side."

"Zevi!"

The call came from across the garden, breaking into what had been the most perfect moments of my life. I growled softly at the intrusion. Especially since, once again, it was Jaru and Teitu barging in on the rare time I had alone with Yochana.

The boys continued calling my name, and for a few moments I considered stealing Yochana away to some other secluded place before they found us among the flowering bushes, but with each shout, their voices grew more urgent.

I grabbed Yochana's hand and tugged her out of our small paradise until Teitu spotted me at the edge of the terrace and dashed toward me. "Zevi! You have to come!"

I reached for his shoulder as the boy skidded to a stop, chest heaving. "What is it?"

"Abba sent for you to come right away. There are men here from Gibeah."

24

Yochana

I clung to Zevi's hand all the way up the mountain, refusing to let him face whatever these men had come for without my support and pleading with Yahweh that they were not here to avenge Asher's blood. We'd been surprised when the boys did not lead us to Natan and Shoshana's home but instead to the compound where most of his clan lived in houses built around a central courtyard or in sturdy tents pitched among the trees.

The first thing I noticed before we entered that courtyard were the horses. Ten of them were tied up nearby, grazing on lush grasses that grew around the large clearing. Whoever these men were, they not only had the resources to afford well-fed beasts but must have been in a rush to arrive in Kiryat-Yearim.

"That's Keziah's horse," Zevi said with surprise, gesturing toward a large black stallion with white speckled forelegs. "I'd recognize that warhorse anywhere."

"Who is Keziah?"

"My cousin Avidan's wife. She's of the tribe of Manasseh across the Jordan, and her father is a breeder of fine horses. She brought that stallion with her when they married."

I remembered him speaking of how much his cousin adored his wife and was curious how such an unlikely union came about. However, the tension in Zevi's form grew with every step, so I held my tongue. A group of men was seated beneath the canopy strung between the pillars, being tended by Yoela, Zevi's grandmother, and a couple of his aunts whose names I could not remember. There were so many people in this large clan that it was difficult to keep track of them all. But I certainly recognized Natan, along with Rezev and Eliyah, who must have returned from Azeka today while Zevi and I had been in the garden.

The Philistine's presence here gave me a small measure of relief. If the men had come for his son as blood avengers, Natan would not be standing there so casually, talking with another tall man whose hair was only a shade deeper than his own golden-brown.

Zevi headed for his father, and I tried to slip my hand out of his grip, but he tightened it, indicating he wanted me to remain at his side in front of everyone. I should have known that once Zevi made a decision, there was no vacillation. I was thrilled he would be so bold in claiming me, even in the midst of whatever upheaval was happening now.

"Avi," Zevi addressed the younger of the two, without the customary greeting to his father. "What's going on?"

"We've come for the Ark," Avi said, his green eyes flashing to me for only a moment before latching onto his cousin. "Saul has called for it."

Shock flashed over Zevi's face. "But why?"

Avi shook his head, his expression grim. "Things are bad, Zev. The Philistines have completely taken Michmash. Saul's army was forced to retreat to Gilgal near the Jordan River."

"How did the Philistines manage to take Michmash so quickly?

It's only been a few weeks since Yonatan attacked the garrison at Geva."

"From what I've heard, once Yonatan struck the garrison, the Philistines amassed an army in what used to be Efraimite territory. They came with thousands of men and hundreds of chariots. I'm not sure how they managed to move that many vehicles over muddy roads with the rain we've had."

"Iron wheels," said Zevi, frowning. "And plenty of horsepower to pull them."

Natan spoke up. "The Philistine chariots are far more sturdy than Egyptian ones. I had a couple of my own in Ashdod. And the Philistines will have plenty of conscripts and slaves to push those chariots, should they bog down."

"However they managed to do it," said Avi, "they swarmed down on Michmash with little warning, so they already hold a good portion of Benjamite territory. Anyone in their way fled with barely the clothes on their back. Thousands of Hebrews are hiding in caves up in the hills with their women and children, which now includes my own pregnant wife and our child. My father has taken them to a well-protected cave system up in the hills above Naioth with the rest of our family. If I'd not been the only person other than Keziah who can ride Sarru, and had my father not vowed to protect them with his own life, I would be there now."

The poor man must be distraught to have to leave his young family behind.

"Are the men of Israel coming to Saul's aid as they did at Yavesh-Gilead?"

Avi shook his head. "Just the opposite. That's why we are here. Once the army retreated down to Gilgal near Jericho, there was so much division and confusion over what was happening that many of them fled. From what the priests tell me"—he gestured to the men he'd come with—"a large number were so terrified they fled over the Jordan."

Zevi's expression went dark. "They *deserted*?"

"They did. Saul sent for Samuel, but after seven days of waiting for the prophet, Saul made his own offerings and pleas to Yahweh. Samuel came just as the smoke began rising to the heavens. No one knows exactly what was said between the two of them; all they know is that Samuel left quickly and went out into the wilderness somewhere, and Saul called for the Ark to be fetched immediately. Ahijah, the high priest, sent these *kohanim* to Naioth." He again gestured toward the priests. "Since few know of its true location, they needed someone to guide them here. They plan to go back with it today."

The situation had to be dire for Saul to call for the Ark to be removed from its hiding place and taken to battle. The last time that had happened was at the terrible battle in Afek, when the Ark was stolen by the Philistines and most of Efraim's territory overtaken. Then, shortly after, the holy city of Shiloh and what remained of the Mishkan complex was destroyed.

"However," Avi said, "I am heading back within the hour—alone. I won't leave my family unprotected, no matter how well-hidden the caves are or how much I trust my abba. We had to come the southern route because of how close the Philistines are to Ramah. They'll need help getting down the backside of the mountain to where we left the wagon and the rest of the guard. Once they are on the road east, the way down to Gilgal is easy."

Zevi stiffened. "And you think I am the man to lead them."

"I know what happened, Zev. Your father just told me everything. I can't imagine a better way for you to prove your loyalty to King Saul than ensuring his command to bring the Ark is carried out. You know every road in these hills. You'll know the smoothest path for a wagon carrying our most sacred object. There's no one better to make certain it gets there safely. I've never known anyone so vigilant in my life."

Zevi huffed a breath, and I knew he was thinking of Kyrum

and how he'd missed any sign the man was a betrayer instead of a friend.

"I'll go with you, son," Natan said.

Zevi was quiet for a few long moments, considering. "No, Abba. I need you to take Yochana back to Maresha."

I flinched. "What?"

"You need to go home, Yochana. I sent your family a message, and they are expecting you within the week."

My jaw dropped. "You sent them a message?"

"We paid a runner in Azeka to deliver a missive to your father," said Natan. "Zevi did not want them worrying over you anymore. To know you were alive and safe."

The kindness toward my family made my love for Zevi double. But he was not simply leaving to guide the priests back to Saul—he was walking toward a king who may command his execution without ever listening to his testimony. And if somehow Saul did believe him and allowed him to do his duty as a soldier, that meant Zevi would be facing down the Philistines—the most brutal army in this region of the world and the very men who'd traumatized him as a child. It was entirely possible that the hour we'd spent in the garden would be the only hour I would ever have alone with him in this life.

But what could I say? *Turn your back on your vow, your king, and your honor? Stay with me because I am terrified you will end up like Ilan?*

Zevi turned to me. "Please, Yochana. Go with my father. He'll make certain you are delivered safely home. I have to know you are far away from all of this and with your family, where you belong."

I belong at your side, my heart cried out.

I frowned at him, my blood pulsing loud in my ears. "You are making my choices for me again. What if I can be of help? I'm the one who knows what Noham and his friend look like—"

248

"No, this is not me making a decision for you." Zevi grabbed both of my hands and pressed them to his chest. "I have to go. You know this as well as I do. I must fight for our people, because if the Philistines take all of Benjamin, they will completely cut our territory in two. And Israel cannot stand if the tribes of the north and the south are not united against our enemies. This is me begging you to remain where I know you are safe."

He leaned closer, pinning me with one of his intense stares, and suddenly it felt as if we were alone again in the garden instead of surrounded by others. "I promise I will not be reckless. I will fight for our people as I have vowed to do, and then I *will* return for you. I will come and speak to your father and hope he does not put me in shackles for snatching his precious daughter."

I let a smile twitch my lips. My father and mother would probably be so thrilled I had found someone I wanted to spend my life with that they would throw a feast in his honor. They would forgive him. I would make sure of it. My father's compassion for Zevi began when he was nine years old and would only expand when I explained some of the reasons why he'd made the choices he had.

"I'll make certain they know I have forgiven you fully and completely. And that even if you made a wrong decision, you are a man of honor. One who I look forward to spending the rest of my *very long* life with." I could not help but give him a subtle command to keep his promise and not take unnecessary risks for the sake of a vow he'd made as a boy.

Zevi would not be the man I'd come to love if he ran like the cowards who'd fled across the Jordan. He was a man of deep loyalty and a powerful sense of justice. And although it made my soul ache, I knew I had to let him go. Just as he'd spoken of El Shaddai being his shield when it came to Kyrum's lies, I would have to trust that the Mighty One would protect him on the battlefield as well. I had no choice but to watch him walk away now.

But that did not mean I was completely powerless to help protect him.

There was a reason Zevi had kidnapped me in the first place, after all—for my perfumes. And thanks to a woman named Eliora, I had an entire garden of wonders at my disposal.

25

Zevi

The path down the backside of the mountain was far more gradual than the one up from Kiryat-Yearim, and as Avi had said, I knew this area and its many winding trails like I knew the lines on my own palm. So it was along that route I led the priests with their precious burden. Since Rezev, Eliyah, and I were not consecrated priests, we were not allowed within two thousand cubits of the Ark, so the journey down into the valley was one of sending messages back and forth via one the priests who was ritually clean and thereby allowed to approach.

I could not help but be curious about the Ark itself. I had no idea where exactly it had been hidden on the mountain for the past twelve years and had only heard loose descriptions of the golden box over the years, but my father cautioned us to take the necessary precautions to remain far away. He'd experienced the effects of its power back in Ashdod and warned us not to take the threat of death lightly. And since I'd determined to never again discount my father's wisdom or experience, I heeded his advice.

However, leaving Yochana in his care had been difficult. Not because I did not trust my father to return her safely to Maresha but because every bone in my body cried out that it was *my* duty to watch over her. We were not betrothed yet, and I already felt as though half of my soul was being ripped away from me as I departed.

She'd been so brave, even though I was certain she was just as devastated by this separation as I was. We'd had only a short time alone as I swiftly packed for my journey while my grandfather led the priests to the secret place he'd stashed the Ark, but I'd stolen a few lingering kisses, wishing I could remain there, drunk on her sweetness. Once I'd reluctantly torn myself away, she insisted that I take the healing balm she'd prepared.

"It has a good portion of terebinth resin," she had said, *"which I feel has done a great deal to heal your wounds, along with honeycomb from the hives here, wine made from grapes that grow on the terraces, and a few other herbs that will guard against infection and help numb any lingering ache. Also, I added the essence of blue lupine. I found a prolific patch on the western terrace."*

Her blush told me she'd done that not for any healing purposes but to give me a piece of her to take with me. I'd have to be careful to ration the balm in order to keep her precious fragrance with me for as long as possible, until I had her in my arms again.

It was astounding how fast I'd healed under her care and skilled use of what grew in Eliora's garden. Yes, there was still some lingering soreness in my left shoulder and especially my gut, but I'd fought before while wounded and would do what I must. The Philistines would not wait for me to heal. I had to face both my king and my enemies, whether I was still in pain or not.

Thankfully, I was far more proficient with my right hand than my left, but Kyrum had taken my sword. All I had to take with me to this battle was an ax my father had handed me—one of his best—and a couple of daggers. But I was still better armed than most Hebrews, who usually fought with little more than stone-tipped spears and javelins and sharpened farm implements, aside from the many well-practiced slingers and archers that filled our ranks. I would make do, even if I desperately missed the iron sword at my side—one my father had procured from a wealthy customer who'd purchased it directly from its Philistine maker in Gath

We made slow progress down the mountain, since the priests had to carry the Ark on their shoulders, but once down in the valley near Shoresh, they loaded their burden onto a wagon and covered it carefully to keep the load inconspicuous. With two of the sturdiest horses they'd brought hooked to the wagon, they were able to move much more quickly. Once the ground leveled out and we joined the well-worn road to Gibeah, they took their leave of us, since the three of us were on foot. Saul would likely have the Ark in his presence before the sun set, and it sounded as if it was none too soon, with Samuel having abandoned the king and half the people of Benjamin hiding or running for their lives.

"Well," Rezev said, as we watched the caravan melt into the distance, "now where do we go, Captain?"

I'd not been called *captain* for weeks, and I flinched at the term. I may no longer be endowed with authority from my commanders, but I still had a job to do. A long-held vow to fulfill. And a determination to clear my name quickly so I could return to Yochana with my honor intact.

Even if I had only two men looking to me for leadership, I would not let them down, nor would I ignore the direction I'd received from Yahweh. It had only been one word—*Go*—but I felt that command implanted in the deepest part of me. It resonated again now as I faced east.

"If things are as bad as Avi says, Saul needs every willing and able body."

"What if we come across Kyrum?" asked Eliyah. "Or someone else who recognizes you?"

"I'll deal with that as it comes. But for now, I say we fight for our people."

Rezev nodded. "Agreed. There'll be time aplenty for clearing your name once the dust settles."

"My father and I will be testifying on your behalf, Captain," said Eliyah. "I hope you know that."

I placed my hand over my heart. "I'm already in your debt for what you did for Yochana and for carrying me home. You honor me with your loyalty. I'll never forget it."

From what I'd learned from Avi and from a couple of the priests sent by Saul, the Philistines had separated their forces into three camps, one on the west side of Michmash, one on the north side, and the third closer to Gibeah in the south.

The three of us were nothing compared to thousands of Philistines, but if I had to choose a region to defend, it would be the one standing between the Philistines and my loved ones, most of whom lived either in Benjamite or Yehudite territory.

So as the wagon with the Ark went southeast on the sloping road toward Gilgal along the River Sorek, Rezev, Eliyah, and I parted from the well-beaten trade road and cut north through the hills and toward the Hebrew encampment west of Michmash to seek out Saul's forces. Hopefully, I could avoid my own division until after the battle was over.

As we hiked the rugged terrain, picking our way through the meandering ridges, narrow wadis, and up and down steep inclines, I considered what I would say when I eventually did come before my leadership. There would be little good in going to Merotai directly. Convincing Kyrum's father that his son was a liar, a traitor, and a killer would be no simple feat, and one that would end with Kyrum's execution for murder. Without question, the path ahead of me was incredibly rocky and steep, but I would take it one step at a time, trusting the Most High would guide each one.

By the time the sun set, we were within sight of Mitzpah—the location of the last major battle with the Philistines when I was twelve years old and just across the valley from the walled city of Ramah. To the east was the narrow pass that led to Michmash, the former Hebrew garrison that was now in Philistine hands. Although we could not see the enemy camp from here, especially with twilight falling, there was only a short distance between it and the deep pass that led to Michmash and Ramah. I hoped Gavi's stepfather, Hanan, had already fled the city with Doda Miri and Gavi's three little sisters, because there was nothing standing between Ramah and thousands of vicious Philistines. It was clear they meant to continue west and take all of Benjamite territory, and it was a wonder they hadn't already done so.

We spent the night not far from the place where my cousins and I had laid on our bellies in the weeds, watching an unknown man named king of Israel by the casting of lots. Although it had only been a little over three years since that day, I somehow felt a decade older.

After all my years of preparation, it was hard to believe it was finally time to meet my enemies on the battlefield. Soon I would stand across from those who'd taken so much from me. I would have my revenge against the monsters who'd destroyed my innocence and that of so many other children of Israel. I was ready to be an instrument of justice in the hand of the Almighty.

Anticipation continued to race through my body until the early hours of the morning, when I knew I had to get some rest before the battle. So, I thought of Yochana. I conjured up her soothing voice, the feel of her soft skin, the taste of her mouth, and, as I inhaled the sweet scent of the healing balm she'd given me, was finally lulled to sleep.

Just before dawn, I awakened with the echo of Adonai's directive in my mind. *Go.*

Rezev, Eliyah, and I quickly ate provisions sent along by my mother before continuing our trek up through the hills while the sun rose through a thick bank of gold-limned clouds in the east. When we came up over the final crest, the three of us slammed to a halt. An enormous horde of Philistines camped in the distance, their tents spread out like a carpet of every color along the floor of the deep canyon leading to Michmash. And this was only a third of their forces?

Rezev gave a low whistle as we surveyed the vast sea of foes. At Yavesh-Gilead, Saul's armies had had the advantage. Tens of thousands of us had broken into three companies, surrounded the Ammonites as they slept, and launched a surprise attack before dawn. How could we possibly be victorious here, when much of the army was now fleeing like sheep scattered by wolves? The Philistines had already devoured a huge swath across the heart of Israel's territories and were practically crouched at Saul's doorstep.

I'd been told to go toward the battle, but had Yahweh sent me here only to witness Saul's short reign brought to a swift and bloody end? If so, I had no doubt the Philistines would come over us like a flood, the vicious pack of idolaters tearing us to pieces as they came.

But as the horrifying thought came to me, I remembered how, in spite of the hopelessness I'd felt in Ashdod, Lukio had come to my rescue. That my salvation had come from the most unlikely of sources only confirmed it had been the All-Knowing One who'd sent him. Just as my father would never abandon me, neither would Yahweh abandon his treasured people. We may have been wrong to demand a human king, but in his mercy, he raised Saul to the throne for a purpose. And no matter our faithlessness, the will of Yahweh would not be thwarted.

Remember your promises, Adonai. For your name's sake.

"What is that?" Eliyah's voice broke into my silent plea to the Almighty. He gestured toward a column of cloud in the far distance to the southeast, rising straight upward from the direction of Gibeah like a thick, swirling pillar of smoke but one that glowed brighter than the morning sun.

Before I could conjure a response, the ground jolted under my feet, nearly sending me to my knees, accompanied by a series of loud booms as the cloud I'd seen in the distance expanded, spreading outward with breathtaking swiftness. More loud percussion echoed around the valley, seeming to come from both the sky and beneath the earth itself at the same time. Rocks began to tumble down the slopes, loose dirt and stones cascading around us, and every tree around us swayed like a drunkard, some coming loose of their moorings and toppling to the ground, roots exposed to the sky.

Desperate to avoid being squashed by one of the large boulders above us, I shouted at Rezev and Eliyah to run for higher ground. Without hesitation, they obeyed while the earth continued to shudder, rattling my bones and knocking my teeth together. We scrambled upward as the entire world seemed to pitch and roll like a ship caught in a tempest on the Great Sea. But even when we reached the top of the ridge, to a place of relative safety, the trembling continued on and on and on, until everything was a terrifying blur of sight and sound.

And then . . . it was over, the stillness nearly as jarring as the shaking had been. My blood rushed like the Jordan during spring runoff, and my insides felt rearranged, but it was over. At least for now.

"What *was* that?" Eliyah repeated in a trembling voice.

"The Ark," said his father. "That cloud was too similar to what we saw at Gilgal to be anything but otherworldly."

Rezev was right. There was simply no other explanation for what had just happened than El Shaddai had reached down his mighty hand and shook the earth. Rationally, I knew that the phenomenon had nothing to do with me, but the timing of the quake alongside my supplications left me in awe.

"But what do we do now?" asked Eliyah.

Rezev put a reassuring arm around him. "Yahweh's intervention means this war is already decided, son. The Mighty One went before us, so there is no need to fear. Now we simply go deal with the aftermath." He turned a wide smile on me. "Which way, Captain?"

I'd seen the changes in Rezev over these past weeks, but his certitude in my leadership was humbling. "We find Saul's army. The cloud has shown us where to go."

So, we began to move southwest but quickly found our progress frustrated by picking our way around boulders on paths, skidding on rivers of stones, and constantly being plagued by smaller tremors that continued to rattle us—as if the earth was still trying to catch its breath after a long and sustained wail.

When we were finally within sight of the mouth of the pass of Michmash but still a good way above the valley floor, we came through a narrow wadi, and the sound of voices floated up to us on the breeze. I threw up a fist, halting Rezev and Eliyah. Then, giving them a quick gesture to let them know I would scout the situation, I crept forward to peer around a boulder that hid whoever was there from my sight.

It was the headdresses I saw first. Bold, unmistakable, feathered headgear that was unique to the Philistine army. It gave them a fearsome aspect, the look of great birds of prey swooping down on their enemies. These were the monsters of my childhood, the destroyers of my innocence, and the thieves of my peace—and that of my people.

And finally—*finally!*—I would have my chance to fulfill the vow I had made.

It didn't matter that I only had an ax and two daggers. There were only six that I could see, and I would rain vengeance on them all by myself. My promise to the people of Zanoah, to Tera and Chelah, would be complete, and I would be whole again.

"And once you've had your vengeance—what then, son?"

The words came from seemingly nowhere, but I heard them as clearly as if my father was standing before me, his one green eye and one brown eye pinning me in place. The sharp reminder of his exhortation on my sickbed made me pause. I'd heard the command of the Almighty to go and had obeyed, but now that weighty presence I'd felt in my room was impressing on me the command to *be still*.

My flesh thrashed hard against the order, and my tongue tasted of bile. This was the perfect opportunity to repay these beasts for their violence. My enemies had been practically dropped at my feet. I gripped my ax in my hand, chest aching, torn between flesh and spirit. Sweat trickled down the back of my neck as my breaths came one upon the other. Surely Yahweh would not have brought me to this place to let the animals who'd terrorized his people go free? No. They could not be allowed to take the innocence of one more child, strip the dignity from one more woman, or burn one more Hebrew town to ash. Belly burning with righteous anger, I lifted my ax and took one step forward—

Be still.

My body jolted at the force of the repeated command. So clear. So unmistakable.

Unable to deny the directive, I hung my head, letting my ax fall to my side and restraining my instinct to plow ahead to mete out justice. I instead listened for my High Commander's voice.

Vengeance is mine.

I nearly gasped aloud at the clarity of the whispered admonition, which was soon followed by the memory of my father's wise words. *"Only Yahweh can stand as a righteous judge. Leave vengeance in his capable hands."*

All the truth I'd spent so long pressing into one of those boxes in my mind burst free. From my earliest days I'd been taught how the justice and mercy of Yahweh was so powerfully displayed in his steadfast love for our people. And yet I'd been so focused on taking an eye for an eye that I'd determined to have my own way instead of seeking his perfect will.

By holding on to bitterness and hatred against those who'd wronged me, instead of giving thanks for how Adonai had rescued me from their grasp, I had become far more like my enemies than my God. It was up to Yahweh alone to execute justice, my job was simply to obey.

As I stood there in silence, stunned by the truth washing over me, I heard the voices of the Philistines a little more clearly this time.

" . . . look for a cave . . ."

"What if they come?"

". . . go past Ramah and then north?"

Although much of the conversation was muffled, my jaw slacked in astonishment while I listened. Because the half-whispered words exchanged between the men only ten paces away, huddled together behind the remains of an enormous oak tree that had fallen during the earthquake, were not Philistine.

They were Hebrew.

26

"What is going on?" Eliyah whispered at my ear as I was trying to make sense of what I'd heard.

I startled to find him so close and whipped around, pushing him backward with a quieting finger to my lips. But I was too late.

Within moments, we were pinned in the narrow wadi, six men surrounding us with javelins and spears, the dust from their swift response floating in the air.

Rezev and Eliyah stood on either side of me, daggers at the ready, but I gestured for them to be still. "Put your weapons down. We are brothers."

"*Brothers?*" Eliyah gaped at me.

The one I assumed to be the leader peered at me, his painted face registering surprise. "You know who we are?"

Even though his speech made his heritage abundantly clear, it was difficult to separate his appearance from the truth. He wore no feathered headdress, but his kilt and corselet were distinctly Philistine. "I heard you talking. You *are* Hebrews, are you not?"

The man let out a heavy breath. "Efraimites."

"I guessed as much."

"But why are you dressed that way?" Eliyah asked. "And fighting for our enemies?"

"They're conscripts, son," said Rezev, and I was glad he'd pieced it together quickly.

"We have no choice," said the leader with a helpless shrug. "They've held our towns for nearly thirty years. If we don't fight for them, they burn our homes. Kill our families. Violate our women."

Most of Efraim's territory had been under Philistine subjugation since the battle at Afek, when they'd stolen the Ark of the Covenant long before I was born. And all this time, these people had been enduring unspeakable oppression. I'd experienced what horrors the Philistines perpetuated against villages like Zanoah that did not capitulate, so when this man spoke of vicious retaliation by their overlords, I could see it clearly in my mind. Going out to battle against fellow Hebrews meant they must have been desperate indeed.

I had to admit that, if it were Yochana and my own family under such threats, it would likely push me to desperation as well.

"Why are you up here?" I asked. "Instead of down with the Philistines?"

The leader ran a hand through his wildly tangled hair. "Did you not feel that earthquake?"

"The ground shaking made you flee?"

"That, on top of everything else." The man sounded exhausted, body and soul.

I slid the waterskin from my shoulder, holding it out to him. "Tell us."

He paused, staring at my offering for a few moments, then gestured for his men to lower their weapons and be at ease before taking the water. At my sides, Rezev and Eliyah relaxed as well.

The Efraimites passed the waterskin between them, slaking their thirst before the leader began. "Nothing has gone according to their plans. Yes, we pushed into Michmash and your army went running. There was a lot of celebration that night." He frowned. "And more than a few bloody sacrifices to their gods. We Hebrews endured days of taunting—mocking Saul, mocking Yahweh. They boasted that Gibeah was next and they'd drag your king naked into Ashdod, Ashkelon, and Gaza before hanging him at one of their gates."

Of course the Philistines would want to humiliate Saul. It would be paramount to parading all of us through their repugnant cities. They were especially talented at stripping dignity from their captives. I myself had been led through Ashdod, shredded to pieces inside, and would never forget the way the people gawked at the pathetic line of us captives—men, women, and children—without a hint of compassion. We were little more than chattel to them.

"After we'd broken into three companies, they told us we'd be sent out on the road toward Ramah with the raiding party." He gestured to the west. "Said we'd be taking whatever villages stood in our way. And, like they did to us, those who did not surrender were to be destroyed."

"What changed?" Eliyah asked.

"Ghosts," said the man.

"Come again?" Rezev said, frowning.

"We only heard rumors, but apparently around twenty Philistines were killed at Michmash. No one knows how. The entire area was guarded heavily, and the pass completely blocked. No way in and no way out. But somehow, those men were slaughtered, left to rot in the sun in an area no bigger than five hundred cubits. There were no footprints left behind. No sign anyone had slipped directly into the middle of the Philistine camp, except for the dead."

"So they think spirits did it?" I asked, incredulous.

He nodded. "We Hebrews are nothing more than a motley group of shepherds and farmers in their minds, after all."

I didn't know who'd had the courage to sneak into a garrison like that, but it was likely a small band of fearless Hebrew soldiers who'd done so. Once again, our enemies had underestimated us. They may think we were nothing to be feared, and they certainly had more weapons and iron chariots, but since the days of

Mosheh, our God had brought powerful nations to their knees with his own hand.

"The thing is, they are a superstitious lot," said the leader. "So by the time the rumor reached us, it had taken on a life of its own. There was a story that it was only two men who appeared just outside the garrison, lured the Philistines out, and then somehow killed them before vanishing into the air." He laughed. "They said they were men with the strength of a hundred and able to melt into the earth like raindrops and appear elsewhere in the span of a breath."

"So these rumors riled them up?"

"They did indeed. And then we heard whispers that the Ark had been spotted somewhere up on the hills above the battlefield. The ghosts of Michmash were all but forgotten when that news washed through the ranks. It may have been three decades ago that Mosheh's golden box was taken into their cities, but they know the stories of the destruction that followed."

I'd heard those stories firsthand from both my father and my aunt Eliora, who'd witnessed the shaking of Ashdod and the destruction of Dagan in his temple and endured the horrifying plague that followed. The Philistines had been so terrified they'd sent the Ark back into Hebrew territory on a driverless wagon—one that led two orphaned Philistine children to a new home in Kiryat-Yearim. It sounded as if the stories of that time were still fresh in the minds of our enemies.

"There was panic in our company," said the leader. "But the commanders refused to let anyone break rank, on pain of death. But when that earthquake struck . . ." He shook his head, wide-eyed. "You should have seen it. Iron-wheeled chariots tossed about like knucklebones in the hand of a child. Horses screaming. People shouting for their gods. We'd seen enough. We fled for the hills."

"Seen enough for what?"

"To realize that we've been cowards," said the man, his gaze steady on mine. "The Philistines may be mighty in the eyes of men, but Yahweh is plainly far more powerful."

"I won't fight for them anymore," said one of the other men.

"Nor I," said another. "It may have seemed like Israel had lost this fight, but not anymore. The Philistines are panic-stricken While we were retreating, we saw plenty of them running for the coastlands."

Rezev spoke up. "You say there are quite a few of you con-scripted into their army?"

"Hundreds. Thousands, if you count those who aren't Hebrew but were subjugated over the years in various battles."

"And many of you fled into the hills?"

"Indeed. The six of us are squad leaders. We came up here to discuss which way to go next. Our troops are awaiting direction just beyond those trees." He gestured to where the wadi widened into a valley about two hundred paces to the south. "There's roughly one hundred and fifty of us. But there are plenty more hiding in the caves around here."

Rezev raised his brows, his expression full of meaning. "You are thinking we should use this opportunity, aren't you, Captain?"

"Be a shame to waste it," I replied, my mind four or five steps down the road already.

"What opportunity?" Eliyah divided a confused frown between the two of us.

"It could not be more perfect had we devised it ourselves," Rezev said, gesturing toward the Philistine-garbed men before us.

I took a few moments to consider the angles. Of course I had no idea what Saul's plan was, and the Hebrews must be regroup-ing after the shaking of the ground, but we had no time to waste.

"It's a good plan," I said. Rezev obviously had the mind of a strategist. And since we'd both fought at Yavesh-Gilead, there was no doubt we had the very same idea.

"What plan?" said Eliyah, frustrated by our unspoken conver-sation.

"If Philistines already think ghosts came to slaughter them, think of what they'll do when they attack themselves." I gestured to the Efraimites.

Understanding came to life on Eliyah's face. "It'll throw them into more of a panic."

Rezev grinned. "Just like Yavesh-Gilead."

"Just like Yavesh-Gilead," I agreed. "We shocked and confused them so much, it was barely a fight."

I turned to the Efraimites. "Are your men willing?"

The leader peered at me, sizing me up. "You're a captain?"

"I was. It's a long story. For now, I am just a soldier."

"No, Zevi," said Rezev. "There is a reason my son and I are still here and not back in Lachish—or worse, with Kyrum. And look." He gestured to the Efraimites. "Yahweh has guided you here for a purpose. You *are* a leader, my friend. A good one. I won't let you take that designation lightly."

Who would have ever imagined that Rezev, who had been so caustic and dismissive of me and my cousins, would be the man to encourage me now? I took his words as further direction from El Shaddai. So I spoke the truth in as concise a way as possible.

"I am a captain in Saul's army," I said to the Efraimite leaders. "I was betrayed by one of my most trusted men and left for dead. When this is over, I plan to go before Saul and clear my name. But for now, I'm here to defend our people."

I took a moment to meet the eyes of each, looking past the unsettling disguises to see varying shadows of indecision on their faces. "I've lived in fear of them. Just like you. But unless we push these ravenous beasts out of our lands, they'll keep coming after our families until all that will be left of us is dust and ash."

Even as I spoke, I realized that something deep inside me had truly shifted. My mission was still to go to battle against the enemy but not because doing so would mend what had been broken so many years ago or because it would undo what had been done to the people of Zanoah. It was wholeheartedly to prevent it from happening to another town, to other women and children, and from happening to Yochana and the little ones I planned to have with her someday. I would leave Yahweh to deal with the past and with those who'd hurt his children—had hurt me—and I would fight with all my strength for Israel's future.

I gestured toward the place where that strange cloud had arisen before the earth began to shake. "The High Commander of the heavenly armies gave us a signal. Are we going to obey?"

I could only hope that my scant explanation would be enough for these strangers to trust me and that their desire to free their families of subjugation would outweigh any misgivings.

"We left for a reason," said their leader, then looked to the others. "He's right. If we don't stand against them now, we'll never be free. Are we in accord?"

One by one, the Efraimite men nodded their agreement. With a glint of excitement in his eye, their leader set his hand on the hilt at his side. "Our swords are yours to command, Captain."

At the words, a surge of something powerful sluiced through my bones, filling me head to toe with certainty. Rezev was right. I'd not only been kept alive for a reason but guided to this place for a purpose I could never have imagined as I lay in that meadow, believing that I'd lost everything. The King of Kings had given me both a clear command to fight for my people and a company of men to lead into battle, and I never disobeyed an order.

I stood with my back to the trees on a small rise, staring out at the unlikely gathering of men in the valley. It had been less than an hour since the earth had tossed the enemy into a state of disarray, but after the obvious display of power by Yahweh, I was certain Saul would not be slow in taking advantage of their confusion.

Therefore, I'd sent two Efraimite scouts to the top of the ridgeline to watch for the army's imminent arrival.

The rest of their squadrons only awaited my signal to set our plans into motion.

To my left, Eliyah was the very picture of a barely restrained young warrior preparing for his first battle. His body was tense as a bowstring, but I had no doubt he was ready. The borrowed Philistine gear he wore was in direct opposition to the strong Hebrew heart that beat in his chest. It galled me to wear one of the feathered helmets myself, but for this plan to work, the enemy had to think they were being attacked by their own. The iron sword one of the Efraimite squad leaders had insisted I carry was nowhere near as fine as the one my father had given me, but it was a sturdy weapon nonetheless.

However, it was not my sword I missed most as I prepared to go into battle. It was Asher. I swallowed hard against the painful lump that formed in my throat as I considered the empty place on my right. Nothing would ever be the same without his steadfast presence. That the injustice against him had stood without recompense this long was a travesty, but I had to believe Yahweh would not allow his killers to go unpunished. For now, I had to focus on the mission before me. But when the dust cleared, I meant to deal with Kyrum and Lemek.

"How's the hand?" I asked Eliyah, trying to distract myself from the void left behind by my loyal friend—both the one who'd been murdered and the one who'd betrayed me.

He showed me his palm, the skin there still pink but well on its way to full healing. "Thanks to Yochana, I can use them both."

The mention of her name seemed to conjure her soothing presence, and I swore I caught a whiff of her lupine sweetness on the breeze. It reminded me of the vow I'd made to not be reckless with my life and to return to her, but it also reminded me why I was here and why this battle was so necessary. I would do anything to make certain that my love, along with our families and everyone else in the Land, never suffered under subjugation like the Efraimites had for the past thirty years.

I nudged Eliyah with an elbow. "After what I've heard of your aim with a sling, the Philistines will regret your presence here today."

"It was my abba who taught me," he said, the tips of his ears going red.

"And I am proud to have you both at my side." I slid my gaze past Eliyah to his father.

The older man grinned at me. "Never thought you'd say that three years ago, eh?"

I took in the sight of the grizzled Yehudite garbed in enemy plumage. "Never thought I'd see you in a feathered headdress either."

He slapped at the back of the bronze helmet before pushing it down tighter atop his balding pate. "I think it suits me. Makes me look like a majestic eagle, no?"

I chuckled, amused by his irreverence and knowing he was doing it for the sake of his son's nerves. But one sharp bleat of a shofar in the distance cut off my playful response.

Saul is almost here.

My heart kicked into a gallop. I'd instructed the scouts to alert me the moment they saw the dust of a thousand marching feet rising to the south.

It was time to set aside everything but the mission given to me by the Most High.

The sound of the ram's horn had brought the Efraimites to attention, and suddenly every eye in the valley was on me. Their squad leaders had wasted no time explaining my plan to their men and ordering them to await my instructions. I'd wondered if perhaps some would refuse to take part in such a bold attack, but every one of them accepted my challenge to turn on their captors.

Yet, as I gazed over the crowd of men who'd suffered under virtual slavery for most—if not all—of their lives, I could see they needed encouragement.

I took in a deep breath at the same time I begged the All-Knowing One for wisdom. And somehow, although my blood pounded like a war drum as I lifted my borrowed sword high, words came to my lips with little effort.

"Brothers," I began, to remind them of our ancient ties, "we are going out today to attack an ancient enemy of our people. This fight will be difficult, I assure you. And lives will be lost. But we *will* have the victory. Because today we fight not only with skill but with power, because we are the army of Israel, united not only under King Saul but also beneath the banner of the Most High."

I swept my sword over the crowd. "*We* are the people who were brought through the Red Sea on dry land. *We* are the ones who watched the walls of Jericho fall. *We* are those who saw the sun stand still as Yehoshua bested the Amorites and who witnessed an entire camp of Assyrians destroyed by three hundred men and oil lamps. And today, *we* felt the power of Yahweh as the earth itself trembled in his presence to prepare the battlefield before us."

Pausing, I let my gaze roam over the men, ignoring the unsettling sight of their Philistine battle gear. "So we will not run. We will not fear. We will fight in that valley. We will fight in the hills. We will fight them wherever they go. Because the people of Efraim are counting on us. The people of Benjamin are counting on us. The people of Yehudah are counting on us, along with the rest of Yaakov's sons who have suffered under the Philistine lash. They need us to run boldly to this battle so that every child within the borders of the Land of Promise can finally sleep in perfect shalom and without fear. Ours *will* be the generation to have victory over the Philistines once and for all."

My final words echoed off the far wall of the valley, returning to me with astounding clarity. I wasn't certain where they'd come from or how I'd managed to deliver a speech to hundreds without the usual sick feeling of horror in my gut. *Asher would be proud* came the errant thought just as the second shofar blasted out the final signal that meant Saul was nearing the mouth of the pass opposite Michmash.

I brought down my sword in a hard swipe and bellowed with all my might, *"GO!"*

Then I turned and ran through the trees toward the battle, trusting that the rest would follow.

And they did, the thunder of hundreds of footsteps at my back bolstering my every stride. I felt, rather than saw, Rezev and Eliyah on one side and the Efraimite leaders on the other as we pressed through the trees, then poured five abreast through the rocky wadi into the valley like the first rush of springtime floods.

It did not take long for those on the edge of the enemy camp to see the horde of false Philistines coming at them and set aside their confusion at the sight to take up their own swords. By the time we were halfway across the valley, a number of them were already coming toward us, leaving off the effort to lift toppled chariots and overturned wagons to defend against what they had to believe were their own soldiers turning against them.

I did not waver as I stretched my gait, pushing toward the brethren of those who'd taken so much from me. But thanks to Yahweh, I no longer carried visions of vengeance with me onto this battlefield or even horrors of Zanoah. I was no longer a frightened and lonely boy riddled with the wounds of my solitary past, but a soldier of the Most High God, overflowing with righteous anger against evil that had taken root here before Avraham had even stepped foot in the Land.

And when we crashed into our enemies like a rolling bank of thunderclouds slamming into a mountainside, I fixed my mind only on my future, the future of Israel, and the Mighty God who shielded her with his unseen hand.

27

My vision blurred as I surveyed the field of destruction in front of me until I blinked away the tinge of red from my eyes. Until now, I'd not noticed a wound near my hairline, but as I wiped my forehead, my hand came away bloody and the cut tingled. I didn't remember which blow did the damage. I took a look down at myself now, gore-splattered and drenched with sweat from head to toe, and saw I'd actually been wounded in a few places. A deep slash curved over one forearm, a gouge had been taken out of my right thigh by a spearhead, and I was certain to be a mess of bruises tomorrow. But for now, I felt none of it. There was still too much euphoria roaring in my blood to care about pain.

Off in the distance, Saul's army was finishing the fight we'd begun, the clash of swords and screams of the wounded already ebbing. So, for the first time since we'd charged at the Philistines, I had a few moments to collect my thoughts.

We were victorious. That was without doubt. Between Yahweh's hand shaking the earth and our company of false Philistines, we'd thrown the enemy into such confusion they'd begun fighting one another, just as I'd guessed they would.

Saul's forces had arrived to find utter chaos.

Two paces from my feet, a Philistine lay belly-down in the dirt, the last of the enemies I'd dispatched to his foul gods. With his face turned in my direction, his sightless eyes stared at me, and blood still trickled from the fatal wound I'd delivered with my father's ax. I still held it in one fist, my knuckles white on its sturdy oak handle. I'd lost the borrowed Philistine sword at some point during combat but left it where it fell and continued on without pause, my focus solely on the next enemy and the next one after that. Each one had been a threat to my people, and each had fallen by my hand.

But now there were no more foes to vanquish, and I realized I'd lost sight of my friends. My throat burned with bile as I turned in a slow circle, searching every blood-speckled face in my vicinity for Rezev and Eliyah. Father and son were nowhere around me, even though they'd most certainly been at my side during the initial attack.

Instead, all I could see was the aftermath of our victory littering the valley floor in every direction. Bodies. Broken weapons. Feathered helmets. More bodies. And so much blood the stones beneath my feet were painted crimson. The only thing left to do now was gather weapons and armor, collect our own dead, and burn the rest. But first I had to find the two loyal men who'd followed me here without question.

I saw a couple of the Efraimite leaders a few paces away, tending to some of their fellow wounded, and made my way toward them, glad I was sidestepping far more Philistine bodies than Hebrew ones.

"Captain!" called one of them, whose name I remembered to be Oneg. "Your plan worked!"

That it had. The confusion that had taken hold of our enemies while attackers in their own feathered helmets shouted the name of El Shaddai had been nearly as satisfying as the way our fairly small company had fanned out and pushed many of them back toward their flattened tents and quake-shattered chariots. But I did not care to rehash the battle just now. I could not face Yochana with no answer as to our friends' fates.

"Have you seen my two companions?"

"Not since this began. They were close together on the front line." Oneg frowned, likely seeing the panic on my face. "But I'm sure they are fine."

My stomach dropped as I dug one hand into my sweat-soaked hair. Eliyah may have the heart of a lion, but he was not an experienced fighter. And even though the Philistines had been thrown by our disguises, they were exceedingly well trained. I didn't know Rezev well but I was positive he would never leave Eliyah's side. He would gladly lay down his own life for his son, just as my own would do for me. In fact, after the miraculous display I'd seen today, I was convinced the Creator himself would probably do the same for his own treasured children, were it possible.

"Zevi?"

The urgent call of my name across the shattered remains of the battlefield had me spinning to find its source. However, it was not Rezev striding over the stretch of bloody dirt between us, or Eliyah, but my commander, Merotai, accompanied by a group of his faithful men.

Cold washed through my body as the icy stare of Kyrum's father fixed to mine. "I did not believe it when one of my men told me they saw you here. Last I heard, you'd run off with some harlot."

Stricken by the aggressive vitriol from a man who'd once treated me like one of his own sons, I bristled at the disgusting label given to Yochana. But even if my battle-riled blood told me to slam a fist into his mouth, this was not the time to defend her honor. I swallowed down my instincts and took a breath before I spoke. "With all respect, Commander, the things you have been told are not true."

Merotai's eyes flared at my insinuation. "How dare you accuse my son of deceit when it is you who stole the king's purse and murdered your closest friend."

I'd prepared for Asher's death to be laid at my feet, but still, pain shot through my chest at the indictment. Every soldier within earshot went silent and still, including the Efraimites who'd followed me so bravely into battle.

"Unfortunately, I must accuse Kyrum of far worse." I kept my gaze firm and steady, knowing any wavering would be interpreted as a lie. "But perhaps we should speak privately."

The man who'd mentored me for the past two years huffed derisively. "I have more important things to do than entertain your fabrications. Yair, Mishal, take this man into custody. He can explain his treachery to a tribunal."

His men shifted forward, and to my surprise, Oneg and Bilhan, two of the Efraimite leaders, stepped to my side.

"The captain has done nothing wrong," said Oneg. "It was he who led us to victory today."

"King Saul led us to victory today. Not this traitor." Merotai's gaze traveled down to the Philistine corselet around Oneg's torso, his jaw twitching as he then took in the other Efraimite's fringed battle kilt. "Who *are* you? And why are you dressed like that?"

Oneg lifted his chin, making a show of courage. "We were conscripted by the Philistines—"

But Merotai had heard enough. He threw up a hand to stop Oneg's explanation as his black eyes snapped back to me with blistering fury. Any chance to persuade him of my innocence had been incinerated by Oneg's attempt to defend me.

"Why does it not surprise me that you led a group of *traitors* onto the field of battle?"

"They are not—" I began, but at some swift and silent gesture, Merotai's men suddenly surrounded us. I was unceremoniously relieved of my ax and daggers, while Oneg and Bilhan were pulled in separate directions. Wide-eyed with confusion, some of the other Efraimites already had their weapons in hand while their friends scuffled with their captors.

"Commander, please," I pleaded, desperate to avoid a disaster. I did not resist the two soldiers who had my arms twisted painfully behind my back. "They have nothing to do with this. These Efraimites fought with Israel today. Let them go. I will come willingly. Tell you everything. I swear it."

Merotai raised a hand, and his men froze in place. He peered at me with intense scrutiny before giving his men a sharp nod. They released Oneg and Bilhan without delay. In response, the rest of their companions lowered their weapons.

I let out a relieved breath, dropping my chin. "Thank you."

Merotai released a caustic chuckle. "I have no need of your worthless gratitude, Zevi, or your flimsy excuses. You are already accused of desertion, theft of the king's purse, and of murder. But it seems the charge of treason will likely be added to the list. You will be taken before a tribunal and then, I expect, sentenced to death. I have no interest in listening to the traitor who ruthlessly killed my son's closest friend. In fact, after the way you have betrayed us, I will gladly hand Kyrum the first stone."

28

Everything hurt.

With no more battle-rush to fend off the pain, I felt every one of my wounds acutely. The gash on my forehead stung; my head itself felt as though it had been slammed against a boulder. My thigh was still bleeding off and on, though the sun had already risen on the second morning after the battle, and the pain of what felt like a hundred different abrasions and bruises had melded into one throbbing ache. Even the places Lemek shot me nearly three weeks before burned deep inside. If only I hadn't been stripped of my pack with Yochana's balm before Merotai's men marched me south of Geva to the war camp and left me tied on the ground in the corner of a supply tent. Thankfully, exhaustion had swiftly eclipsed both my pain and my roaring hunger, and I'd fallen into a heavy, dreamless sleep. I'd awakened the following day desperately trying to recall Yochana's lupine-and-honey scent but smelling only the filth, sweat, and gore that covered me. I spent the long hours alternately thanking Yahweh that she was safe in Maresha with her family and wishing she were with me now.

She'd probably find a measure of amusement in my humbled position, bound hand and foot among sacks of grain, just as she'd been. I knew she'd already forgiven me but wished I could ask her once again to pardon my stupidity and selfishness. If ever I got the chance to hold that woman in my arms after this, I'd never let go. I'd make her my wife, even if I had to work seven years, or fourteen, to earn her father's forgiveness and blessing.

The tent flap parted, and light blazed through the opening. As my eyes adjusted to the searing brightness, four of Merotai's men entered. "Time to stand for your crimes," said one, while the rest hauled me upright. Then, forcing me to shuffle forward with fettered ankles, they dragged me into the sunlight.

Although I'd been relieved of my weapons, I still wore the leather armor Gavi had made, the same set that had saved me from the full force of Lemek's arrow. Fitting, since it felt very much as if I was heading into yet another battle—one that I might lose. I had no one to stand witness to my innocence against the wicked testimony of Kyrum and Lemek, except for the God Who Sees.

Go before me and behind me, O Mighty One, I prayed, determined to surrender myself and my instinct for vengeance on Asher's behalf to his unknowable ways. *Shield me with your truth and let justice reign.*

I was hauled through camp like a prisoner of war while the soldiers I'd aspired to be like for most of my life looked on with disgust. A few spat in my direction, calling me a traitor.

We arrived at a large clearing in the sea of tents, where I was thrown to the ground at the center and told to get on my knees. Shoulders aching from how tightly my arms were tied at my back and body screaming in pain as the ropes dug into my bruises, I forced myself into the submissive position. And there I remained for what felt like a thousand years, sharp stones digging into my knees as a crowd gathered around me.

Head bowed, I refused to let myself waver, though my insides were trembling with the effort. Having pushed my body to its limits many times before, I was grateful for the way I'd beaten any physical weaknesses into submission during my years of training.

The murmurs around me rose as Merotai, along with his direct superior, Eyal, and two more grim-faced commanders, parted the crowd and came to stand in front of me. I lifted my chin to meet Merotai's eyes as he loudly began to list the charges against me—treason, theft, desertion, cowardice, and murder. He hadn't included kidnapping, the one crime I was actually guilty of, but I felt its weight nonetheless.

"And who bears witness to these charges?" asked Eyal.

"I do." Kyrum must have stepped out of the crowd behind me, but I did not turn as the man I'd once trusted with my life began his lies. "I loved Zevi like my own brother. I served at his side, along with Asher ben Zered, since Yavesh-Gilead. He was fearless in battle. Wise in leadership. And although younger than me by a couple of years, a man to look up to." His voice cracked on the last three words, as if deeply wounded by my accused lack of integrity. As Yochana had said, he was a skilled deceiver.

"But Zevi is highly secretive," he continued. "Kept most everything close to his chest, including that he was taken captive and enslaved in Philistia as a boy."

The shock of his revelation vibrated through the courtyard. My mind spun backward to when he possibly could have overheard me reveal my past and landed on the night I'd taken Yochana to the stream. It made me sick to think he was listening as I opened my wounds to the woman I'd come to love.

"And apparently," he continued, his tone full of disdain, "he was raised in the household of a Philistine."

My blood flared hot. He could accuse me all he wanted but to make my abba sound like just another enemy was the strike of flint on iron. "My father is loyal to Israel—" I began but was immediately cut off by Eyal.

"You'll have your chance to speak, young man."

Trained to obey my superiors without hesitation, I slammed my mouth shut and counted my breaths to slow the thundering of my pulse.

"How does any of this relate to the charges against Zevi now?" Eyal asked Kyrum, brows raised.

"Because it wasn't until we were given the mission in Yehudite territory that I began to think he was not the man he portrayed himself to be. He showed a lack of interest in recruiting, was far too finicky about who was chosen, and drove away some of our best possibilities with his overly demanding training regimen. Asher and I tried to reason with him, but by the time we reached Maresha, he'd given up any pretense of obeying his orders. He said there was no use trying, since the elders of that town considered Saul a usurper to the throne and were involved in funding Yehudite factions whose goal is to raise up one of their own to crown as king."

All the breath left my lungs. Kyrum had just laid the entire town of Maresha on the altar of his ambitions. How had I never seen that he was utterly devoid of honor?

"By the time he took up with a woman from that same town, pretending to bring her along because she'd be worth something to King Saul, both Asher and I were suspicious of his intentions and his loyalty."

I'd been honest with Asher the morning I took Yochana up to the meadow, about why I'd taken her and why I planned to send her home. He'd been more than willing to escort her back to Maresha and said my humility in admitting my sins only made him admire me more. We'd parted on the best of terms, as brothers. That was my only comfort as Kyrum exaggerated Asher's confusion about my odd decisions in the preceding days.

"The fact that he took off with a large sum of the king's purse, at the behest of the harlot he'd conspired with, and then murdered Asher when he tried to stop him, was unfortunately not a surprise by that point. The only thing that is shocking is that he would dare show his traitorous face here now. However, he was spotted fighting *with* the Philistines, so perhaps it's not such a surprise after all."

No wonder he'd had me fooled into believing he was a loyal friend. He was the most capable liar I'd ever met.

"We'll deal with that issue later," said Eyal. "Please tell us what happened on the day he fled."

"As I said, Asher and I suspected he was up to something. We took a few other trusted men with us and followed him up to a meadow where he and the woman were engaged in . . ." The conniver cleared his throat, seemingly embarrassed to say more. "Well, I'm certain you can imagine what the two of them were up to."

Laughter traveled through the crowd of soldiers, and my stomach lurched at the assault on Yochana's character. If I ever got my hands on Kyrum ben Merotai, he would rue the moment he besmirched my love.

"They had a couple bags of silver with them, apparently thinking they'd gotten away easily, and when Asher confronted Zevi, he charged him, knocked him to the ground, and then plunged a dagger into the poor man's neck." He paused, as if affected by the telling of his own filthy lie.

"And what happened then?" Eyal prompted.

"Zevi took the bags of silver, left the woman, and ran. Lemek got in a good shot or two as he sped out of the meadow like the coward he is, but it seems he survived. And now he's slithered back here with his mouth full of falsehood. If his hidden past and his association with those Efraimite liars is any indication, he may be a spy sent by the Philistines."

Whispers about this accusation traveled through the crowd, but I refused to flinch. I had to believe that somehow the truth would be revealed. *Let justice shine in this darkness, Adonai.*

"Thank you, Kyrum," said Eyal before calling for additional witnesses. Of course Lemek repeated nearly word for word what Kyrum had said, and Sakar and the others from Lachish who'd been in the meadow that day backed up the story. The silver I was supposed to have stolen must've been divided evenly between them.

"All right, Zevi," Eyal said. "What do you have to say in your defense?"

What could I say to change their minds? Kyrum had formulated a highly detailed account that obviously had everyone convinced of my guilt. But I felt the prompting to speak anyhow.

"All I can say is that I took a vow of fidelity to King Saul two years ago. I served my people and my sovereign with honor during the battle with the Philistines. The only crime I accept full responsibility for is one of kidnapping."

More shocked whispers murmured through the crowd.

"I took an innocent perfumer from her home. I could give you a list of reasons why I did so, some justified and some perhaps not, but it began with an order from my commander to bring back the most talented artisans and ended with a realization that I had been wrong to force her into serving the king instead of simply inviting her to offer her gifts freely. She is blameless and pure of heart, and no matter what lies these men tell about me, I won't stand for her honor being tarnished."

"So you deny the charge of treason? And of murder?" Eyal pressed.

"The Efraimites I fought alongside during the battle had been enslaved to the Philistines and, like the rest of us, were desperate to keep their families safe and free from tyranny. For the sake of Israel, they bravely ran into the battle disguised as Philistines, and I will not apologize for leading them."

Eyal's silvering brows pulled together in bewilderment at my words.

"As for Asher . . ." My throat burned to speak his name aloud. "I would no more kill my own brothers than I would such a valiant and loyal friend."

"Where are the witnesses to your innocence?"

I shrugged. "Real truth needs no one to defend it. It speaks for itself. My conscience is clear before Adonai."

Eyal stared down at me, seeming to digest what I'd said. But before he or anyone else could say another word, a great commotion arose off to the right. A group of men was pushing through the crowd toward us, voices lifted as they ordered the gawking group of soldiers to make way.

And then, to my absolute astonishment, the king of Israel, Saul ben Kish, came into sight, surrounded by his royal retinue and a large number of decorated guards. But the truly astonishing thing was not that the king—and therefore the High Commander of Israel—had joined this military tribunal. It was the sight of two people trailing a few paces behind him.

The woman I loved. And my father.

29

Yochana

The shock on Zevi's face would have been comical had the situation not been so dire. As it was, the poor man not only looked astounded but as though he'd been dragged behind a chariot for a few hours. Kneeling before his accusers, he was still covered in dirt and battle gore and was far too pale for my liking—almost the same ghastly shade as when he'd been on the edge of death.

I wanted to fly to him and throw my arms around his shoulders, to assure myself that he was alive and whole and to shield him from this horrible, gawking crowd and whatever lies Kyrum had told this hastily arranged tribunal. At my side, Zevi's father stiffened at the sight of his son, and I knew he felt the same.

Saul strode to the center of the gathering, which had been struck silent by his appearance. "Why was I not informed of this tribunal?"

The four commanders in charge of Zevi's trial looked cowed by the king's question. Only one, an imposing man with silvering hair, was brave enough to respond.

"This is a disciplinary trial, my lord. A soldier accused of col-luding with enemies and—"

"And murder," Saul spoke over him. "Yes, I know the charges, Eyal."

Eyal frowned in confusion. "If I'd known the case was of particular interest, I would certainly have informed you. We did not want to trouble you over the actions of one soldier so soon after . . . yesterday's events."

I wasn't certain which events the man spoke of, although something told me it was not simply the battle to which he was referring. Saul waved a dismissive hand. "That's all settled. But after what I've heard this morning, the fate of this man is absolutely of particular interest to me."

It had not been easy to gain an audience with Saul. When Eliyah had arrived in Kiryat-Yearim, having run directly from the battlefield with news that Zevi had been taken into custody, it had taken little to convince Natan to leave earlier than we'd planned. The man had driven the poor mules hooked to his timber wagon as if the entire Philistine army was at our backs, but when we arrived at the war camp near dusk yesterday, we were told by the king's steward that Saul had just returned from the north and was far too busy to speak with us.

But I had brought the only weapons I had—a jar of perfume and the warning of a possible coup.

Whether it was the perfume or the danger of overthrow that caught his attention, first thing this morning, we were called before the king of Israel. I'd been grateful to have Natan's large and sturdy presence at my right, and Eliyah's loyal and reassuring one on my left, as I admitted how I'd blamed Saul for my husband's tragic death and my own small part in Noham's scheme, and then explained how Rezev's testimony about the storm at Gilgal had caused me to reconsider everything.

Saul had barely reacted to my confession, his handsome face

stoic as he regarded me from a wooden throne at the center of his royal tent. Perhaps the fact I was a woman meant my word held no weight for him, as it would for most men. I could only hope that my skill as a perfumer outshined any prejudice against my gender.

"It is highly unlikely that two men sneaking about camp would have any chance at getting anywhere close to me. I have a personal guard of at least twelve warriors around me," he'd said. "My food and drink is prepared by my own personal cook. However, I am grateful you went to such lengths to bring this to my attention, and these traitors will be found and brought to justice. It seems as though we have much more work to do in convincing the men of Yehudah that my claim to the throne is legitimate."

"With respect, my lord, I believe Yahweh's continued favor upon you is more than sufficient in that regard."

Saul's brows lifted at my statement. "Perhaps so." The king of Israel peered at me for a few long moments, the tense silence in the room causing my knees to tremble as the man Yahweh himself had set on the throne scrutinized me. He alone could grant me leave to speak in his presence. I could do nothing but pray my gift curried enough favor to plead for Zevi's life.

"If your purpose was to simply warn me, you could have left descriptions of these traitors with my steward. Why the perfume?" He gestured to the table beside him where my offering sat, housed in an alabaster vase Natan had procured from one of his timber customers. "What is it you want in exchange for such an exquisite fragrance?"

A wash of pure relief came over me. Adonai had heard my prayers.

"The perfume is a gift, my lord, but also a promise. Although you do have two traitors in your camp, you also have a loyal soldier here who is being accused of treachery and murder." I placed my hand on my heart. "And I am willing to do anything, even remain here permanently as a royal perfumer, if you will listen to evidence of his innocence."

I'd felt Natan's gaze on the side of my face. I'd convinced him to help me intervene for Zevi but had not told him I'd planned to offer myself to gain the king's ear. Saul straightened. "You are the one who made that fragrance?"

I nodded. "A unique scent I crafted with your beautiful wife in mind, but I have others if that one is not to her preference."

He leaned forward on his throne. I had indeed piqued his interest. Thankfully Zevi had told me how much the sovereign valued his wife. "You have more with you?"

"I do." It was fortunate I'd spent the long days of waiting for Zevi to regain his strength by experimenting with everything the garden had to offer. I'd come up with at least six new perfumes in the past few weeks, all of them far more potent than anything I'd created in Maresha.

He'd peered at me so intensely a bead of sweat trickled down my spine. Even seated, the king was beyond intimidating, and I had guessed that when he stood he may top Natan's superior height. He may not be Yehudite, but there was a distinctly regal air about the man that was undeniable. The sight of such a warrior-king striding across the battlefield would terrify many an enemy.

What a fool I'd been to believe Noham's scheme would ever succeed against the anointed of the Most High. Yahweh alone had raised him to power and Yahweh alone would determine the length of his reign.

Leaning back against his throne, Saul scratched at his beard in contemplation. "Tell me more about this soldier accused of murder."

Relieved that he'd not had us immediately banished from his presence, I'd told the king about the false charges leveled at Zevi, and what I'd witnessed in the meadow when Kyrum revealed himself as the true killer of their friend. When I was finished, Eliyah was given permission to explain what happened after the earthquake and how courageously Zevi had led former conscripts into battle against the Philistines before Saul arrived.

Having overheard our pleas for justice, the king's steward then alerted Saul that a military tribunal was indeed being conducted this morning. Within moments, I was struggling to keep up with the long-legged strides of both the king and Natan as we wound through the war camp toward this unjust trial.

Flanked by Natan and Eliyah, I glared at Kyrum now, but the coward refused to look my way. I hoped he was panicking at the sight of us.

"Tell me, Eyal," Saul continued, "what evidence is there against this young man?"

"Numerous eyewitnesses have testified that he murdered one of his own friends," said the commander. "And he has freely admitted to associating with Efraimites who fought on the side of the Philistines. He has little to say in his own defense."

"I see," said the king, his dark-eyed gaze moving over the gathering of onlookers. "And are there no witnesses on his behalf?"

"I will testify!" came a familiar gruff voice from somewhere behind me. I peered over my shoulder to see Rezev, aided by two strangers, slowly pushing through the crowd, a thick swath of bandages wrapped around his middle and another over half his face. My throat constricted at the sight. Eliyah had said his father was wounded during the battle, but I'd not known the extent. Though he was in considerable pain, he'd still come to stand with Zevi.

Once in front of the king and his commanders, Rezev testified to Zevi's loyalty, how he'd insisted on returning to fight for Israel though gravely wounded and falsely accused of murder, and further explained his successful strategy during the battle at Michmash. Although I'd already heard the story twice, I was truly astounded by the courage of the man I'd come to love. Once

Rezev was finished, some of the Efraimites Zevi had led into battle testified how he'd inspired them to turn away from their cowardly flight and instead to fight for the future of Israel.

An Efraimite named Oneg said that a large number of Benjamites hiding in the hills with their families had realized what was happening and joined in the initial assault as well. From the look on Zevi's face, he'd not been aware of their involvement in the victory.

"The captain is far from a traitor, my lord," concluded Oneg. "I would gladly serve Israel under the leadership of such a man." The rest of his companions murmured their agreement.

"I must admit, I am perplexed," said Saul, his eyes back on Zevi. "These do not sound like the actions of a traitor. In fact, I'd wondered why the Philistines were in such disarray when I arrived at Michmash, aside from the earthquake, of course. Sounds as though you should be commended."

"With respect, my lord," said another of the commanders, "the more serious charge here is murder. And there are plenty of witnesses who said Zevi killed Asher, including my own son."

"And which is your son, Merotai?" asked Saul.

Kyrum stepped forward to bow before the king, somehow looking unaffected as he stood beside his father.

"I've already heard this young woman's account of that day, but since I missed your testimony," said Saul, "perhaps you will indulge me by recounting exactly what happened that day."

"Of course," said Kyrum, with a tight smile. "I'm happy to refute whatever lies you've been told by that woman. And my men too will attest to her harlotry."

Zevi glanced up at me, lips pressed into a hard line. I gave a little shake of my head. Nothing could be gained by him coming to my defense right now. This was the time to prove *his* innocence, not mine.

With smug confidence, Kyrum launched into his fabricated tale of Asher's death, once again displaying his slimy ability to act distraught over his loss when it was he who'd caused the tragedy.

"And you say that Zevi stole silver meant for the royal treasury in order to run off with this young woman?" questioned Saul.

"He did indeed."

"But your man shot him with an arrow as he fled?"

He nodded. "I'm not certain how the coward survived the hit by Lemek."

"I see." Saul made a thoughtful noise in the back of his throat. "Well, that's easily enough proved."

Kyrum flinched. "Well, it happened so fast—"

Saul put up a palm, halting Kyrum's lying tongue. "Merotai, cut the captain's bonds."

Unable to do anything but comply with a direct order from the king, Kyrum's father did as he was told, cutting the ropes from Zevi's wrists and ankles.

Once free, Zevi struggled to his feet, and it was all I could do not to run to his aid. But I refused to make him look weak before his king. Instead, I prayed that Yahweh would infuse him with fresh strength.

"Captain," said Saul, "remove your armor."

Zevi complied, then held the dusty, gore-spattered leather breastplate aloft. A hole was plainly visible on its front right where the arrow had pierced his abdomen, and the stain of old blood ringed the hole on both sides.

"Now your tunic," said the king.

Kyrum had gone pale, his earlier smugness wiped away, while his father appeared dumbfounded.

Perhaps I should have been embarrassed as Zevi obeyed Saul's order, stripping off his grimy tunic, which left him clad only in a linen undergarment and naked to the waist, but I was so glad to see that he'd not been seriously injured during the battle that I did not bother averting my eyes. I'd seen as much while tending him in Kiryat-Yearim, after all.

290

And now everyone could see the truth carved into Zevi's strong body. Aside from the one arrow that had sliced through his shoulder and been removed by the healer in Azeka, the other had plainly not pierced his back—as it would a coward fleeing with stolen goods. It had penetrated knuckle-deep into the flesh of his abdomen. The evidence was irrefutable.

"It was Kyrum!" The outburst came from Lemek, the terrible scar on his face standing out starkly against the flush of his complexion. "He promised me silver to shoot Zevi, but I didn't kill Asher. I swear on my own life. Kyrum had already cut his throat when I arrived on the scene."

The chaos that followed was as shocking as it was swift. On a sharp command from Saul, his personal guards rushed forward to take both Kyrum and Lemek into custody. Lemek wisely acquiesced without a fight, but Kyrum struggled against his captors, accusing Lemek of lying on Zevi's behalf while the crowd around us erupted into surprised chatter.

"That's enough!"

The bellowed command from Saul caused everyone to go silent and even Kyrum to cease his struggle. But his wide eyes were latched onto his stricken father.

"Abba, please, listen to me. They are lying. Zevi has them fooled, just like he hoodwinked you into believing he was the best man to lead the squad."

Merotai frowned. "He *was* the best man to lead."

"No!" Kyrum spat out, all semblance of control gone. "That should have been *my* command from the start. It was my *right*, as your son. But no, you just had to teach me a lesson, didn't you? Make me submit to some upstart Yehudite."

Merotai's face went ashen. "So, what, you betrayed him out of jealousy?"

A brittle laugh came from Kyrum's mouth. "Of course you would believe him over me. Zevi can do no wrong."

"You weren't ready yet, Kyrum—"

"Yes I was!" Kyrum's face went red as he unraveled before our eyes. "But you chose him. Everyone did. Even Asher, who was *my* friend first, practically worshiped the ground Zevi walked on." He huffed, sneering. "Little good his devotion did him in the end. The fool."

Merotai went still as stone, eyes locked on his son as his voice dropped low. "You really did kill him. Didn't you?"

Kyrum's mouth pinched shut, and he looked away from his father defiantly. Merotai's head dropped to his chest in resignation, as if no longer in doubt of his son's guilt.

"Take them away," said Saul to his men. "They'll be dealt with later."

As Kyrum and Lemek were led out of the clearing, a visibly shocked Eyal declared the tribunal dismissed, and the assembly of soldiers scattered off to spread word of the dramatic events they'd just witnessed.

And then, somehow, I was locked in Zevi's arms, my face pressed into the crook of his neck. "You're *here*," he murmured into my hair. "Why did you come?"

I burrowed farther into his embrace. "You said Saul would do anything for my perfumes."

He pulled back to look at me. "What did you do?"

"What I had to, to make certain he would listen."

"*Yochana*," his voice dropped low, his brown eyes penetrating, "what did you *do*?"

From a few paces away, Saul answered for me. "I'm told I have you to thank for hand-selecting such a talented perfumer."

Zevi flinched, as if he'd been so focused on having me in his arms that he'd completely forgotten anyone else was nearby, least of all the king of Israel. Releasing me so the two of us could face Saul, he made a simple bow. "My lord, I must express my gratitude."

"You have this young woman to thank," said Saul, with a gesture toward me. "She is very determined, as well as a skilled arti-san. My wife and daughters are already desperate for more of her perfumes. She'll be of great value in my court."

Zevi's body went very still. But he had to know that I'd had no choice but to offer my skills to Saul in exchange for his interven-tion. And it was worth it. Zevi was free. Truth had prevailed. And I could not regret that, even if it meant remaining in Gibeah. At least I'd be near him.

Saul turned to me. "I expect a detailed description of those men from your town so they can be brought in for questioning."

"Of course," I replied, grateful for his mercy regarding my own misguided support of such a scheme.

"I am aware that not everyone is happy about my kingship, especially among Yehudites. But I hope you will make it clear to the elders of Maresha that I am committed to protecting all of Israel, regardless of their enthusiasm for my leadership."

Shocked that he seemed to know exactly where the elders of Maresha stood, I nodded mutely.

"And you, Captain," Saul continued, turning to Zevi, "it seems we have your quick thinking to thank for the Philistines turning on themselves at Michmash."

"I only stoked the confusion already fomenting in their camp after Yahweh shook the earth."

"A man of humility, I see," said Saul. "And yet, from what Eyal says, you are one of my youngest captains, promoted soon after Yavesh-Gilead for extraordinary courage on the battlefield. You are exactly the sort of leader this army needs."

"And if I may interject, my lord," said Eyal, at his side, "Zevi created a unique training regimen that has made his squad known for their endurance, strength, and agility."

"Ah, the famously difficult training regimen. I'll have to hear more about that later. For now, Eyal, make it known that Zevi is restored to leadership, with the king's full support."

The endorsement would go a long way to ensuring no one questioned whether Zevi actually deserved to be reinstated, even if there may still be speculation over what exactly happened to Asher.

Saul continued, "Add to his company whatever Efraimites volunteer to serve Israel. I expect we'll add at least a couple of hundred to our ranks after such an inspiring victory." He smiled at Zevi's shocked expression. "Hopefully, the Philistines will stay in their nests for a good long while, but they certainly won't roll over forever. We must be ready for them. Perhaps this training of yours will be a means to that end."

With only a few words, Saul had made Zevi the leader of hundreds, fulfilling his ambition since childhood. At some point, Natan had come to his son's opposite side, and pride was written on every line of his fierce countenance.

"I am incredibly honored by the opportunity to serve my people in such a way," said Zevi, "but first I must ask for a provision."

Saul frowned in confusion, looking none too pleased. "What sort of provision?"

"Please do not misunderstand," said Zevi, palms lifted in supplication. "It has been my fervent desire to be a soldier for Israel since I was a boy, and I am truly honored by your confidence in my leadership. But, in keeping with the Torah law, I ask to be released from military service for the first year of my marriage, in order to build my household and bring happiness to my wife." He reached for my hand and tugged me into his side.

My jaw dropped, and I blinked at Zevi in bewilderment as he continued, "I would, of course, appoint capable men to keep my company fit for battle."

"This is your wife?" Saul asked, his gaze moving back and forth between us.

"She will be," Zevi replied, giving my hand a squeeze. "If I can convince her father to forgive me for taking her away in the first place."

Tears pricked my eyes. Not only was this beautiful man claiming me as his own before the king of Israel, but he was choosing to place me above his sworn duty. It was a bold request, but one that Saul would have difficulty ignoring, since it was clearly commanded by the Torah.

"Then all is well," said Saul. "She'll be serving as my royal perfumer in Gibeah. There should be no issue with you remaining at your post. If the Philistines lift their chins at us again over the next year, you have my permission to remain behind."

Zevi cleared his throat. "Yochana is without doubt a talented woman, my lord, but she must also have access to the finest of ingredients in order to create such extraordinary fragrances. The garden from which she harvests such things is in Kiryat-Yearim. Near where our home will be."

"Kiryat-Yearim? Where the Ark has been?"

Zevi nodded. "My grandfather is Elazar, the Levite responsible for its care."

"Is he?" Saul's gaze turned thoughtful. "And yet you fight as a Yehudite?"

"I was adopted into the family," Zevi said, gesturing to Natan. "Like my father before me."

"Ah yes. The Philistine who claims you as a son." He turned his interested gaze on Natan. "You told me earlier that you honor the Covenant of Mosheh. Does this allegiance extend to Israel herself?"

Natan's mismatched eyes widened ever so slightly. "I consider myself as much an Israelite as Avraham, who came out of a far country at the behest of Yahweh."

Saul peered at him curiously, as if sizing up the enormous man. "And yet you are not among my ranks?"

"I took a vow before the Almighty, decades ago, not to go to war or to use my hands for anything but peaceful endeavors. A vow I will keep until the day I die. Unless, of course, my family is in imminent danger. Although I would be more than happy to lend my ax to the kingdom of Israel by supplying fine timber for any building projects you may have in the future."

For a moment, the tattooed and pierced Philistine stood opposite the king of Israel, nearly the same height and both exuding such natural strength and authority it felt like the meeting of two immovable mountains. To my surprise, it was Saul who blinked.

"That will be acceptable," he said dryly, then turned to me. "You may return to Kiryat-Yearim for now in order to utilize this garden of yours. But I expect regular deliveries of perfumes and whatever unguents my wife and daughters desire. As well, be prepared to provide gifts for emissaries and other dignitaries at my request."

"With pleasure," I said. "I will devise scents and balms exclusive to your court."

"And you," he said to Zevi, "will teach my commanders this training regimen *before* you marry. And will appoint trusted men to keep your company in hand during your absence."

Zevi bowed his head, hand on his heart. "It will be an honor, my king."

Saul gave him a regal nod, then turned to stride away.

"I cannot believe you did that," I said in a low tone as the king's guardsmen trailed after him like lambs.

"Announced I was marrying you?"

"No, although, it might have been nice to make certain I was in agreement first."

"Are you?" His eyes danced with mischief. "In agreement?"

I paused, holding the moment long as I frowned at him. "I thought I told you not to be reckless. And then I hear you dressed as a *Philistine* and ran directly into their camp."

His grin turned sheepish. "I didn't *fully* dress as a Philistine. I only carried one of their swords and wore a helmet. But I tossed it aside the moment Saul's men arrived."

"Oh, well, that changes everything," I said tonelessly.

He drew me closer. "My only defense is that Yahweh was in it, Yochana. He placed me there, at the right time, and provided me with the perfect opportunity to join a work he'd already begun. I obeyed my orders."

I huffed a sigh. "You and your orders."

He leaned in to speak into my ear, his breath warm on my skin. "My orders now are to spend an entire year making my wife happy."

Heat rose in my cheeks at the low rasp in his voice. "I cannot believe you asked such a thing of the king himself."

"Don't you know by now that I would do anything to be near you?" He gave me an enticing grin, his brown eyes full of promise.

"All right, the two of you," Natan interjected. "I need to get back home before your mother marches to Gibeah and storms the fortress."

Shoshana was more than supportive of my efforts to save Zevi, but she was not happy that Natan had refused to let her come along.

"The last thing we need is you going after the king of Israel in Zevi's defense. You might spark a civil war," Natan had said to her with a teasing note in his voice before unashamedly kissing her in front of me. *"We'll get your son back, Tesi. Have no fear."*

"Thank you, Abba," said Zevi, "for coming. And for bringing Yochana."

Natan gazed at his son with so much affection it made my heart squeeze tightly. "From the first moment I saw you—a young boy taking on Philistine soldiers in defense of innocent girls—I knew you were fearless, Zevi, and so very strong. It is no surprise to me that you are a warrior and a leader of men. But I am more proud that you have grown into a man of deep honor and steadfast love."

There was a sheen in Zevi's brown eyes as he took in the heart-felt compliment, and I could almost see the boy he once was, looking up in awe at the man I knew he adored more than any other.

Zevi swallowed hard before speaking in a strangled tone. "Of course I am. I've had the very best of examples to follow."

Zevi

I wiped sweat from my eyes with the back of my hand and reached for the skin of water Mahir held out for me.

"A little out of practice, are we?"

"You try running through those exercises a month after being shot in the gut," I said, taking up my sword from the bench where I'd left it to join my men in their training. It had been disconcerting to leave it behind so soon after getting it back, but running hills for hours with a weapon slapping against my thigh would have been restrictive, and I would never ask my men to do anything I myself would not do.

Merotai himself had returned the iron sword Kyrum had stolen from me the day after the trial, along with my father's ax. He'd been deeply ashamed of his son and also for refusing to believe me. But I did not blame him. He'd been just as deceived as I had been by Kyrum's duplicity, and of course he'd wanted to assume the best of his child.

However, it was likely that his own ruthless ambitions had influenced Kyrum's poor decisions, and in some small way, my own. It had been his threat to towns like Maresha that I'd used to justify taking Yochana. Although the culpability ultimately lay with me for that sin, I was certain he'd exaggerated Saul's position so he could take credit for my success and move up in the ranks as well.

There was nothing satisfying in Kyrum's inevitable conviction for Asher's murder, only a deep sadness over the loss of both my friends. It had been gut-wrenching to have to testify against the man I'd once considered as close as a brother. But for Asher's sake, I'd boldly spoken the truth, then gladly left the atonement for his blood in the hands of my superiors, refusing to be enslaved to vengeance ever again.

Shortly after his son's swift execution for treason and murder, Merotai had withdrawn from leadership. As the commander of three hundred men, I now reported directly to Eyal, who himself answered only to Abner, the High Commander of Saul's forces, and the king himself.

"They're coming along nicely," said Shimi, his eyes on the group of recruits who'd just returned from the hours-long midday run and had already flopped on the ground in the shade of a sprawling oak. "Hopefully they'll keep up the regimen at home."

Roughly two-thirds of my company would return to their homes within the next couple of weeks. There was little need for so many soldiers around Gibeah, unless another considerable threat reared up. Although there had been a fair amount of tribute collected over the past couple of months, it was certainly not enough for Saul to sustain a large standing army for any length of time. It would likely take many years of building his kingdom before such a thing would be possible.

Egypt and Assyria may have such resources after hundreds of years of empire-building, but regardless of his designation as king, Saul was little more than a very powerful warlord reigning over tribes that still deeply mistrusted one another. The fortress he'd built at Gibeah was sturdy, but it was certainly nothing compared to the luxurious palace I'd seen as a boy in Ashdod. Perhaps someday Israel would enjoy wealth like the Philistines and a well-equipped army clad in gleaming helmets and bronze-scaled armor, but for now, we would remain mostly a volunteer force made up of shepherds and farmers. But one whose Highest Commander shook the earth with his ancient voice and sent enemies scattering like roaches.

Thankfully, I trusted Mahir and Shimi to keep the troops that remained in excellent shape for the next skirmish with whatever brazen nation dared harass the beloved of El Shaddai. Even though I would be in Kiryat-Yearim building a home for Yochana, I expected the two of them to keep me well informed of both the progress of my company and any activity on our borders. Since Eliyah had proved himself a capable runner, if not quite as fleet-footed as Asher had been, it would undoubtedly be him delivering those messages to my door.

Rezev had returned home to recover but not before promising to watch for Shalem among the many traders who streamed through the gates of Lachish. *"I remember your cousin well,"* he'd said. *"That flimsy disguise you boys contrived did nothing to conceal that he was far too young for the battle at Yavesh-Gilead, nor did it hide that silver streak in his hair. If I find him, I'll bring him to you. You just take good care of my son. And that lovely woman of yours. She's a brave one, for certain."*

And that she was. I'd hated watching her leave with my father the day after Noham and his friend were arrested on her identification, leaving King Saul more in her debt when they confessed and gave up names of other conspirators. But knowing I would be with her once my obligations to Saul were complete had kept me going for the past couple of weeks. Only a few more days should be sufficient to ensure that the rest of the captains and commanders in Saul's army were familiar enough with my training regimen to teach it to their own soldiers.

After giving the men a short period of rest and an order to get a quick drink from the nearby stream, Mahir and Shimi directed the troops to seek out a rock to carry above their heads for yet another run through the hills around Gibeah. This time I remained in place, watching which man chose which stone.

A few were far too sure of themselves, choosing the heaviest rocks possible, and would most certainly have to give up early. Some anticipated the long run under the blazing sun and chose stones that were barely a burden. But it was those like Eliyah, who selected a stone with plenty of weight to be a challenge but not enough to keep him from completing the run, that I most had my eye on. Careful forethought was far more valuable in my eyes than brute strength. Perhaps one day the loyal young man would lead a unit himself, something I knew would make his father burst with pride.

"Impressive," said a voice I knew as well as my own. "Uncle Natan must be proud."

Keeping my eyes on my men as they took off running at Shimi's command, the rocks hefted above their heads, I hummed agreement with both of Gavi's assessments. My company *was* impressive, especially considering that many of them had been dragged through the confusion of thinking I was a traitor and then discovering they'd been lied to by a murderer. And vow of pacifism notwithstanding, my father had been greatly honored to learn the exercises he'd devised to prepare himself for the wrestling grounds as the feared Champion of Ashdod were now being used to shape the entire army of Israel into a force to be reckoned with among the nations.

"In charge of your own men yet?" I asked without turning my head.

Gavi barked a laugh. "As if I had any desire to mother a bunch of half-grown men."

"You're barely of age yourself."

"Exactly," he replied with a snort. "And I mean to stay that way for a good long while. I'll leave the henpecking to you."

I'd always wondered why Gavi never seemed to be interested in leading our little group. He was younger than Avi and me but far exceeded us both in talent. There was no weapon he could not master, be it sling or bow or sword, and his eye for craftsmanship was unparalleled by any but the Philistine metalsmiths. I had no doubt he would outshine them if he too had the benefit of metals from Caphtor and other nations around the Great Sea and beyond.

"I see you survived the battle," I said, although it had not been in doubt. I'd heard Yonatan's division had nearly annihilated the Philistines that had flown north after the battle.

"Of course," Gavi said, then under his breath, "though no thanks to Saul."

Shocked, I turned to face him. He'd aged quite a bit in the last couple of years, his youthful innocence scoured away by the realities of war. His dark hair was past his shoulders now, lightened by the sun, and his thick beard long and unruly. A scar traveled the length of his cheekbone from a near miss with an Amorite javelin thrown at close range a few months after Yavesh-Gilead. The man who threw it took only two more breaths before Gavi had pierced his lungs with a jab of his favorite serrated dagger.

But I could still see my younger cousin inside the rough-hewn shell of a warrior. The boy who'd been enamored of my abba from the very beginning of our acquaintance and begged him for descriptions of various Philistine weapons, along with details about his time as the Champion of Ashdod. The boy who watched over his little sisters like a hawk, even if he hated their father, and regarded his mother as nothing less than a queen. And the boy who had grown increasingly sullen as the years went on, for some reason that I didn't quite understand but felt a kinship with all the same. We'd both lost the fathers who'd given us life at young ages, but whereas I'd had Natan to shepherd me, Gavi's stepfather

Hanan was a cold and unaffectionate man. His singular goal in life was to be wealthy, one he'd achieved long ago, but it seemed that no amount of silver was ever enough.

I furrowed my brows at my cousin. "What do you mean? Saul's victory is undisputed."

Gavi scowled. "Perhaps. But he nearly drove us into the ground in the process. I was ready to gnaw on my bracers by the time the sun finally went down."

"What are you talking about?"

"The vow?" He lifted his hands, exasperated with my ignorance. "The order Saul gave not to eat or drink until the battle was completely won?"

I shook my head. "I didn't march out with the army. I came in from the west with a group of Efraimites." In brief terms, I told him of what had happened over the past couple of months, from the order to recruit soldiers in Yehudite territory up until I'd rushed into battle with the false Philistines and then the outcome of both trials.

Arms crossed over a chest that had grown significantly wider since he'd joined Yonatan's division, Gavi stared at me in disbelief. "Kyrum was a traitor?"

"Unfortunately so." I'd introduced the two of them the last time we'd run across each other, before Gavi left Gibeah with a group of Yonatan's men on a secret mission. But I did not want to talk about Kyrum anymore. "Tell me more about this vow."

Gavi's expression turned hard and his voice went low. "It was foolishness is what it was. Saul declared the morning of the battle, before the ground shook, that none of us were to eat or drink until the enemy had been completely overtaken. And of course it took until well after nightfall before the order came to stop the chase. By that time, everyone was famished. Faint with hunger. It was a miracle the Philistines didn't realize how vulnerable we were. They could have turned around at any moment and knocked the lot of us down easily."

"Why would the king make such an unwise vow?"

"He's a fool," snapped Gavi. "That's why."

I sucked in a breath and took a quick look over my shoulder to ensure no one had heard his traitorous statement. "Best not use such terms around Gibeah, cousin."

He gritted his teeth. "There's no other word for a man who nearly executed his own son."

I flinched. "*What?*"

"Yonatan and his armor-bearer weren't present when that order was given," said Gavi. "They'd already gone to sneak into the Philistine garrison. It took them a while to get down into the wadi and then climb up the cliff and back to camp after they killed the lookouts."

Realization struck me. "Yonatan and his armor-bearer were the ghosts?"

Gavi gave a snort of amusement. "Ghosts?"

I told him how the Efraimites said the Philistines had ascribed the slaughter of twenty men to two spirits who'd disappeared into the air.

"Oh, Yonatan will love that." My cousin tipped his head back and let out a gusty laugh, one I'd not heard in a long while.

"So he missed the order from Saul because he was off stirring up the enemy?"

"He did. And when he saw a fallen tree in the forest, filled by an overflowing beehive, he stuck his staff into the honey. He didn't know the king had made this foolish decree. We could have finished off the Philistines that night if we'd not been ready to eat our sandals. I heard that after nightfall, a bunch of Saul's men took livestock from captured herds in Efraimite territory and ate the meat still full of blood. At least Yonatan made certain we bled the animals first."

"And how exactly did any of this put Yonatan in danger?"

"Because the king wanted to pursue the Philistines in the morning, so he called a priest to see if Yahweh gave him leave to do so. But Yahweh refused to answer. Saul called the commanders together and threatened to kill whoever had sinned and caused Adonai to turn away."

"And the lots fell on Yonatan?"

He nodded, a look of disgust on his face. "Saul's back was against a wall. He'd made a vow to kill his own son. But there was immediate outcry. Nearly a riot. Saul would have lost most of his army if he'd executed Yonatan for something as ridiculous as a bite of honey. I don't understand why a man like him was chosen to sit on that throne." Gavi spat on the ground. "The son is worth three of the father."

I was infinitely grateful to the king. He'd not only given me my freedom but allowed me a year with Yochana *and* my own company of men. Yet Gavi's story unsettled me. Added to the uneven leadership Saul had shown after Yavesh-Gilead when we'd at first pursued the Ammonites with a vengeance and then suddenly stopped and retreated across the Jordan, along with the hesitation that had allowed the Philistines to take so much of our territory in the first place, I'd begun to have a few doubts about the man Yahweh had chosen.

"They say Samuel is furious with him," said Gavi. "He took it upon himself to offer the sacrifices before battle instead of waiting for the prophet. Samuel stormed out of the fortress like a whirlwind after a very heated private conversation."

I'd have to ask Avi if he'd heard anything about that situation when I traveled through Naioth on my way home. "Seems I missed quite a bit of excitement while recovering in Kiryat-Yearim."

Gavi narrowed his eyes on me. "So, tell me more about this woman. The perfumer you took from Maresha. She nice to look at?"

I'd skimmed over the mention of Yochana during my initial explanation of recent events, but Gavi never missed a chance to talk about beautiful women. However, Yochana was not just any beautiful woman. She was *mine*.

"I'm marrying her."

Gavi's brows flew high. "You are getting *married*?"

I nodded. "As soon as I'm done with training. Then I'll be taking a year off duty."

His dark eyes went wide, his jaw gaping. "*You* are taking a year off being a soldier? Is that possible? I haven't seen you without a sword at your side since you were fifteen."

I shrugged. "She's worth it."

He pressed his lips into a flat line, shaking his head. "First Avi. Now you."

"You'll be next."

"Not in a thousand years, my friend." He gave me a feral grin. "There are far too many pretty mouths out there to taste. Besides, I'm happily shackled for life to the army of Israel."

I wondered what Doda Miri might have to say over her firstborn refusing to marry. "Been home lately?"

A sour look came over his face. "Not for a few months. And even then, just long enough for Hanan to stir me up. I had to leave before my fist took on a mind of its own."

"What about your sisters?"

A genuine smile spread across his face, displaying just how much he adored them. "Growing up far too quickly. They clung to me like moss when I had to go."

"Won't be too long before young men come around."

His eyes narrowed. "I told Hanan if he so much as thought about handing over any of them before they are ready and willing, I'd slit his throat myself."

The threat sounded genuine. Miri had been married off very young to a man who was drunk more than he was sober, so it was likely Gavi feared history might repeat itself. But I doubted my aunt would tolerate anything like that happening to her girls. She was a woman of fierce determination and a mother who'd defend her own with her life—including her eldest.

The thought reminded me of another doting mother, our grief-stricken aunt Hodiyah. "I ran across Shalem's trail. Down in Lachish."

"What? I thought you were convinced he was dead."

"I was wrong. He's with Phoenician traders like Avi said. But they went into Philistine territory before I could find him."

Head down, he let out a slow breath, hands splayed on his hips. "You told Avi yet?"

"I did. Had to apologize for not believing him. And for leaving him to look for Shay on his own." It had been humbling to do so, but Avidan had been more than gracious in receiving my apology.

Instead of gloating, Avi had assured me that Yahweh knew where Shay was and that all would be made right in his time. I'd marveled at the change in my once restless and impetuous cousin. Over the past couple of years, he'd grown into a man of honor and found peace with his sacred duties. Perhaps it was marriage that had tempered him, but it seemed he too had learned to bend his knee to the Most High.

However, I had a feeling it might take more than a simple earthquake to shake sense into Gavriel.

"I plan to ask my men to keep an eye out for Shalem as they go back to their homes," I said. "Perhaps you can do the same for the men in your own company."

"Doubt it'd do much good. He could be anywhere by now."

"It's worth a try."

He grunted a noncommittal response, and the two of us remained silent as the first group of my men returned from their run, arms shaking from the effort of carrying those stones over their heads for so long. Eliyah was the first to drop his stone five paces away from me, and then one by one the rest dumped their burdens on the pile before dashing off to find water.

"Come find me before you leave," Gavi said, already backing away. "We'll drink a few cups in honor of your bride."

I took a long look at my cousin, wishing I had Avi's silver tongue or a few words to express what he meant to me. Instead, I simply nodded. "I'll do that."

He strode away, and for a brief moment, I wondered whether I should chase him down, force him to tell me the burdens he carried, but I doubted he would. Probably would make some sort of crass jest to deflect from my prying, like he usually did. Besides, I had a duty to fulfill, and men who counted on me. And the faster I completed my obligations, the faster I would have Yochana in my arms again.

EPILOGUE

Zevi

Maresha, Israel

The house I'd been born in still stood.

It looked much smaller now than it had the day I'd been sent away. Some other family lived there now. An oleander grew in a hefty pot near the door my father and I had built together when the old one rotted on its hinges. A few geese toddled about near the side of the house, scratching and pecking at the grassy spot where my little sisters used to play. And a small garden grew in the same place my mother had once tended spindly bean plants, cabbages, and leeks with as much tenderness as she did her children.

For the first time in two decades, I allowed myself to remain inside my happy memories of her, letting them wash over me instead of pushing them away. As if it were only yesterday I'd sat in her lap beneath one of the nearby terebinth trees, I could feel the warmth

311

of her arms around me. Could feel the vibration of her musical laughter against my cheek. Could clearly see the large brown eyes I'd inherited looking down at me with such adoration that my heart seemed to leap toward her. Somehow, I even felt her kiss on my forehead like it had been pressed there only a moment before.

And then, the precious whisper from the past was gone, replaced by the twitter of birds in the trees celebrating the clear blue sky above Maresha. This town had once been a place of bitter memories. But now it was the place I'd found the one my soul loved.

It had been five long weeks since I'd seen her last. Five long weeks since I'd held her. And five weeks since I'd kissed her lips. I could wait no longer. I turned away from the past and its bittersweetness and hurried toward my future. With every step closer to her, my heart pounded harder.

She had no idea that I'd already been in Maresha for hours. I'd arrived at her father's home soon after she'd left in the morning and had, to my great surprise, been invited into the house without a moment's hesitation.

Her father had listened to my profuse apology for stealing his daughter and then told me that he'd forgiven me weeks ago, as soon as Yochana had explained the entire story. Then, to my astonishment, he'd proceeded to ask *my* forgiveness for having sent me away all those years before and expressed his great regret for not taking me into his own home. I could barely speak through the pinch of emotion in my throat as I told him that there was no forgiveness necessary and that Yahweh had used the ugly situation to bring me into Natan and Shoshana's family, for which I would be eternally grateful.

Then, although I'd been aching to go to Yochana, her mother had insisted on feeding me, and her younger sisters took me out to the courtyard, where the puppies from the cave now lived with their mother. Apparently Yochana's father had helped the girls bring the little dog and her litter to the house in an attempt to soothe their grief after their sister's disappearance. The kindness the entire family showed me, along with their astounding lack of anger for how I'd wronged them, made me understand the woman I loved a little more. No wonder she'd been so quick to forgive me if she'd grown up in a household of grace.

I hoped she would forgive me, once again, for taking so long to come for her. Although it had taken only three weeks to ensure Saul's commanders and captains were familiar with the rigors of my training regimen, there had been an issue with some Jebusites raiding vineyards just south of Gibeah, and Eyal had asked my company to deal with the problem. My men had performed admirably, including the new recruits, and it had taken little effort to find the gang of Jebusites and give them several strong reasons not to bother the Hebrew inhabitants of the local farms. It had been accomplished without bloodshed, and I was fairly sure they'd keep to their mountaintop stronghold for a good long while. Hopefully much longer than the precious uninterrupted year we would have together.

The scent of blue lupine and spiced honey wafted by on the gentle breeze when I was still ten paces away from the shop. I'd carefully rationed the balm Yochana had given me over the past few weeks, but the little jar was empty now. I'd been desperate enough for her that I continued to press my nose into it every night to soak up the final notes of remaining scent. And now here it was again, drawing me toward her just like it had done the first time I stood outside her doorway.

The door was open, and as I stood before the threshold, I could see her across the room. With her back to me, she was searching about in her wooden box—the same one Mahir had rescued from the wagon before Kyrum could toss it aside or destroy it.

"No," she murmured to herself as she held something that looked to me like nothing more than a weed. "That's not right.

Too sharp. Perhaps rosemary instead? Or those poppies I found yesterday . . ."

Smitten by her ever-meandering mind as much as by her gorgeous face, I smiled at her back as she riffled through the box again, pulling out packets of herbs, smelling them, and then tossing them aside with small huffs of displeasure. "These herbs are just not the same as Eliora's. . . ."

I could not wait any longer. I stepped over the threshold. "Shalom. Are you open for business?"

She whirled at my voice, dropping a handful of dried yarrow to the ground as her hand flew to her mouth. Her eyes glistened as she took me in.

"I'm sorry if I startled you," I said, valiantly keeping my tone even, as if I were speaking to a stranger and not the woman who held my heart in her talented fingers. "I was walking by your door, and there was just something in the air . . . some sort of beautiful flower, perhaps? But sweet and spicy too."

She narrowed her eyes at me, catching on to my game. She cleared her throat, then arranged her features into a merchant's inviting smile.

"I am open, but I've been expecting a visitor for some time now. Once he arrives, I'll close up the shop. Is there something I can help you with?"

"I've been told this is the best place in the region to find perfumes, among other things."

"Then you've been informed correctly," she said. "I have a wide variety of scents for you to sample, along with medicinal tinctures and unguents, balms to sooth the skin, and creams to keep it supple and youthful. Do you have something particular in mind?"

I stepped closer, and she matched my move with one of her own. "Well, I came to this town to ask the woman I love to marry me. I spent the morning with her father and mother, begging their forgiveness for a very foolish decision I made, and then pleaded with them for her hand."

Her eyes went wide. "You did?"

I nodded. "But she might not be happy with me, as it has taken longer than I guessed to return."

"Understandable," she said, with a little frown. "She may have thought you changed your mind."

"Never. She is everything I want and everything I never knew I needed."

Her eyes glistened. "Is she?"

I stepped closer. "Indeed she is. And so very brave . . . you cannot *fathom* what courage this woman has. She stood before a king for my sake. Saved my life—twice. My family adores her. As do my men. And though she is as sweet as honeycomb and more graceful than lupine, her spine is made of iron. So, naturally, she lets me get away with nothing."

She grinned. "She sounds quite perfect, then."

"Perfect for me," I said, finally closing the distance between us and settling my hands on her waist where they belonged. "In every way."

"You're here," she whispered. "Finally."

"I am."

"And you spoke to my father already?"

"I had to, because I can't be close to you without having you in my arms, and I didn't want to end up in front of the council on a charge of debauching innocent young women."

She huffed a laugh. "I'm hardly innocent."

"Beautiful young women, then." I leaned closer, inhaling deeply as I slid one hand into her soft hair and tugged her into my embrace with the other. "Ones who smell like lupine and honey and whose lips I need on mine—now."

She gave me my wish, letting me indulge in a long, slow kiss that melted every other thought from my mind. Saul and his entire army could come crashing through the door right now and I would not care.

I was not certain how I would ever wrench myself away when I was needed back in Gibeah in a year. But I would spend every moment of the next cycle of seasons making her happy and letting her love soak deep into my bones before I had to leave her again. And hopefully Saul's reputation would spread among the enemies of Israel and we'd have no need to be separated for any longer than short periods of time. I had a feeling that once we had children of our own, it would be even harder to leave.

For the first time in my life, I wondered whether I should follow my father's path instead of the one I'd chosen. Perhaps a life in the woods of Kiryat-Yearim, cutting timber and watching my family grow, would be far more gratifying than I'd ever imagined. But no matter what I decided, I would always give Yochana a say.

I finally loosened my embrace, letting her move just a hairsbreadth from my mouth. "Do you want to stay here?"

She frowned at me. "In the shop?"

"Your shop. Maresha. Am I forcing you to come with me again?"

She caressed my cheek. "Zevi. I want to be where you are. These weeks without you have been awful. You are not forcing anything. Besides, I love my little shop, but I *need* to be near Eliora's garden. Other than the wildflowers around Maresha, the only ingredients I can find here are dried, imported from other places. If I am going to make perfumes for a king and queen, I must have direct access to the freshest and most exotic plants."

Little did she know that my father was already gathering timber for the two of us to build an extension onto the family home, including a workshop fit for a master perfumer, one with plenty of shelves and underground storage for her perfumes. And she already had the perfect apprentice in Galit's daughter, along with Ami and a couple of my other young cousins, who were nearly as enamored by Yochana as I was.

"So it's the garden you really want, then?" I teased. "Not me?"

She poked a finger into my chest. "You fool. There's nothing I want more than to be with you. How long do we have to wait to marry?"

Heat rushed through me, and I bent to press my lips at the corner of her jaw. "If I had my choice, I'd take you home right now."

Her fingers dug into my shoulders. "Zevi . . ." she breathed, only half-chiding.

"Two weeks," I said. "My mother, aunts, and grandmother have been planning the celebration since the moment you took off to intercede with Saul on my behalf. Your father, mother, and sisters have already agreed to return with us."

"They have?"

"The clan of Elazar does nothing in half-measures and never misses a chance for a celebration. It's more than likely that a good portion of my family from Ramah and Naioth will already be there when we arrive, preparing enough food to feed the entire army."

Her gray eyes went wide, full of anticipation. "Even Eliora?"

"Yes, you'll finally get to meet my aunt, but she *cannot* steal you away from me. I've waited too long to have you to myself." I kissed the edge of her jaw, then worked my way up to that tender spot behind her earlobe. "In fact, let's just stay here in your shop for the next two weeks instead. We won't have a moment to ourselves until our wedding night."

She shook her head. "I love your big, wonderful family. I can't wait to be a part of it."

"And I cannot wait to begin making a family of our own," I said with a teasing grin.

Yochana's cheeks were tinged with pink, but she glossed over my suggestive comment. "Will Avi and Keziah come to the wedding? I'm anxious to meet her."

"I certainly hope so." It had been far too long since I'd spent any length of time with my cousin, and I hoped to continue to mend the rift I'd caused between us.

"And Gavi?"

"I'd not count on it. He hasn't been in Kiryat-Yearim for years. And from what I heard, Yonatan assigned him to a special division that will be keeping an eye on the far northern borders. There have been some issues with Amorites near Har Hermon. It may be a long while before we see him."

I'd been so occupied in the past weeks of training that by the time I'd found Gavi again, it was the morning of my departure. I'd gone into Yonatan's camp and asked around until I found the tent he shared with a few other soldiers.

"He's sleeping off last night," said one of his companions with a shrug. *"Good luck getting the bear to wake."*

I'd entered the dim tent to find Gavi snoring on his bedroll, mouth wide open and breath stinking of stale beer. I called his name a couple of times, tried to shake him awake, but he murmured a curse and then turned over to give me his back.

He was a disaster. And I could not help but wonder whether it was partially my fault. He and I had never been as close as he had been with Avi, and we'd parted ways soon after Yavesh-Gilead. But perhaps if I'd set aside my own ambitions and fought beside Gavi instead, he might not be so unraveled.

I vowed right then that, in the future, I would make a more concerted effort to seek him out and make certain he was well. We'd made a blood pact, after all, and promised to always have each other's backs. I'd not lived up to that commitment, but I would not neglect it anymore. The things that had been broken inside me for so many years were slowly healing, thanks to Yochana's love and that of the merciful God who brought us together. It may take walking through some valleys of his own before Gavi found the peace he so desperately needed, but I had faith that someday he too would find rest for his turbulent soul.

Reminded of our boyhood oath, I had reached into my pack and taken out Shalem's little stone knife, the one Gavi had made when we were children and that Avi had come across in a market shortly after Shay had disappeared. For the past two years, I'd had it wrapped in a small piece of wool and kept it with me as a reminder of my failure to protect our young cousin, but I'd tucked it carefully into Gavi's own leather pack, which had been serving as a makeshift pillow beneath his head, as an unspoken token of the renewal of our vow of brotherhood.

Instead of the knife, I now kept a white shell engraved with the childish sketch of a giant dog in my pack to remind me that when things seemed bleak, there was always hope. Igo had been my greatest comfort in Ashdod, a gift from Yahweh to a frightened child who'd endured so much. Avi had kept it safe for me since he'd found it in the dirt near the place Shay had disappeared, knowing I would someday want it back.

I could only pray that the same unseen hand that guided and shielded me would eventually lead Shalem home, and that the steadfast love of the Great Healer would mend whatever was broken inside Gavriel as well. Because although there were still plenty of scars deep inside me, and perhaps always would be, once I surrendered everything to Yahweh—past, present, and future—the bitterness that had nearly consumed me for so long was finally gone.

I reached for Yochana's hand, tangling my fingers in hers and pulling her toward the doorway. "For now, we need to get back to your parents' house. I told your father I would fetch you. And I am determined to prove that I am trustworthy with his precious daughter."

Her gray eyes were full of mischief. "So, you are kidnapping me again?"

I swooped her up into my arms, and she let out a squeak of surprise, throwing her arms around my neck. I pressed my nose into her chestnut hair and inhaled deeply of her intoxicating lupine-and-honey scent. "Oh no, it is you who holds me captive, my love. And I cannot wait to be bound to you for the rest of our days."

With my precious bride in my arms, I stepped over the threshold of her shop and into the sun.

AUTHOR'S NOTE

Over the past three years, the road I've traversed has been over some of the rockiest terrain I've ever encountered. It began with my cancer diagnosis in June 2021, then chemotherapy, a double mastectomy, a medical emergency that led to both of my parents being diagnosed with severe dementia and having to be moved from their home (while I was in the middle of six weeks of radiation treatments), the passing of my dad, major reconstructive surgery and months of recovery, all while dealing with some really hard family issues. Any one of those things by themselves would be tough to handle. So much at once has been, to say the least, overwhelming. But *God* . . .

He has been so kind to me. He has shown me his steadfast love in hundreds of ways, through his Word, his people, and his comforting Spirit. He has taught me things about himself I never would have known had I not walked these valleys. He has shown me in the heights of the storm how deep the roots of my faith truly go. He has shown me that he is my shield, my rock, and my refuge. And he has shown me that my preparation for these battles began years ago, long before I was anywhere near a battlefield. In fact, the foundations were laid with the solid and abiding faith of my mother and grandmother even before I was born.

So as I wrote Zevi's story, which had been percolating in my mind since the fierce little boy who took on grown Philistines in protection of two little girls appeared on the page (because he was in no way planned beforehand), I was reminded of all the ways the Lord prepared me over the years for the war against defeat, despair, pride, shame, and all the other spiritual forces whose goal is to seek and destroy. Looking back at the hard lessons I learned when I was younger, I can see with astounding clarity how he has worked all things together for my good (Romans 8:28). And I will continue to cling to that promise for the future and for the battles that lie ahead of me.

So I hope that, along with being a page-turning adventure that illuminates biblical history and a romantic story that entertains, this book will be a reminder that "He is the shield that protects you, the sword you boast in. Your enemies will cringe before you, and you will tread on their backs" (Deuteronomy 33:29 HCSB).

We serve the God who spoke the universe into existence. The God who split the sea to rescue his people. The God who conquered death with an empty tomb. There is nothing at all that he cannot do. So keep your eyes on the Lord, my friend, for he is at your right hand. Do not be shaken (Psalm 16:8).

Soli Deo Gloria.

FOR MORE FROM
CONNILYN COSSETTE,
read on
for an excerpt from

Between the Wild Branches

After a heartbreaking end to her friendship with Lukio, Shoshana thought she'd never see him again. But when, years later, she is captured in a Philistine raid and enslaved, she is surprised to find Lukio is now a famous and brutal fighter. With deadly secrets and unbreakable vows standing between them, finding a way to freedom may cost them everything.

Available now wherever books are sold.

ONE

Lukio

1052 BC
ASHDOD, PHILISTIA

M y fist slammed into my opponent's jaw, the collision so jarring that I felt the vibration of it all the way to my shoulder. His head snapped back, blood trickling from his mouth. Perhaps he'd bitten his tongue all the way through, like my last opponent, but I did not relent. Before he'd steadied himself, I struck again, this time with a kick to the knee. Leg buckling, he lurched sideways but somehow remained standing, shaking off my blow. With a growl he charged at me again, a sneer on his face.

Before his punch could connect, I spun, the action so ingrained in my bones that I barely had to think before I was behind him, driving my elbow between his shoulder blades. He tripped forward, nearly going down, but somehow found his balance before he landed in the dirt, where it would have been all over. No one could beat me on the ground. No one. Not even this champion of Tyre, who had a reputation that stretched all the way here to Ashdod.

Myriad voices hummed around me like the constant buzz of a disturbed hive, but I remained immune to their bidding. For years now, the cheers and chanting of my name had been little more than an irritant, not the impetus for the pulse-pounding rush of anticipation I used to crave more than anything.

The one voice that broke through the haze was Mataro's—and only then because he was at the edge of the fighting grounds, screaming at me to finish the man, as if I actually planned to let my opponent get the best of me. My cousin knew me better than that; I didn't know why he bothered goading me. I'd not lost a fight in years. Not one that counted, anyhow.

Even as I threw my weight forward, slamming full force into the Phoenician, my mouth soured at the proprietary tone of Mataro's commands, As if it was him and not me who knew the correct placement of my feet, which weaknesses to look for, and how to clinch victory. The thought almost made me laugh as I wrenched my opponent's dominant arm back. Mataro was little more than an overfed jackal these days. Nothing like the man who'd opened the door to me ten years ago—the man who had been on the verge of ruin, inebriated and unsteady on his feet as I explained who I was and that I'd come back to Philistia to build the fortune he'd promised me.

Mataro may have arranged the first of my matches and coached me to fight like the ruthless demon I was rumored to be, but the urge to wrap my fingers around his fat neck and squeeze was increasing. It seemed that the fuller his purse, the larger it grew, always making room for more. And along with the accumulation of his wealth, his mouth seemed to grow larger and larger as well, boasts gushing out like rancid wine with every ridiculous demand and every public declaration that it was *his* guidance that had made me an unmatched champion on the fighting grounds.

The Phoenician snarled a curse as I jerked his arm harder, then hissed as pain I knew well shot through his body. I took advantage of the momentary distraction and swung, grunting as I jammed my leather-wrapped knuckles into his ribs in a series of unrelenting blows. He hissed out a pained curse that told me this bout was nearly finished. A jolt of triumph surged in my chest, but instead of lingering the way it used to and curling around my bones in a delicious embrace, it burned away like mist on a summer morning. I'd claimed countless victories since I returned to Ashdod as a fifteen-year-old boy with my hopes crushed and my blood boiling with betrayal, and yet each one seemed to matter less than the last.

My opponent wavered on his feet, catching his breath from the relentless attack I'd delivered to his torso, and in that brief moment my attention flitted up to the balcony that surrounded this royal courtyard. The crowd was thick today, gathered to revel in the violence between us and the events that would follow, but somehow my gaze snagged on one face out of the multitude that were gleefully screaming for the Phoenician's downfall. Everything inside me slammed to a halt.

Surely it was only a trick of the light that familiar hazel eyes gazed down at me, their depths filled with an expression of stricken recognition that swiftly flared into panicked horror.

It could not be her. Could not be the one who'd left my heart in tatters ten years ago.

Sweat rolled into my eyes, blurring my vision for a moment, and I blinked it away, heart pounding as shock and confusion gripped me in an iron hold. But by the time I could see again, whatever illusion that had deceived me had vanished—nothing left of it but a ghost of a memory that had taunted me for far too long.

A fist hit my cheekbone, rattling my teeth as I tasted metal. Lights flashed and pain radiated across my face as I realized that I'd been far too absorbed in the absurd vision I'd seen among the raving crowd to notice my opponent had regrouped.

Cursing myself for such a foolish mistake, I shook off the blur in my sight, spat out the blood that coated my tongue, and plowed forward into him. Grunting as I rammed my knuckles directly into his side once again and felt a rib give, I let out a foul word of my own as he recoiled from the hit. He tripped back a step, chest heaving, but his eyes never lost their focus on me, even though he had to be in extraordinary pain. Although he was heavier than I was, he was younger by a few years, his face free of the many scars that marred my own, and the glint in his eyes told me he was hungry enough for this win to ignore any and all injuries.

I, however, was undefeated. A record that would remain unbroken because I refused to let the last year of planning and maneuvering go to waste, especially for the elusive memory of a girl who'd tossed me aside like a soiled garment. The Phoenician and I both braced ourselves for the next strike—panting, sweating, and bloody.

"What are you waiting for?" screamed Mataro. "This should already have been over! Stop hesitating!"

I blinked the sweat from my eyes again, every muscle in my body going still as granite. But instead of letting my cousin's taunting words crawl under my skin and steal my focus, I allowed them to burn in my belly, stoking the fire higher and higher until everything outside this match was nothing but ash. Mataro could rant all he wanted today; he could seethe and snarl and hiss out demands, but this would be the last time. Tomorrow I would cut the cord I'd too-willingly bound myself with, and he could hang himself with it for all I cared.

I unleashed the rage I'd been harnessing, giving it permission to flood my limbs and propel me forward as quick as a wildcat to grab the Phoenician's head with both hands. My fingers locked around his neck and dug into his skull as I yanked it forward to collide with a powerful knee strike. Before he'd even hit the ground, I'd turned away, not bothering to wait for the announcement that he'd been knocked insensible and my victory was secure. I left the fighting grounds, ignoring the clamoring crowd as they parted before me, the multitude of hands that slithered over my bare skin as I pressed past, and the lurid invitations that followed in my wake. I'd long ceased being flattered by the attention I'd once reveled in.

Even more bodies than I'd guessed were packed into this space, stirring up the dust with their sandals and adding their voices to the cacophony. Now that the long-anticipated fight between myself and the Phoenician had been decided, the dancing and storytelling would begin. This festival, dedicated to the gods and goddesses credited with leading our forefathers across the sea, would culminate with the impossible and fascinating leaping of the bulls like our ancestors had enjoyed on the island of Caphtor so long ago. It was a celebration I'd dreamed about participating in when I was a boy, before my sister Risi forced me to leave Ashdod in pursuit of a magical golden box.

I tried to shut down the memory and the ache that never failed to build in the center of my chest whenever I gave myself permission to think of Risi or her beloved mountaintop in Hebrew territory that I'd never fully been able to call home. But whatever delusion had gripped me earlier must have forced open a door I'd been certain was nailed securely closed.

Helpless against the urge, I paused to peer over my shoulder, allowing my eyes to swiftly scrutinize the face of every dark-haired female on the balcony where I'd seen the apparition. Then, disgusted with my own weakness, I headed for the gates, shaking off the ridiculous notion that the girl I'd once thought to be my future would be here in Ashdod, among people who hated her kind so vehemently. The sooner this day was over, the better.

TWO

Shoshana

I pushed my way back through the crowd on the balcony, bones vibrating and eyes burning. But I had to get away before anyone saw the grief on my face. I'd been reckless enough as it was today, slithering closer and closer to the parapet so I could catch a glimpse of him down below. Too helpless against the pull he had on me to restrain myself any longer.

When I was finally safe in the shadows, I slumped back against the wall and dropped my chin, doing my best to restrain the hot tears that glutted my throat.

Lukio. *My* Lukio was here.

After over an entire year and a half of avoiding him, of praying that he and I would never cross paths, I'd finally given in to my fierce curiosity and slipped in among the revelers, my greedy eyes feasting on the sight of the boy I'd loved since I was nine years old. But that boy was now a man. One who'd far surpassed even

330

the superior height of his youth and whose enormous body was cut into lines that even the fiercest warrior might envy.

His golden-brown hair was nearly to the center of his back, the curls I'd once adored now oiled and pulled back, secured by a series of gold clasps that ran the length of the long queue. His face was clean-shaven, revealing the sharp lines of his strong jaw, and his earlobes were studded with ornate ivory plugs. Dark tattoos in distinct Philistine shapes swirled around both of his arms and across his impressively broad chest as well. He'd been handsome as a boy, far more than any of the other young men in Kiryat-Yearim, but now he was devastating—a trait not lost on the hundreds of people in this courtyard who'd been screaming for him, their suggestions becoming more violent and more lewd as the fight went on.

And then, he'd seen me. And everything had stopped for the space of five eternal heartbeats. In those moments he was not the brutal champion of Ashdod, known for his unapologetic and emotionless method of beating men senseless on the fighting grounds, but the boy who'd taught me how to climb trees and differentiate between bird calls, who'd left sycamore figs on my windowsill as a sign to meet in our special place. For the four years that he and I had enjoyed a secret friendship, he'd insisted that I call him by his Philistine name instead of the one he'd been given by his sister Eliora and the Hebrew family that had adopted him. They'd known him as Natan, but he'd always been Lukio to me—the designation something sweet and sacred between just the two of us. So much had transpired since those quiet days when our innocent friendship had slowly shifted into something deeper as we explored the woods outside Kiryat-Yearim together under full moons. But I could not help but hope that behind that vicious façade my tenderhearted friend was still there.

However, at the same moment that his opponent regathered his wits and struck Lukio with a ferocious hit that jerked his head to the side, a woman beside me screamed encouragement to "Demon Eyes," and those hopes shattered to pieces.

Not only was he no longer using the name Natan, but he'd embraced the horrific moniker used to mock and humiliate him as a child because he had one brown eye and one green. A jeer that had been invented by none other than Medad, his former friend and my own husband. Why Lukio would use such a demeaning name to fight under, something meant to strip away his humanity and highlight the fact that he'd been an outsider in our town, was far beyond me; but it had been the reason I'd known it was him in the first place.

For months I'd heard tales of a ruthless fighter whose fame had spread throughout the Five Cities of Philistia, heard my mistress and her sisters exclaim over his dangerous beauty. But it was not until I'd heard him called Demon Eyes that I realized it must be Lukio, the young man who'd run away from my hometown after I'd trampled his heart into the dust. The one whose pleas I'd ignored as I fled our last conversation and ran toward the destiny chosen for me, even if it meant my own heart was left in pieces beside his.

An even louder swell of shouts and cries of joy from the mass of people gathered on the balcony told me that Lukio had thrown off whatever hesitation he'd had the moment our gazes met. The sounds of delight at his victory, undoubtedly achieved with the same cold-blooded execution of the final blows he was famous for, jerked me away from my childhood memories and reminded me of my true purpose here today.

My mistress had given me leave to watch the match from the upper level of the palace, and now I had only a short time to deliver a message before she sent someone to find me. I should not have paused to indulge in foolhardy curiosity. Lukio was no longer the boy he'd been, but neither was I the same girl, so it did no good to wish away the chasm between us. It was just as immovable as the mountain I'd grown up on and as deep as the valley I'd walked since he'd left Kiryat-Yearim.

Besides, for as much pain as I'd endured in my marriage to Medad, and even after I'd been enslaved by the Philistines, there were three very important reasons that I would not change the outcome of that fateful last conversation with Lukio. And right now, I had much more important things to deal with than thoughts of a man who'd likely forgotten me long ago anyhow.

Pushing away from the wall, I was glad that I'd not allowed any tears to slip down my face. To any of the revelers around me, I was nothing more than one of the many slaves in Ashdod, albeit garbed in a linen tunic that gave away my status as a maidservant to a family of means. No one would notice me spiriting through the shadows behind the vibrantly painted columns that held aloft the top story of the sprawling residence of the king of Ashdod.

Descending the wide stone stairs that led to the ground level, I strode down the shady hallway away from the central courtyard and toward the farthest corner of the palace, keeping my head down and my steps measured so as not to draw any attention. Thankfully, with all the excitement of the festival that had begun at sunrise with a series of sacrifices to the Philistines' gods and that would end with debauched rituals I'd rather not dwell upon, none of the revelers took any notice of me. I made my way toward the small storage shed on the southernmost outside corner of the palace, one that held garden tools that would certainly not be of any use in the midst of a festival and therefore a perfect place for meeting in secret today.

After a quick sweep of my gaze to ensure that no one's eyes were on me, I unlatched the door and slipped into the black room. Holding my breath, I waited, my heartbeat the only sound for a few long moments in which I wondered whether the detour to slake my curiosity about Lukio had meant that I'd missed my contact. Or whether he'd even come in the first place.

"Do you have the names?" said a low voice, one that was familiar now after a few months of meetings like this one. However, since I'd never seen the face that matched that deep voice, nothing about this encounter was safe. It was not wise to remain here any longer than I must.

"I do," I said. "The house of Kaparo the High Priest took in two young boys of perhaps ten or eleven, and that of Rumit the scribe purchased a girl of fourteen or so."

"Any others that gave you cause to worry?"

"They all give me cause to worry," I retorted. "They are my countrymen. Brothers and sisters from the tribes of Yaakov."

He paused, only his slow, measured breaths reaching out to me from the blackness. When he spoke again, there was a deep note of compassion in his voice. "You know what I mean. We can only do so much, my friend."

I cleared my throat of the thick coating of remorse. I had no cause to snap at this man who risked so much to meet me and who relayed the names of recently sold slaves on to people who carried out more dangerous tasks than I could imagine for the sake of the most vulnerable.

This man I met in the dark could be anyone. I'd never seen his face, and for his sake and mine, had never even considered breaching the trust between us to tarry outside the storage shed and discern his identity. He did not sound Hebrew, so either he'd been in Philistia so long that the peculiar sound of our tongue had been washed away or he had chosen to help with this mission purely from a sense of compassion. I had no idea. But whatever his motivations and however he'd fallen in with those of us who did our best to help other slaves escape their bonds, he'd never given me cause to doubt his trustworthiness.

"From what I was told, there were not more than ten brought in before the festival, likely a raid on a small hamlet, and most of them were men," I said. "Only two were sold locally. The rest were taken to the port." They were probably already on a ship bound for some unknown destination so far from the shores of the Land of Promise that they would never return.

I had not seen the captives with my own eyes, of course, being only one link in a chain, but every time I received information about new victims of the Philistines' campaign of targeted attacks on Hebrew villages, my chest ached with empathy. I did not have to guess what it was like to be dragged from your home, to watch your neighbors and friends slaughtered, to pray that the vicious men who'd stolen everything from you would simply kill you instead of—

I pressed down those disturbing memories and the swell of nausea that always accompanied them.

"I'll pass the information on to my contact," he said. "Send word when more arrive."

And there would be more. Whatever fear had been put into the Philistines' hearts by the resulting plagues and famine from stealing the Ark of the Covenant had eroded with every passing year. By the time my husband moved us to Beth Shemesh just after we were married, raids on villages in the *shephelah* were commonplace. True, our enemy had not come at us with their collective might like they had at Afek, when the five kings of Philistia took the Ark from the battlefield and then laid waste to Shiloh, but they'd been relentless in nipping at our heels, making certain that the people of Yahweh were never able to rest in the peace we'd been promised a thousand years ago. Peace I would never have again but hoped that I might give others a chance to reclaim.

"I should go," I said. "My mistress will be looking for me now that the fight is over."

"Who won?" he asked, the question dragging me right back to that balcony when I'd looked into Lukio's eyes for the first time in ten years.

I swallowed down a sharp response. He would have no reason to know of my connection with one of the fighters in that match today and had not meant to wound me by asking.

"The champion of Ashdod," I replied, the words feeling like rusted blades in my throat.

"Of course," said the man with a chuckle. "He doesn't lose. Perhaps I should have put a piece of silver or two into the pot."

With that comment, one of my many questions about the man I'd been passing information to was answered. No kind of slave would have a piece of silver to gamble on a fight. And certainly not two. This man was free. Someone able to walk about unfettered in the city, to come and go when he pleased.

I left the room without further comment. I had no interest in discussing Lukio's violent tendencies with anyone, let alone a faceless person in the dark.

Slipping back into the palace through a rear entrance, I made my way toward the opposite side of the complex, where those with more than enough silver to waste had gathered to observe the festivities and make their own wagers. By the time I found my mistress, any evidence of the fight on the courtyard grounds was gone, replaced by a troupe of half-naked dancers who were performing a complicated sequence of movements, leaping and contorting their bodies in impossible ways. To my profound relief, Lukio was nowhere in the vicinity.

As was my duty, I took my place behind her shoulder, grateful that she was so absorbed in an animated conversation with her two sisters about the dancers that she did not seem to notice my return at all.

Once my heartbeat returned to a normal rhythm, my eyes dropped to the infant in the arms of her oldest sister. The little one gazed over the woman's shoulder toward the vibrant blue-and-red walls at my back, drawn to the ornate shapes and swirls, even though she could not yet comprehend the mural depicting the subjugation of my people by the Philistine ancestors who'd arrived on our shores hundreds of years before. Then the baby turned her eyes toward me, peering up at me with her wispy brows drawn together, and I was nearly leveled by an overwhelming wave of grief and longing.

Ten years ago, I'd lost the boy I'd thought I would marry, and at that time, it had been the most devastating thing in my life—even more than my mother slipping away after a long illness when I was eight. But nothing compared to the soul-shattering loss of my children, and nothing ever would.

Connilyn Cossette is a Christy Award–winning and bestselling author of fiction that illuminates the ancient world of the Bible, in hopes that readers will dig deeper into the Word and encounter the Great Storyteller himself within its pages. A recent breast cancer survivor and adoptive mom of her two greatest gifts, she lives in a small town south of Dallas, Texas. Connect with her at ConnilynCossette.com.

Sign Up for Connilyn's Newsletter

Keep up to date with Connilyn's latest news
on book releases and events by signing up
for her email list at the link below.

ConnilynCossette.com

More from Connilyn Cossette

When a nearby city is attacked, Avidan fights for the newly crowned King Saul. When one of his cousins goes missing during the battle, he searches for him and instead stumbles across Keziah—the daughter of a powerful man. Traveling together, they must rely on each other to stay alive and learn to trust the King of Israel to guide their every step.

Voice of the Ancient
THE KING'S MEN #1

Determined to bring the Ark of the Covenant to a proper resting place, Levite musician Ronen never expected that Eliora, the Philistine girl he rescued years ago, would be part of the family he's to deceive. As his attempts to charm her lead in unexpected directions, they question their loyalties when their beliefs about the Ark and themselves are shaken.

To Dwell among Cedars
THE COVENANT HOUSE #1

After a heartbreaking end to her friendship with Lukio, Shoshana thought she'd never see him again. But when, years later, she is captured in a Philistine raid and enslaved, she is surprised to find Lukio is now a famous and brutal fighter. With deadly secrets and unbreakable vows standing between them, finding a way to freedom may cost them everything.

Between the Wild Branches
THE COVENANT HOUSE #2

◈BETHANYHOUSE

 Bethany House Fiction

 @BethanyHouseFiction

 @Bethany_House

 @BethanyHouseFiction

 Free exclusive resources for your book group at BethanyHouseOpenBook.com

 Sign up for our fiction newsletter today at BethanyHouse.com